SOUTHERN STORIES

SOUTHERN STORIES

Edited with an Introduction by

ARLIN TURNER

HOLT, RINEHART AND WINSTON, INC.

NEW YORK · CHICAGO · SAN FRANCISCO · ATLANTA · DALLAS

MONTREAL · TORONTO

Introduction, Chronology, and Notes Copyright © 1960 by Arlin Turner

All Rights Reserved

Typography by Stefan Salter

Printed in the United States of America

Library of Congress Catalog Card Number: 60–7870

SBN: 03-009790-8

0123   68   9876543

CONTENTS

INTRODUCTION

The tales chosen for this collection are Southern in matter and in authorship, and they are also good stories. As authors and examples have been winnowed in the process of selection, several conclusions have asserted themselves. For one, short prose fiction, whether the pieces are best labeled tales and sketches in the earlier periods or short stories more recently, has been important from the beginnings of literary production in the South to the present. One collateral fact is that among the major authors of the region a fair number have been primarily story writers, and another is that the South has produced a good proportion of the best short stories written in America. A large percentage of the Southern stories, moreover, bear within their pages clear marks of the region and, taken together, they convey a full portrait of the South in its variety of terrain, people, and history. It can be added that the tales have reflected the literary tendencies of the successive periods, while occupying an integral and as a rule a prominent station in the national literature.

Captain John Smith hardly belongs in any history of prose fiction, for all the liberties he took in reporting the scene and events at the founding of Virginia, but his Pocahontas story might stand without apology in a collection of fictional narratives. A hundred years after Smith, William Byrd of Westover in Virginia, wrote under promptings from his associations at Will's Coffee House during a long residence in London. It was his habit to turn ideas and phrases in the manner of Addison and Steele, and he characterized the Lubberlanders back of the Dismal Swamp and reported happenings among them in ways to suggest the Southern fiction writers in generations after him. More than one of the episodes narrated in his *History of the Dividing Line* and *A Journey to the Land of Eden* have characterization and structure suitable to a fictional tale. Historical narratives such as John Smith's continued to be printed long after him, as in the reports of Daniel Boone's adventures, but they remained as a rule close to fact, and paid deference to literal accuracy; likewise oral tales, most often anecdotal in nature, were never out of fashion; but the short narrative as an acknowledged literary form dates of course from Edgar Allan Poe.

The impetus given the writing of short tales by Poe's example and by his description and defense of the form was supported also by external circumstances of the time. Gift books and annuals flourished, and magazines were founded, such as the *Cosmopolitan* (1833) and the *Southern Literary Journal* (1835), both at Charleston, and the *Southern Literary Messenger* (1834) at Richmond. These publications required short pieces, and they especially welcomed tales and sketches to their pages. William Gilmore Simms apparently saw little difference except length between the tales he wrote occasionally and the romances to which his pen was most accustomed. His tales tended to be long, in fact, and his correspondence testifies that their length was governed by the needs of a magazine or an annual rather than any design he had chosen. When Simms wrote his early stories, he was likely more aware of Washington Irving's leisurely tales than of the strictly focused stories of Poe. The tellers of raucous anecdotes and tall tales from the backwoods or the frontier as a rule found the normal avenues of publication closed to them and often turned to local newspapers and the New York sportsman's weekly, *The Spirit of the Times,* but their wares like more conventional fiction had a readier market because new magazines and series of gift-books had been founded.

The flowering of the short tale which might have been expected to follow Poe was delayed by the Civil War and did not occur in fact until the 1870's and 1880's, when stories or tales or sketches proved admirably suited to the needs of the local-color school. When Albion Tourgée, a novelist writing in North Carolina, remarked in 1888 that on the evidence of current production American literature was mainly Southern and the hero was the Confederate soldier, he might have added that the authors were more successful with the tale than the novel in recording the elements of character, scene, and action peculiar to one region. In this period Joel Chandler Harris's tales of Uncle Remus claimed a distinct place in world literature, and George W. Cable, Kate Chopin, James Lane Allen, Mary Noailles Murfree, and Grace King, joining Bret Harte, Harriet Beecher Stowe, and others outside the South, gave the short story a prominence it had never had before. Toward the end of the century, Thomas Nelson Page found the tale of moderate length and leisurely movement well suited to the reminiscent portraits he wanted to draw of the South "befo' de war."

Even more than the nineteenth, the twentieth has proved to be the century of the novel, no less in the South than elsewhere. And along with the novel, short fiction has flourished and has been produced by enough of the major authors such as William Faulkner to give it a place of importance. Katherine Anne Porter has won her considerable reputation with work restricted to short stories and novelettes. Periodicals ranging from the little magazines on one hand to the slick weeklies and monthlies on the other have furnished the prestige or the pay or both needed to encourage writers of short fiction, though it is as true now as it was in the 1830's or the 1880's that books of stories have a relatively small market.

It may be that writers in the South have been more steadily aware of their section than writers elsewhere. It is certain that in many of them the regional affiliation is conspicuous and also that a book of representative tales will display in some fullness the multiple facets of the South. Poe stands off in contradiction at this point, for his tales often seem to belong not to the earth at all, and surely not to a particular region on its surface. Even so, a few of them employ recognizable settings in the South. "The Gold Bug," for one, has its setting on Sullivan's Island, off the South Carolina coast, where Poe was stationed in the army. The Jupiter of this story has only the stiffest of action and speech, but close observation will disclose in him the primitive lineaments which later become dominant among his descendants in stories of the slave South. The climactic episode of "The Premature Burial" is placed on the James River near Richmond, Virginia; the action of "The Oblong Box" occurs on a ship which has sailed from Charleston, South Carolina; and the scene of "A Tale of the Ragged Mountains" is "the chain of wild and dreary hills that lie westward and southward of Charlottesville," Virginia.

But in none of these stories does it matter what the locality is; place names appear only as if by the merest chance. William Gilmore Simms championed in his early years nationalism rather than localism, and though he set his novels and tales mainly in South Carolina or elsewhere on the Southern frontier, he employed his materials with no more sectional purpose than did the "great Elizabethans," whom he so much admired, or the Greeks. He used whatever was at hand, but only for the reason that it was his own and he knew it best. Even when later he was the apostle of sectional ideas and attitudes, his fiction showed little trace of his sectional bias. A man robustly active in the world about him and frank in his manner, Simms achieved greater realism than was usual in his time in presenting the scenes, characters, and action of his fiction. There is probably no great exaggeration in his statement in the preface to *The Wigwam and the Cabin* of the characters drawn in that work, "in their delineation I have mostly drawn from living portraits and in frequent instances from actual scenes and circumstances within the memories of men." In such stories as "The Lazy Crow" he gave a fuller view of the Negro character than Poe ever attempted.

Locality was of first importance among the humorists who flourished in the Old Southwest. Alert to what was distinctive or picturesque in the life about them, they proposed to record that life before change engulfed it. The presence of Andrew Jackson in the White House and David Crockett in the Senate increased general awareness of the frontier and the backwoods and in turn encouraged authors and editors to exploit what was peculiar in the remote localities. Augustus Baldwin Longstreet looked about him in his native Georgia and began writing newspaper sketches which later in the preface to *Georgia Scenes* (1835) he described as "fanciful *combinations* of *real* incidents and characters." Reviewing *Georgia Scenes* in *The Southern Literary Messenger* (March, 1836), Poe credited the author with "an exquisitely discriminative understanding of character in general and Southern character in particular" and pointed to his "forcible, accurate and original generic delineations of real existences to be found" in regions of the South. James Glover Baldwin undertook in the sketches making up *The Flush Times of Alabama and Mississippi* (1853) to report what seemed to him, a Virginian

moved to the new country, novel or interesting in the world of law-
yers and judges and hangers-on at the frontier law courts. Thomas
Bangs Thorpe, to name another, came from New England to live in
Louisiana and wrote down the yarns he heard in hunting camps and
on the Mississippi River steamboats about unhuntable bears like the
one appearing in his masterpiece, "The Big Bear of Arkansas,"
about bee hunters like the Tom Owen he wrote about, and about
the coming of civilization to the backwoods, as in the introduction
of the first piano into an Arkansas community. Longstreet wrote of
rough-and-tumble fighting, horse trading, and such frontier public
functions as a gander pulling and a shooting match. Baldwin described courthouse characters and gave them roles in native anecdotes. Johnson Jones Hooper, like most of the other humorists the
author of one major book of tales, the *Adventures of Simon Suggs*
(1845), epitomized in his title character the sharp dealings which
flourished in boom days on the frontier. George Washington Harris,
in recounting the escapades of his quintessential hillbilly in *Sut Lovingood Yarns* (1867), abstracted from the immediate and the local
a complex of human qualities which are at the same time elemental
and universal and also poetic in both concept and statement.

To these writers may be added William Tappan Thompson, crea-
tor of Major Jones; Henry Clay Lewis, who under the name of
Madison Tensas wrote of doctors and their patients in the swamp
country of Louisiana and Mississippi; Richard Malcolm Johnston;
and others writing in the same genre but with less talent. Taken together, their pages furnish a panoramic view from Virginia to Texas,
but the greatest number and the best of the tales were written in the
six states of the Old Southwest: Georgia, Alabama, Mississippi,
Louisiana, Arkansas, and Tennessee. Georgia was most productive.
These writers are all properly called humorists, but in most of them
an interest in the local remains apparent. It was their habit, in fact,
to speak slightingly if at all about the humor of their pieces and to
stress the local reporting. Even when his first concern apparently
was to tell a hilarious story, an author was likely to approach his
readers as a social historian. Longstreet is reported to have regretted
in later years that he had written the crude sketches of *Georgia
Scenes,* and many of the earthy tales printed in *The Spirit of the*

Times came from authors who wrote under pen names in order to guard their public respectability.

These frontier yarns stand off in contrast to the polite literature of the time. They belonged to a subliterary stratum where it was possible to employ realism of both material and presentation which would have outraged the readers whom most authors and publishers kept in mind. Even William Gilmore Simms, himself a man of robust naturalness and unsqueamish tastes, said in reviewing a book of humorous sketches that a reader would enjoy it on a steamboat or a train but of course would not bring it inside when he reached home. The evidence seems clear, moreover, that the authors of these tales wrote in conscious variance from the prevalent artificial refinement. Madison Tensas includes in one sentence of "The Indefatigable Bear-Hunter" a firm protest against the artificial literary language the humorists avoided: "The sun, in despair at the stern necessity which compelled him to yield up his tender offspring, day, to the gloomy grave of darkness, had stretched forth his long arms, and, with the tenacity of a drowning man clinging to a straw, had clutched the tender whispering straw-like topmost branches of the trees—in other words it was near sunset. . . ." Just as Sut Lovingood, according to a statement in what is supposedly a preface from his pen, wants his tales for a "gineral skeer—speshually fur the wimmen," so many of the frontier authors wrote with obvious relish in thinking of the prudishness they were violating. From the low characters of the back country they collected incidents and expressions, especially earthy figures of speech, which challenged the guardians of polite letters and prepared the way for Mark Twain's rebellion at a later time and the still greater freedom to be claimed by authors in the twentieth century.

At the same time that these ante-bellum humorists were moving in the direction of literary realism, they picked characters and incidents out of folk tradition, as humorists in other parts of the country were doing also, and, in keeping with the myth-making propensity of the folk imagination, built them into what is America's closest approach to a native mythology. Thus Davy Crockett, Mike Fink, John Henry, Annie Christmas, and Pecos Bill grew into characters who might rival the exploits of the Homeric gods. They might live in the "creation" state of Arkansas, where the soil runs down to the center of the earth; they might ride a streak of lightning straight through a crabapple orchard; they might pursue the phantom white stallion of the prairies or might track an unhuntable bear. They might walk up Daybreak Hill on a cold morning, as reported in "David Crockett and a Frozen Daybreak," and squeeze hot bear oil on the earth's axes to thaw them out and start the sun moving. They were close to the elements and elemental creatures. They had unbelievable strength and skill and gargantuan appetites, whether for food, drink, or love-making. Thus the early humorists combined a realism of circumstance and language with a fantasy of thought and expression in a way to foretell the realists of a later time, and more significantly still, the authors like William Faulkner whose implements are fused from realism, fantasy, symbolism, and elemental myths.

The early Southern humorists seem to have contributed also something to the technique of the short story as it developed from Poe to O. Henry. The humorists had as a model the oral tale, which normally is shaped to hold the listener for a brief period and then to release him after a quick and final turn of affairs. Such a tale is more effective if there is a second turn which, in the fashion of the anecdote, modifies and improves the first turn just at the moment the reader has comprehended it. Edgar Allan Poe, in his review of Longstreet's *Georgia Scenes* in 1836, showed that the book impressed him most favorably; and it is likely that even earlier, before writing the first of his stories, he had read or heard tales displaying the same compactness he found in Longstreet and the same concentration toward a resolution in the final paragraph or sentence. These are qualities Poe did not find in the tales of Irving. Some of Poe's stories are best called anecdotes, and a few of them, such as "Why the Little Frenchman Wears His Hand in a Sling" and "The Man That Was Used Up," suggest a kinship with the tales existing on the subliterary level. When Mark Twain wrote later on "How to Tell a Story" (1895), his topic was really the oral story, and no less surely O. Henry still later owed a considerable debt to the oral tale.

The concern which the ante-bellum humorists had for the local became still more conspicuous in the authors who came on the scene after the Civil War. Humor was an ingredient no less prominent in the local tales of the South than it was in Bret Harte's stories of the mining camps, but what was distinctive in terrain, character, speech, manners, and action normally had greatest prominence. The remote settlements were brought forward on the pages of fiction, and the magazine stories became a force for information and reconciliation in the decades when the wounds of sectional warfare were being healed. The reading public won by George W. Cable, Joel Chandler Harris, Charles Egbert Craddock, Thomas Nelson Page, and others of their generation held over into the next century, but it was not until the 1930's that the earlier Southern vogue was duplicated. In the depression years there was published an escape literature, which in the manner of Margaret Mitchell's *Gone with the Wind* recreated the heroic and satisfying past of Thomas Nelson Page's earlier works. Beside it and sharing with it an extensive reading public there grew a branch of realistic or naturalistic fiction which looked at the current South clinically, as in Erskine Caldwell's work, or symbolically, as in William Faulkner's. In recent years several authors of first importance, though employing local color simply as convenient material rather than for its own sake, have kept the Southern region prominent on the shelf of American fiction.

If Southern tales have displayed especially strong ties to the region, the reason may lie in the especially rich and varied materials the South affords. Clearly the ante-bellum humorists, the local colorists following the war, and the writers in the regional vogue of the 1930's were tempted to display the strange or the picturesque for its own sake. One consequence was that they often wrote sketches rather than stories and were satisfied with stock characters and generalized speech and action, when they needed to cultivate subtlety of matter and presentation and excellence of style.

The varieties of race and nationality have been especially inviting. Poe and Simms employed Negro characters but made them only the merest pieces of machinery and equipped them with conventional speech. With George W. Cable, Joel Chandler Harris, and Thomas Nelson Page in the decades following the Civil War, however, the Negro became a full-scale character, and down to William Faulkner and Flannery O'Connor his psychological and social problems, whether he has been pictured in slavery or emancipated, have filled a large share of Southern tales. Less necessarily associated with social and personal tragedy than the Negroes, the descendants of the early French and Spanish in Louisiana, the Creoles of the towns and plantations and the Cajuns of the prairies west of the Mississippi, were drawn by Cable, Grace King, Kate Chopin, and others as peoples delightfully foreign and picturesque. These peoples, along with the Negroes and the illiterate whites, have been given appropriate speech.

When Cable first began to reproduce accurately the speech of the New Orleans Creole, the Negro slave, and the backwoods white (all three of whom appear in his story "Posson Jone'"), his editors in New York were reluctant and some of his readers were outraged. And Thomas Nelson Page's first story, "Marse Chan," lay four years in the editor's drawer at the *Century Magazine* before it was published. Page's dialect has a compressed or elliptical quality which denies it the naturalness of movement Cable and Harris achieved; but it was the presence of the dialect, not any flaws in it, which caused the story to be held up. These writers first undertook to give a literal rendering of the speech, but they learned, or others after them did, that the flavor of the speech and in turn the desired aid to characterization could be gained without needlessly burdening the reader. Roark Bradford's Negro dialect reaches something like the ultimate in this direction; in it exact distinctions of word formation and pronunciation are sloughed off, leaving what will be recognized certainly and readily, but vaguely, as Southern Negro speech. Although reduced to a common denominator not so low as Bradford's, the dialect in Faulkner, Caldwell, and other recent authors has been so reduced that it is much less troublesome to the reader than the dialect in Joel Chandler Harris and Thomas Nelson Page.

The mulattoes, with their special problems, have attracted Southern authors, particularly Cable in the last century and Faulkner more recently. Ada Jack Carver has written about a special people, the Redbones, who bear a mixture of French, Spanish, and Indian blood, and bear also a special cross. The Indians, who have been pariahs only slightly less than the Negroes, appear in Faulkner's microcosm of the South, Yoknapatawpha County, and they share with his

Negroes and mulattoes the elemental and persevering qualities and the efficacious faith which he seems to say the whites have lost.

The classes of Southern society appear over and over in the stories. The plantation legend, with its grand ladies and generous masters at one extreme and the happy, faithful slaves at the other, appears in epitome in such stories as "Marse Chan" and "Unc' Edinburg's Drowndin'" by Thomas Nelson Page. This legend, welcomed and honored in the North as well as the South, dominated Southern fiction half a century after it took shape in the 1880's, and it is by no means dead. Yet there have been divergent notes. In the early years of the twentieth century Ellen Glasgow delivered in her novels kindly but telling thrusts at the plantation mistress and other figures in the legend, and O. Henry, born in the South but not born to the Southern manor, turned on the plantation legend the ironic view that was customary with him. The outlook on feuding reflected in "A Blackjack Bargainer" is duplicated in others of his stories in which elements in the Southern tradition are surveyed.

The legend proper contained only the planters and their slaves, with now and then a poor white or a free Negro skulking at the boundaries of the plantation. Yet, the various groups of poor whites have been drawn repeatedly. The ante-bellum humorists dealt mainly with illiterate whites and other low characters who existed beyond the older settlements or below the ken of the dominant class. After the Civil War Cable portrayed low-class characters from both the French-speaking and the English-speaking segments of Louisiana society, as did Grace King, Kate Chopin, and Ruth McEnery Stuart after him. Similarly Joel Chandler Harris, Charles Egbert Craddock, and John Fox, Jr., wrote of the Southern Mountaineers. Among the later story writers Caldwell, Faulkner, Marjorie Kinnan Rawlings, Paul Green, Eudora Welty, and Flannery O'Connor have continued to treat the lowest stratum of the Southern population. But middle-class folk have not appeared in large numbers, perhaps for no reason except that they have seemed less interesting than those at the extremes of the social scale. Authors under urging from publishers and readers, whom they all along have known to reside outside the South, and perhaps from their own inclinations to display the picturesque of their region, were not likely to search along Main Street for Howellsian commonplace characters. In the plantation tradition, moreover, the middle ground of Southern society was largely unoccupied, though in actuality such was not the case.

One conspicuous result of the search in Southern fiction for the strange and the remote has been that the peoples and the society have been pictured from an external position. The authors have written not about themselves but about the people off there in the slave quarters, or on the mountain farms, or along Tobacco Road, or in the settlements where a brand of French or Spanish is the hereditary speech, or in the white-columned mansion where once lived parents or grandparents or still more distant ancestors. White authors portraying Negroes or mulattoes could approach them only as outsiders, no matter how intimate their understanding and how great their sympathy. Joel Chandler Harris knew the plantation darky of Central Georgia as few authors have known the generic prototypes of their characters, and in the tales of Uncle Remus are displayed, in the animals and the darkies, elemental and universal human qualities. Still, Harris's characters are the slaves in the quarters or the cotton fields or the kitchen as they appeared to the master. Harris was a close observer, and he had an acute ear for the finer variations of speech. As a consequence, he caught with undoubted accuracy such externals as the language of the unsophisticated rural Negro and his way of dealing with his white folks, but he could portray the essential character of the Negro only as the white man thought him to be. And until recently, Negro authors, such as Paul Lawrence Dunbar and Charles W. Chesnutt, pictured their own people in a manner little different from the manner of white authors.

This way of drawing the Negro as the whites believed him to be, or wanted to believe him to be, continued in Thomas Nelson Page. As with the narrator in "Unc' Edinburg's Drowndin'," Page employed the affectionate old Negro as the most sympathetic of mirrors in which to reflect the glorious, lamented past. The portrayal here employs double reflecting surfaces: the Negroes as the whites imagine them look at the whites as the whites want to appear and as they imagine they appear to the Negroes. The result in Page is a fascinating portrayal of both whites and blacks of the plantation era, however unreal they may be.

Without exception the authors stressing the local have stood at some distance from their characters, and the intervening distance appears greatest when the stress on the strange and the picturesque is greatest. An extreme instance appears in Mary Noailles Murfree's stories of the mountaineers she observed during her summer vacations among them. Grace King, herself a Creole, seems no closer to her Creole characters than Cable, not a Creole, seems to his. Since the 1930's, writers of talent have rarely undertaken to exploit the local as of major interest. William Faulkner has set his works almost exclusively in his particular Southern region and has drawn heavily and with relish upon his own observations in that region. His first concern, however, has been for something besides a realistic portrayal of the local scene. The surroundings of Aunt Het in "Mule in the Yard" convey a degree of actuality, and the incident has the farcical humor and the earthy, anecdotal quality common to the early humorous tales; but the story is only secondarily local.

Thomas Wolfe wrote of his own people—of himself and his family; Eudora Welty has written mainly of her own region in Mississippi, and at times she portrays her immediate associates as closely as did Jane Austen, but again, as in "The Wide Net," she deals with a level which she knows only as an outside observer. Much the same is true of Elizabeth Madox Roberts, and in "The Haunted Palace" the two extremes of her milieu are brought together, the tenant farmers occupying the front of the stage and reflecting the highest social level as they attempt to understand the former owners of the mansion which is now a sheep barn. Faulkner as author and narrator becomes absorbed in the impersonality of carefully managed point of view. Thus his characters and their actions are in effect lifted out of any apparent relationship with the author or a specific setting. In contrast, Flannery O'Connor's reader remains sharply aware of her particular outlook. The characters in "Greenleaf" seem to have clear and positive relations with the author; as a consequence the personality of the author is a major element in the story, and in turn both author and characters seem to belong to a real scene.

Southern short fiction since 1930 has shown greater variety and greater experimentation than in any earlier period. It has displayed also greater complexity of both content and technique. On the one hand is Thomas Wolfe's pained searching within his own consciousness, presented in a rich and breathless pictorial method; on the other is the deliberate exploring in Katherine Anne Porter of the delicate threads of human connections. The grimly impersonal, point-blank report of human and social depravity in Caldwell's "Saturday Afternoon" has an antithesis in the deft handling of irony and symbolism in Elizabeth Madox Roberts's story of "The Haunted Palace." The authors have remained aware of the richness and variety of the Southern materials, and though not local colorists, they have not hesitated to employ those materials for full effect as the vehicle to carry their studies of characters, society, and ideas. They have profited from the immensely varied foreground of the Southern tale, and the sequel they have added shows no evidence of diminishing variety or strength.

A BIBLIOGRAPHICAL NOTE

The best history of Southern literature is Jay B. Hubbell, *The South in American Literature, 1607–1900* (1954), which contains excellent bibliographies. Earlier books of similarly inclusive scope are Montrose J. Moses, *The Literature of the South* (1910), and Carl Holliday, *A History of Southern Literature* (1906). In *The Southern Plantation* (1924) Francis Pendleton Gaines analyzes the plantation legend in the literary tradition. The *Library of Southern Literature,* edited by Edwin A. Alderman and others (17 volumes, 1907–1923), is a mine of selections accompanied by biographical and bibliographical information. *Southern Renascence: The Literature of the Modern South,* edited by Louis D. Rubin and Robert D. Jacobs (1953), contains good essays on several of the recent authors.

Works valuable for portraying the Southern background are W. J. Cash, *The Mind of the South* (1941); Shields McIlwaine, *The Southern Poor-White from Lubberland to Tobacco Road* (1939); the symposium *I'll Take My Stand* (1930); and the several volumes of *A History of the South,* edited by Wendell Holmes Stephenson and E. Merton Coulter (1947—).

Useful books on the short story are F. L. Pattee, *The Development of the American Short Story* (1923), Ray B. West, Jr., *The Short Story in America, 1900–1950* (1952), and Robert Cecil Beale, *The Development of the Short Story in the South* (1911). In A. H. Quinn, *American Fiction: An Historical and Critical Survey* (1936) the short story is given perspective alongside the novel.

The most helpful guide to the humorists of the Old Southwest is Walter Blair, *Native American Humor, 1800–1900* (1937), which contains, besides representative selections, the fullest bibliography on the subject available and an introduction which surveys the development of the native humor. The same author wrote also *Horse*

Sense in American Humor (1942). Constance Rourke's *American Humor: A Study of the National Character* (1931) was a pioneering work and is still valuable. Bernard DeVoto's *Mark Twain's America* (1932) surveys the humorous tradition, oral and literary, which lay back of Mark Twain. See also Norris W. Yates, *William T. Porter and the Spirit of the Times: A Study of the Big Bear School of Humor* (1957).

For general bibliography see the third volume of Robert E. Spiller and others, *Literary History of the United States* (1948) and the Supplement (1959); Lewis Leary, *Articles on American Literature, 1900–1950* (1954); the quarterly listing of articles in the issues of *American Literature;* and the annual bibliography in the *Publications of the Modern Language Association.*

A SOUTHERN CHRONOLOGY

1565   St. Augustine founded.

1585   Raleigh's "Lost Colony."

1607   Jamestown founded.

1608   John Smith (1580–1631), *A True Relation*.

1616   Smith, *A Description of New England*.

1624   Smith, *The Generall Historie of Virginia*.

1634   Maryland settlement.

1670   Charleston founded.

1676   Nathaniel Bacon's Rebellion.

1693   William and Mary College founded.

1705   Robert Beverley (1673–1722), *History and Present State of Virginia*.

1718   New Orleans founded.

1727   *Maryland Gazette* founded, the earliest Southern newspaper.

1728   Survey of the dividing line between Virginia and North Carolina by William Byrd II (1674–1744); *History of the Dividing Line* published in 1841; *Secret History*, 1929.

1732   Byrd's journal published in 1841 as *Progress to the Mines*.

1733   Byrd's journal published in 1841 as *Journey to the Land of Eden*. Oglethorpe's settlement of Georgia.

1755   French Acadians deported by the British.

1762   Louisiana ceded by France to Spain.

1763–67   Mason and Dixon line surveyed.

1769–71   Daniel Boone's exploration in Kentucky.

1775–83   American Revolution.

1784   Thomas Jefferson (1743–1826), *Notes on the State of Virginia.*

1785   University of Georgia founded.

1789   University of North Carolina founded.

1796   George Washington (1732–1799), "Farewell Address."

1803   Louisiana Purchase.

1811   Steamboats appear on the Mississippi.

1812–15   War with England.

1814   Francis Scott Key (1778–1843), "The Star-Spangled Banner."

1815   Battle of New Orleans.

1819   University of Virginia founded.

1820   Missouri Compromise.

1821   Florida annexed.

1824   George Tucker (1775–1861), *The Valley of the Shenandoah.*

1825   Edward Coote Pinkney (1802–1828), *Poems.*

1827   Edgar Allan Poe (1809–1849), *Tamerlane and Other Poems.*

1827–38   John James Audubon (1785–1851), *Birds of America.*

1829   Poe, *Al Aaraaf, Tamerlane, and Minor Poems.*

1831   Poe, *Poems.*

1832   John Pendleton Kennedy (1785–1870), *Swallow Barn.* Thomas Holley Chivers (1809–1858), *The Path of Sorrow.*

1833   Poe, "MS. Found in a Bottle," prize story. William Gilmore Simms (1806–1870), *Martin Faber.*

1834   Chivers, *Conrad and Eudora.* David Crockett (1786–1836), *Life of David Crockett of Tennessee.* Simms, *Guy Rivers.*

1834–64   *Southern Literary Messenger.*

1835   Kennedy, *Horse-Shoe Robinson.* Augustus Baldwin Longstreet (1790–1870), *Georgia Scenes.* Simms, *The Partisan; The*

Yemassee. Poe becomes editor of the *Southern Literary Messenger.* First of the "Crockett Almanacs."

1836   Simms, *Mellichampe.* Texas independence.

1837   Chivers, *Nacoochee.* Poe leaves the *Messenger.*

1838   Kennedy, *Rob of the Bowl.* Simms, *Richard Hurdis.*

1839   Simms, *The Damsel of Darien.*

1840   Kennedy, *Quodlibet.* Poe, *Tales of the Grotesque and Arabesque,* Simms, *Border Beagles.*

1841   Thomas Bangs Thorpe (1815–1878), "The Big Bear of Arkansas." Poe, "The Murders in the Rue Morgue." Simms, *The Kinsman.*

1842   Poe, review of Hawthorne's *Twice-Told Tales.* Simms, *Beauchampe.*

1843   Poe, *Prose Romances.* William Tappan Thompson (1812–1882), *Major Jones's Courtship.*

1845   Chivers, *The Lost Pleiad.* Johnson Jones Hooper (1815–1862), *Simon Suggs.* Poe, *Tales; The Raven and Other Poems.* Simms, *Count Julian; The Wigwam and the Cabin.* Thompson, *Chronicles of Pineville.* Annexation of Texas.

1846   Simms, *The Wigwam and the Cabin,* second series. Thorpe, *The Mysteries of the Backwoods; Our Army on the Rio Grande.*

1846–48   War with Mexico.

1847   Stephen Collins Foster (1826–1864), "Oh! Susannah." Thompson, *Major Jones's Sketches of Travel.* Thorpe, *Our Army at Monterey.*

1848   Foster, *Songs of the Sable Harmonists.* Poe, *Eureka.*

1850   Madison Tensas (Henry Clay Lewis, 1825–1850), *Odd Leaves from the Life of a Louisiana Swamp Doctor.* Compromise of 1850.

1851   Chivers, *Eonchs of Ruby.* Foster, "Old Folks at Home."

Hooper, *The Widow Rugby's Husband*. Simms, *Katherine Walton*.

1852   Harriet Beecher Stowe (1811–1896), *Uncle Tom's Cabin*.

1853   Chivers, *Virginalia*. Joseph Glover Baldwin (1815–1864), *Flush Times of Alabama and Mississippi*. Stowe, *A Key to Uncle Tom's Cabin*.

1854   John Esten Cooke (1830–1886), *Leather Stocking and Silk; The Virginia Comedians*. William J. Grayson (1788–1863), *The Hireling and the Slave*. Simms, *Woodcraft*. Thorpe, *The Hive of the Bee-Hunter*.

1855   Baldwin, *Party Leaders*. Paul Hamilton Hayne (1830–1886), *Poems*. Simms, *The Forayers*.

1856   Simms, *Eutaw; Charlemont*. Stowe, *Dred*.

1857   Hayne, *Sonnets and Other Poems*.

1857–60   *Russell's Magazine,* Charleston.

1857–61   Mark Twain (Samuel Langhorne Clemens, 1835–1910) a river pilot.

1858   Hooper, *Dog and Gun*. Thorpe, *Colonel Thorpe's Scenes in Arkansas*.

1859   Simms, *The Cassique of Kiawah*. John Brown's raid and his execution.

1860   Henry Timrod (1828–1867), *Poems*.

1861–65   Civil War.

1863   Cooke, *Life of Stonewall Jackson*.

1864   Longstreet, *Master William Mitten*.

1865   Mark Twain, "The Jumping Frog of Calavaras County."

1866   Cooke, *Surry of Eagle's Nest*. Charles Henry Smith (1826–1903), *Bill Arp, So Called*.

1867   George Washington Harris (1814–1869), *Sut Lovingood Yarns*. Sidney Lanier (1842–1881), *Tiger-Lilies*. Mark Twain,

The Celebrated Jumping Frog of Calavaras County and Other Sketches.

1868   Charles Henry Smith, *Bill Arp's Letters.* Fourteenth Amendment to the Constitution.

1869   Cooke, *Hilt to Hilt; Mohun.* Mark Twain, *The Innocents Abroad.*

1870   Cooke, *The Heir of Gaymount.* Fifteenth Amendment to the Constitution.

1871   Richard Malcolm Johnston (1822–1898), *Dukesborough Tales.*

1872   Hayne, *Legends and Lyrics.* Mark Twain, *Roughing It.*

1873   George W. Cable (1844–1925), " 'Sieur George." Mark Twain and Charles Dudley Warner, *The Gilded Age.* Charles Henry Smith, *Bill Arp's Peace Papers.* Timrod, *Poems.*

1874   Albion Tourgée (1838–1905), *'Toinette* (republished as *A Royal Gentleman,* 1881).

1875   Edward King, *The Great South.*

1876   Joel Chandler Harris (1848–1908) joined the Atlanta *Constitution.* Mark Twain, *Tom Sawyer.*

1877   Lanier, *Poems.* End of Reconstruction.

1878   Lanier, "The Marshes of Glynn."

1879   Cable, *Old Creole Days.* Lanier, *The Boy's Froissart.* Tourgée, *A Fool's Errand; Figs and Thistles.*

1880   Cable, *The Grandissimes.* Joel Chandler Harris, *Uncle Remus: His Songs and Sayings.* Lanier, *The Boy's King Arthur; The Science of English Verse.* Mark Twain, *A Tramp Abroad.* Tourgée, *Bricks without Straw.*

1881   Cable, *Madame Delphine.* Lanier, *The Boy's Mabinogion.*

1882   Hayne, *Collected Poems.* Lafcadio Hearn (1850–1904), *One of Cleopatra's Nights.* Lanier, *The Boy's Percy.* Mark Twain, *The Prince and the Pauper.* Tourgée, *John Eax and Mamelon.*

1883   Joel Chandler Harris, *Nights with Uncle Remus.* Lanier, *The*

English Novel. Mark Twain, *Life on the Mississippi*. Tourgée, *Hot Plowshares*.

1884   Cable, *Dr. Sevier*. Charles Egbert Craddock (Mary Noailles Murfree, 1850–1922), *In the Tennessee Mountains; Where the Battle Was Fought*. Joel Chandler Harris, *Mingo, and Other Sketches in Black and White*. Hearn, *Stray Leaves from Strange Literature*. Lanier, *Poems*. Thomas Nelson Page (1853–1922), "Marse Chan." Mark Twain, *Huckleberry Finn*.

1885   Craddock, *Down the Ravine; The Prophet of the Great Smoky Mountains*. Hearn, *Gombo Zhébes*.

1886   Henry W. Grady (1850–1889), "The New South."

1887   Joel Chandler Harris, *Free Joe, and Other Georgian Sketches*. Thomas Nelson Page, *In Ole Virginia*.

1888   Cable, *Bonaventure*. Thomas Nelson Page, *Befo' de War*.

1889   Cable, *Strange True Stories of Louisiana*. Hearn, *Chita*. Mark Twain, *A Connecticut Yankee in King Arthur's Court*.

1890   Madison Cawein (1865–1914), *Lyrics and Idylls*. Kate Chopin (1851–1904), *At Fault*. Hearn, *Two Years in the French West Indies*. Tourgée, *Pactolus Prime*.

1891   James Lane Allen (1849–1925), *Flute and Violin*. Thomas Nelson Page, *Elsket and Other Stories*. Francis Hopkinson Smith (1838–1915), *Colonel Carter of Cartersville*.

1891–95   Walter Hines Page (1855–1918) editor of the *Forum*.

1892   James Lane Allen, *The Blue-Grass Region of Kentucky*. Joel Chandler Harris, *Uncle Remus and His Friends*. Grace King (1851–1932), *Tales of a Time and Place*. Thomas Nelson Page, *The Old South*. The *Sewanee Review* founded by W. P. Trent.

1893   Grace King, *Balcony Stories*. F. J. Turner, "The Significance of the Frontier in American History."

1894   Allen, *A Kentucky Cardinal*. Cable, *John March, Southerner*. Chopin, *Bayou Folk*. Hearn, *Glimpses of Unfamiliar Japan*.

Thomas Nelson Page, *The Burial of the Guns*. Mark Twain, *Pudd'nhead Wilson*.

1895   Craddock, *The Mystery of Witchface Mountain*. Joel Chandler Harris, *Mr. Rabbit at Home*.

1895–99   Walter Hines Page editor of the *Atlantic Monthly*.

1896   Allen, *Aftermath; A Summer in Arcady*. Paul Laurence Dunbar (1872–1906), *Lyrics of Lowly Life*. John Fox, Jr. (1863–1919), *A Cumberland Vendetta*. Mark Twain, *Joan of Arc*.

1897   Allen, *The Choir Invisible*. Chopin, *A Night in Arcadie*. Craddock, *The Young Mountaineers*. Fox, *"Hell-fer-sartin."* Ellen Glasgow (1874–1945), *The Descendant*. Thomas Nelson Page, *Social Life in Old Virginia; The Old Gentleman of the Black Stock*.

1898   Fox, *The Kentuckians*. Thomas Nelson Page, *Red Rock*. Spanish-American War.

1899   Cable, *Strong Hearts*. Charles Waddell Chesnutt (1858–1932), *The Conjure Woman; The Wife of His Youth*. Chopin, *The Awakening*. Craddock, *The Story of Old Fort Loudon*. Fox, *A Mountain Europa*. Booker T. Washington (1856–1915), *The Future of the Negro*.

1900   Allen, *The Reign of Law*. Fox, *Crittenden*. Glasgow, *The Voice of the People*. Mark Twain, "The Man That Corrupted Hadleyburg." The cause of yellow fever discovered. *Uncle Remus's Magazine* founded.

1900–13   Walter Hines Page editor of the *World's Work*.

1901   Cable, *The Cavalier*. Washington, *Up from Slavery*.

1902   Thomas Dixon (1864–1946), *The Leopard's Spots*. Glasgow, *The Battle Ground; The Freeman and Other Poems*. Joel Chandler Harris, *Gabriel Tolliver*. The *South Atlantic Quarterly* founded by John Spencer Bassett.

1903   Allen, *The Mettle of the Pasture*. Craddock, *A Spectre of Power*. Fox, *The Little Shepherd of Kingdom Come*. Thomas

Nelson Page, *Gordon Keith*. Francis Hopkinson Smith, *Colonel Carter's Christmas*.

1904 James Branch Cabell (1879–), *The Eagle's Shadow*. Craddock, *The Frontiersman*. Glasgow, *The Deliverance*. Joel Chandler Harris, *The Tar-Baby and Other Rhymes of Uncle Remus*. O. Henry (William Sydney Porter, 1862–1910), *Cabbages and Kings*. Thomas Nelson Page, *Bred in the Bone*.

1905 Craddock, *The Storm Centre*. Dixon, *The Clansman*.

1906 Craddock, *The Amulet*. Glasgow, *The Wheel of Life*. O. Henry, *The Four Million*. Stark Young (1881–), *The Blind Man at the Window; Guenevere*.

1907 Dixon, *The Traitor*. Joel Chandler Harris, *Uncle Remus and Brer Rabbit*. O. Henry, *Heart of the West; The Trimmed Lamp*.

1908 Fox, *The Trail of the Lonesome Pine*. Glasgow, *The Ancient Law*. O. Henry, *The Gentle Grafter; The Voice of the City*. Thomas Nelson Page, *The Old Dominion*.

1909 Cabell, *The Cords of Vanity*. Glasgow, *The Romance of a Plain Man*. O. Henry, *Options; Roads of Destiny*. Thomas Nelson Page, *John Marvel, Assistant*. Washington, *The Story of the Negro*.

1910 O. Henry, *Whirligigs; Strictly Business*. John A. Lomax (1872–1948), *Cowboy Songs and Other Frontier Ballads*.

1911 Glasgow, *The Miller of Old Church*. O. Henry, *Sixes and Sevens*.

1912 O. Henry, *Rolling Stones*.

1913 Dunbar, *Complete Poems*. Glasgow, *Virginia*.

1915 Cabell, *The Rivet in Grandfather's Neck*. John Gould Fletcher (1886–1950), *Irradiations*. Elizabeth Madox Roberts (1886–1941), *In the Great Steep's Garden*.

1915–24 The *Texas Review*.

1916 Cabell, *The Certain Hour*. Fletcher, *Goblins and Pagodas*.

Glasgow, *Life and Gabriella*. Mark Twain, "The Mysterious Stranger."

1917   Cabell, *The Cream of the Jest*. O. Henry, *Waifs and Strays*.

1917–18   The United States in World War I.

1918   Carolina Playmakers founded.

1919   Cabell, *Jurgen; Beyond Life*. John Crowe Ransom (1888–   ), *Poems about God*.

1921   Cabell, *Figures of Earth*. Fletcher, *Breakers and Granite*.

1922   Dubose Heyward (1885–1940) and Hervey Allen (1889–1952), *Carolina Chansons*. Roberts, *Under the Tree*.

1922–25   The *Fugitive* published at Nashville.

1923   Glasgow, *The Shadowy Third*. O. Henry, *Postscripts*.

1924   Donald Davidson (1893–   ), *An Outland Piper*. William Faulkner (1897–   ), *The Marble Faun*. Heyward, *Skylines and Horizons*. Mark Twain, *Autobiography*. Julia Peterkin (1880–   ), *Green Thursday*. Ransom, *Chills and Fever; Grace After Meat*. Young, *The Three Fountains; The Colonnade*. The *Southwest Review* founded.

1925   Allen, *The Landmark*. Glasgow, *Barren Ground*. Paul Green 1894–   ), *The Lord's Will and Other Carolina Plays*. Heyward, *Porgy*. Scopes trial in Tennessee. The *Virginia Quarterly Review* founded.

1926   Cabell, *The Music from Behind the Moon*. Faulkner, *Soldiers' Pay*. Fletcher, *Branches of Adam*. Green, *In Abraham's Bosom*, Pulitzer Prize; *Lonesome Road*. Roberts, *The Time of Man*. T. S. Stribling (1881–   ), *Teeftallow*. Young, *Heaven Trees*.

1927   Davidson, *The Tall Men*. Faulkner, *Mosquitoes*. Green, *The Field God*. Peterkin, *Black April*. Ransom, *Two Gentlemen in Bonds*. Roberts, *My Heart and My Flesh*.

1928   Roark Bradford (1896–1948), *Ol' Man Adam an' His Chillun*. Fletcher, *The Black Rock*. Peterkin, *Scarlet Sister Mary*,

Pulitzer Prize. Roberts, *Jingling in the Wind*. Allen Tate (1899–   ), *Mr. Pope and Other Poems*.

1929   Bradford, *This Side Jordan*. Erskine Caldwell (1903–   ), *The Bastard*. Faulkner, *The Sound and the Fury; Sartoris*. Glasgow, *They Stooped to Folly*. Heyward, *Mamba's Daughters*. Merrill Moore (1903–1957), *The Noise That Time Makes*. Robert Penn Warren (1905–   ), *John Brown*. Thomas Wolfe (1900–1938), *Look Homeward, Angel*. Young, *River House*. Stock market crash.

1930   Bradford, *Ol' King David an' the Philistine Boys*. Caldwell, *Poor Fool*. Faulkner, *As I Lay Dying; I'll Take My Stand*. Katherine Anne Porter (1894–   ), *Flowering Judas*. Ransom, *God Without Thunder*. Roberts, *The Great Meadow*. Tate, *Three Poems*. *The Green Pastures* adapted for the stage from Bradford's *Ol' Man Adam an' His Chillun*.

1931   Bradford, *John Henry*. Caldwell, *American Earth*. Faulkner, *Sanctuary; These 13; Idyll in the Desert*. Caroline Gordon (1895–   ), *Penhally*. Green, *The House of Connelly*. Heyward, *Jasbo Brown*. Roberts, *A Buried Treasure*. Stribling, *The Forge*.

1932   Caldwell, *Tobacco Road*. Virginius Dabney (1901–   ), *Liberalism in the South*. Faulkner, *Light in August; Miss Zilphia Gant; Salmagundi*. Glasgow, *The Sheltered Life*. Heyward, *Peter Ashley*. Peterkin, *Bright Skin*. Roberts, *The Haunted Mirror*. Stribling, *The Store,* Pulitzer Prize, 1933. Tate, *Poems, 1928–1931*.

1933   Hervey Allen, *Anthony Adverse*. Bradford, *Kingdom Coming*. Caldwell, *God's Little Acre; We Are the Living*. Faulkner, *A Green Bough*. Marjorie Kinnan Rawlings (1896–1953), *South Moon Under*.

1933–41   *Tobacco Road* on the stage.

1934   Hamilton Basso (1904–   ), *Cinnamon Seed*. Bradford, *How Come Christmas,* private printing in 1930. Faulkner, *Dr. Martino and Other Stories*. Gordon, *Aleck Maury, Sportsman*.

Green, *Roll, Sweet Chariot.* Lomax, *American Ballads and Folk Songs.* Porter, *Hacienda.* Stribling, *Unfinished Cathedral.* Jesse Stuart (1905–   ), *Man with a Bull-Tongue Plow.* Young, *So Red the Rose.*

1935   Caldwell, *Journeyman; Kneel to the Rising Sun.* Faulkner, *Pylon.* Fletcher, *XXIV Elegies.* Glasgow, *Vein of Iron.* Green, *This Body the Earth.* Porgy and Bess, an opera adapted from Heyward's *Porgy.* Rawlings, *Golden Apples.* Roberts, *He Sent Forth a Raven.* Wolfe, *Of Time and the River; From Death to Morning.* Young, *Feliciana.* 1935–1939 Federal Writers Project.

1935–42   The *Southern Review* published at Louisiana State University.

1936   Basso, *Courthouse Square.* Faulkner, *Absalom, Absalom!* Fletcher, *The Epic of Arkansas.* Andrew Lytle (1903–   ), *The Long Night.* Margaret Mitchell (1900–1949), *Gone with the Wind.* Stuart, *Head O' W-Hollow.* Tate, *Reactionary Essays on Poetry and Ideas; The Mediterranean and Other Poems. Who Owns America?*

1936–39   Federal Theater Project.

1937   Caldwell, *You Have Seen Their Faces.* Clifford Dowdey (1904–   ), *Bugles Blow No More.* Fletcher, *Life Is My Song.* Gordon, *None Shall Look Back; The Garden of Adonis.* Green, *Johnny Johnson; The Lost Colony.* Porter, *Noon Wine.* Tate, *Selected Poems; The Fathers.*

1938   Hervey Allen, *Action at Aquila.* Cabell, *The King Was in His Counting House.* Caldwell, *Southways.* Davidson, *Lee in the Mountains; The Attack on Leviathan.* Faulkner, *The Unvanquished.* Fletcher, *Selected Poems,* Pulitzer Prize. Merrill Moore, *M.* Ransom, *The World's Body.* Rawlings, *The Yearling.* Roberts, *Black Is My Truelove's Hair.* Stuart, *Beyond Dark Hills.* Richard Wright (1909–   ), *Uncle Tom's Children.*

1939   Basso, *Days Before Lent.* Dixon, *The Flaming Sword.* Faulkner, *The Wild Palms.* Heyward, *The Star Spangled Virgin.*

Porter, *Pale Horse, Pale Rider*. Warren, *Night Rider*. Wolfe, *The Web and the Rock*.

1940 Caldwell, *Trouble in July; Jackpot*. Faulkner, *The Hamlet*. Carson McCullers (1917–), *The Heart Is a Lonely Hunter*. Rawlings, *When the Whippoorwill*. Roberts, *Song in the Meadow*. Stuart, *Trees of Heaven*. Wolfe, *You Can't Go Home Again*. Wright, *Native Son*.

1941 Basso, *Wine of the Country*. Fletcher, *South Star*. Glasgow, *In This Our Life,* Pulitzer Prize. Gordon, *Green Centuries*. Lomax, *Our Singing Country*. McCullers, *Reflections in a Golden Eye*. Ransom, *The New Criticism*. Roberts, *Not by Strange Gods*. Stuart, *Man of the Mountains*. Tate, *Reason in Madness*. Eudora Welty (1909–), *A Curtain of Green*. Wright, *12 Million Black Voices*.

1941–45 The United States in World War II.

1942 Basso, *Sun in Capricorn*. Cabell, *The First Gentleman of America*. Faulkner, *Go Down, Moses*. Randall Jarrell (1914–), *Blood for a Stranger*. Rawlings, *Cross Creek*. James Street (1903–), *Tap Roots*. Welty, *The Robber Bridegroom*.

1943 Caldwell, *Georgia Boy*. Glasgow, *A Certain Measure*. Green, *The Hawthorn Tree*. Warren, *At Heaven's Gate*. Welty, *The Wide Net, and Other Stories*.

1944 Caldwell, *Tragic Ground*. Hodding Carter (1907–), *Winds of Fear*. Porter, *The Leaning Tower and Other Stories*. Lillian Smith (1897–), *Strange Fruit*. Stuart, *Taps for Private Tussie; Mountain Mettle; Album of Destiny*. Tate, *The Winter Sea*. Warren, *Selected Poems 1923-43*.

1944–46 Tate editor of the *Sewanee Review*.

1945 Gordon, *The Forest of the South*. Jarrell, *Little Friend, Little Friend*. Ransom, *Selected Poems*. Tennessee Williams (1914–), *The Glass Menagerie; Battle of Angels*. Wright, *Black Boy*.

1946 Caldwell, *A House in the Uplands*. Fletcher, *The Burning Mountain*. McCullers, *The Member of the Wedding*. Stuart,

Tales from the Plum Grove Hills. Warren, *All the King's Men,* Pulitzer Prize. Welty, *Delta Wedding.* Williams, *27 Wagons Full of Cotton.*

1947 Cabell, *Let Me Lie.* Caldwell, *The Sure Hand of God.* Lomax, *Adventures of a Ballad Hunter.* Williams, *A Streetcar Named Desire,* Pulitzer Prize; *You Touched Me.*

1948 Caldwell, *This Very Earth.* Truman Capote (1925–), *Other Voices, Other Rooms.* Faulkner, *Intruder in the Dust.* Jarrell, *Losses.* Elizabeth Spencer (1921–), *Fire in the Morning.* Tate, *On the Limits of Poetry.* Peter Taylor (1917–), *A Long Fourth and Other Stories.* Williams, *Summer and Smoke; American Blues.* Welty, *Music from Spain.*

1949 Basso, *The Greenroom.* Caldwell, *A Place Called Estherville.* Capote, *A Tree of Night and Other Stories.* Faulkner, *Knight's Gambit.* Lillian Smith, *Killers of the Dream.* Stuart, *The Thread That Runs So True.* Tate, *The Hovering Fly.* Warren, *Circus in the Attic.* Welty, *The Golden Apples.*

1950 Caldwell, *Episode in Palmetto.* Capote, *Local Color.* Faulkner, *Collected Stories;* Nobel Prize for 1949. McCullers, *The Member of the Wedding* dramatized. Stuart, *Hie to the Hunters.* Taylor, *A Woman of Means.* Warren, *World Enough and Time.* Williams, *The Roman Spring of Mrs. Stone.*

1950–53 The Korean War.

1951 Caldwell, *Call It Experience.* Capote, *The Grass Harp,* dramatized in 1952. Faulkner, *Requiem for a Nun.* Jarrell, *The Seven-League Crutches.* McCullers, *The Ballad of the Sad Cafe.* Williams, *The Rose Tattoo.*

1952 Caldwell, *The Courting of Susie Brown.* Flannery O'Connor (1925–), *Wise Blood.* Porter, *The Days Before.* Spencer, *This Crooked Way.*

1953 Jarrell, *Poetry and the Age.* Tate, *The Forlorn Demon.* Warren, *Brother to Dragons.* Williams, *Camino Real.* Wright, *The Outsider. Southern Renascence,* ed. Louis D. Rubin, Jr., and Robert D. Jacobs.

1954   Basso, *The View from Pompey's Head*. Faulkner, *A Fable*.
Glasgow, *The Woman Within*. Jay B. Hubbell (1885–   ),
The South in American Literature. Jarrell, *Pictures from an
Institution*. Frances Gray Patton, *Good Morning, Miss Dove*.
Lillian Smith, *The Journey*. Taylor, *The Widows of Thorn-
ton*. Welty, *The Ponder Heart*. Williams, *Hard Candy; Cat on
a Hot Tin Roof,* Pulitzer Prize. Wright, *Black Power*. United
States Supreme Court rules racial segregation in schools is un-
constitutional.

1955   Capote, *House of Flowers*. Jarrell, *Selected Poems*. Moore, *A
Doctor's Book of Hours*. O'Connor, *A Good Man Is Hard to
Find*. Lillian Smith, *Now Is the Time*. Warren, *Band of
Angels*. Welty, *The Bride of the Innisfallen*.

1956   Capote, *The Muses Are Heard*. Spencer, *The Voice at the
Back Door*. Street, *Captain Little Axe*. Wolfe, *Letters,* ed.
Elizabeth Nowell. Warren, *Segregation*.

1957   Faulkner, *The Town*. Lytle, *The Velvet Horn*.

1958   Capote, *Breakfast at Tiffany's*. Dowdey, *The Death of a Na-
tion*. Glasgow, *Letters,* ed. Blair Rouse. Lytle, *A Novel, A
Novella, and Four Stories*. Stuart, *Plowshare in Heaven*.
Warren, *Selected Essays*. Wright, *The Long Dream*.

1959   Basso, *The Light Infantry Ball*. Carter, *The Angry Scar*.
Faulkner, *The Mansion*. Warren, *The Cave*.

SOUTHERN STORIES

A TALE OF THE
RAGGED MOUNTAINS

Edgar Allan Poe

First published in *Godey's Lady's Book*, April, 1844; then in the *Broadway Journal*, November 29, 1845. Not collected by Poe.

Although Edgar Allan Poe (1809-1849) grew up in Richmond, attended the University of Virginia, edited *The Southern Literary Messenger* at Richmond from 1835 to 1837, and remained conscious of his Southern ties even when in his later years he lived outside the South, only a few of his stories have identifiable Southern connections. His most characteristic stories gain their effects in part from being placed in unspecified or remote or unearthly settings, and they rarely touch on matters which belong to any one section or country.

In an essay-review of Hawthorne's *Twice-Told Tales* published in *Graham's Magazine* for May, 1842, Poe enunciated what became in effect the principles by which short stories were written and judged during the next hundred years. He published three collections of his stories: *Tales of the Grotesque and Arabesque* (1840), *Prose Romances* (1843), and *Tales* (1845). The standard edition of his works is that edited by James A. Harrison in seventeen volumes (1902); Thomas O. Mabbott is now preparing a new edition of the complete works. Poe's letters have been published in two volumes by John W. Ostrom (1948). A reliable factual account of his life is Arthur Hobson Quinn, *Edgar Allan Poe: A Critical Biography* (1941). Jay B. Hubbell has published in *Eight American Authors*, edited by Floyd Stovall (1956), an excellent bibliographical essay on Poe.

The vision which Bedloe had of Cheyte Sing and Hastings and the massacre at Benares was paraphrased from the account in Thomas Babington Macaulay's essay on "Warren Hastings" (1841), in which occurs the name Bedloe, though in a different context from that in Poe's tale.

During the fall of the year 1827, while residing near Charlottesville, Virginia, I casually made the acquaintance of Mr. Augustus Bedloe. This young gentleman was remarkable in every respect, and excited in me a profound interest and curiosity. I found it impossible to comprehend him either in his moral or his physical relations. Of his family I could obtain no satisfactory account. Whence he came, I never ascertained. Even about his age—although I call him a young gentleman—there was something which perplexed me in no little degree. He certainly *seemed* young—and he made a point of speaking about his youth—yet there were moments when I should have had little trouble in imagining him a hundred years of age. But in no regard was he more peculiar than in his personal appearance. He was singularly tall and thin. He stooped much. His limbs were exceedingly long and emaciated. His forehead was broad and low. His complexion was absolutely bloodless. His mouth was large and flexible, and his teeth were more wildly uneven, although sound, than I had ever before seen teeth in a human head. The expression of his smile, however, was by no means unpleasing, as might be supposed; but it had no variation whatever. It was one of profound melancholy—of a phaseless and unceasing gloom. His eyes were abnormally large, and round like those of a cat. The pupils, too, upon any accession or diminution of light, underwent contraction or dilation, just such as is observed in the feline tribe. In moments of excitement the orbs grew bright to a degree almost inconceivable; seeming to emit luminous rays, not of a reflected, but of an intrinsic lustre, as does a candle or the sun; yet their ordinary condition was so totally vapid, filmy, and dull, as to convey the idea of the eyes of a long-interred corpse.

These peculiarities of person appeared to cause him much annoyance, and he was continually alluding to them in a sort of half explanatory, half apologetic strain, which, when I first heard it, impressed me very painfully. I soon, however, grew accustomed to it, and my uneasiness wore off. It seemed to be his design rather to insinuate than directly to assert that, physically, he had not always been what he was—that a long series of neuralgic attacks had reduced him from a condition of more than usual personal beauty, to that which I saw. For many years past he had been attended by a physician, named Templeton—an old gentleman, perhaps seventy years of age—whom he had first encountered at Saratoga, and from whose attention, while there, he either received, or fancied that he received, great benefit. The result was that Bedloe, who was wealthy, had made an arrangement with Dr. Templeton, by which the latter, in consideration of a liberal annual allowance, had consented to devote his time and medical experience exclusively to the care of the invalid.

Doctor Templeton had been a traveller in his younger days, and, at Paris, had become a convert, in great measure, to the doctrines of Mesmer. It was altogether by means of magnetic remedies that he had succeeded in alleviating the acute pains of his patient; and this success had very naturally inspired the latter with a certain degree of confidence in the opinions from which the remedies had been educed. The Doctor, however, like all enthusiasts, had struggled hard to make a thorough convert of his pupil, and finally so far gained his point as to induce the sufferer to submit to numerous experiments.—By a frequent repetition of these, a result had arisen, which of late days has become so common as to attract little or no attention, but which, at the period of which I write, had very rarely been known in America. I mean to say, that between Dr. Templeton and Bedloe there had grown up, little by little, a very distinct and strongly marked *rapport,* or magnetic relation. I am not prepared to assert, however, that this *rapport* extended beyond the limits of the simple sleep-producing power; but this power itself had attained great intensity. At the first attempt to induce the magnetic somnolency, the mesmerist entirely failed. In the fifth or sixth he succeeded very partially, and after long continued effort. Only at the twelfth was the triumph complete. After this the will of the patient succumbed rapidly to that of the physician, so that, when I first became acquainted with the two, sleep was brought about almost instantaneously, by the mere volition of the operator, even when the invalid was unaware of his presence. It is only now, in the year 1845, when similar miracles are witnessed daily by thousands, that I dare venture to record this apparent impossibility as a matter of serious fact.

The temperature of Bedloe was, in the highest degree, sensitive, excitable, enthusiastic. His imagination was singularly vigorous and creative; and no doubt it derived additional force from the habitual use of morphine, which he swallowed in great quantity, and without which he would have found it impossible to exist. It was his practice to take a very large dose of it immediately after breakfast, each morning—or rather immediately after a cup of strong coffee, for he ate nothing in the forenoon—and then set forth alone, or attended only by a dog, upon a long ramble among the chain of wild and dreary hills that lie westward and southward of Charlottesville, and are there dignified by the title of the Ragged Mountains.

Upon a dim, warm, misty day, towards the close of November, and during the strange *interregnum* of the seasons which in America is termed the Indian Summer Mr. Bedloe departed, as usual, for the hills. The day passed, and still he did not return.

About eight o'clock at night, having become seriously alarmed at his protracted absence, we were about setting out in search of him, when he unexpectedly made his appearance, in health no worse than usual, and in rather more than ordinary spirits. The account which he gave of his expedition, and of the events which had detained him, was a singular one indeed.

"You will remember," said he, "that it was about nine in the morning when I left Charlottesville. I bent my steps immediately to the mountains, and, about ten, entered a gorge which was entirely new to me. I followed the windings of this pass with much interest.—The scenery which presented itself on all sides, although scarcely entitled to be called grand, had about it an indescribable and to me, a delicious aspect of dreary desolation. The solitude seemed absolutely virgin. I could not help believing that the green sods and the gray rocks upon which I trod, had been trodden never before by the foot of a human being. So entirely secluded, and in fact inaccessible, except through a series of accidents, is the entrance of the ravine, that it is by no means impossible that I was indeed the first adventurer —the very first and sole adventurer who had ever penetrated its recesses.

"The thick and peculiar mist, or smoke, which distinguishes the Indian Summer, and which now hung heavily over all objects, served, no doubt, to deepen the vague impressions which these objects created. So dense was this pleasant fog, that I could at no time see more than a dozen yards of the path before me. This path was excessively sinuous, and as the sun could not be seen, I soon lost all idea of the direction in which I journeyed. In the meantime the morphine had its customary effect—that of enduing all the external world with an intensity of interest. In the quivering of a leaf—in the hue of a blade of grass—in the shape of a trefoil—in the humming of a bee—in the gleaming of a dew-drop—in the breathing of the wind—in the faint odors that came from the forest—there came a whole universe of suggestion—a gay and motly train of rhapsodical and immethodical thought.

"Busied in this, I walked on for several hours, during which the mist deepened around me to so great an extent, that at length I was reduced to an absolute groping of the way. And now an indescribable uneasiness possessed me—a species of nervous hesitation and tremor.—I feared to tread, lest I should be precipitated into some abyss. I remembered, too, strange stories told about these Ragged Hills, and of the uncouth and fierce races of men who tenanted their groves and caverns. A thousand vague fancies oppressed and disconcerted me—fancies the more distressing because vague. Very suddenly my attention was arrested by the loud beating of a drum.

"My amazement was, of course, extreme. A drum in these hills was a thing unknown. I could not have been more surprised at the sound of the trump of the Archangel. But a new and still more astounding source of interest and perplexity arose. There came a wild rattling or jingling sound, as if of a bunch of large keys—and upon the instant a dusky-visaged and half-naked man rushed past me with a shriek. He came so close to my person that I felt his hot breath upon my face. He bore in one hand an instrument composed of an assemblage of steel rings, and shook them vigorously as he ran. Scarcely had he disappeared in the mist, before, panting after him, with open mouth and glaring eyes, there darted a huge beast. I could not be mistaken in its character. It was a hyena.

"The sight of this monster rather relieved than heightened my terrors—for I now made sure that I dreamed, and endeavored to arouse myself to waking consciousness. I stepped boldly and briskly forward. I rubbed my eyes. I called aloud. I pinched my limbs. A small spring of water presented itself to my view, and here, stooping,

I bathed my hands and my head and neck. This seemed to dissipate the equivocal sensations which had hitherto annoyed me. I arose, as I thought, a new man, and proceeded steadily and complacently on my unknown way.

"At length, quite overcome by exertion, and by a certain oppressive closeness of the atmosphere, I seated myself beneath a tree. Presently there came a feeble gleam of sunshine, and the shadow of the leaves of the tree fell faintly but definitely upon the grass. At this shadow I gazed wonderingly for many minutes. Its character stupified me with astonishment. I looked upward. The tree was a palm.

"I now rose hurriedly, and in a state of fearful agitation—for the fancy that I dreamed would serve me no longer. I saw—I felt that I had perfect command of my senses—and these senses now brought to my soul a world of novel and singular sensation. The heat became all at once intolerable. A strange odor loaded the breeze.—A low continuous murmur, like that arising from a full, but gently-flowing river, came to my ears, intermingled with the peculiar hum of multitudinous human voices.

"While I listened in an extremity of astonishment which I need not attempt to describe, a strong and brief gust of wind bore off the incumbent fog as if by the wand of an enchanter.

"I found myself at the foot of a high mountain, and looking down into a vast plain, through which wound a majestic river. On the margin of this river stood an Eastern-looking city, such as we read of in the Arabian Tales, but of a character even more singular than any there described. From my position, which was far above the level of the town, I could perceive its every nook and corner, as if delineated on a map. The streets seemed innumerable, and crossed each other irregularly in all directions, but were rather long winding alleys than streets, and absolutely swarmed with inhabitants. The houses were wildly picturesque. On every hand was a wilderness of balconies, of verandahs, of minarets, of shrines, and fantastically carved oriels. Bazaars abounded; and in these were displayed rich wares in infinite variety and profusion—silks, muslins, the most dazzling cutlery, the most magnificent jewels and gems. Besides these things, were seen, on all sides, banners and palanquins, litters with stately dames close veiled, elephants gorgeously caparisoned, idols grotesquely hewn, drums, banners and gongs, spears, silver and gilded maces. And amid the crowd, and the clamor, and the general intricacy and confusion—amid the million of black and yellow men, turbaned and robed, and of flowing beard, there roamed a countless multitude of holy filleted bulls, while vast legions of the filthy but sacred ape clambered, chattering and shrieking, about the cornices of the mosques, or clung to the minarets and oriels. From the swarming streets to the banks of the river, there descended innumerable flights of steps leading to bathing places, while the river itself seemed to force a passage with difficulty through the vast fleets of deeply-burthened ships that far and wide encumbered its surface. Beyond the limits of the city arose, in frequent majestic groups, the palm and the cocoa, with other gigantic and weird trees of vast age; and here and there might be seen a field of rice, the thatched hut of a peasant, a tank, a stray temple, a gypsy camp, or a solitary graceful maiden taking her way, with a pitcher upon her head, to the banks of the magnificent river.

"You will say now, of course, that I dreamed; but not so. What I saw—what I heard—what I felt—what I thought—had about it nothing of the unmistakable idiosyncrasy of the dream. All was rigorously self-consistent. At first, doubting that I was really awake, I entered into a series of tests, which soon convinced me that I really was. Now, when one dreams, and, in the dream, suspects that he dreams, the suspicion *never fails to confirm itself,* and the sleeper is almost immediately aroused. Thus Novalis errs not in saying that 'we are near waking when we dream that we dream.' Had the vision occurred to me as I describe it, without my suspecting it as a dream, then a dream it might absolutely have been, but, occurring as it did, and suspected and tested as it was, I am forced to class it among other phenomena."

"In this I am not sure that you are wrong," observed Dr. Templeton, "but proceed. You arose and descended into the city."

"I arose," continued Bedloe, regarding the Doctor with an air of profound astonishment, "I arose as you say, and descended into the city. On my way, I fell in with an immense populace, crowding, through every avenue, all in the same direction, and exhibiting in every action the wildest excitement. Very suddenly, and by some in-

conceivable impulse, I became intensely imbued with personal interest in what was going on. I seemed to feel that I had an important
part to play, without exactly understanding what it was. Against
the crowd which environed me, however, I experienced a deep sentiment of animosity. I shrank from amid them, and, swiftly, by a
circuitous path, reached and entered the city. Here all was the wildest tumult and contention. A small party of men, clad in garments
half-Indian, half-European, and officered by gentlemen in a uniform
partly British, were engaged, at great odds, with the swarming rabble of the alleys. I joined the weaker party, arming myself with the
weapons of a fallen officer, and fighting I knew not whom with the
nervous ferocity of despair. We were soon overpowered by numbers, and driven to seek refuge in a species of kiosk. Here we barricaded ourselves, and, for the present, were secure. From a loop-hole
near the summit of the kiosk, I perceived a vast crowd, in furious
agitation, surrounding and assaulting a gay palace that overhung
the river. Presently, from an upper window of this palace, there descended an effeminate-looking person, by means of a string made of
the turbans of his attendants. A boat was at hand, in which he escaped to the opposite bank of the river.

"And now a new object took possession of my soul. I spoke a few
hurried but energetic words to my companions, and, having succeeded in gaining over a few of them to my purpose, made a frantic
sally from the kiosk. We rushed amid the crowd that surrounded it.
They retreated, at first, before us. They rallied, fought madly, and
retreated again. In the mean time we were borne far from the kiosk, and became bewildered and entangled among the narrow
streets of tall overhanging houses, into the recesses of which the sun
had never been able to shine. The rabble pressed impetuously upon
us, harassing us with their spears, and overwhelming us with flights
of arrows. These latter were very remarkable, and resembled in
some respects the writhing creese of the Malay. They were made to
imitate the body of a creeping serpent, and were long and black,
with a poisoned barb. One of them struck me upon the right temple.
I reeled and fell. An instantaneous and deadly sickness seized me. I
struggled—I gasped—I died."

"You will hardly persist *now*," said I, smiling, "that the whole of your adventure was not a dream. You are not prepared to maintain that you are dead?"

When I said these words, I of course expected some lively sally from Bedloe in reply; but, to my astonishment, he hesitated, trembled, became fearfully pallid, and remained silent. I looked towards Templeton. He sat erect and rigid in his chair—his teeth chattered, and his eyes were starting from their sockets. "Proceed!" he at length said hoarsely to Bedloe.

"For many minutes," continued the latter, "my sole sentiment—my sole feeling—was that of darkness and nonentity, with the consciousness of death. At length, there seemed to pass a violent and sudden shock through my soul, as if of electricity. With it came the sense of elasticity and of light. This latter I felt—not saw. In an instant I seemed to rise from the ground. But I had no bodily, no visible, audible, or palpable presence. The crowd had departed. The tumult had ceased. The city was in comparative repose. Beneath me lay my corpse, with the arrow in my temple, the whole head greatly swollen and disfigured. But all these things I felt—not saw. I took interest in nothing. Even the corpse seemed a matter in which I had no concern. Volition I had none, but appeared to be impelled into motion, and flitted buoyantly out of the city, retracing the circuitous path by which I had entered it. When I had attained that point of the ravine in the mountains at which I had encountered the hyena, I again experienced a shock as of a galvanic battery; the sense of weight, of volition, of substance, returned. I became my original self, and bent my steps eagerly homewards—but the past had not lost the vividness of the real—and not now, even for an instant, can I compel my understanding to regard it as a dream."

"Nor was it," said Templeton, with an air of deep solemnity, "yet it would be difficult to say how otherwise it should be termed. Let us suppose only, that the soul of the man of today is upon the verge of some stupendous psychal discoveries. Let us content ourselves with this supposition. For the rest I have some explanation to make. Here is a water-color drawing, which I should have shown you before, but which an unaccountable sentiment of horror has hitherto prevented me from showing."

We looked at the picture which he presented. I saw nothing in it of an extraordinary character; but its effect upon Bedloe was prodigious. He nearly fainted as he gazed. And yet it was but a miniature portrait—a miraculously accurate one, to be sure—of his own very remarkable features. At least this was my thought as I regarded it.

"You will perceive," said Templeton, "the date of this picture—it is here, scarcely visible, in this corner—1780. In this year was the portrait taken. It is the likeness of a dead friend—a Mr. Oldeb—to whom I became much attached at Calcutta, during the administration of Warren Hastings. I was then only twenty years old.—When I first saw you, Mr. Bedloe, at Saratoga, it was the miraculous similarity which existed between yourself and the painting, which induced me to accost you, to seek your friendship, and to bring about those arrangements which resulted in my becoming your constant companion. In accomplishing this point, I was urged partly, and perhaps principally, by a regretful memory of the deceased, but also, in part, by an uneasy, and not altogether horrorless curiosity respecting yourself.

"In your detail of the vision which presented itself to you amid the hills, you have described, with the minutest accuracy, the Indian city of Benares, upon the Holy River. The riots, the combats, the massacre, were the actual events of the insurrection of Cheyte Sing, which took place in 1780, when Hastings was put in imminent peril of his life. The man escaping by the string of turbans, was Cheyte Sing himself. The party in the kiosk were sepoys and British officers, headed by Hastings. Of this party I was one, and did all I could to prevent the rash and fatal sally of the officer who fell, in the crowded alleys, by the poisoned arrow of a Bengalee. That officer was my dearest friend. It was Oldeb. You will perceive by these manuscripts" (here the speaker produced a note-book in which several pages appeared to have been freshly written) "that at the very period in which you fancied these things amid the hills, I was engaged in detailing them upon paper here at home."

In about a week after this conversation, the following paragraphs appeared in a Charlottesville paper.

"We have the painful duty of announcing the death of Mr. Augustus Bedlo, a gentleman whose amiable manners and many virtues have long endeared him to the citizens of Charlottesville.

"Mr. B., for some years past, has been subject to neuralgia, which has often threatened to terminate fatally; but this can be regarded only as the mediate cause of his decease. The proximate cause was one of especial singularity. In an excursion to the Ragged Mountains, a few days since, a slight cold and fever were contracted, attended with great determination of blood to the head. To relieve this, Dr. Templeton resorted to topical bleeding. Leeches were applied to the temples. In a fearfully brief period the patient died, when it appeared that, in the jar containing the leeches, had been introduced, by accident, one of the venomous vermicular sangsues which are now and then found in the neighboring ponds. This creature fastened itself upon a small artery in the right temple. Its close resemblance to the medicinal leech caused the mistake to be overlooked until too late.

"N.B. The poisonous sangsue of Charlottesville may always be distinguished from the medicinal leech by its blackness, and especially by its writhing or vermicular motions, which very nearly resemble those of a snake."

I was speaking with the editor of the paper in question, upon the topic of this remarkable accident, when it occurred to me to ask how it happened that the name of the deceased had been given as Bedlo.

"I presume," said I, "you have authority for this spelling, but I have always supposed the name to be written with an *e* at the end."

"Authority?—no," he replied. "It is a mere typographical error. The name is Bedlo with an *e,* all the world over, and I never knew it to be spelt otherwise in my life."

"Then," said I mutteringly, as I turned upon my heel, "then indeed has it come to pass that one truth is stranger than any fiction—for Bedlo, without the *e,* what is it but Oldeb conversed? And this man tells me it is a typographical error."

THE TWO CAMPS

A LEGEND OF THE OLD NORTH STATE

William Gilmore Simms

From *The Wigwam and the Cabin* by William Gilmore Simms, first series, 1845; first published in *The Gift,* 1844, pages 149-181.

A native of South Carolina, William Gilmore Simms (1806-1870) was prominent in public affairs and had a long career as newspaper and magazine editor. A voluminous author in both poetry and prose, he is best known for his prose romances. *The Partisan* (1835), a story of the American Revolution, is representative of his historical romances; *The Yemassee* (1835), of his Indian tales; and *Border Beagles* (1840), of his romances of life in the South. W. P. Trent wrote the life of Simms for the American Men of Letters series (1892). A new life is being written by C. Hugh Holman. Simms's letters have been published in a scholarly edition of five volumes (1952-1956). See Jay B. Hubbell, *The South in American Literature, 1607-1900* (1954) for an evaluation of Simms's work, pages 572-602, and a useful bibliography, pages 958-961. A list of Simms's short stories is included in J. Allen Morris, "The Stories of William Gilmore Simms," *American Literature,* XIV (March, 1942), 20-35.

John Pendleton Kennedy's romance of the Revolution, *Horse-Shoe Robinson* (1835), which is mentioned in the first chapter of "The Two Camps," was based on experiences related to the author by a man who became the title character in the book, or so Kennedy avowed in his preface.

> "These, the forest born
> And forest nurtured—a bold, hardy race,
> Fearless and frank, unfettered, with big souls
> In hour of danger."

CHAPTER 1

It is frequently the case, in the experience of the professional novelist or tale-writer, that his neighbour comes in to his assistance when he least seeks, and, perhaps, least desires any succour. The worthy person, man or woman, however,—probably some excellent octogenarian whose claims to be heard are based chiefly upon the fact that he himself no longer possesses the faculty of hearing,—has some famous incident, some wonderful fact, of which he has been the eyewitness, or of which he has heard from his great-grandmother, which he fancies is the very thing to be woven into song or story. Such is the strong possession which the matter takes of his brain, that, if the novelist whom he seeks to benefit does not live within trumpet-distance, he gives him the narrative by means of post, some three sheets of stiff foolscap, for which the hapless tale-writer, whose works are selling in cheap editions at twelve or twenty cents, pays a sum of one dollar sixty-two postage. Now, it so happens, to increase the evil, that, in ninety-nine cases in the hundred, the fact thus laboriously stated is not worth a straw—consisting of some simple deed of violence, some mere murder, a downright blow with gun-butt or cudgel over the skull, or a hidden thrust, three inches deep, with dirk or bowie knife, into the abodmen, or at random among the lower ribs. The man dies and the murderer gets off to Texas, or is prematurely caught and stops by the way—and still stops by the way! The thing is fact, no doubt. The narrator saw it himself, or his brother saw it, or—more solemn, if not more certain testimony still—his grandmother saw it, long before he had eyes to see at all. The circumstance is attested by a cloud of witnesses—a truth solemnly sworn to—and yet, for the purposes of the tale-writer, of no manner of value. This assertion may somewhat conflict with the received opinions of many, who, accustomed to find deeds of violence recorded in almost every work of fiction, from the time of Homer to the present day, have rushed to the conclusion that this is all, and overlook that labour of the artist, by which an ordinary event is made to assume the character of novelty; in other words, to become an extraordinary event. The least difficult thing in the world, on the part of the writer of fiction, is to find the assassin and the bludgeon; the art is to make them appear in the right place, strike at the right time, and so adapt one fact to another, as to create mystery, awaken curiosity, inspire doubt as to the result, and bring about the catastrophe, by processes which shall be equally natural and unexpected. All that class of sagacious persons, therefore, who fancy they have found a mare's nest, when, in fact, they are only gazing at a goose's, are respectfully counselled that no fact—no tradition—is of any importance to the artist, unless it embodies certain peculiar characteristics of its own, or unless it illustrates some history about which curiosity has already been awakened. A mere brutality, in which John beats and bruises Ben, and Ben in turn shoots John, putting eleven slugs, or thereabouts, between his collar-bone and vertebræ—or, maybe, stabs him under his left pap, or any where you please, is just as easily conceived by the novelist, without the help of history. Nay, for that matter, he would perhaps rather not have any precise facts in his way, in such cases, as then he will be able to regard the picturesque in the choice of his weapon, and to put the wounds in such parts of the body, as will better bear the examination of all persons. I deem it right to throw out this hint, just at this moment, as well for the benefit of my order as for my own protection. The times are hard, and the post-office requires all its dues in hard money. Literary men are not proverbially prepared at all seasons for any unnecessary outlay—and to be required to make advances for commodities of which they have on hand, at all times, the greatest abundance, is an injustice which, it is to be hoped, that this little intimation will somewhat lessen. We take for granted, therefore, that our professional brethren will concur with us in saying to the public, that we are all sufficiently provided with "disastrous chances" for some time to come—that our "moving accidents by flood and field" are particularly numerous, and of "hair-breadth 'scapes" we have enough to last a century. Murders, and such matters, as they are among the most ordinary events of the day, are decidedly vulgar; and, for mere cudgelling and bruises, the taste of the belles-lettres reader, rendered delicate by the monthly magazines, has voted them equally gross and unnatural.

But, if the character of the materials usually tendered to the novelist by the incident-mongers, is thus ordinarily worthless as we describe it, we sometimes are fortunate in finding an individual, here and there, in the deep forests,—a sort of recluse, hale and lusty, but white-headed,—who unfolds from his own budget of experience a rare chronicle, on which we delight to linger. Such an one breathes life into his deeds. We see them as we listen to his words. In lieu of the dead body of the fact, we have its living spirit—subtle, active, breathing and burning, and fresh in all the provocations and associations of life. Of this sort was the admirable characteristic narrative of Horse-Shoe Robinson, which we owe to Kennedy, and for which he was indebted to the venerable hero of the story. When we say that the subject of the sketch which follows was drawn from not dissimilar sources, we must beg our readers not to understand us as inviting any reference to that able and national story—with which it is by no means our policy or wish to invite or provoke comparison.

CHAPTER II

There are probably some old persons still living upon the upper dividing line between North and South Carolina, who still remember the form and features of the venerable Daniel Nelson. The old man was still living so late as 1817. At that period he removed to Mississippi, where, we believe, he died in less than three months after his change of residence. An old tree does not bear transplanting easily, and does not long survive it. Daniel Nelson came from Virginia when a youth. He was one of the first who settled on the southern borders of North Carolina, or, at least in that neighbourhood where he afterwards passed the greatest portion of his days.

At that time the country was not only a forest, but one thickly settled with Indians. It constituted the favourite hunting-grounds for several of their tribes. But this circumstance did not discourage young Nelson. He was then a stalwart youth, broad-chested, tall, with a fiery eye, and an almost equally fiery soul—certainly with a very fearless one. His companions, who were few in number, were like himself. The spirit of old Daniel Boone was a more common one than is supposed. Adventure gladdened and excited their hearts, —danger only seemed to provoke their determination,—and mere hardship was something which their frames appeared to covet. It was as refreshing to them as drink. Having seen the country, and struck down some of its game,—tasted of its bear-meat and buffalo, its deer and turkey,—all, at that time, in the greatest abundance,— they returned for the one thing most needful to a brave forester in a new country,—a good, brisk, fearless wife, who, like the damsel in Scripture, would go whithersoever went the husband to whom her affections were surrendered. They had no fear, these bold young hunters, to make a home and rear an infant family in regions so remote from the secure walks of civilization. They had met and made an acquaintance and a sort of friendship with the Indians, and, in the superior vigour of their own frames, their greater courage, and better weapons, they perhaps had come to form a too contemptuous estimate of the savage. But they were not beguiled by him into too much confidence. Their log houses were so constructed as to be fortresses upon occasion, and they lived not so far removed from one another, but that the leaguer of one would be sure, in twenty-four hours, to bring the others to his assistance. Besides, with a stock of bear-meat and venison always on hand, sufficient for a winter, either of these fortresses might, upon common calculations, be maintained for several weeks against any single band of the Indians, in the small numbers in which they were wont to range together in those neighbourhoods. In this way these bold pioneers took possession of the soil, and paved the way for still mightier generations. Though wandering, and somewhat averse to the tedious labours of the farm, they were still not wholly unmindful of its duties; and their open lands grew larger every season, and increasing comforts annually spoke for the increasing civilization of the settlers. Corn was in plenty in proportion to the bear-meat, and the squatters almost grew indifferent to those first apprehensions, which had made them watch the approaches of the most friendly Indian as if he had been an enemy. At the end of five years, in which they had suffered no hurt and but little annoyance of any sort from their wild neighbours, it would seem as if this confidence in the security of their situation was not without sufficient justification.

But, just then, circumstances seemed to threaten an interruption of this goodly state of things. The Indians were becoming discon-

tented. Other tribes, more frequently in contact with the larger settlements of the whites,—wronged by them in trade, or demoralized
by drink,—complained of their sufferings and injuries, or, as is more
probable, were greedy to obtain their treasures, in bulk, which they
were permitted to see, but denied to enjoy, or only in limited quantity. Their appetites and complaints were transmitted, by inevitable
sympathies, to their brethren of the interior, and our worthy settlers
upon the Haw, were rendered anxious at signs which warned them
of a change in the peaceful relations which had hitherto existed in
all the intercourse between the differing races. We need not dwell
upon or describe these signs, with which, from frequent narratives
of like character, our people are already sufficiently familiar. They
were easily understood by our little colony, and by none more
quickly than Daniel Nelson. They rendered him anxious, it is true,
but not apprehensive; and, like a good husband, while he strove
not to frighten his wife by what he said, he deemed it necessary to
prepare her mind for the worst that might occur. This task over, he
felt somewhat relieved, though, when he took his little girl, now five
years old, upon his knee that evening, and looked upon his infant
boy in the lap of his mother, he felt his anxieties very much increase;
and that very night he resumed a practice which he had latterly
abandoned, but which had been adopted as a measure of strict pre-
caution, from the very first establishment of their little settlement.
As soon as supper was over, he resumed his rifle, thrust his *couteau
de chasse* into his belt, and, taking his horn about his neck, and calling up his trusty dog, Clinch, he proceeded to scour the woods immediately around his habitation. This task, performed with the
stealthy caution of the hunter, occupied some time, and, as the night
was clear, a bright starlight, the weather moderate, and his own
mood restless, he determined to strike through the forest to the settlement of Jacob Ransom, about four miles off, in order to prompt
him, and, through him, others of the neighbourhood, to the continued exercise of a caution which he now thought necessary. The
rest of this night's adventure we propose to let him tell in his own
words, as he has been heard to relate it a thousand times in his old
age, at a period of life when, with one foot in his grave, to suppose

him guilty of falsehood, or of telling that which he did not himself fervently believe, would be, among all those who knew him, to suppose the most impossible and extravagant thing in the world.

CHAPTER III

"Well, my friends," said the veteran, then seventy, drawing his figure up to its fullest height, and extending his right arm, while his left still grasped the muzzle of his ancient rifle, which he swayed from side to side, the butt resting on the floor—"Well, my friends, seeing that the night was cl'ar, and there was no wind, and feeling as how I didn't want for sleep, I called to Clinch and took the path for Jake Ransom's. I knew that Jake was a sleepy sort of chap, and if the redskins caught any body napping, he'd, most likely, be the man. But I confess, 'twarn't so much for his sake, as for the sake of all,—of my own as well as the rest;—for, when I thought how soon, if we warn't all together in the business, I might see, without being able to put in, the long yellow hair of Betsy and the babies twirling on the thumbs of some painted devil of the tribe,—I can't tell you how I felt, but it warn't like a human, though I shivered mightily like one,—'twas wolfish, as if the hair was turned in and rubbing agin the very heart within me. I said my prayers, where I stood, looking up at the stars, and thinking that, after all, all was in the hands and the marcy of God. This sort o' thinking quieted me, and I went ahead pretty free, for I knew the track jest as well by night as by day, though I didn't go so quick, for I was all the time on the look-out for the enemy. Now, after we reached a place in the woods where there was a gully and a mighty bad crossing, there were two roads to get to Jake's—one by the hollows, and one jest across the hills. I don't know why, but I didn't give myself time to think, and struck right across the hill, though that was rather the longest way.

"Howsomedever, on I went, and Clinch pretty close behind me. The dog was a good dog, with a mighty keen nose to hunt, but jest then he didn't seem to have the notion for it. The hill was a sizeable one, a good stretch to foot, and I began to remember, after awhile, that I had been in the woods from blessed dawn; and that made me see how it was with poor Clinch, and why he didn't go for'ad; but I was more than half way, and wasn't guine to turn back till I had said my say to Jake. Well, when I got to the top of the hill, I stopped, and rubbed my eyes. I had cause to rub 'em, for what should I see at a distance but a great fire. At first I was afeard lest it was Jake's house, but I considered, the next moment, that he lived to the left, and this fire was cl'ar to the right, and it did seem to me as if 'twas more near to my own. Here was something to scare a body. But I couldn't stay there looking, and it warn't now a time to go to Jake's; so I turned off, and, though Clinch was mighty onwilling, I bolted on the road to the fire. I say road, but there was no road; but the trees warn't over-thick, and the land was too poor for undergrowth; so we got on pretty well, considering. But, what with the tire I had had, and the scare I felt, it seemed as if I didn't get for'ad a bit. There was the fire still burning as bright and almost as far off as ever. When I saw this I stopt and looked at Clinch, and he stopped and looked at me, but neither of us had any thing to say. Well, after a moment's thinking, it seemed as if I shouldn't be much of a man to give up when I had got so far, so I pushed on. We crossed more than one little hill, then down and through the hollow, and then up the hill again. At last we got upon a small mountain the Indians called Nolleehatchie, and then it seemed as if the fire had come to a stop, for it was now burning bright, on a little hill below me, and not two hundred yards in front. It was a regular camp fire, pretty big, and there was more than a dozen Indians sitting round it. 'Well,' says I to myself, 'it's come upon us mighty sudden, and what's to be done? Not a soul in the settlement knows it but myself, and nobody's on the watch. They'll be sculped, every human of them, in their very beds, or, moutbe, waken up in the blaze, to be shot with arrows as they run.' I was in a cold sweat to think of it. I didn't know what to think and what to do. I looked round to Clinch, and the strangest thing of all was to see him sitting quiet on his haunches, looking at me, and at the stars, and not at the fire jest before him. Now, Clinch was a famous fine hunting dog, and jest as good on an Indian trail as any other. He know'd my ways, and what I wanted, and would give tongue, or keep it still, jest as I axed him. It was sensible enough, jest then, that he shouldn't bark, but, dang it!—he

didn't even seem to see. Now, there warn't a dog in all the settlement so quick and keen to show sense as Clinch, even when he
didn't say a word;—and to see him looking as if he didn't know and
didn't care what was a-going on, with his eyes sot in his head and
glazed over with sleep, was, as I may say, very onnatural, jest at that
time, in a dog of any onderstanding. So I looked at him, half angry,
and when he saw me looking at him, he jest stretched himself off,
put his nose on his legs, and went to sleep in 'arnest. I had half a
mind to lay my knife-handle over his head, but I considered better
of it, and though it did seem the strangest thing in the world that
he shouldn't even try to get to the fire, for warm sake, yet I recollected that dog natur', like human natur', can't stand every thing, and
he hadn't such good reason as I had, to know that the Indians were
no longer friendly to us. Well, there I stood, a pretty considerable
chance, looking, and wondering, and onbeknowing what to do. I
was mighty beflustered. But at last I felt ashamed to be so oncertain,
and then again it was a needcessity that we should know the worst
one time or another, so I determined to push for'ad. I was no slouch
of a hunter, as you may suppose; so, as I was nearing the camp, I
begun sneaking; and, taking it sometimes on hands and knees, and
sometimes flat to the ground, where there was neither tree nor bush
to cover me, I went ahead, Clinch keeping close behind me, and not
showing any notion of what I was after. It was a slow business, because it was a ticklish business; but I was a leetle too anxious to be
altogether so careful as a good sneak ought to be, and I went on
rather faster than I would advise any young man to go in a time of
war, when the inimy is in the neighbourhood. Well, as I went, there
was the fire, getting larger and larger every minute, and there were
the Indians round it, getting plainer and plainer. There was so much
smoke that there was no making out, at any distance, any but their
figures, and these, every now and then, would be so wrapt in the
smoke that not more than half of them could be seen at the same
moment. At last I stopped, jest at a place where I thought I could
make out all that I wanted. There was a sizeable rock before me,
and I leaned my elbows on it to look. I reckon I warn't more than
thirty yards from the fire. There were some bushes betwixt us, and
what with the bushes and the smoke, it was several minutes be-

fore I could separate man from man, and see what they were all
adoing, and when I did, it was only for a moment at a time, when
a puff of smoke would wrap them all, and make it as difficult as
ever. But when I did contrive to see clearly, the sight was one to
worry me to the core, for, in the midst of the redskins, I could see a
white one, and that white one a woman. There was no mistake.
There were the Indians, some with their backs, and some with their
faces to me; and there, a little a-one side, but still among them, was
a woman. When the smoke blowed off, I could see her white face,
bright like any star, shining out of the clouds, and looking so pale
and ghastly that my blood cruddled in my veins to think lest she
might be dead from fright. But it couldn't be so, for she was sitting
up and looking about her. But the Indians were motionless. They
jest sat or lay as when I first saw them—doing nothing—saying
nothing, but jest as motionless as the stone under my elbow. I
couldn't stand looking where I was, so I began creeping again, getting nigher and nigher, until it seemed to me as if I ought to be
able to read every face. But what with the paint and smoke, I
couldn't make out a single Indian. Their figures seemed plain
enough in their buffalo-skins and blankets, but their faces seemed
always in the dark. But it wasn't so with the woman. I could
make her out clearly. She was very young; I reckon not more than
fifteen, and it seemed to me as if I knew her looks very well. She
was very handsome, and her hair was loosed upon her back. My
heart felt strange to see her. I was weak as any child. It seemed as
if I could die for the gal, and yet I hadn't strength enough to raise
my rifle to my shoulder. The weakness kept on me the more I
looked; for every moment seemed to make the poor child more and
more dear to me. But the strangest thing of all was to see how motionless was every Indian in the camp. Not a word was spoken—
not a limb or finger stirred. There they sat, or lay, round about the
fire, like so many effigies, looking at the gal, and she looking at
them. I never was in such a fix of fear and weakness in my life.
What was I to do? I had got so nigh that I could have stuck my
knife, with a jerk, into the heart of any one of the party, yet I hadn't
the soul to lift it; and before I knew where I was, I cried like a child.
But my crying didn't make 'em look about 'em. It only brought my

poor dog Clinch leaping upon me, and whining, as if he wanted to give me consolation. Hardly knowing what I did, I tried to set him upon the camp, but the poor fellow didn't seem to understand me; and in my desperation, for it was a sort of madness growing out of my scare, I jumped headlong for'ad, jest where I saw the party sitting, willing to lose my life rather than suffer from such a strange sort of misery.

CHAPTER IV

"Will you believe me! there were no Indians, no young woman, no fire! I stood up in the very place where I had seen the blaze and the smoke, and there was nothing! I looked for'ad and about me—there was no sign of fire any where. Where I stood was covered with dry leaves, the same as the rest of the forest. I was stupefied. I was like a man roused out of sleep by a strange dream, and seeing nothing. All was dark and silent. The stars were overhead, but that was all the light I had. I was more scared than ever, and, as it's a good rule when a man feels that he can do nothing himself, to look to the great God who can do every thing, I kneeled down and said my prayers—the second time that night that I had done the same thing, and the second time, I reckon, that I had ever done so in the woods. After that I felt stronger. I felt sure that this sign hadn't been shown to me for nothing; and while I was turning about, looking and thinking to turn on the back track for home, Clinch began to prick up his ears and waken up. I clapped him on his back, and got my knife ready. It might be a *painter* that stirred him, for he could scent that beast a great distance. But, as he showed no fright, only a sort of quickening, I knew there was nothing to fear. In a moment he started off, and went boldly ahead. I followed him, but hadn't gone twenty steps down the hill and into the hollow, when I heard something like a groan. This quickened me, and keeping up with the dog, he led me to the foot of the hollow, where was a sort of pond. Clinch ran right for it, and another groan set me in the same direction. When I got up to the dog, he was on the butt-end of an old tree that had fallen, I reckon, before my time, and was half buried in the water. I jumped on it, and walked a few steps for'ad, when, what should I see but a human, half across the log, with his legs hanging in the water, and his head down. I called Clinch back out of my way, and went to the spot. The groans were pretty constant. I stooped down and laid my hands upon the person, and, as I felt the hair, I knew it was an Indian. The head was clammy with blood, so that my fingers stuck, and when I attempted to turn it, to look at the face, the groan was deeper than ever; but 'twarn't a time to suck one's fingers. I took him up, clapped my shoulders to it, and, fixing my feet firmly on the old tree, which was rather slippery, I brought the poor fellow out without much trouble. Though tall, he was not heavy, and was only a boy of fourteen or fifteen. The wonder was how a lad like that should get into such a fix. Well, I brought him out and laid him on the dry leaves. His groans stopped, and I thought he was dead, but I felt his heart, and it was still warm, and I thought, though I couldn't be sure, there was a beat under my fingers. What to do was the next question. It was now pretty late in the night. I had been all day a-foot, and, though still willing to go, yet the thought of such a weight on my shoulders made me stagger. But 'twouldn't do to leave him where he was to perish. I thought, if so be I had a son in such a fix, what would I think of the stranger who should go home and wait till daylight to give him help! No, darn my splinters, said I,—though I had just done my prayers,—if I leave the lad—and, tightening my girth, I give my whole soul to it, and hoisted him on my shoulders. My cabin, I reckoned, was good three miles off. You can guess what trouble I had, and what a tire under my load, before I got home and laid the poor fellow down by the fire. I then called up Betsy, and we both set to work to see if we could stir up the life that was in him. She cut away his hair, and I washed the blood from his head, which was chopped to the bone, either with a knife or hatchet. It was a God's blessing it hadn't gone into his brain, for it was fairly enough aimed for it, jest above the ear. When we come to open his clothes, we found another wound in his side. This was done with a knife, and, I suppose, was pretty deep. He had lost blood enough, for all his clothes were stiff with it. We knew nothing much of doctoring, but we had some rum in the cabin, and after washing his wounds clean with it, and pouring some down his throat, he began to groan more freely, and by that we knew he was coming to a nateral feeling. We rubbed his body down with warm cloths, and after a little while, seeing that he made some signs, I give him water as much as he could drink. This seemed to do him good, and having done every thing that we thought could help him, we wrapped him up warmly before the fire, and I stretched myself off beside him. 'Twould be a long story to tell, step by step, how he got on. It's enough to say that he didn't die that bout. We got him on his legs in a short time, doing little or nothing for him more than we did at first. The lad was a good lad, though, at first, when he first came to his senses, he was mighty shy, wouldn't look steadily in our faces, and, I do believe, if he could have got out of the cabin, would have done so as soon as he could stagger. But he was too weak to try that, and, meanwhile, when he saw our kindness, he was softened. By little and little, he got to play with my little Lucy, who was not quite six years old; and, after a while, he seemed to be never better pleased than when they played together. The child, too, after her first fright, leaned to the lad, and was jest as willing to play with him as if he had been a cl'ar white like herself. He could say a few words of English from the beginning, and learnt quickly; but, though he talked tolerable free for an Indian, yet I could never get him to tell me how he was wounded, or by whom. His brow blackened when I spoke of it, and his lips would be shut together, as if he was ready to fight sooner than to speak. Well, I didn't push him to know, for I was pretty sure the head of the truth will be sure to come some time or other, if you once have it by the tail, provided you don't jerk it off by straining too hard upon it.

CHAPTER V

"I suppose the lad had been with us a matter of six weeks, getting better every day, but so slowly that he had not, at the end of that time, been able to leave the picket. Meanwhile, our troubles with the Indians were increasing. As yet, there had been no bloodshed in our quarter, but we heard of murders and sculpings on every side, and we took for granted that we must have our turn. We made our preparations, repaired the pickets, laid in ammunition, and took turns for scouting nightly. At length, the signs of Indians got to be thick in our parts, though we could see none. Jake Ransom had come upon one of their camps after they had left it; and we had reason to apprehend every thing, inasmuch as the outlyers didn't show themselves, as they used to do, but prowled about the cabins and went from place to place, only by night, or by close skulking in the thickets. One evening after this, I went out as usual to go the rounds, taking Clinch with me, but I hadn't got far from the gate, when the dog stopped and gave a low bark;—then I knew there was mischief, so I turned round quietly, without making any show of scare, and got back safely, though not a minute too soon. They trailed me to the gate the moment after I had got it fastened, and were pretty mad, I reckon, when they found their plan had failed for surprising me. But for the keen nose of poor Clinch, with all my skill in scouting,—and it was not small even in that early day,—they'd 'a had me, and all that was mine, before the sun could open his eyes to see what they were after. Finding they had failed in their ambush, they made the woods ring with the war-whoop, which was a sign that they were guine to give us a regular siege. At the sound of the whoop, we could see the eyes of the Indian boy brighten, and his ears prick up, jest like a hound's when he first gets scent of the deer, or hears the horn of the hunter. I looked closely at the lad, and was dub'ous what to do. He moutbe only an enemy in the camp, and while I was fighting in front, he might be cutting the throats of my wife and children within. I did not tell you that I had picked up his bow and arrows near the little lake where I had found him, and his hunting-knife was sticking in his belt when I brought him home. Whether to take these away from him, was the question. Suppose I did, a billet of wood would answer pretty near as well. I thought the matter over while I watched him. Thought runs mighty quick in time of danger! Well, after turning it over on every side, I concluded 'twas better to trust him jest as if he had been a sure friend. I couldn't think, after all we had done for him, that he'd be false, so I said to him—'Lenatewá!'—'twas so he called himself—'those are your people!' 'Yes!' he answered slowly, and lifting himself up as if

he had been a lord—he was a stately-looking lad, and carried himself like the son of a Micco,* as he was—'Yes, they are the people of
Lenatewá—must he go to them?' and he made the motion of going
out. But I stopped him. I was not willing to lose the security which
I had from his being a sort of prisoner. 'No,' said I; 'no, Lenatewá,
not to-night. To-morrow will do. To-morrow you can tell them I
am a friend, not an enemy, and they should not come to burn my
wigwam.' 'Brother—friend!' said the lad, advancing with a sort of
freedom and taking my hand. He then went to my wife, and did the
same thing,—not regarding she was a woman,—'Brother—friend!'
I watched him closely, watched his eye and his motions, and I said
to Betsy, 'The lad is true; don't be afeard!' But we passed a weary
night. Every now and then we could hear the whoop of the Indians.
From the loop-holes we could see the light of three fires on different sides, by which we knew that they were prepared to cut off
any help that might come to us from the rest of the settlement. But
I didn't give in or despair. I worked at one thing or another all
night, and though Lenatewá gave me no help, yet he sat quietly, or
laid himself down before the fire, as if he had nothing in the world
to do in the business. Next morning by daylight, I found him already dressed in the same bloody clothes which he had on when I
found him. He had thrown aside all that I gave him, and though
the hunting-shirt and leggins which he now wore, were very much
stained with blood and dirt, he had fixed them about him with a
good deal of care and neatness, as if preparing to see company. I
must tell you that an Indian of good family always has a nateral
sort of grace and dignity which I never saw in a white man. He
was busily engaged looking through one of the loop-holes, and
though I could distinguish nothing, yet it was cl'ar that he saw
something to interest him mightily. I soon found out that, in spite
of all my watchfulness, he had contrived to have some sort of correspondence and communication with those outside. This was a
wonder to me then, for I did not recollect his bow and arrows. It
seems that he had shot an arrow through one of the loop-holes, to
the end of which he had fastened a tuft of his own hair. The effect
of this was considerable, and to this it was owing that, for a few

* A prince or chief.

hours afterwards, we saw not an Indian. The arrow was shot at the very peep of day. What they were about, in the meantime, I can only guess, and the guess was only easy, after I had known all that was to happen. That they were in council what to do was cl'ar enough. I was not to know that the council was like to end in cutting some of their own throats instead of ours. But when we did see the enemy fairly, they came out of the woods in two parties, not actually separated, but not moving together. It seemed as if there was some strife among them. Their whole number could not be less than forty, and some eight or ten of these walked apart under the lead of a chief, a stout, dark-looking fellow, one-half of whose face was painted black as midnight, with a red circle round both his eyes. The other party was headed by an old white-headed chief, who couldn't ha' been less than sixty years—a pretty fellow, you may be sure, at his time of life, to be looking after sculps of women and children. While I was kneeling at my loop-hole looking at them, Lenatewá came to me, and touching me on the arm, pointed to the old chief, saying—'Micco Lenatewá Glucco,' by which I guessed he was the father or grandfather of the lad. 'Well,' I said, seeing that the best plan was to get their confidence and friendship if possible,—'Well, lad, go to your father and tell him what Daniel Nelson has done for you, and let's have peace. We can fight, boy, as you see; we have plenty of arms and provisions; and with this rifle, though you may not believe it, I could pick off your father, the king, and that other chief, who has so devilled himself up with paint.' 'Shoot!' said the lad quickly, pointing to the chief of whom I had last spoken. 'Ah! he is your enemy then?' The lad nodded his head, and pointed to the wound on his temple, and that in his side. I now began to see the true state of the case. 'No,' said I; 'no, Lenatewá, I will shoot none. I am for peace. I would do good to the Indians, and be their friend. Go to your father and tell him so. Go, and make him be my friend.' The youth caught my hand, placed it on the top of his head, and exclaimed, 'Good!' I then attended him down to the gate, but, before he left the cabin, he stopped and put his hand on the head of little Lucy,—and I felt glad, for it seemed to say, 'you shan't be hurt—not a hair of your head!' I let him out, fastened up, and then hastened to the loop-hole.

CHAPTER VI

"And now came a sight to tarrify. As soon as the Indians saw the young prince, they set up a general cry. I couldn't tell whether it was of joy, or what. He went for'ad boldly, though he was still quite weak, and the king at the head of his party advanced to meet him. The other and smaller party, headed by the black chief, whom young Lenatewá had told me to shoot, came forward also, but very slowly, and it seemed as if they were doubtful whether to come or go. Their leader looked pretty much beflustered. But they hadn't time for much study, for, after the young prince had met his father, and a few words had passed between them, I saw the finger of Lenatewá point to the black chief. At this, he lifted up his clenched fists, and worked his body as if he was talking angrily. Then, sudden, the war-whoop sounded from the king's party, and the other troop of Indians began to run, the black chief at their head; but he had not got twenty steps when a dozen arrows went into him, and he tumbled for'a'ds, and grappled with the earth. It was all over with him. His party was scattered on all sides, but were not pursued. It seemed that all the arrows had been aimed at the one person, and when he sprawled, there was an end to it: the whole affair was over in five minutes.

CHAPTER VII

"It was a fortunate affair for us. Lenatewá soon brought the old Micco to terms of peace. For that matter, he had only consented to take up the red stick because it was reported by the black chief— who was the uncle of the young Micco, and had good reasons for getting him out of the way—that he had been murdered by the whites. This driv' the old man to desperation, and brought him down upon us. When he knew the whole truth, and saw what friends we had been to his son, there was no end to his thanks and promises. He swore to be my friend while the sun shone, while the waters run, and while the mountains stood, and I believe, if the good old man had been spared so long, he would have been true to his oath. But, while he lived, he kept it, and so did his son when he succeeded him as Micco Glucco. Year after year went by, and though there was frequent war between the Indians and the whites, yet Lenatewá kept it from our doors. He himself was at war several times with our people, but never with our settlement. He put his *totem* on our trees, and the Indians knew that they were sacred. But, after a space of eleven years, there was a change. The young prince seemed to have forgotten our friendship. We now never saw him among us, and, unfortunately, some of your young men—the young men of our own settlement—murdered three young warriors of the Ripparee tribe, who were found on horses stolen from us. I was very sorry when I heard it, and began to fear the consequences; and they came upon us when we least looked for it. I had every reason to think that Lenatewá would still keep the warfare from my little family, but I did not remember that he was the prince of a tribe only, and not of the nation. This was a national warfare, in which the whole Cherokee people were in arms. Many persons, living still, re-member that terrible war, and how the Carolinians humbled them at last; but there's no telling how much blood was shed in that war, how many sculps taken, how much misery suffered by young and old, men, women, and children. Our settlement had become so large and scattered that we had to build a sizeable blockhouse, which we stored, and to which we could retreat whenever it was necessary. We took possession of it on hearing from our scouts that Indian trails had been seen, and there we put the women and children, un-der a strong guard. By day we tended our farms, and only went to our families at night. We had kept them in this fix for five weeks or thereabouts, and there was no attack. The Indian signs disappeared, and we all thought the storm had blown over, and began to hope and to believe that the old friendship of Lenatewá had saved us. With this thinking, we began to be less watchful. The men would stay all night at the farms, and sometimes, in the day, would carry with them the women, and sometimes some even the children. I cautioned them agin this, but they mocked me, and said I was gitting old and scary. I told them, 'Wait and see who'll scare first.' But, I confess, not seeing any Indians in all my scouting, I began to feel and think like the rest, and to grow careless. I let Betsy go now and then with me to the farm, though she kept it from me that she had gone there more than once with Lucy, without any man protector. Still, as it was only a short mile and a half from the block, and we could hear of no Indians, it did not seem so venturesome a thing. One day we heard of some very large b'ars among the thickets—a famous range for them, about four miles from the settlement; and a party of us, Simon Lorris, Hugh Darling, Jake Ransom, William Harkless, and myself, taking our dogs, set off on the hunt. We started the b'ar with a rush, and I got the first shot at a mighty big she b'ar, the largest I had ever seen—lamed the critter slightly, and dashed into the thickets after her! The others pushed, in another direction, after the rest, leaving me to finish my work as I could.

"I had two dogs with me, Clap and Claw, but they were young things, and couldn't be trusted much in a close brush with a b'ar. Old Clinch was dead, or he'd ha' made other guess-work with the varmint. But, hot after the b'ar, I didn't think of the quality of the dogs till I found myself in a fair wrestle with the brute. I don't brag, my friends, but that *was* a fight. I tell you my breath was clean gone, for the b'ar had me about the thin of my body, and I thought I was doubled up enough to be laid down without more handling. But my heart was strong when I thought of Betsy and the children, and I got my knife, with hard *jugging*—though I couldn't use my arm above my elbow—through the old critter's hide, and in among her ribs. That only seemed to make her hug closer, and I reckon I was clean gone, if it hadn't been that she blowed out before me. I had worked a pretty deep window in her waist, and then life run out plentiful. Her nose dropped agin my breast, and then her paws; and when the strain was gone, I fell down like a sick child, and she fell on top of me. But she warn't in a humour to do more mischief. She roughed me once or twice more with her paws, but that was only because she was at her last kick. There I lay a matter of half an hour, with the dead b'ar alongside o' me. I was almost as little able to move as she, and I vomited as if I had taken physic. When I come to myself and got up, there was no sound of the hunters. There I was with the two dogs and the b'ar, all alone, and the sun already long past the turn. My horse, which I had fastened outside of the thicket, had slipped his bridle, and, I reckoned, had either strayed off grazing, or had pushed back directly for the block. These things didn't make me feel much better. But, though my stomach didn't feel altogether right, and my ribs were as sore as if I had been sweating under a coating of hickory, I felt that there was no use and no time to stand there grunting. But I made out to skin and to cut up the b'ar, and a noble mountain of fat she made. I took the skin with me, and, covering the flesh with bark, I whistled off the dogs, after they had eat to fill, and pushed after my horse. I followed his track for some time, till I grew fairly tired. He had gone off in a scare and at a full gallop, and, instead of going home, had dashed down the lower side of the thicket, then gone aside, to round some of the hills, and thrown himself out of the track, it moutbe seven miles or more. When I found this, I saw there was no use to hunt him that day and afoot, and I had no more to do but turn about, and push as fast as I could for the block. But this was work enough. By this time the sun was pretty low, and there was now a good seven miles, work it how I could, before me. But I was getting over my b'ar-sickness, and though my legs felt weary enough, my stomach was better, and my heart braver; and, as I was in no hurry, having the whole night before me, and knowing the way by night as well as by light, I began to feel cheerful enough, all things considering. I pushed on slowly, stopping every now and then for rest, and recovering my strength this way. I had some parched meal and sugar in my pouch which I ate, and it helped me mightily. It was my only dinner that day. The evening got to be very still. I wondered I had seen and heard nothing of Jake Ransom and the rest, but I didn't feel at all oneasy about them, thinking that, like all other hunters, they would naterally follow the game to any distance. But, jest when I was thinking about them, I heard a gun, then another, and after that all got to be as quiet as ever. I looked to my own rifle and felt for my knife, and put forward a little more briskly. I suppose I had walked an hour after this, when it came on close dark, and I was still four good miles from the block. The night was cloudy, there were no stars, and the feeling in the air was damp and oncomfortable. I began to wish I was safe home, and felt queerish, almost as bad as I did when the b'ar was 'bracing me; but it warn't so much the body-sickness as the heart-sickness. I felt as if something was going wrong. Jest as this feeling was most worrisome, I stumbled over a human. My blood cruddled, when, feeling about, I put my hand on his head, and found the sculp was gone. Then I knew there was mischief. I couldn't make out who 'twas that was under me, but I reckoned 'twas one of the hunters. There was nothing to be done but to push for'ad. I didn't feel any more tire. I felt ready for fight, and when I thought of our wives and children in the block, and what might become of them, I got wolfish, though the Lord only knows what I was minded to do. I can't say I had any raal sensible thoughts of what was to be done in the business. I didn't trust myself to think whether the Indians had been to the block yet or no; though ugly notions came across me when I remembered how we let the women and children go about to the farms. I was in a complete fever and agy. I scorched one time and shivered another, but I pushed on, for there was now no more feeling of tire in my limbs than if they were made of steel. By this time I had reached that long range of hills where I first saw that strange camp-fire, now eleven years gone, that turned out to be a deception, and it was nateral enough that the thing should come fresh into my mind, jest at that moment. While I was thinking over the wonder, and asking myself, as I had done over and often before, what it possibly could mean, I reached the top of one of the hills, from which I could see, in daylight, the whole country for a matter of ten miles or more on every side. What was my surprise, do you reckon, when there, jest on the very same hill opposite where I had seen that apparition of a camp, I saw another, and this time it was a raal one. There was a rousing blaze, and though the woods and undergrowth were thicker on this than on the other side, from which I had seen it before, yet I could make out that there were several figures, and them Indians. It sort o' made me easier to see the enemy before, and then I could better tell what I had to do. I was to spy out the camp, see what the red-devils were thinking to do, and what they had already done. I was a little better scout and hunter this time than when I made the same sort o' search before, and I reckoned that I could get nigh enough to see all that was going on, without stirring up any dust among 'em. But I had to keep the dogs back. I couldn't tie 'em up, for they'd howl; so I stripped my hunting-shirt and put it down for one to guard, and I gave my cap and horn to another. I knew they'd never leave 'em, for I had l'arned 'em all that sort of business—to watch as well as to fetch and carry. I then said a sort of short running prayer, and took the trail. I had to work for'ad slowly. If I had gone on this time as I did in that first camp transaction, I'd ha' lost my sculp to a sartainty. Well, to shorten a long business, I tell you that I got nigh enough, without scare or surprise, to see all that I cared to see, and a great deal more than I wished to see; and now, for the first time, I saw the meaning of that sight which I had, eleven years before, of the camp that come to nothing. I saw that first sight over again, the Indians round the fire, a young woman in the middle, and that young woman my own daughter, my child, my poor, dear Lucy!

CHAPTER VIII

"That was a sight for a father. I can't tell you—and I won't try—how I felt. But I lay there, resting upon my hands and knees, jest as if I had been turned into stone with looking. I lay so for a good half hour, I reckon, without stirring a limb; and you could only tell that life was in me, by seeing the big drops that squeezed out of my eyes now and then, and by a sort of shivering that shook me as you sometimes see the canebrake shaking with the gust of the pond inside. I tried to pray to God for help, but I couldn't pray, and as for thinking, that was jest as impossible. But I could do nothing by looking, and, for that matter, it was pretty cla'r to me, as I stood, with no help—by myself—one rifle only and knife—I couldn't do much by moving. I could have lifted the gun, and in a twinkle, tumbled the best fellow in the gang, but what good was that guine to do me? I was never fond of blood-spilling, and if I could have been made sure of my daughter, I'd ha' been willing that the red devils should have had leave to live for ever. What was I to do? Go to the block? Who know'd if it warn't taken, with every soul in it? And where else was I to look for help? Nowhere, nowhere but to God! I groaned—I groaned so loud that I was dreadful 'feared that they'd hear me; but they were too busy among themselves, eating supper, and poor Lucy in the midst, not eating, but so pale, and looking so miserable—jest as I had seen her, when she was only a child—in the same fix, though 'twas only an appearance—eleven years ago! Well, at last, I turned off. As I couldn't say what to do, I was too miserable to look, and I went down to the bottom of the hill and rolled about on the ground, pulling the hair out of my head and groaning, as if that was to do me any good. Before I knew where I was, there was a hand on my shoulder. I jumped up to my feet, and flung my rifle over my head, meaning to bring the butt down upon the stranger—but his voice stopped me.

" 'Brother,' said he, 'me Lenatewá!'

"The way he talked, his soft tones, made me know that the young prince meant to be friendly, and I gave him my hand; but the tears gushed out as I did so, and I cried out like a man struck in the very heart, while I pointed to the hill—'My child, my child!'

" 'Be man!' said he, 'come!' pulling me away.

" 'But, will you save her, Lenatewá?'

"He did not answer instantly, but led me to the little lake, and pointed to the old tree over which I had borne his lifeless body so many years ago. By that I knew he meant to tell me, he had not forgotten what I had done for him; and would do for me all he could. But this did not satisfy me. I must know how and when it was to be done, and what was his hope; for I could see from his caution, and leading me away from the camp, that he did not command the party, and had no power over them. He then asked me, if I had not seen the paint of the warriors in the camp. But I had seen nothing but the fix of my child. He then described the paint to me, which was his way of showing me that the party on the hill were his deadly enemies. The paint about their eyes was that of the great chief, his uncle, who had tried to murder him years ago, and who had been shot, in my sight, by the party of his father. The young chief, now in command of the band on the hill was the son of his uncle, and sworn to revenge the death of his father upon him, Lenatewá. This he made me onderstand in a few minutes. And he gave me farther to onderstand, that there was no way of getting my child from them onless by cunning. He had but two followers with him, and they were even then busy in making preparations. But of these preparations he either would not or could not give me any account; and I had to wait on him with all the patience I could muster; and no easy trial it was, for an Indian is the most cool and slow-moving creature in the world, unless he's actually fighting, and then he's about the quickest. After awhile, Lenatewá led me round the hill. We fetched a pretty smart reach, and before I knew where I was, he led me into a hollow that I had never seen before. Here, to my surprise, there were no less than twelve or fourteen horses fastened, that these red devils had stolen from the settlement that very day, and mine was among them. I did not know it till the young prince told me.

" 'Him soon move,' said he, pointing to one on the outside, which a close examination showed me to be my own—'Him soon move,'—and these words gave me a notion of his plan. But he did not allow me to have any hand in it—not jest then, at least. Bidding me keep a watch on the fire above, for the hollow in which we stood was at the foot of the very hill the Indians had made their camp on—though the stretch was a long one between—he pushed for'ad like a shadow, and so slily, so silently, that, though I thought myself a good deal of a scout before, I saw then that I warn't fit to hold a splinter to him. In a little time he had unhitched my horse, and quietly led him farther down the hollow, half round the hill, and then up the opposite hill. There was very little noise, the wind was from the camp, and, though they didn't show any alarm, I was never more scary in my life. I followed Lenatewá, and found where he had fastened my nag. He had placed him several hundred yards from the Indians, on his way to the block; and, where we now stood, owing to the bend of the hollow, the camp of the Indians was between us and where they had hitched the stolen horses. When I saw this, I began to guess something of his plan. Meantime, one after the other, his two followers came up, and made a long report to him in their own language. This done, he told me that three of my hunting companions had been sculped, the other, who was Hugh Darling, had got off cl'ar, though fired upon twice, and had alarmed the block, and that my daughter had been made prisoner at the farm to which she had gone without any company. This made me a little easier, and Lenatewá then told me what he meant to do. In course, I had to do something myself towards it. Off he went, with his two men, leaving me to myself. When I thought they had got pretty fairly round the hill, I started back for the camp, trying my best, you may be sure, to move as slily as Lenatewá. I got within twenty-five yards, I

reckon, when I thought it better to lie by quietly and wait. I could
see every head in the huddle, and my poor child among them, looking whiter than a sheet, beside their ugly painted skins. Well, I
hadn't long to wait, when there was such an uproar among the
stolen horses in the hollow on the opposite side of the hill—such a
trampling, such a whinnying and whickering, you never heard the
like. Now, you must know, that a stolen horse, to an Indian, is jest
as precious as a sweetheart to a white man; and when the rumpus
reached the camp, there was a rush of every man among them, for
his critter. Every redskin, but one, went over the hill after the horses,
and he jumped up with the rest, but didn't move off. He stood over
poor Lucy with his tomahawk, shaking it above her head, as if
guine to strike every minute. She, poor child—I could see her as
plain as the fire-light, for she sat jest on one side of it—her hands
were clasped together. She was praying, for she must have looked
every minute to be knocked on the head. You may depend, I found
it very hard to keep in. I was a'most biling over, the more when I
saw the red devil making his flourishes, every now and then, close to
the child's ears, with his bloody we'pon. But it was a needcessity to
keep in till the sounds died off pretty much, so as not to give them
any scare this side, till they had dashed ahead pretty far 'pon the
other. I don't know that I waited quite as long as I ought to, but
I waited as long as my feelings would let me, and then I dropped
the sight of my rifle as close as I could fix it on the breast of the Indian
that had the keeping of my child. I took aim, but I felt I was a little
tremorsome, and I stopped. I know'd I had but one shoot, and if I
didn't onbutton him in that one, it would be a bad shoot for poor
Lucy. I didn't fear to hit *her,* and I was pretty sure I'd hit him. But it
must be a dead shot to do good, for I know'd if I only hurt him, that
he'd sink the tomahawk in her head with what strength he had left
him. I brought myself to it again, and this time I felt strong. I could
jest hear a little of the hubbub of men and horses afar off. I knew it
was the time, and, resting the side of the muzzle against a tree, I give
him the whole blessing of the bullet. I didn't stop to ask what luck,
but run in, with a sort o' cry, to do the finishing with the knife. But
the thing was done a'ready. The beast was on his back, and I only
had to use the knife in cutting the vines that fastened the child to the

sapling behind her. The brave gal didn't scream or faint. She could only say, 'Oh, my father!' and I could only say, 'Oh! my child!' And what a precious hug followed; but it was only for a minute. We had no time to waste in hugging. We pushed at once for the place where I had left the critter, and if the good old nag ever used his four shanks to any purpose, he did that night. I reckon it was a joyful surprise to poor Betsy when we broke into the block. She had given it out for sartin that she'd never see me or the child again, with a nateral sculp on our heads.

CHAPTER IX

"There's no need to tell you the whole story of this war between our people and the redskins. It's enough that I tell you of what happened to us, and our share in it. Of the great affair, and all the fights and burnings, you'll find enough in the printed books and newspapers. What I tell you, though you can't find it in any books, is jest as true, for all that. Of our share in it, the worst has already been told you. The young chief, Oloschottee—for that was his name—the cousin and the enemy of Lenatewá, had command of the Indians that were to surprise our settlements; and though he didn't altogether do what he expected and intended, he worked us quite enough of mischief as it was. He soon put fire to all our farms to draw us out of the block, but finding that wouldn't do, he left us; for an Indian gets pretty soon tired of a long siege where there is neither rum nor blood to git drunk on. His force was too small to trouble us in the block, and so he drawed off his warriors, and we saw no more of him until the peace. That followed pretty soon after General Middleton gave the nation that licking at Echotee,—a licking, I reckon, that they'll remember long after my day. At that affair Lenatewá got an ugly bullet in his throat, and if it hadn't been for one of his men, he'd ha' got a bag'net in his breast. They made a narrow run with him, head foremost down the hill, with a whole swad of the mounted men from the low country at their heels. It was some time after the peace before he got better of his hurt, though the Indians are naterally more skilful in cures than white men. By this time we had all gone home to our farms, and had planted and rebuilt, and begun to forget our troubles, when who should pop into our cabin one day, but Lenatewá. He had got quite well of his hurts. He was a monstrous fine-looking fellow, tall and handsome, and he was dressed in his very best. He wore pantaloons, like one of us, and his hunting shirt was a raally fine blue, with a white fringe. He wore no paint, and was quite nice and neat with his person. We all received him as an old friend, and he stayed with us three days. Then he went, and was gone for a matter of two weeks, when he came back and stayed with us another three days. And so, off and on, he came to visit us, until Betsy said to me one day, 'Daniel, that Indian, Lenatewá, comes here after Lucy. Leave a woman to guess these things.' After she told me, I recollected that the young prince was quite watchful of Lucy, and would follow her out into the garden, and leave us, to walk with her. But then, again, I thought —'What if he is favourable to my daughter? The fellow's a good fellow; and a raal, noble-hearted Indian, that's sober, is jest as good, to my thinking, as any white man in the land.' But Betsy wouldn't hear to it. 'Her daughter never should marry a savage, and a heathen, and a redskin, while her head was hot':—and while her head was so hot, what was I to do? All I could say was this only, 'Don't kick, Betsy, till you're spurred. 'Twill be time enough to give the young Chief his answer when he asks the question; and it won't do for us to treat him rudely, when we consider how much we owe him.' But she was of the mind that the boot was on the other leg,— that it was he and not us that owed the debt; and all that I could do couldn't keep her from showing the lad a sour face of it whenever he came. But he didn't seem much to mind this, since I was civil and kind to him. Lucy too, though her mother warned her against him, always treated him civilly as I told her; though she naterally would do so, for she couldn't so easily forget that dreadful night when she was a prisoner in the camp of the enimy, not knowing what to expect, with an Indian tomahawk over her head, and saved, in great part, by the cunning and courage of this same Lenatewá. The girl treated him kindly, and I was not sorry she did so. She walked and talked with him jest as if they had been brother and sister, and he was jest as polite to her as if he had been a born Frenchman.

"You may be sure, it was no pleasant sight to my wife to see them two go out to walk. 'Daniel Nelson,' said she, 'do you see and keep an eye on those people. There's no knowing what may happen. I do believe that Lucy has a liking for that redskin, and should they run!'—'Psho!' said I,—but that wouldn't do for her, and so she made me watch the young people sure enough. 'Twarn't a business that I was overfond of, you may reckon, but I was a rough man and didn't know much of woman natur'. I left the judgment of such things to my wife, and did pretty much what she told me. Whenever they went out to walk, I followed them, rifle in hand; but it was only to please Betsy, for if I had seen the lad running off with the girl, I'm pretty sure, I'd never ha' been the man to draw trigger upon him. As I said before, Lenatewá was jest as good a husband as she could have had. But, poor fellow, the affair was never to come to that. One day, after he had been with us almost a week, he spoke softly to Lucy, and she got up, got her bonnet and went out with him. I didn't see them when they started, for I happened to be in the upper story,—a place where we didn't so much live, but where we used to go for shelter and defence whenever any Indians came about us. 'Daniel,' said my wife, and I knew by the quickness and sharpness of her voice what 'twas she had to tell me. But jest then I was busy, and, moreover, I didn't altogether like the sort of business upon which she wanted me to go. The sneaking after an enimy, in raal warfare, is an onpleasant sort of thing enough; but this sneaking after one that you think your friend is worse than running in a fair fight, and always gave me a sheepish feeling after it. Besides, I didn't fear Lenatewá, and I didn't fear my daughter. It's true, the girl treated him kindly and sweetly, but that was owing to the nateral sweetness of her temper, and because she felt how much sarvice he had been to her and all of us. So, instead of going out after them, I thought I'd give them a look through one of the loop-holes. Well, there they went, walking among the trees, not far from the picket, and no time out of sight. As I looked at them, I thought to myself, 'Would n't they make a handsome couple!' Both of them were tall and well made. As for Lucy, there wasn't, for figure, a finer set girl in all the settlement, and her face was a match for her figure. And then she was so easy in her motion, so graceful, and walked, or sate, or danced,—jest, for all the world, as if she was born only to do the particular thing she was doing. As for Lenatewá, he was a lad among a thousand. Now, a young Indian warrior, when he don't drink, is about the noblest-looking creature, as he carries himself in the woods, that God ever did make. So straight, so proud, so stately, always as if he was doing a great action—as if he knew the whole world was looking at him. Lenatewá was pretty much the handsomest and noblest Indian I had ever seen; and then, I know'd him to be raally so noble. As they walked together, their heads a little bent downwards, and Lucy's pretty low, the thought flashed across me that, jest then, he was telling her all about his feelings; and perhaps, said I to myself, the girl thinks about it pretty much as I do. Moutbe now, she likes him better than any body she has ever seen, and what more nateral? Then I thought, if there is any picture in this life more sweet and beautiful than two young people jest beginning to feel love for one another, and walking together in the innocence of their hearts, under the shady trees,—I've never seen it! I laid the rifle on my lap, and sat down on the floor and watched 'em through the loop until I felt the water in my eyes. They walked backwards and for'ads, not a hundred yards off, and I could see all their motions, though I couldn't hear their words. An Indian don't use his hands much generally, but I could see that Lenatewá was using his,—not a great deal, but as if he felt every word he was saying. Then I began to think, what was I to do, if so be he was raally offering to marry Lucy, and she willing! How was I to do? what was I to say?—how could I refuse him when I was willing? how could I say 'yes,' when Betsy said 'no!'

"Well, in the midst of this thinking, what should I hear but a loud cry from the child, then a loud yell,—a regular war-whoop,— sounded right in front, as if it came from Lenatewá himself. I looked up quickly, for, in thinking, I had lost sight of them, and was only looking at my rifle; I looked out, and there, in the twinkle of an eye, there was another sight. I saw my daughter flat upon the ground, lying like one dead, and Lenatewá staggering back as if he was mortally hurt; while, pressing fast upon him, was an Indian warrior, with his tomahawk uplifted, and striking—once, twice, three times—hard and heavy, right upon the face and forehead of the young prince. From the black paint on his face, and the red ring about his eyes, and from his figure and the eagle feathers in his head, I soon guessed it was Oloschottee and I then knew it was the old revenge for the killing of his father; for an Indian never forgets that sort of obligation. Of course, I didn't stand quiet to see an old friend, like Lenatewá, tumbled in that way, without warning, like a bullock; and there was my own daughter lying flat, and I wasn't to know that he hadn't struck her too. It was only one motion for me to draw sight upon the savage, and another to pull trigger; and I reckon he dropped jest as soon as the young Chief. I gave one whoop for all the world as if I was an Indian myself, and run out to the spot; but Lenatewá had got his discharge from further service. He warn't exactly dead, but his sense was swimming. He couldn't say much, and that warn't at all to the purpose. I could hear him, now and then, making a sort of singing noise, but that was soon swallowed up in a gurgle and a gasp, and it was all over. My bullet was quicker in its working than Oloschottee's hatchet; he was stone dead before I got to him. As for poor Lucy, she was not hurt, either by bullet or hatchet; but she had a hurt in the heart, whether from the scare she had, or because she had more feeling for the young prince than we reckoned, there's no telling. She warn't much given to smiling after that. But, whether she loved Lenatewá, we couldn't know, and I never was the man to ask her. It's sartain she never married, and she had about as many chances, and good ones, too, as any girl in our settlement. You've seen her—some among you—and warn't she a beauty—though I say it myself—the very flower of the forest!"

DAVID CROCKETT AND A
FROZEN DAYBREAK

Anonymous

This selection was quoted from one of the Crockett almanacs by Constance Rourke in *American Humor* (1931), pages 58-59. Here is suggested in small compass the myth-making propensity of the folk imagination.

One January morning it was so all screwen cold that the forest trees were stiff and they couldn't shake, and the very daybreak froze fast as it was trying to dawn. The tinder box in my cabin would no more ketch fire than a sunk raft at the bottom of the sea. Well, seein' daylight war so far behind time I thought creation war in a fair way for freezen fast: so, thinks I, I must strike a little fire from my fingers, light my pipe, an' travel out a few leagues, and see about it. Then I brought my knuckles together like two thunderclouds, but the sparks froze up afore I could begin to collect 'em, so out I walked, whistlin' "Fire in the mountains!" as I went along in three double quick time. Well, arter I had walked about twenty miles up the Peak O'Day and Daybreak Hill I soon discovered what war the matter. The airth had actually friz fast on her axes, and couldn't turn round; the sun had got jammed between two cakes o' ice under the wheels, an' thar he had been shinin' an' workin' to get loose till he friz fast in his cold sweat. C-r-e-a-t-i-o-n! thought I, this ar the toughest sort of suspension, an' it mustn't be endured. Somethin' must be done, or human creation is done for. It war then so anteluvian an' premature cold that my upper and lower teeth an' tongue war all collapsed together as tight as a friz oyster; but I took a fresh twenty-pound bear off my back that I'd picked up on my road, and beat the animal agin the ice till the hot ile began to walk out on him at all sides. I then took an' held him over the airth's axes an' squeezed him till I'd thawed 'em loose, poured about a ton on't over the sun's face, give the airth's cog-wheel one kick backward till I got the sun loose—whistled "Push along, keep movin'!" an' in about fifteen seconds the airth gave a grunt, an' began movin'. The sun walked up beautiful, salutin' me with sich a wind o' gratitude that it made me sneeze. I lit my pipe by the blaze o' his top-knot, shouldered my bear, an' walked home, introducin' people to the fresh daylight with a piece of sunrise in my pocket.

THE SHOOTING-MATCH

———

Augustus Baldwin Longstreet

From *Georgia Scenes* by Augustus Baldwin Longstreet, 1835.

Augustus Baldwin Longstreet (1790-1870), lawyer, journalist, and Methodist preacher, served as college and university president in his native Georgia and also in Mississippi, Louisiana, and South Carolina. Besides *Georgia Scenes* (1835), he wrote *William Mitten* (1864), a novel based on his early life in Georgia. Two biographies have been published: John Donald Wade, *Augustus Baldwin Longstreet: A Study of the Development of Culture in the South* (1924) and O. P. Fitzgerald, *Judge Longstreet: A Life Sketch* (1891). See also Walter Blair, *Native American Humor* (1937), pages 65-66, 76-78; and Jay B. Hubbell, *The South in American Literature, 1607-1900* (1954), pages 666-669, 947-948.

Shooting-matches are probably nearly coeval with the colonization of Georgia. They are still common throughout the Southern States, though they are not as common as they were twenty-five or thirty years ago. Chance led me to one about a year ago. I was travelling in one of the northeastern counties, when I overtook a swarthy, bright-eyed, smerky little fellow, riding a small pony, and bearing on his shoulder a long, heavy rifle, which, judging from its looks, I should say had done service in Morgan's corps.

"Good morning, sir!" said I, reining up my horse as I came beside him.

"How goes it, stranger?" said he, with a tone of independence and self-confidence that awakened my curiosity to know a little of his character.

"Going driving?" inquired I.

"Not exactly," replied he, surveying my horse with a quizzical smile; "I haven't been a driving *by myself* for a year or two; and my nose has got so bad lately, I can't carry a cold trail *without hounds to help me.*"

Alone, and without hounds as he was, the question was rather a silly one; but it answered the purpose for which it was put, which was only to draw him into conversation, and I proceeded to make as decent a retreat as I could.

"I didn't know," said I, "but that you were going to meet the huntsmen, or going to your stand."

"Ah, sure enough," rejoined he, "that *mout* be a bee, as the old woman said when she killed a wasp. It seems to me I ought to know you."

"Well, if you *ought,* why *don't* you?"

"What *mout* your name be?"

"It *might* be anything," said I, with borrowed wit; for I knew my man, and knew what kind of conversation would please him most.

"Well, what *is* it, then?"

"It *is* Hall," said I; "but you know it might as well have been anything else."

"Pretty digging!" said he. "I find you're not the fool I took you to be; so here's to a better acquaintance with you."

"With all my heart," returned I; "but you must be as clever as I've been, and give me your name."

"To be sure I will, my old coon; take it, take it, and welcome. Anything else about me you'd like to have?"

"No," said I, "there's nothing else about you worth having."

"Oh, yes there is, stranger! Do you see this?" holding up his ponderous rifle with an ease that astonished me. "If you will go with me to the shooting-match, and see me knock out the *bull's-eye* with her a few times, you'll agree the old *Soap-stick's* worth something when Billy Curlew puts his shoulder to her."

This short sentence was replete with information to me. It taught me that my companion was *Billy Curlew;* that he was going to a *shooting-match;* that he called his rifle the *Soap-stick,* and that he was very confident of winning beef with her; or, which is nearly, but not quite the same thing, *driving the cross with her*.

"Well," said I, "if the shooting-match is not too far out of my way, I'll go to it with pleasure."

"Unless your way lies through the woods from here," said Billy, "it'll not be much out of your way; for it's only a mile ahead of us, and there is no other road for you to take till you get there; and as that thing you're riding in an't well suited to fast travelling among brushy knobs, I reckon you won't lose much by going by. I reckon you hardly ever was at a shooting-match, stranger, from the cut of your coat?"

"Oh yes," returned I, "many a time. I won beef at one when I was hardly old enough to hold a shotgun off-hand."

"*Children* don't go to shooting-matches about here," said he, with a smile of incredulity. "I never heard of but one that did, and he was a little *swinge* cat. He was born a shooting, and killed squirrels before he was weaned."

"Nor did *I* ever hear of but one," replied I, "and that one was myself."

"And where did you win beef so young, stranger?"

"At Berry Adams's."

"Why, stop, stranger, let me look at you good! Is your name *Lyman* Hall?"

"The very same," said I.

"Well, dang my buttons, if you an't the very boy my daddy used to tell me about. I was too young to recollect you myself; but I've heard daddy talk about you many a time. I believe mammy's got a neck-handkerchief now that daddy won on your shooting at Collen Reid's store, when you were hardly knee high. Come along, Lyman, and I'll go my death upon you at the shooting-match, with the old Soap-stick at your shoulder."

"Ah, Billy," said I, "the old Soap-stick will do much better at your own shoulder. It was my mother's notion that sent me to the shooting-match at Berry Adams's; and, to tell the honest truth, it was altogether a chance shot that made me win beef; but that wasn't generally known; and most everybody believed that I was carried there on account of my skill in shooting; and my fame was spread far and wide, I well remember. I remember too, perfectly well, your father's bet on me at the store. *He* was at the shooting-match, and nothing could make him believe but that I was a great shot with a rifle as well as a shotgun. Bet he would on me, in spite of all I could say, though I assured him that I had never shot a rifle in my life. It so happened, too, that there were but two bullets, or, rather, a bullet and a half; and so confident was your father in my skill, that he made me shoot the half bullet; and, strange to tell, by another chance shot, I like to have drove the cross and won his bet."

"Now I know you're the very chap; for I heard daddy tell that very thing about the half bullet. Don't say anything about it, Lyman, and darn my old shoes if I don't tare the lint off the boys with you at the shooting-match. They'll never 'spect such a looking man as you are of knowing anything about a rifle. I'll risk your *chance* shots."

I soon discovered that the father had eaten sour grapes, and the son's teeth were on edge; for Billy was just as incorrigibly obstinate in his belief of my dexterity with a rifle as his father had been before him.

We soon reached the place appointed for the shooting-match. It went by the name of Sims's Cross Roads, because here two roads intersected each other; and because, from the time that the first had been laid out, Archibald Sims had resided there. Archibald had been a justice of the peace in his day (and where is the man of his age in Georgia who has not?); consequently, he was called *'Squire* Sims. It is the custom in this state, when a man has once acquired a title, civil or military, to force it upon him as long as he lives; hence the countless number of titled personages who are introduced in these sketches.

We stopped at the 'squire's door. Billy hastily dismounted, gave me the shake of the hand which he had been reluctantly reserving for a mile back, and, leading me up to the 'squire, thus introduced me: "Uncle Archy, this is Lyman Hall; and for all you see him in these fine clothes, he's a *swinge* cat; a darn sight cleverer fellow than he looks to be. Wait till you see him lift the old Soap-stick, and draw a bead upon the bull's-eye. You *gwine* to see fun here to-day. Don't say nothing about it."

"Well, Mr. Swinge-cat," said the 'squire, "here's to a better acquaintance with you," offering me his hand.

"How goes it, Uncle Archy?" said I, taking his hand warmly (for I am always free and easy with those who are so with me; and in this course I rarely fail to please). "How's the old woman?"

"Egad," said the 'squire, chuckling, "there you're too hard for me; for she died two-and-twenty years ago, and I haven't heard a word from her since."

"What! and you never married again!"

"Never, as God's my judge!" (a solemn asseveration, truly, upon so light a subject).

"Well, that's not my fault."

"No, nor it's not mine *ni*ther," said the 'squire.

Here we were interrupted by the cry of another Rancey Sniffle. "Hello, here! All you as wish to put in for the shoot'n'-match, come on here! for the putt'n' in's *riddy* to begin."

About sixty persons, including mere spectators, had collected; the most of whom were more or less obedient to the call of Mealy White-cotton, for that was the name of the self-constituted commander-in-chief. Some hastened and some loitered, as they desired to be first or last on the list; for they shoot in the order in which their names are entered.

The beef was not present, nor is it ever upon such occasions; but several of the company had seen it, who all concurred in the opinion that it was a good beef, and well worth the price that was set upon it—eleven dollars. A general inquiry ran round, in order to form some opinion as to the number of shots that would be taken; for, of course, the price of a shot is cheapened in proportion to the increase of that number. It was soon ascertained that not more than twenty persons would take chances; but these twenty agreed to take the number of shots, at twenty-five cents each.

The competitors now began to give in their names; some for one, some for two, three, and a few for as many as four shots.

Billy Curlew hung back to the last; and when the list was offered him, five shots remained undisposed of.

"How many shots left?" inquired Billy.

"Five," was the reply.

"Well, I take 'em all. Put down four shots to me, and one to Ly-man Hall, paid for by William Curlew."

I was thunder-struck; not at his proposition to pay for my shot, because I knew that Billy meant it as a token of friendship, and he would have been hurt if I had refused to let him do me this favour; but at the unexpected announcement of my name as a competitor for beef, at least one hundred miles from the place of my residence. I was prepared for a challenge from Billy to some of his neighbours for a *private* match upon me; but not for this.

I therefore protested against his putting in for me, and urged every reason to dissuade him from it that I could, without wounding his feelings.

"Put it down!" said Billy, with the authority of an emperor, and with a look that spoke volumes intelligible to every bystander. "Reckon I don't know what I'm about?" Then wheeling off, and muttering in an under, self-confident tone, "Dang old Roper," continued he, "if he don't knock that cross to the north corner of creation and back again before a cat can lick her foot."

Had I been king of the cat tribe, they could not have regarded me with more curious attention than did the whole company from this moment. Every inch of me was examined with the nicest scrutiny; and some plainly expressed by their looks that they never would have taken me for such a bite. I saw no alternative but to throw myself upon a third chance shot; for though, by the rules of the sport, I would have been allowed to shoot by proxy, by all the rules of good breeding I was bound to shoot in person. It would have been unpardonable to disappoint the expectations which had been raised on me. Unfortunately, too, for me, the match differed in one respect from those which I had been in the habit of attending in my younger days. In olden time the contest was carried on chiefly with *shot-guns,* a generic term which, in those days, embraced three descriptions of firearms: *Indian-traders* (a long, cheap, but sometimes excellent kind of gun, that mother Britain used to send hither for traffic with the Indians); *the large musket,* and the *shot-gun,* properly so called. Rifles were, however, always permitted to compete with them, under equitable restrictions. These were, that they should be fired off-hand, while the shot-guns were allowed a rest, the distance being equal; or that the distance should be one hundred yards for a rifle, to sixty for the shot-gun, the mode of firing being equal.

But this was a match of rifles exclusively; and these are by far the most common at this time.

Most of the competitors fire at the same target; which is usually a board from nine inches to a foot wide, charred on one side as black as it can be made by fire, without impairing materially the uniformity of its surface; on the darkened side of which is *pegged* a square piece of white paper, which is larger or smaller, according to the distance at which it is to be placed from the marksmen. This is almost invariably sixty yards, and for it the paper is reduced to about two and a half inches square. Out of the centre of it is cut a rhombus of about the width of an inch, measured diagonally; this is the *bull's eye,* or *diamond,* as the marksmen choose to call it: in the centre of this is the cross. But every man is permitted to fix his target to his own taste; and accordingly, some remove one fourth of the paper, cutting from the centre of the square to the two lower corners, so as to leave a large angle opening from the centre downward; while others reduce the angle more or less; but it is rarely the case that all are not satisfied with one of these figures.

The beef is divided into five prizes, or, as they are commonly termed, five *quarters*—the hide and tallow counting as one. For several years after the revolutionary war, a sixth was added; the *lead* which was shot in the match. This was the prize of the sixth best shot; and it used to be carefully extracted from the board or tree in which it was lodged, and afterward remoulded. But this grew out of the exigency of the times, and has, I believe, been long since abandoned everywhere.

The three master shots and rivals were Moses Firmby, Larkin Spivey, and Billy Curlew; to whom was added, upon this occasion, by common consent and with awful forebodings, your humble servant.

The target was fixed at an elevation of about three feet from the ground; and the judges (Captain Turner and 'Squire Porter) took their stands by it, joined by about half the spectators.

The first name on the catalogue was Mealy Whitecotton. Mealy stepped out, rifle in hand, and toed the mark. His rifle was about three inches longer than himself, and near enough his own thickness to make the remark of Darby Chislom, as he stepped out, tolerably appropriate: "Here comes the corn-stock and the sucker!" said Darby.

"Kiss my foot!" said Mealy. "The way I'll creep into that bull's-eye's a fact."

"You'd better creep into your hind sight," said Darby. Mealy raised and fired.

"A pretty good shot, Mealy!" said one.

"Yes, a blamed good shot!" said a second.

"Well done, Meal!" said a third.

I was rejoiced when one of the company inquired, "Where is it?" for I could hardly believe they were founding these remarks upon the evidence of their senses.

"Just on the right-hand side of the bull's-eye," was the reply.

I looked with all the power of my eyes, but was unable to discover the least change in the surface of the paper. Their report, however, was true; so much keener is the vision of a practised than an unpractised eye.

The next in order was Hiram Baugh. Hiram was like some race-horses which I have seen; he was too good not to contend for every prize, and too good for nothing ever to win one.

"Gentlemen," said he, as he came to the mark, "I don't say that I'll win beef; but if my piece don't blow, I'll eat the paper, or be mighty apt to do it, if you'll b'lieve my racket. My powder are not good powder, gentlemen; I bought it *thum* (from) Zeb Daggett, and gin him three quarters of a dollar a pound for it; but it are not what I call good powder, gentlemen; but if old Buck-killer burns it clear, the boy you call Hiram Baugh eats paper, or comes mighty near it."

"Well, blaze away," said Mealy, "and be d—d to you, and Zeb Daggett, and your powder, and Buck-killer, and your powder-horn and shot-pouch to boot! How long you gwine stand thar talking 'fore you shoot?"

"Never mind," said Hiram, "I can talk a little and shoot a little too; but that's nothin'. Here goes!"

Hiram assumed the figure of a note of interrogation, took a long sight, and fired.

"I've eat paper," said he, at the crack of the gun, without looking, or seeming to look, towards the target. "Buck-killer made a clear racket. Where am I, gentlemen?"

"You're just between Mealy and the diamond," was the reply.

"I said I'd eat paper, and I've done it; haven't I, gentlemen?"

"And 'spose you have!" said Mealy, "what do that 'mount to? You'll not win beef, and never did."

"Be that as it mout be, I've beat Meal 'Cotton mighty easy; and the boy you call Hiram Baugh are able to do it."

"And what do that 'mount to? Who the devil an't able to beat Meal 'Cotton! I don't make no pretense of bein' nothin' great, no how: but you always makes out as if you were gwine to keep 'em makin' crosses for you constant, and then do nothin' but *'eat paper'* at last; and that's a long way from *eatin' beef,* 'cordin' to Meal 'Cotton's notions, as you call him."

Simon Stow was now called on.

"Oh Lord!" exclaimed two or three: "now we have it. It'll take him as long to shoot as it would take 'Squire Dobbins to run round a *track* o' land."

"Good-by, boys," said Bob Martin.

"Where are you going, Bob?"

"Going to gather in my crop; I'll be back agin though by the time Sime Stow shoots."

Simon was used to all this, and therefore it did not disconcert him in the least. He went off and brought his own target, and set it up with his own hand.

He then wiped out his rifle, rubbed the pan with his hat, drew a piece of tow through the touch-hole with his wiper, filled his charger with great care, poured the powder into the rifle with equal caution, shoved in with his finger the two or three vagrant grains that lodged round the mouth of his piece, took out a handful of bullets, looked them all over carefully, selected one without flaw or wrinkle, drew out his patching, found the most even part of it, sprung open the grease-box in the breech of his rifle, took up just so much grease, distributed it with great equality over the chosen part of his patching, laid it over the muzzle of his rifle, grease side down, placed his ball upon it, pressed it a little, then took it up and turned the neck a little more perpendicularly downward, placed his knife handle on it, just buried it in the mouth of the rifle, cut off the redundant patching just above the bullet, looked at it, and shook his head, in token that he had cut off too much or too little, no one knew which, sent down the ball, measured the contents of his gun with his first and second fingers on the protruding part of the ramrod, shook his head again, to signify there was too much or too little powder, primed carefully, placed an arched piece of tin over the hind sight to shade it, took his place, got a friend to hold his hat over the foresight to shade it, took a very long sight, fired, and didn't even eat the paper.

"My piece was badly *loadned,*" said Simon, when he learned the place of his ball.

"Oh, you didn't take time," said Mealy. "No man can shoot that's in such a hurry as you is. I'd hardly got to sleep 'fore I heard the crack o' the gun."

The next was Moses Firmby. He was a tall, slim man, of rather sallow complexion; and it is a singular fact, that though probably no part of the world is more healthy than the mountainous parts of Georgia, the mountaineers have not generally robust frames or fine complexions: they are, however, almost inexhaustible by toil.

Moses kept us not long in suspense. His rifle was already charged, and he fixed it upon the target with a steadiness of nerve and aim that was astonishing to me and alarming to all the rest. A few seconds, and the report of his rifle broke the deathlike silence which prevailed.

"No great harm done yet," said Spivey, manifestly relieved from anxiety by an event which seemed to me better calculated to produce despair. Firmby's ball had cut out the lower angle of the diamond, directly on a right line with the cross.

Three or four followed him without bettering his shot; all of whom, however, with one exception, "eat the paper."

It now came to Spivey's turn. There was nothing remarkable in his person or manner. He took his place, lowered his rifle slowly from a perpendicular until it came on a line with the mark, held it there like a vice for a moment, and fired.

"Pretty *sevigrous,* but nothing killing yet," said Billy Curlew, as he learned the place of Spivey's ball.

Spivey's ball had just broken the upper angle of the diamond; beating Firmby about half its width.

A few more shots, in which there was nothing remarkable, brought us to Billy Curlew. Billy stepped out with much confidence, and brought the Soap-stick to an order, while he deliberately rolled up his shirt sleeves. Had I judged of Billy's chance of success from the looks of his gun, I should have said it was hopeless. The stock of Soap-stick seemed to have been made with a case-knive; and had it been, the tool would have been but a poor apology for its clumsy appearance. An auger-hole in the breech served for a grease-box; a cotton string assisted a single screw in holding on the lock; and the thimbles were made, one of brass, one of iron, and one of tin.

"Where's Lark Spivey's bullet?" called out Billy to the judges, as he finished rolling up his sleeves.

"About three quarters of an inch from the cross," was the reply.

"Well, clear the way! the Soap-stick's coming, and she'll be along in there among 'em presently."

Billy now planted himself astraddle, like an inverted V; shot forward his left hip, drew his body back to an angle of about forty-five degrees with the plane of the horizon, brought his cheek down close to the breech of old Soap-stick, and fixed her upon the mark with untrembling hand. His sight was long, and the swelling muscles of his left arm led me to believe that he was lessening his chance of success with every half second that he kept it burdened with his ponderous rifle; but it neither flagged nor wavered until Soap-stick made her report.

"Where am I?" said Billy, as the smoke rose from before his eye.

"You've jist touched the cross on the lower side," was the reply of one of the judges.

"I was afraid I was drawing my bead a *leetle* too fine," said Billy. "Now, Lyman, you see what the Soap-stick can do. Take her, and show the boys how you used to do when you was a baby."

I begged to reserve my shot to the last; pleading, rather sophistically, that it was, in point of fact, one of Billy's shots. My plea was rather indulged than sustained, and the marksmen who had taken more than one shot commenced the second round. This round was a manifest improvement upon the first. The cross was driven three times: once by Spivey, once by Firmby, and once by no less a personage then Mealy Whitecotton, whom chance seemed to favour for this time, merely that he might retaliate upon Hiram Baugh; and the bull's-eye was disfigured out of all shape.

The third and fourth rounds were shot. Billy discharged his last shot, which left the rights of parties thus: Billy Curlew first and fourth choice, Spivey second, Firmby third, and Whitecotton fifth. Some of my readers may perhaps be curious to learn how a distinction comes to be made between several, all of whom drive the cross. The distinction is perfectly natural and equitable. Threads are stretched from the uneffaced parts of the once intersecting lines, by means of which the original position of the cross is precisely ascertained. Each bullet-hole being nicely pegged up as it is made, it is easy to ascertain its circumference. To this I believe they usually, if not invariably, measure, where none of the balls touch the cross; but if the cross be driven, they measure from it to the centre of the bullet-hole. To make a draw shot, therefore, between two who drive the cross, it is necessary that the centre of both balls should pass directly through the cross; a thing that very rarely happens.

The Bite alone remained to shoot. Billy wiped out his rifle carefully, loaded her to the top of his skill, and handed her to me. "Now," said he, "Lyman, draw a fine bead, but not too fine; for Soap-stick bears up her ball well. Take care and don't touch the trigger until you've got your bead; for she's spring-trigger'd, and goes mighty easy: but you hold her to the place you want her, and if she don't go there, dang old Roper."

I took hold of Soap-stick, and lapsed immediately into the most hopeless despair. I am sure I never handled as heavy a gun in all my life. "Why, Billy," said I, "you little mortal, you! What do you use such a gun as this for?"

"Look at the bull's-eye yonder!" said he.

"True," said I, "but *I* can't shoot her; it is impossible."

"Go 'long, you old coon!" said Billy; "I see what you're at;"

intimating that all this was merely to make the coming shot the more remarkable; "Daddy's little boy don't shoot anything but the old Soap-stick here to-day, I know."

The judges, I knew, were becoming impatient, and, withal, my situation was growing more embarrassing every second; so I e'en resolved to try the Soap-stick without farther parley.

I stepped out, and the most intense interest was excited all around me, and it flashed like electricity around the target, as I judged from the anxious gaze of all in that direction.

Policy dictated that I should fire with a falling rifle, and I adopted this mode; determining to fire as soon as the sights came on a line with the diamond, *bead* or no *bead*. Accordingly, I commenced lowering old Soap-stick; but, in spite of all my muscular powers, she was strictly obedient to the laws of gravitation, and came down with a uniformly accelerated velocity. Before I could arrest her downward flight, she had not only passed the target, but was making rapid encroachments on my own toes.

"Why, he's the weakest man in the arms I ever seed," said one, in a half whisper.

"It's only his fun," said Billy; "I know him."

"It may be fun," said the other, "but it looks mightily like yearnest to a man up a tree."

I now, of course, determined to reverse the mode of firing, and put forth all my physical energies to raise Soap-stick to the mark. The effort silenced Billy, and gave tongue to all his companions. I had just strength enough to master Soap-stick's obstinate proclivity, and, consequently, my nerves began to exhibit palpable signs of distress with her first imperceptible movement upward. A trembling commenced in my arms; increased, and extended rapidly to my body and lower extremities; so that, by the time that I had brought Soap-stick up to the mark, I was shaking from head to foot, exactly like a man under the continued action of a strong galvanic battery. In the mean time my friends gave vent to their feelings freely.

"I swear poin' blank," said one, "that man can't shoot."

"He used to shoot well," said another; "but can't now, nor never could."

"You better *git* away from 'bout that mark!" bawled a third, "for I'll be dod darned if Broadcloth don't give some of you the dry gripes if you stand too close thare."

"The stranger's got the *peedoddles*," * said a fourth, with humorous gravity.

"If he had bullets enough in his gun, he'd shoot a ring round the bull's-eye big as a spinning wheel," said a fifth.

As soon as I found that Soap-stick was high enough (for I made no farther use of the sights than to ascertain this fact), I pulled trigger, and off she went. I have always found that the most creditable way of relieving myself of derision was to heighten it myself as much as possible. It is a good plan in all circles, but by far the best which can be adopted among the plain, rough farmers of the country. Accordingly, I brought old Soap-stick to an order with an air of triumph; tipped Billy a wink, and observed, "Now, Billy, 's your time to make your fortune. Bet 'em two to one that I've knocked out the cross."

"No, I'll be dod blamed if I do," said Billy; "but I'll bet you two to one you han't hit the plank."

"Ah, Billy," said I, "I was joking about *betting,* for I never bet; nor would I have you to bet: indeed, I do not feel exactly right in shooting for beef; for it is a species of gaming at last: but I'll say this much: if that cross isn't knocked out, I'll never shoot for beef again as long as I live."

"By dod," said Mealy Whitecotton, "you'll lose no great things at that."

"Well," said I, "I reckon I know a little about wabbling. Is it possible, Billy, a man who shoots as well as you do, never practised shooting with the double wabble? It's the greatest take in in the world when you learn to drive the cross with it. Another sort for getting bets upon, to the drop-sight, with a single wabble! And the Soap-stick's the very yarn for it."

"Tell you what, stranger," said one, "you're too hard for us all here. We never *hearn* o' that sort o' shoot'n' in these parts."

---

* This word was entirely new to me: but like most, if not all words in use among the common people, it is doubtless a legitimate English word, or, rather, a compound of two words, the last a little corrupted, and was very aptly applied in this instance. It is a compound of *"pee,"* to peep with one eye, and *"daddle,"* to totter or wabble.

"Well," returned I, "you've seen it now, and I'm the boy that can do it."

The judges were now approaching with the target, and a singular combination of circumstances had kept all my party in utter ignorance of the result of my shot. Those about the target had been prepared by Billy Curlew for a great shot from me; their expectations had received assurance from the courtesy which had been extended to me; and nothing had happened to disappoint them but the single caution to them against the "dry gripes," which was as likely to have been given in irony as in earnest; for my agonies under the weight of the Soap-stick were either imperceptible to them at the distance of sixty yards, or, being visible, were taken as the flourishes of an expert who wished to "astonish the natives." The other party did not think the direction of my ball worth the trouble of a question; or if they did, my airs and harangue had put the thought to flight before it was delivered. Consequently, they were all transfixed with astonishment when the judges presented the target to them, and gravely observed, "It's only second best, after all the fuss."

"Second best!" exclaimed I, with uncontrollable transports.

The whole of my party rushed to the target to have the evidence of their senses before they would believe the report: but most marvellous fortune decreed that it should be true. Their incredulity and astonishment were most fortunate for me; for they blinded my hearers to the real feelings with which the exclamation was uttered, and allowed me sufficient time to prepare myself for making the best use of what I had said before with a very different object.

"Second best!" reiterated I, with an air of despondency, as the company turned from the target to me. "Second best only? Here, Billy, my son, take the old Soap-stick; she's a good piece, but I'm getting too old and dimsighted to shoot a rifle, especially with the drop-sight and double wabbles."

"Why, good Lord a'mighty!" said Billy, with a look that baffles all description, "an't you *driv* the cross!"

"Oh, driv the cross!" rejoined I, carelessly. "What's that! Just look where my ball is! I do believe in my soul its centre is a full quarter of an inch from the cross. I wanted to lay the centre of the bullet upon the cross, just as if you'd put it there with your fingers."

Several received this palaver with a contemptuous but very appropriate curl of the nose; and Mealy Whitecotton offered to bet a half pint "that I couldn't do the like again with no sort o' wabbles, he didn't care what." But I had already fortified myself on this quarter by my morality. A decided majority, however, were clearly of opinion that I was serious; and they regarded me as one of the wonders of the world. Billy increased the majority by now coming out fully with my history, as he had received it from his father; to which I listened with quite as much astonishment as any other one of his hearers. He begged me to go home with him for the night, or, as he expressed it, "to go home with him and swap lies that night, and it shouldn't cost me a cent"; the true reading of which is, that if I would go home with him, and give him the pleasure of an evening's chat about old times, his house should be as free to me as my own. But I could not accept his hospitality without retracing five or six miles of the road which I had already passed, and therefore I declined it.

"Well, if you won't go, what must I tell the old woman for you? for she'll be mighty glad to hear from the boy that won the silk handkerchief for her, and I expect she'll lick me for not bringing you home with me."

"Tell her," said I, "that I send her a quarter of beef, which I won, as I did the handkerchief, by nothing in the world but mere good luck."

"Hold your jaw, Lyman!" said Billy; "I an't a gwine to tell the old woman any such lies; for she's a *rael* reg'lar built Meth'dist."

As I turned to depart, "Stop a minute, stranger!" said one: then lowering his voice to a confidential but distinctly audible tone, "What you offering for?" continued he. I assured him I was not a candidate for anything; that I had accidentally fallen in with Billy Curlew, who begged me to come with him to the shooting-match, and, as it lay right on my road, I had stopped. "Oh," said he, with a conciliatory nod, "if you're up for anything, you needn't be mealy-mouthed about it 'fore us boys; for we'll all go in for you here up to the handle."

"Yes," said Billy, "dang old Roper if we don't go our death for you, no matter who offers. If ever you come out for anything, Lyman, jist let the boys of Upper Hogthief know it, and they'll go for you to the hilt, against creation, tit or no tit, that's the *tatur*."

I thanked them kindly, but repeated my assurances. The reader will not suppose that the district took its name from the character of the inhabitants. In almost every county in the state there is some spot or district which bears a contemptuous appellation, usually derived from local rivalships, or from a single accidental circumstance.

A PIANO IN ARKANSAS

Thomas Bangs Thorpe

From *The Hive of "The Bee-Hunter," a Repository of Sketches* by Thomas Bangs Thorpe, 1854; first published in *The Spirit of the Times,* XI (October 30, 1841), 409-410.

Thomas Bangs Thorpe (1815-1878) was a native of Massachusetts who went to Louisiana in 1833 and stayed twenty years. He was a painter and a journalist, and in narratives and sketches he undertook to record the scene and the life he observed about him. He contributed often to *The Spirit of the Times,* of which he later became editor, and he published two collections of his tales and sketches: *The Mysteries of the Backwoods; or, Sketches of the Southwest* . . . (1846) and *The Hive of the "Bee-Hunter," A Repository of Sketches* (1854). See Walter Blair, *Native American Humor* (1937), pages 63-67, 93-95; also Eugene Current-Garcia, "Thomas Bangs Thorpe and the Literature of the Ante-Bellum Southwestern Frontier," *The Louisiana Historical Quarterly,* XXXIX (April, 1956), 199-222. Milton Rickels has published "A Bibliography of the Writings of Thomas Bangs Thorpe," *American Literature,* XXIX (May, 1957), 169-197, and "Thomas Bangs Thorpe in the Felicianas, 1836-1842," *The Louisiana Historical Quarterly,* XXXIX (April, 1956), 169-197; and he is writing a book-length biography.

We shall never forget the excitement which seized upon the inhabitants of the little village of Hardscrabble, as the report spread through the community, that a real piano had actually arrived within its precincts.

Speculation was afloat as to its appearance and its use. The name was familiar to everybody; but what it precisely meant, no one could tell. That it had legs was certain;—for a stray volume of some

literary traveller was one of the most conspicuous works in the floating library of Hardscrabble; and said traveller stated, that he had
seen a piano somewhere in New England with pantalettes on—
also, an old foreign paper was brought forward, in which there was
an advertisement headed "Soiree," which informed the "citizens
generally," that Mr. Bobolink would preside at the piano.

This was presumed by several wiseacres, who had been to a
menagerie, to mean, that Mr. Bobolink stirred the piano up with a
long pole, in the same way that the showman did the lions and rhi-
no-ce-rus.

So, public opinion was in favor of its being an animal, though a
harmless one; for there had been a land speculator through the village a few weeks previously, who distributed circulars of a "Female
Academy," for the accomplishment of young ladies. These circulars
distinctly stated "the use of the piano to be one dollar per month."

One knowing old chap said, if they would tell him what so-i-ree
meant, he would tell them what a piano was, and no mistake.

The owner of this strange instrument was no less than a very
quiet and very respectable late merchant of a little town somewhere
"north," who having failed at home, had emigrated into the new
and hospitable country of Arkansas, for the purpose of bettering his
fortune, and escaping the heartless sympathy of his more lucky
neighbors, who seemed to consider him a very bad and degraded
man because he had become honestly poor.

The new comers were strangers, of course. The house in which
they were setting up their furniture was too little arranged "to admit of calls"; and as the family seemed very little disposed to court
society, all prospects of immediately solving the mystery that hung
about the piano seemed hopeless. In the meantime public opinion
was "rife."

The depository of this strange thing was looked upon by the
passers-by with indefinable awe; and as noises unfamiliar, sometimes reached the street, it was presumed that the piano made them,
and the excitement rose higher than ever—in the midst of it, one or
two old ladies, presuming upon their age and respectability, called
upon the strangers and inquired after their health, and offered their
services and friendship; meantime every thing in the house was

eyed with the greatest intensity, but seeing nothing strange, a hint was given about the piano. One of the new family observed carelessly, "that it had been much injured by bringing out, that the damp had affected its tones, and that one of its legs was so injured that it would not stand up, and for the present it would not ornament the parlor."

Here was an explanation, indeed: injured in bringing out—damp affecting its tones—leg broken. "Poor thing!" ejaculated the old ladies with real sympathy, as they proceeded homeward; "travelling has evidently fatigued it; the Mass-is-sip fogs have given it a cold, poor thing!" and they wished to see it with increased curiosity.

The "village" agreed, that if Moses Mercer, familiarly called "Mo Mercer," was in town, they would have a description of the piano, and the uses to which it was put; and fortunately, in the midst of the excitement, "Mo" arrived, he having been temporarily absent on a hunting expedition.

Moses Mercer was the only son of "old Mercer," who was, and had been, in the State Senate ever since Arkansas was admitted into the "Union." Mo, from this fact, received great glory, of course; his father's greatness alone would have stamped him with superiority; but his having been twice to the "Capitol" when the legislature was in session, stamped his claims to pre-eminence over all competitors.

Mo Mercer was the oracle of the renowned village of Hard-scrabble.

"Mo" knew every thing; he had all the consequence and complacency of a man who had never seen his equal, and never expected to. "Mo" bragged extensively upon his having been to the "Capitol" twice,—of his there having been in the most "fashionable society,"—of having seen the world. His return to town was therefore received with a shout. The arrival of the piano was announced to him, and *he alone* of all the community, was not astonished at the news.

His insensibility was considered wonderful. He treated the piano as a thing that he was used to, and went on, among other things to say, that he had seen more pianos in the "Capitol" than he had ever seen woodchucks; and that it was not an animal, but a musical instrument, played upon by the ladies; and he wound up his description by saying that the way "the dear creeters could pull music out of it was a caution to hoarse owls."

The new turn given to the piano excitement in Hardscrabble by Mo Mercer, was like pouring oil on fire to extinguish it, for it blazed out with more vigor than ever. That it was a musical instrument, made it a rarer thing in that wild country than if it had been an animal, and people of all sizes, colors, and degrees, were dying to see and hear it.

Jim Cash was Mo Mercer's right-hand man; in the language of refined society, he was "Mo's toady,"—in the language of Hardscrabble, he was "Mo's wheel-horse." Cash believed in Mo Mercer with an abandonment that was perfectly ridiculous. Mr. Cash was dying to see the piano, and the first opportunity he had alone with his Quixote, he expressed the desire that was consuming his vitals.

"We'll go at once and see it," said Mercer.

"Strangers!" echoed the frightened Cash.

"Humbug! Do you think I have visited the 'Capitol' twice, and don't know how to treat fashionable society? Come along at once, Cash," said Mercer.

Off the pair started, Mercer all confidence, and Cash all fears, as to the propriety of the visit. These fears Cash frankly expressed; but Mercer repeated, for the thousandth time, his experience in the fashionable society of the "Capitol, and pianos," which he said "was synonymous"—and he finally told Cash, to comfort him, that however abashed and ashamed he might be in the presence of the ladies, "that he needn't fear of sticking, for he would pull him through."

A few minutes' walk brought the parties on the broad galleries of the house that contained the object of so much curiosity. The doors and windows were closed, and a suspicious look was on every thing.

"Do they always keep a house closed up this way that has a piano in it?" asked Cash, mysteriously.

"Certainly," replied Mercer; "the damp would destroy its tones."

Repeated knocks at the doors, and finally at the windows, satisfied both Cash and Mercer that nobody was at home. In the midst of their disappointment Cash discovered a singular machine at the end of the gallery, crossed by bars and rollers, and surmounted with an enormous crank. Cash approached it on tiptoe; he had a presentiment that he beheld the object of his curiosity, and as its intricate character unfolded itself, he gazed with distended eyes, and asked Mercer, with breathless anxiety, "What that strange and incomprehensible box was?"

Mercer turned to the thing as coolly as a north wind to an icicle, and said "that was *it*."

"That *It!!*" exclaimed Cash, opening his eyes still wider; and then recovering himself, he asked to see "the tones."

Mercer pointed to the cross-bars and rollers. With trembling hands, with a resolution that would enable a man to be scalped without winking, Cash reached out his hand, and seized the handle of the crank (Cash, at heart, was a brave and fearless man); he gave it a turn, the machinery grated harshly, and seemed to clamor for something to be put in its maw.

"What delicious sounds!" said Cash.

"Beautiful!" observed the complacent Mercer, at the same time seizing Cash's arm, and asking him to desist, for fear of breaking the instrument, or getting it out of tune.

The simple caution was sufficient; and Cash, in the joy of the moment, at what he had done and seen, looked as conceited as Mo Mercer himself.

Busy, indeed, was Cash, from this time forward, in explaining to gaping crowds the exact appearance of the piano, how he had actually taken hold of it, and, as his friend Mo Mercer observed, "pulled music out of it."

The curiosity of the village was thus allayed, and consequently died comparatively away; Cash, however, having risen to almost as much importance as Mo Mercer, for having seen and handled the thing.

Our "Northern family" knew little or nothing of all this excitement; they received meanwhile the visits and congratulations of the hospitable villagers, and resolved to give a grand party to return some of the kindness they had received, and the piano was, for the first time, moved into the parlor. No invitation on this occasion was neglected; early at the post was every visitor, for it was rumored that Miss Patience Doolittle would, in the course of the evening, "perform on the piano."

The excitement was immense. The supper was passed over with a contempt, rivalling that which is cast upon an excellent farce played preparatory to a dull tragedy, in which the *star* is to appear. The furniture was all critically examined; but nothing could be discovered answering Cash's description. An enormously *thick-leafed table,* with a "spread" upon it, attracted little attention, *timber* being so very cheap in a new country, and so every body expected soon to see the piano "brought in."

Mercer, of course, was the hero of the evening; he talked much and loudly. Cash, as well as several young ladies, went into hysterics at his wit. Mercer, as the evening wore away, grew exceedingly conceited, even for him; and he graciously asserted that the company present reminded him of his two visits to the "Capitol," and other associations, equally exclusive and peculiar.

The evening wore on apace, and still—no piano. That hope deferred which maketh the heart sick, was felt by some elderly ladies, and by a few younger ones; and Mercer was solicited to ask Miss Patience Doolittle, to favor the company with the presence of the piano.

"Certainly," said Mercer, and with the grace of a city dandy he called upon the lady to gratify all present with a little music, prefacing his request with the remark, that if she was fatigued, "his friend Cash would give the machine a *turn."*

Miss Patience smiled, and looked at Cash.

Cash's knees trembled.

All eyes in the room turned upon him.

Cash sweat all over.

Miss Patience said she was gratified to hear that Mr. Cash was a musician; she admired people who had a musical taste. Whereupon Cash fell into a chair, as he afterwards observed, "chawed-up."

Oh that Beau Brummel, or any of his admirers could have seen Mo Mercer all this while! Calm as a summer morning—complacent as a newly-painted sign—he smiled and patronized, and was the only unexcited person in the room.

Miss Patience rose,—a sigh escaped from all present,—the piano was evidently to be brought in. She approached the thick-leafed table, and removed the covering, throwing it carelessly and gracefully aside; opened the instrument, and presented the beautiful arrangement of dark and white keys.

Mo Mercer at this, for the first time in his life, looked confused; he was Cash's authority in his descriptions of the appearance of the piano; while Cash himself, began to recover the moment that he ceased to be an object of attention. Many a whisper now ran through the room as to the "tones," and more particularly the "crank"; none could see them.

Miss Patience took her seat, ran her fingers over a few octaves, and if "Moses in Egypt" was not perfectly *executed,* Moses in Hardscrabble *was.* The dulcet sounds ceased. "Miss," said Cash, the moment that he could express himself, so entranced was he by the music,—"Miss Doolittle, what was that instrument Mo Mercer showed me in your gallery once, that went by a crank, and had rollers in it?"

It was now the time for Miss Patience to blush; so away went the blood from confusion to her cheeks; she hesitated, stammered, and said, "if Mr. Cash must know, it was a—a—a—*Yankee washing machine.*"

The name grated on Mo Mercer's ears as if rusty nails had been thrust into them; the heretofore invulnerable Mercer's knees trembled; the sweat started to his brow as he heard the taunting whispers of "visiting the Capitol twice," and seeing pianos as plenty as woodchucks.

The fashionable vices of envy and maliciousness, were that moment sown in the village of Hardscrabble; and Mo Mercer—the great—the confident—the happy and self-possessed—surprising as it may seem, was the first victim sacrificed to their influence.

Time wore on, and pianos became common, and Mo Mercer less popular; and he finally disappeared altogether, on the evening of the day on which a Yankee peddler of notions sold, to the highest bidder, "six patent, warranted, and improved Mo Mercer pianos."

THE INDEFATIGABLE
BEAR-HUNTER

———

Madison Tensas

[HENRY CLAY LEWIS]

From *Odd Leaves from the Life of a Louisiana "Swamp Doctor"* by Madison Tensas (Henry Clay Lewis), 1850, in which the story first appeared; printed immediately afterward in *The Spirit of the Times*, XX (April 20, 1850), 9.

Henry Clay Lewis (1825-1850) was a native of South Carolina who grew up in Mississippi, attended medical school in Louisville, Kentucky, and practiced medicine in northeast Louisiana. His tales and sketches appeared in *The Spirit of the Times* before being collected in his only book, *Odd Leaves from the Life of a Louisiana "Swamp Doctor"* (1850). John Q. Anderson has established Lewis as the author of the *Odd Leaves* and has discovered the main facts of his career. See his "Henry Clay Lewis, Alias 'Madison Tensas,' M.D., The Louisiana Swamp Doctor," *Bulletin of the Medical Library Association*, XLIII (January, 1955), 58-73. He has published also "Folklore in the Writings of 'The Louisiana Swamp Doctor,'" *Southern Folklore Quarterly*, XIX (December, 1955), 243-251; and he is editing Lewis's book for publication along with a biographical introduction.

"The Big Bear of Arkansas" mentioned early in this tale is a reference to Thomas Bangs Thorpe's masterpiece with that title, which had appeared first in *The Spirit of the Times* on March 27, 1841, and had been reprinted several times afterward.

In my round of practice, I occasionally meet with men whose peculiarities stamp them as belonging to a class composed only of themselves. So different are they in appearance, habits, taste, from the majority of mankind, that it is impossible to classify them, and you have therefore to set them down as queer birds "of a feather," that none resemble sufficiently to associate with.

I had a patient once who was one of these queer ones; gigantic in stature, uneducated, fearless of real danger, yet timorous as a child of superstitious perils, born literally in the woods, never having been in a city in his life, and his idea of one being that it was a place where people met together to make whiskey, and form plans for swindling country folks. To view him at one time, you would think him only a whiskey-drinking, bear-fat-loving mortal; at other moments, he would give vent to ideas, proving that beneath his rough exterior there ran a fiery current of high enthusiastic ambition.

It is a favourite theory of mine, and one that I am fond of consoling myself with, for my own insignificance, that there is no man born who is not capable of attaining distinction, and no occupation that does not contain a path leading to fame. To bide our time is all that is necessary. I had expressed this view in the hearing of Mik-hoo-tah, for so was the subject of this sketch called, and it seemed to chime in with his feelings exactly. Born in the woods, and losing his parents early, he had forgotten his real name, and the bent of his genius inclining him to the slaying of bears, he had been given, even when a youth, the name of Mik-hoo-tah, signifying "the grave of bears," by his Indian associates and admirers.

To glance in and around his cabin, you would have thought that the place had been selected for ages past by the bear tribe to yield up their spirits in, so numerous were the relics. Little chance, I ween, had the cold air to whistle through that hut, so thickly was it tap-estried with the soft, downy hides, the darkness of the surface re-lieved occasionally by the skin of a tender fawn, or the short-haired irascible panther. From the joists depended bear-hams and tongues innumerable, and the ground outside was literally white with bones. Ay, he was a bear-hunter, in its most comprehensive sense—the chief of that vigorous band, whose occupation is nearly gone—crushed beneath the advancing strides of romance-destroying civilization. When his horn sounded—so tradition ran—the bears be-gan to draw lots to see who should die that day, for painful experi-ence had told them the uselessness of all endeavouring to escape.

The "Big Bear of Arkansas" would not have given him an hour's extra work, or raised a fresh wrinkle on his already care-corrugated brow. But, though almost daily imbruing his hands in the blood of Bruin, Mik-hoo-tah had not become an impious or cruel-hearted man. Such was his piety, that he never killed a bear without getting down on his knees—to skin it—and praying to be d—ned if it warn't a buster; and such his softness of heart, that he often wept, when he, by mistake, had killed a suckling bear—depriving her poor offspring of a mother's care—and found her too poor to be eaten. So indefatigable had he become in his pursuit, that the bears bid fair to disappear from the face of the swamp, and be known to posterity only through the one mentioned in Scripture, that assisted Elisha to punish the impertinent children, when an accident occurred to the hunter, which raised their hopes of not being entirely exterminated.

One day, Mik happened to come unfortunately in contact with a stray grizzly fellow, who, doubtless in the indulgence of an adventurous spirit, had wandered away from the Rocky Mountains, and formed a league for mutual protection with his black and more effeminate brethren of the swamp. Mik saluted him, as he approached, with an ounce ball in the forehead, to avenge half a dozen of his best dogs, who lay in fragments around; the bullet flattened upon his impenetrable skull, merely infuriating the monster; and before Mik could reload, it was upon him. Seizing him by the leg, it bore him to the ground, and ground the limb to atoms. But before it could attack a more vital part, the knife of the dauntless hunter had cloven its heart, and it dropped dead upon the bleeding form of its slayer, in which condition they were shortly found by Mik's comrades. Making a litter of branches, they placed Mik upon it, and proceeded with all haste to their camp, sending one of the company by a near cut for me, as I was the nearest physician. When I reached their temporary shelter I found Mik doing better than I could have expected, with the exception of his wounded leg, and that, from its crushed and mutilated condition, I saw would have to be amputated immediately, of which I informed Mik. As I expected, he opposed it vehemently; but I convinced him of the impossibility of saving it, assuring him if it were not amputated, he would certainly die, and appealed to his good sense to grant permission, which he did at last. The next difficulty was to procure amputating instruments, the rarity of surgical operations, and the generally slender purse of the "Swamp Doctor," not justifying him in purchasing expensive instruments. A couple of bowie-knives, one ingeniously hacked and filed into a saw—a tourniquet made of a belt and piece of stick—a gun-screw converted for the time into a tenaculum—and some buckskin slips for ligatures, completed my case of instruments for amputation. The city physician may smile at this recital, but I assure him many a more difficult operation than the amputation of a leg, has been performed by his humble brother in the "swamp," with far more simple means than those I have mentioned. The preparations being completed, Mik refused to have his arms bound, and commenced singing a bear song; and throughout the whole operation, which was necessarily tedious, he never uttered a groan, or missed a single stave. The next day, I had him conveyed by easy stages to his pre-emption; and tending assiduously, in the course of a few weeks, he had recovered sufficiently for me to cease attentions. I made him a wooden leg, which answered a good purpose; and with a sigh of regret for the spoiling of such a good hunter, I struck him from my list of patients.

A few months passed over and I heard nothing more of him. Newer, but not brighter, stars were in the ascendant, filling with their deeds the clanging trump of bear-killing fame, and, but for the quantity of bear-blankets in the neighbouring cabins, and the painful absence of his usual present of bear-hams, Mik-hoo-tah bid fair to suffer that fate most terrible to aspiring ambitionists—forgetfulness during life. The sun, in despair at the stern necessity which compelled him to yield up his tender offspring, day, to the gloomy grave of darkness, had stretched forth his long arms, and, with the tenacity of a drowning man clinging to a straw, had clutched the tender whispering straw-like topmost branches of the trees—in other words it was near sunset—when I arrived at home from a long wearisome semi-ride-and-swim through the swamp. Receiving a negative to my inquiry whether there were any new calls, I was felicitating myself upon a quiet night beside my tidy bachelor hearth, undisturbed by crying children, babbling women, or amorous cats—

the usual accompaniments of married life—when, like a poor hen-pecked Benedick crying for peace when there is no peace, I was doomed to disappointment. Hearing the splash of a paddle in the bayou running before the door, I turned my head towards the bank, and soon beheld, first the tail of a coon, next his body, a human face, and, the top of the bank being gained, a full-proportioned form clad in the garments which, better than any printed label, wrote him down raftsman, trapper, bear-hunter. He was a messenger from the indefatigable bear-hunter, Mik-hoo-tah. Asking him what was the matter, as soon as he could get the knots untied which two-thirds drunkenness had made in his tongue, he informed me, to my sincere regret, that Mik went out that morning on a bear-hunt, and in a fight with one had got his leg broke all to flinders, if possible worse than the other, and that he wanted me to come quickly. Getting into the canoe, which awaited me, I wrapped myself in my blanket, and yielding to my fatigue, was soon fast asleep. I did not awaken until the canoe striking against the bank, as it landed at Mik's pre-emption, nearly threw me in the bayou, and entirely succeeded with regard to my half-drunken paddler, who—like the sailor who circumnavigated the world and then was drowned in a puddle-hole in his own garden—had escaped all the perils of the tortuous bayou to be pitched overboard when there was nothing to do but step out and tie the dug-out. Assisting him out of the water, we proceeded to the house, when, to my indignation, I learnt that the drunken messenger had given me the long trip for nothing, Mik only wanting me to make him a new wooden leg, the old one having been completely demolished that morning.

Relieving myself by a satisfactory oath, I would have returned that night, but the distance was too great for one fatigued as I was, so I had to content myself with such accommodations as Mik's cabin afforded, which, to one blessed like myself with the happy faculty of ready adaptation to circumstances, was not a very difficult task.

I was surprised to perceive the change in Mik's appearance. From nearly a giant, he had wasted to a mere huge bony frame-work; the skin of his face clung tightly to the bones, and showed nothing of those laughter-moving features that were wont to adorn his visage; only his eye remained unchanged, and it had lost none of its brilliancy—the flint had lost none of its fire.

"What on earth is the matter with you, Mik? I have never seen any one fall off so fast; you have wasted to a skeleton—surely you must have the consumption."

"Do you think so, Doc? I'll soon show you whether the old bellows has lost any of its force!" and hopping to the door, which he threw wide open, he gave a death-hug rally to his dogs, in such a loud and piercing tone, that I imagined a steam whistle was being discharged in my ear, and for several moments could hear nothing distinctly.

"That will do! stop!" I yelled, as I saw Mik drawing in his breath preparatory to another effort of his vocal strength; "I am satisfied you have not got consumption; but what has wasted you so, Mik? Surely, you ain't in love?"

"Love! h-ll! you don't suppose, Doc, even if I was 'tarmined to make a cussed fool of myself, that there is any gal in the swamp that could stand that hug, do you?" and catching up a huge bull-dog, who lay basking himself by the fire, he gave him such a squeeze that the animal yelled with pain, and for a few moments appeared dead. "No, Doc, it's grief, pure sorrur, sorrur, Doc! when I looks at what I is now and what I used to be! Jes think, Doc, of the fust hunter in the swamp having his sport spilte, like bar-meat in summer without salt! Jes think of a man standin' up one day and blessing old Master for having put bar in creation, and the next cussing high heaven and low h-ll 'cause he couldn't 'sist in puttin' them out! Warn't it enough to bring tears to the eyes of an Injun tater, much less take the fat off a bar-hunter? Doc, I fell off like 'simmons arter frost, and folks as doubted me, needn't had asked whether I war 'ceitful or not, for they could have seed plum threw me! The bar and painter got so saucy that they'd cum to the tother side of the bayou and see which could talk the impudentest! 'Don't you want some bar-meat or painter blanket?' they'd ask; 'bars is monstrous fat, and painter's hide is mighty warm!' Oh! Doc, I was a miserable man! The sky warn't blue for me, the sun war always cloudy, and the shade-trees gin no shade for me. Even the dogs forgot me, and the little children quit coming and asking, 'Please, Mr. Bar-Grave, cotch me a young bar or a painter kitten.' Doc, the tears would cum in my eyes and the hot blood would cum biling up from my heart, when I'd hobble out of a sundown and hear the boys tell, as they went by, of the sport they'd had that day, and how the bar fit 'fore he was killed, and how fat he war arter he was slayed. Long arter they was gone, and the whip-poor-will had eat up their voices, I would sit out there on the old stump, and think of the things that used to hold the biggest place in my mind when I was a boy, and p'raps sense I've bin a man.

"I'd heard tell of distinction and fame, and people's names never dying, and how Washington and Franklin, and Clay and Jackson, and a heap of political dicshunary-folks, would live when their big hearts had crumbled down to a rifle-charge of dust; and I begun, too, to think, Doc, what a pleasant thing it would be to know folks a million years off would talk of me like them, and it made me 'tarmine to 'stinguish myself, and have my name put in a book with a yaller kiver. I warn't a genus, Doc, I nude that, nor I warn't dicshunary; so I determined to strike out in a new track for glory, and 'title myself to be called the 'bear-hunter of Ameriky.' Doc, my heart jumpt up, and I belted my hunting-shirt tighter for fear it would lepe out when I fust spoke them words out loud.

"'The bar-hunter of Ameriky!' Doc, you know whether I war ernin' the name when I war ruined. There is not a child, white, black, Injun, or nigger, from the Arkansas line to Trinity, but what has heard of me, and I were happy when"—here a tremor of his voice and a tear glistening in the glare of the fire told the old fellow's emotion—"when—but les take a drink—Doc, I found I was dying—I war gettin' weaker and weaker—I nude your truck warn't what I needed, or I'd sent for you. A bar-hunt war the medsin that my systum required, a fust class bar-hunt, the music of the dogs, the fellers a screaming, the cane poppin', the rifles crackin', the bar growlin', the fight hand to hand, slap goes his paw, and a dog's hide hangs on one cane and his body on another, the knife glistenin' and then goin' plump up to the handle in his heart!—Oh! Doc, this was what I needed, and I swore, since death were huggin' me, anyhow, I mite as well feel his last grip in a bar-hunt.

"I seed the boys goin' long one day, and haled them to wait

awhile, as I believed I would go along too. I war frade if I kept
out of a hunt much longer I wood get outen practis. They laughed
at me, thinkin' I war jokin'; for wat cood a sick, old, one-legged
man do in a bar-hunt? how cood he get threw the swamp, and
vines, and canes, and backwater? and s'pose he mist the bar, how
war he to get outen the way?

"But I war 'tarmined on goin'; my dander was up, and I swore I
wood go, tellin' them if I coodent travel 'bout much, I could take
a stand. Seein' it war no use tryin' to 'swade me, they saddled my
poney, and off we started. I felt better right off. I knew I cuddent
do much in the chase, so I told the fellers I would go to the cross-
path stand, and wate for the bar, as he would be sarten to cum by
thar. You have never seed the cross-path stand, Doc. It's the singu-
larest place in the swamp. It's rite in the middle of a canebrake,
thicker than har on a bar-hide, down in a deep sink, that looks like
the devil had cummenst diggin' a skylite for his pre-emption. I
knew it war a dangersome place for a well man to go in, much
less a one-leg cripple; but I war 'tarmined that time to give a deal
on the dead wood, and play my hand out. The boys gin me time
to get to the stand, and then cummenst the drive. The bar seemed
'tarmined on disappinting me, for the fust thing I heard of the dogs
and bar, they was outen hearing. Everything got quiet, and I got
so wrathy at not being able to foller up the chase, that I cust till the
trees cummenst shedding their leaves and small branches, when I
herd them lumbrin back, and I nude they war makin' to me. I
primed old 'bar death' fresh, and rubbed the frizin, for it war no
time for rifle to get to snappin'. Thinks I, if I happen to miss, I'll
try what virtue there is in a knife—when, Doc, my knife war gone.
H-ll! bar, for God's sake have a soft head, and die easy, for I *can't*
run!

"Doc, you've hearn a bar bustin' threw a cane-brake, and know
how near to a harrycane it is. I almost cummenst dodgin' the trees,
thinkin' it war the best in the shop one a comin', for it beat the
loudest thunder ever I heard; that ole bar did, comin' to get his
death from an ole, one-legged cripple, what had slayed more of his
brethren than his nigger foot had ever made trax in the mud. Doc,
he heerd a *monstrus long ways ahead of the dogs.* I warn't skeered,

but I must own, as I had but one shot, an' no knife, I wud have prefurd they had been closer. But here he cum! he bar—big as a bull—boys off h-ll-wards—dogs nowhar—no knife—but one shot— *and only one leg that cood run!*

"The bar 'peered s'prised to see me standin' ready for him in the openin'; for it war currently reported 'mong his brethren that I war either dead, or no use for bar. I thought fust he war skeered; and, Doc, I b'leve he war, till he cotch a sight of my wooden leg, and that toch his pride, for he knew he would be hist outen every she bear's company, ef he run from a poor, sickly, one-legged cripple, so on he cum, a small river of slobber pourin from his mouth, and the blue smoke curlin outen his ears. I tuck good aim at his left, and let drive. The ball struck him on the eyebrow, and glanced off, only stunnin' him for a moment, jes givin' me time to club my rifle, an' on he kum, as fierce as old grizzly. As he got in reach, I gin him a lick 'cross the temples, brakin' the stock in fifty pieces, an' knockin' him senseless. I struv to foller up the lick, when, Doc, I war fast—my timber toe had run inter the ground, and I cuddent git out, though I jerked hard enuf almost to bring my thigh out of joint. I stuped to unscrew the infurnal thing, when the bar cum too, and cum at me agen. Vim! I tuck him over the head, and, cochunk, he keeled over. H-ll! but I cavorted and pitched. Thar war my wust enemy, watin' for me to giv him a finisher, an' *I cuddent* git at him. I'd cummense unscrewin' leg—here cum bar— vim—cochunk—he'd fall out of reach—and, Doc, *I cuddent git to him.* I kept workin' my body round, so as to unscrew the leg, and keep the bar off till I cood 'complish it, when jes as I tuck the last turn, and got loose from the d——d thing, here cum bar, more venimous than ever, and I nude thar war death to one out, and comin' shortly. I let him get close, an' then cum down with a perfect tornado on his head, as I thought; but the old villin had learnt the dodge—the barrel jes struck him on the side of the head, and glanst off, slinging itself out of my hands bout twenty feet 'mongst the thick cane, and thar I war in a fix sure. Bar but little hurt— no gun—no knife—no dogs—no frens—no chance to climb—*an' only one leg that cood run.* Doc, I jes cummenst makin' 'pologies to ole Master, when an idee struck me. Doc, did you ever see a piney woods nigger pullin at a sassafras root? or a suckin' pig in a tater patch arter the big yams? You has! Well, you can 'magin how I jurkt at that wudden leg, for it war the last of pea-time with me, sure, if I didn't rise 'fore bar did. At last, they both cum up, bout the same time, and I braced myself for a death struggle.

"We fit all round that holler! Fust I'd foller bar, and then bar would chase me! I'd make a lick, he'd fend off, and showin' a set of teeth that no doctor, 'cept natur, had ever wurkt at, cum tearin' at me! We both 'gan to git tired, I heard the boys and dogs cumin', so did bar, and we were both anxshus to bring the thing to a close 'fore they cum up, though I wuddent thought they were intrudin' ef they had cum up some time afore.

"I'd worn the old leg pretty well off to the second jint, when, jest 'fore I made a lick, the noise of the boys and the dogs cummin' sorter confused bar, and he made a stumble, and bein' off his guard I got a fair lick! The way that bar's flesh giv in to the soft impres-shuns of that leg war an honor to the mederkal perfeshun for hav-ing invented sich a weepun! I hollered—but you have heered me holler an' I won't describe it—I had whipped a bar in a fair hand to hand fight—me, an old sickly one-legged bar-hunter! The boys cum up, and, when they seed the ground we had fit over, they swore they would hav thought, 'stead of a bar-fight, that I had been cuttin' cane and deadenin' timber for a corn-patch, the sile war so worked up, they then handed me a knife to finish the work.

"Doc, les licker, it's a dry talk—when will you make me another leg? for bar-meat is not over plenty in the cabin, and I feel like tryin' another!"

PARSON JOHN BULLEN'S
LIZARDS

————

George Washington Harris

From *Sut Lovingood Yarns* by George Washington Harris, 1867.

A native of Tennessee, George Washington Harris (1814-1869) knew life on the river steamboats and among the mountaineers, and he undertook to report in tales and sketches the essential qualities of the life he observed. He was a contributor to *The Spirit of the Times* by 1845, and he published sketches in various local newspapers before bringing out his one book, *Sut Lovingood Yarns* (1867). Three additional sketches have been collected by Edd W. Parks in *Sut Lovingood's Travels with Old Abe Lincoln* (1937), and there are others which have not been reprinted from the newspapers in which Harris published them. See Walter Blair, *Native American Humor* (1937), pages 96-101; Donald Day, "The Humorous Works of George W. Harris," *American Literature,* XIV (January, 1943), 391-406; "The Life of George Washington Harris," *Tennessee Historical Quarterly,* VI (March, 1947), 3-38; and Milton Rickels, "The Imagery of George Washington Harris," *American Literature,* XXXI (May, 1959), 173-187.

————

AIT ($8) DULLARS REW-ARD.

'TENSHUN BELEVERS AND KONSTABLES! KETCH 'IM!
KETCH 'IM!

This kash wil be pade in korn, ur uther projuce, tu be kolected at ur about nex camp-meetin, *ur thararter,* by eny wun what ketches him, fur the karkus ove a sartin wun Sut Lovingood, dead ur alive, ur ailin, an' safely giv over tu the purtectin care ove Parson John Bullin, ur lef' well tied, at Squire Mackjunkins, fur the raisin ove the devil pussonely, an' permiskusly discumfurtin the wimen very powerful, an' skeerin ove folks generly a heap, an' bustin up a promisin, big warm meetin, an' a makin the wickid larf, an' wus, an' wus, insultin ove the passun orful.

Test,   Jehu Wethero.

Sined by me,

John Bullen, the passun.

I found written copies of the above highly intelligible and vindictive proclamation, stuck up on every blacksmith shop, doggery, and store door, in the Frog Mountain Range. Its blood-thirsty spirit, its style, and above all, its chirography, interested me to the extent of taking one down from a tree for preservation.

In a few days I found Sut in a good crowd in front of Capehart's Doggery, and as he seemed to be about in good tune, I read it to him.

"Yas, George, that ar dockymint am in dead yearnist sartin. Them hard shells over thar dus want me the wus kine, powerful bad. *But,* I spect ait dullers won't fetch me, nither wud ait hundred, bekase thar's nun ove 'em fas' enuf tu ketch me, nither is thar hosses by the livin jingo! Say, George, much talk 'bout this fuss up whar yu're been?" For the sake of a joke I said yes, a great deal.

"Jis' es I 'spected, durn 'em, all git drunk, an' skeer thar fool sefs ni ontu deth, an' then lay hit ontu me, a poor innersent youf, an' es soun' a belever es they is. Lite, lite, ole feller an' let that roan ove yourn blow a litil, an' I'll 'splain this cussed misfortnit affar: hit hes ruinated my karacter es a pius pusson in the s'ciety roun' yere, an' is a spreadin faster nur meazils. When ever yu hear eny on 'em a spreadin hit, gin hit the dam lie squar, will yu? I haint dun nuffin tu one ove 'em. Hits true, I did sorter frustrate a few lizzards a littil, but they haint members, es I knows on.

"You see, las' year I went tu the big meetin at Rattlesnake Springs, an' wer a sittin in a nice shady place convarsin wif a frien' ove mine, intu the huckilberry thickit, jis' duin nuffin tu nobody an' makin no fuss, when, the fust thing I remembers, I woke up frum a trance what I hed been knocked inter by a four-year old hickory-stick, hilt in the paw ove ole Passun Bullin, durn his alligator hide; an' he wer standin a striddil ove me, a foamin at the mouf, a-chompin his teeth—gesterin wif the hickory club—an' a-preachin tu me so you cud a-hearn him a mile, about a sartin sins gineraly, an' my wickedness pussonely; an' mensunin the name ove my frien' loud enuf tu be hearn tu the meetin 'ous. My poor innersent frien' wer dun gone an' I wer glad ove hit, fur I tho't he ment tu kill me rite whar I lay, an' I didn't want her tu see me die."

"Who was she, the friend you speak of, Sut?" Sut opened his eyes wide.

"Hu the devil, an' durnashun tole *yu* that hit wer a she?"

"Why, you did, Sut"——

"I *didn't,* durn ef I did. Ole Bullin dun hit, an' I'll hev tu kill him yet, the cussed, infernel ole tale-barer!"——

"Well, well, Sut, who was she?"

"Nun ove y-u-r-e b-i-s-n-i-s-s, durn yure littil ankshus picter! I *sees yu* a lickin ove yure lips. I *will* tell you one thing, George; that night, a neighbor gal got a all-fired, overhandid stroppin frum her mam, wif a stirrup leather, an' ole Passun Bullin, hed et supper thar, an' what's wus nur all, that poor innersent, skeer'd gal hed dun her levil bes' a cookin hit fur 'im. She begged him, a trimblin, an' a-cryin not tu tell on her. He et her cookin, he promised her he'd keep dark—an' then went strait an' tole her mam. Warnt that rale low down, wolf mean? The durnd infunel, hiperkritikal, pot-bellied, scaley-hided, whisky-wastin, stinkin ole groun'-hog. He'd heap better a stole sum *man's* hoss; I'd a tho't more ove 'im. But I paid him plum up fur hit, an' I means tu keep a payin him, ontil one ur tuther, ove our toes pints up tu the roots ove the grass.

"Well, yere's the way I lifted that note ove han'. At the nex big meetin at Rattilsnaik—las' week hit wer—I wer on han' es solemn es a ole hat kivver on collection day. I hed my face draw'd out intu the shape an' perporshun ove a taylwer's sleeve-board, pint down. I hed put on the convicted sinner so pufeckly that an' ole obsarvin she pillar ove the church sed tu a ole he pillar, es I walked up tu my bainch:

" 'Law sakes alive, ef thar ain't that *orful* sinner, Sut Lovingood, pearced plum thru; hu's nex?'

"Yu see, by golly, George, I *hed* tu promis the ole tub ove soap-greas tu cum an' hev myself convarted, jis' tu keep him frum killin me. An' es I know'd hit wudn't interfare wif the relashun I bore tu the still housis roun' thar, I didn't keer a durn. I jis' wanted tu git *ni* ole Bullin, onst onsuspected, an' this wer the bes' way tu du hit. I tuk a seat on the side steps ove the pulpit, an' kivvered es much ove my straitch'd face es I could wif my han's, tu prove I wer in yearnis. Hit tuck powerful—fur I hearn a sorter thankful kine ove buzzin all over the congregashun. Ole Bullin hissef looked down at me, over his ole copper specks, an' hit sed jis' es plain es a look cud say hit: 'Yu am thar, ar you—durn yu, hits well fur yu that yu cum.' I tho't sorter diffrent frum that. I tho't hit wud a been well fur *yu,* ef I hadent a-cum, but I didn't say hit jis then. Thar wer a monstrus crowd in that grove, fur the weather wer fine, an' b'levers wer plenty roun' about Rattilsnaik Springs. Ole Bullin gin out, an' they sung that hyme, yu know:

> "Thar will be mournin, mournin yere, an' mournin thar,
>   On that dredful day tu cum."

"Thinks I, ole hoss, kin hit be possibil enybody hes tole yu what's a gwine tu happin; an' then I tho't that nobody know'd hit but me, and I wer cumforted. He nex tuck hisself a tex pow'fly mixed wif brimstone, an' trim'd wif blue flames, an' then he open'd. He cummenced ontu the sinners; he threaten'd 'em orful, tried tu skeer 'em wif all the wust varmints he cud think ove, an' arter a while he got ontu the idear ove Hell-sarpints, and he dwelt on it sum. He tole 'em how the ole Hell-sarpints wud sarve 'em if they didn't repent; how cold they'd crawl over thar nakid bodys, an' how like ontu pitch they'd stick tu 'em es they crawled; how they'd rap thar tails roun' thar naiks chokin clost, poke thar tungs up thar noses, an' hiss intu thar years. This wer the way they wer tu sarve men folks. Then he turned ontu the wimmen: tole 'em how they'd quile intu thar buzzims, an' how they *wud* crawl down onder thar frock-strings, no odds how tite they tied 'em, an' how sum ove the oldes' an' wus ones wud crawl up thar laigs, an' travil *onder* thar garters, no odds how tight they tied *them,* an' when the two armys ove Hell-sarpents met, then—— That las' remark *fotch 'em.* Ove all the screamin, an' hollerin, an' loud cryin, I ever hearn, begun all at onst, all over the hole groun' jis' es he hollered out that word 'then.' He kep on a bellerin, but I got so buisy jis' then, that I didn't listen tu him much, fur I saw that my time fur ackshun hed cum. Now yu see, George, I'd cotch seven ur eight big pot-bellied lizzards, an' hed 'em in a littil narrer bag, what I had made a-purpus. Thar tails all at the bottim, an' so crowdid fur room that they cudent turn roun'. So when he wer a-ravin ontu his tip-toes, an' a-poundin the pulpit wif his fis'—onbenowenst tu enybody, I ontied my bag ove reptiles, put the mouf ove hit onder the bottim ove his britches-laig, an' sot intu pinchin thar tails. Quick es gunpowder they all tuck up his bar laig, makin a nise like squirrils a-climbin a shell-bark hickory. He stop't preachin rite in the middil ove the word 'damnation,' an' looked fur a moment like he wer a listenin fur sumthin—sorter like a ole sow dus, when she hears yu a-whistlin fur the dorgs. The tarifick shape ove his feeters stopp't the shoutin an' screamin; instuntly yu cud hearn a cricket chirp. I gin a long groan, an' hilt my head a-twixt my knees. He gin hisself sum orful open-handed slaps wif fust one han' an' then tuther, about the place whar yu cut the bes' steak outen a beef. Then he'd fetch a vigrus ruff rub whar a hosses tail sprouts; then he'd stomp one foot, then tuther, then bof at onst. Then he run his han' atween his waisbun an' his shut an' reach'd way down, an' roun' wif hit; then he spread his big laigs, an' gin his back a good rattlin rub agin 'e pulpit, like a hog scratches hisself agin a stump, leanin tu hit pow'ful, an' twitchin, an' squirmin all over, es ef he'd slept in a dorg bed, ur ontu a pisant hill. About this time, one ove my lizzards scared an' hurt by all this poundin' an' feelin, an' scratchin, popp'd out his head frum the passun's shut collar, an' his ole brown naik, an' wer a-surveyin the crowd, when ole Bullin struck at 'im, jis' too late, fur he'd dodged back agin. The hell desarvin ole raskil's speech now cum tu 'im, an' sez he, 'Pray fur me brethren an' sisteren, fur I is a-rastilin wif the great inimy rite now! an' his voice wer the mos' pitiful, trimblin thing I ever hearn. Sum ove the wimmen fotch a painter yell, an' a young docter, wif ramrod laigs, lean'd toward me monstrus knowin like, an' sez he, 'Clar case ove Delishus Tremenjus.' I nodded my head, an' sez I, 'Yas, spechuly the tremenjus part, an' Ise feard hit haint at hits worst.' Ole Bullin's eyes wer a-stickin out like ontu two buckeyes flung agin a mud wall, an' he wer a-cuttin up more shines nor a cockroach in a hot skillet. Off went the clamhammer coat, an' he flung hit ahine 'im like he wer a-gwine intu a fight; he hed no jackid tu take off, so he unbuttoned his galluses, an' vigrusly flung the ainds back over his head. He fotch his shut over-handed a durnd site faster nor I got outen my pasted one, an' then flung hit strait up in the air, like he jis' wanted hit tu keep on up furever; but hit lodged ontu a black-jack, an' I sed one ove my lizzards wif his tail up, a-racin about all over the ole dirty shut, skared too bad tu jump. Then he gin a sorter shake, an' a stompin kine ove twis', an' he cum outer his britches. He tuck 'em by the bottim ove the laigs, an' swung 'em roun' his head a time ur two, an' then fotch 'em down cherall-up over the frunt ove the pulpit. You cud a hearn the smash a quarter ove a mile! Ni ontu fifteen shorten'd biskits, a boiled chicken, wif hits laigs crossed, a big dubbil-bladed knife, a hunk ove terbacker, a cob-pipe, sum copper ore, lots ove broken glass, a cork, a sprinkil ove whisky, a squirt, an' three lizzards flew permiskusly all over that meetin-groun', outen the upper aind ove them big flax britches. One ove the smartes' ove my lizzards lit head-fust intu the buzzim ove a fat 'oman, es big es a skin'd hoss, an' ni ontu es ugly, who sot thuty yards off, a fannin herself wif a tucky-tail. Smart tu the las', by golly, he imejuntly commenced runnin down the centre ove her breas'-bone, an' kep on, I speck. She wer jis' boun' tu faint; an' she did hit fust rate—flung the tucky-tail up in the air, grabbed the lap ove her gown, gin hit a big histin an' fallin shake, rolled down the hill, tangled her laigs an' garters in the top ove a huckilberry bush, wif her head in the branch an' jis' lay still. She wer interestin, she wer, ontil a serious-lookin, pale-faced 'oman hung a nankeen ridin skirt over the huckilberry bush. That wer all that wer dun to'ards bringin her too, that I seed. Now ole Bullin hed nuffin left ontu 'im but a par ove heavy, low quarter'd shoes, short woolen socks, an' eel-skin garters tu keep off the cramp. His skeer hed druv him plum crazy, fur he felt roun' in the air, abuv his head, like he wer huntin sumthin in the dark, an' he beller'd out, 'Brethren, brethren, take keer ove yerselves, the Hell-sarpints *hes got me!'* When this cum out, yu cud a-hearn the screams tu Halifax. He jis' spit in his han's, an' loped over the frunt ove the pulpid *kerdiff!* He lit on top ove, an' rite amung the mos' pius part ove the congregashun. Ole Misses Chaneyberry sot wif her back tu the pulpit, sorter stoopin forrid. He lit astradil ove her long naik, a shuttin her up wif a snap, her head atwix her knees, like shuttin up a jack-knife, an' he sot intu gittin away his levil durndest; he went in a heavy lumberin gallop, like a ole fat waggon hoss, skared at a locomotive. When he jumpt a bainch he shook the yeath. The bonnets, an' fans clar'd the way an' jerked most ove the children wif 'em, an' the rest he scrunched. He open'd a purfeckly clar track tu the woods, ove every livin thing. He weighed ni ontu three hundred, hed a black stripe down his back, like ontu a ole bridil rein, an' his belly wer 'bout the size an' color ove a beef paunch, an' hit a-swingin out frum side tu side; he leand back frum hit, like a littil feller a-totin a big drum, at a muster, an' I hearn hit plum tu whar I wer. Thar wer cramp-knots on his laigs es big es walnuts, an' mottled splotches on his shins; an' takin him all over, he minded ove a durnd crazy ole elephant, pussessed ove the devil, rared up on hits hind aind, an' jis' *gittin* frum sum imijut danger ur tribulashun. He did the loudest, an' skariest, an' fussiest runnin I ever seed, tu be no faster nur hit wer, since dad tried tu outrun the ho'nets.

"Well, he disapear'd in the thicket jis' bustin—an' ove all the noises yu ever hearn, wer made thar on that camp groun': sum wimen screamin—they wer the skeery ones; sum larfin—they wer the wicked ones; sum cryin—they wer the fool ones (sorter my stripe yu know); sum tryin tu git away wif thar faces red—they wer the modest ones; sum lookin arter ole Bullin—they wer the curious ones; sum hangin clost tu thar sweethearts—they wer the sweet ones; sum on thar knees wif thar eyes shot, but facin the way the ole mud turtil wer a-runnin—they wer the 'saitful ones; sum

duin nuthin—they wer the waitin ones; an' the mos' dangerus ove
all ove em by a durnd long site.

"I tuck a big skeer mysef arter a few rocks, an' sich like fruit,
spattered ontu the pulpit ni ontu my head; an' es the Lovingoods,
durn em! knows nuffin but tu run, when they gits skeerd, I jis' put
out fur the swamp on the krick. As I started, a black bottil ove
bald-face smashed agin a tree furninst me, arter missin the top ove
my head 'bout a inch. Sum durn'd fool professor dun this, who hed
more zeal or sence; fur I say that eny man who wud waste a quart
ove even mean sperrits, fur the chance ove knockin a poor ornary
devil like me down wif the bottil, is a bigger fool nor ole Squire
Mackmullen, an' he tried tu shoot hissef wif a onloaded hoe-han-
dle."

"Did they catch you Sut?"

"Ketch thunder! *No sir!* jis' look at these yere laigs! Skeer me,
hoss, jis' skeer me, an' then watch me while I stay in site, an' yu'll
never ax that fool question agin. Why, durn it, man, that's what the
ait dullers am fur.

"Ole Barbelly Bullin, es they calls 'im now, never preached ontil
yesterday, an' he hadn't the fust durn'd 'oman tu hear 'im, *they hev
seed too much ove 'im.* Passuns ginerly hev a pow'ful strong holt
on wimen; but, hoss, I tell yu thar ain't meny ove em kin run
start nakid over an' thru a crowd ove three hundred wimen an' not
injure thar karacters *sum*. Enyhow, hits a kind ove show they'd
ruther see one at a time, an' pick the passun at that. His tex' wer,
'Nakid I cum intu the world, an' nakid I'm a gwine outen hit, ef
I'm spard ontil then.' He sed nakidness warnt much ove a sin,
purtickerly ove dark nights. That he wer a weak, frail wum ove
the dus', an' a heap more sich truck. Then he totch ontu me; sed
I wer a livin proof ove the hell-desarvin nater ove man, an' that
thar warnt grace enuf in the whole 'sociation tu saften my outside
rind; that I wer 'a lost ball' forty years afore I wer born'd, an'
the bes' thing they cud du fur the church, wer tu turn out, an' still
hunt fur me ontil I wer shot. An' he never said Hell-sarpints onst
in the hole preach. I b'leve, George, the durnd fools am at hit.

"Now, I wants yu tu tell ole Barbelly this fur me, ef he'll let me an' Sall alone, I'll let him alone—a-while; an' ef he don't, ef I don't lizzard him agin, I jis' wish I may be dod durnd! *Skeer him if yu ken.*

"Let's go tu the spring an' take a ho'n.

"Say George, didn't that ar Hell-sarpint sermon ove his'n, hev sumthin like a Hell-sarpint aplicashun? Hit looks sorter so tu me."

POSSON JONE'

George W. Cable

From *Old Creole Days,* by George W. Cable, 1879. First published in *Appletons' Journal,* XV (April 1, 1876), 422-426.

George W. Cable (1844-1925) was born in New Orleans and lived there until he moved to Northampton, Massachusetts, at the age of forty. In a real sense he introduced French Louisiana to American literature and also brought realism to Southern fiction. His best work is in the collection of stories *Old Creole Days* (1879) and the novels *The Grandissimes* (1880), *Dr. Sevier* (1884), and *John March, Southerner* (1894). Other books of tales are *Bonaventure* (1888), *Strange True Stories of Louisiana* (1889), and *Strong Hearts* (1899).

A volume of Cable's social criticism, *The Negro Question: A Selection of Writings on Civil Rights in the South* (1958), and a collection of his stories, *Creoles and Cajuns: Stories of Old Louisiana* (1959), have been published by the present editor, who is also the author of *George W. Cable: A Biography* (1956). See also L. L. C. Biklé, *George W. Cable: His Life and Letters* (1928); Kjell Ekström, *George Washington Cable: A Study of His Early Life and Works* (1950); and Philip Butcher, *George W. Cable: The Northampton Years* (1959).

To Jules St.-Ange—elegant little heathen—there yet remained at manhood a remembrance of having been sent to school, and of having been taught by a stony-headed Capuchin that the world is round —for example, like a cheese. This round world is a cheese to be eaten through, and Jules had nibbled quite into his cheese-world already at twenty-two.

He realized this as he idled about one Sunday morning where the intersection of Royal and Conti Streets some seventy years ago

formed a central corner of New Orleans. Yes, yes, the trouble was
he had been wasteful and honest. He discussed the matter with that
faithful friend and confidant, Baptiste, his yellow body-servant.
They concluded that, papa's patience and *tante's* pin-money having
been gnawed away quite to the rind, there were left open only these
few easily enumerated resorts: to go to work—they shuddered; to
join Major Innerarity's filibustering expedition; or else—why not?
—to try some games of confidence. At twenty-two one must begin
to be something. Nothing else tempted; could that avail? One could
but try. It is noble to try; and, besides, they were hungry. If one
could "make the friendship" of some person from the country, for
instance, with money, not expert at cards or dice, but, as one would
say, willing to learn, one might find cause to say some "Hail Marys."

The sun broke through a clearing sky, and Baptiste pronounced
it good for luck. There had been a hurricane in the night. The
weed-grown tile-roofs were still dripping, and from lofty brick and
low adobe walls a rising steam responded to the summer sunlight.
Up-street, and across the Rue du Canal, one could get glimpses of
the gardens in Faubourg Ste.-Marie standing in silent wretchedness,
so many tearful Lucretias, tattered victims of the storm. Short rem-
nants of the wind now and then came down the narrow street in
erratic puffs heavily laden with odors of broken boughs and torn
flowers, skimmed the little pools of rain-water in the deep ruts of
the unpaved street, and suddenly went away to nothing, like a jug-
gler's butterflies or a young man's money.

It was very picturesque, the Rue Royale. The rich and poor met
together. The locksmith's swinging key creaked next door to the
bank; across the way, crouching mendicant-like in the shadow of a
great importing house, was the mud laboratory of the mender of
broken combs. Light balconies overhung the rows of showy shops
and stores open for trade this Sunday morning, and pretty Latin
faces of the higher class glanced over their savagely prolonged rail-
ings upon the passers below. At some windows hung lace curtains,
flannel duds at some, and at others only the scraping and sighing
one-hinged shutter groaning toward Paris after its neglectful master.

M. St.-Ange stood looking up and down the street for nearly an
hour. But few ladies, only the inveterate mass-goers, were out.

About the entrances of the frequent *cafés* the masculine gentility stood leaning on canes, with which now one and now another beckoned to Jules, some even adding pantomimic hints of the social cup.

M. St.-Ange remarked to his servant without turning his head that somehow he felt sure he should soon return those *bons* that the mulatto had lent him.

"What will you do with them?"

"Me!" said Baptiste, quickly; "I will go and see the bull-fight in the Place Congo."

"There is to be a bull-fight? But where is M. Cayetano?"

"Ah, got all his affairs wet in the tornado. Instead of his circus, they are having a bull-fight—not an ordinary bull-fight with sick horses, but a buffalo-and-tiger fight. I would not miss it—"

Two or three persons ran to the opposite corner and began striking at something with their canes. Others followed. Can M. St.-Ange and servant, who hasten forward—can the Creoles, Cubans, Spaniards, St. Domingo refugees, and other loungers—can they hope it is a fight? They hurry forward. Is a man in a fit? The crowd pours in from the side-streets. Have they killed a so-long snake? Bareheaded shopmen leave their wives, who stand upon chairs. The crowd huddles and packs. Those on the outside make little leaps into the air, trying to be tall.

"What is the matter?"

"Have they caught a real live rat?"

"Who is hurt?" asks some one in English.

"*Personne,*" replies a shopkeeper; "a man's hat blow' in the gutter; but he has it now. Jules pick it. See, that is the man, head and shoulders on top the res'."

"He in the homespun?" asks a second shopkeeper. "Humph! an *Américain*—a West-Floridian; bah!"

"But wait; 'st! he is speaking; listen!"

"To who' is he speak—?"

"Sh-sh-sh! to Jules."

"Jules who?"

"Silence, you! To Jules St.-Ange, what h-owe me a bill since long time. Sh-sh-sh!"

Then the voice was heard.

Its owner was a man of giant stature, with a slight stoop in his shoulders, as if he were making a constant, good-natured attempt to accommodate himself to ordinary doors and ceilings. His bones were those of an ox. His face was marked more by weather than age, and his narrow brow was bald and smooth. He had instantaneously formed an opinion of Jules St.-Ange, and the multitude of words, most of them lingual curiosities, with which he was rasping the wide-open ears of his listeners, signified, in short, that, as sure as his name was Parson Jones, the little Creole was a "plumb gentleman."

M. St.-Ange bowed and smiled, and was about to call attention, by both gesture and speech, to a singular object on top of the still uncovered head, when the nervous motion of the *Américain* anticipated him, as, throwing up an immense hand, he drew down a large roll of bank-notes. The crowd laughed, the West-Floridian joining, and began to disperse.

"Why, that money belongs to Smyrny Church," said the giant.

"You are very dangerous to make your money expose like that, Misty Posson Jone'," said St.-Ange, counting it with his eyes.

The countryman gave a start and smile of surprise.

"How d'd you know my name was Jones?" he asked; but, without pausing for the Creole's answer, furnished in his reckless way some further specimens of West-Floridian English; and the conciseness with which he presented full intelligence of his home, family, calling, lodging-house, and present and future plans, might have passed for consummate art, had it not been the most run-wild nature. "And I've done been to Mobile, you know, on busi*ness* for Bethesdy Church. It's the on'yest time I ever been from home; now you wouldn't of believed that, would you? But I admire to have saw you, that's so. You've got to come and eat with me. Me and my boy ain't been fed yit. What might one call yo' name? Jools? Come on, Jools. Come on, Colossus. That's my niggah—his name's Colossus of Rhodes. Is that yo' yallah boy, Jools? Fetch him along, Colossus. It seems like a special provi*dence*.—Jools, do you believe in a special provi*dence?*"

Jules remembered the roll of bank-notes and said he did.

The new-made friends moved briskly off, followed by Baptiste and a short, square, old negro, very black and grotesque, who had introduced himself to the mulatto, with many glittering and cavernous smiles, as "d'body-sarvant of d'Rev'n' Mr. Jones."

Both pairs enlivened their walk with conversation. Parson Jones descanted upon the doctrine he had mentioned, as illustrated in the perplexities of cotton-growing, and concluded that there would always be "a special provi*dence* again' cotton untell folks quits a-pressin' of it and haulin' of it on Sundays!"

"*Je dis,*" said St.-Ange, in response, "I thing you is juz right. I believe, me, strong-strong in the improvidence, yes. You know my papa he h-own a sugah-plantation, you know. 'Jules, my son,' he say one time to me, 'I goin' to make one baril sugah to fedge the moze high price in New Orleans.' Well, he take his bez baril sugah —I nevah see a so careful man like my papa always to make a so beautiful sugah *et sirop.* 'Jules, go at Father Pierre an' ged this lill pitcher fill with holy-water, an' tell him sen' his tin bucket, and I will make it fill with *quitte.*' I ged the holy-water; my papa sprinkle it over the baril, an' make one cross on the 'ead of the baril."

"Why, Jools," said Parson Jones, "that didn't do no good."

"Din do no good! Id broughd the so great value! You can strike me dead if thad baril sugah din fedge the more high cost than any other in the city. *Parceque,* the man what buy that baril sugah he make a mistake of one hundred pound' "—falling back—"*Mais* certainlee!"

"And you think that was growin' out of the holy-water?" asked the parson.

"*Mais,* what could make it else? Id could not be the *quitte,* because my papa keep the bucket, an' forget to sen' the *quitte* to Father Pierre."

Parson Jones was disappointed.

"Well, now, Jools, you know, I don't think that was right. I reckon you must be a plumb Catholic."

M. St.-Ange shrugged. He would not deny his faith.

"I am a *Catholique, mais*"—brightening as he hoped to recommend himself anew—"not a good one."

"Well, you know," said Jones—"where's Colossus? Oh! all right. Colossus strayed off a minute in Mobile, and I plumb lost him for two days. Here's the place; come in. Colossus and this boy can go to the kitchen.—Now, Colossus, what *air* you a-beckonin' at me faw?"

He let his servant draw him aside and address him in a whisper.

"Oh, go 'way!" said the parson with a jerk. "Who's goin' to throw me? What? Speak louder. Why, Colossus, you shayn't talk so, saw. 'Pon my soul, yo're the mightiest fool I ever taken up with. Jest you go down that alley-way with this yallah boy, and don't show yo' face untell yo' called!"

The negro begged; the master wrathily insisted.

"Colossus, will you do ez I tell you, or shell I hev' to strike you, saw?"

"O Mahs Jimmy, I—I's gwine; but"—he ventured nearer—"don't on no account drink nothin', Mahs Jimmy."

Such was the negro's earnestness that he put one foot in the gutter, and fell heavily against his master. The parson threw him off angrily.

"Thar, now! Why, Colossus, you most of been dosted with sumthin'; yo' plumb crazy.—Humph, come on, Jools, let's eat: Humph! to tell me that when I never taken a drop, exceptin' for chills, in my life—which he knows so as well as me!"

The two masters began to ascend a stair.

"*Mais,* he is a sassy; I would sell him, me," said the young Creole.

"No, I wouldn't do that," replied the parson; "though there is people in Bethesdy who says he is a roscal. He's a powerful smart fool. Why, that boy's got money, Jools; more money than religion, I reckon. I'm shore he fallen into mighty bad company"—they passed beyond earshot.

Baptiste and Colossus, instead of going to the tavern kitchen, went on to the next door and entered the dark rear corner of a low grocery, where, the law notwithstanding, liquor was covertly sold to slaves. There, in the quiet company of Baptiste and the grocer, the colloquial powers of Colossus, which were simply prodigious, began very soon to show themselves.

"For whilst," said he, "Mahs Jimmy has eddication, you know—

whilst he has eddication, I has 'scretion. He has eddication and I has 'scretion, an' so we gits along."

He drew a black bottle down the counter, and, laying half his length upon the damp board, continued:

"As a p'inciple I discredits de imbimin' of awjus liquors. De imbimin' of awjus liquors, de wiolution of de Sabbaf, de playin' of de fiddle, and de usin' of by-words, dey is de fo' sins of de conscience; an' if any man sin de fo' sins of de conscience, de debble done sharp his fork fo' dat man.—Ain't dat so boss?"

The grocer was sure it was so.

"Neberdeless, mind you"—here the orator brimmed his glass from the bottle and swallowed the contents with a dry eye—"mind you, a roytious man, sech as ministers of de gospel and deir bodysarvants, can take a *leetle* for de weak stomach."

But the fascination of Colossus's eloquence must not mislead us; this is the story of a true Christian; to wit, Parson Jones.

The parson and his new friend ate. But the coffee M. St.-Ange declared he could not touch; it was too wretchedly bad. At the French Market, near by, there was some noble coffee. This, however, would have to be bought, and Parson Jones had scruples.

"You see, Jools, every man has his conscience to guide him, which it does so in—"

"Oh, yes!" cried St.-Ange, "conscien'; thad is the bez, Posson Jone'. Certainlee! I am a *Catholique,* you is a *schismatique;* you thing it is wrong to dring some coffee—well, then, it *is* wrong; you thing it is wrong to make the sugah to ged the so large price—well, then, it *is* wrong; I thing it is right—well, then it *is* right; it is all 'abit; *c'est tout.* What a man thing is right, *is right;* 'tis all 'abit. A man muz nod go again' his conscien'. My faith! do you thing I would go again' my conscien'? *Mais allons,* led us go and ged some coffee."

"Jools."

"W'at?"

"Jools, it ain't the drinkin' of coffee, but the buyin' of it on a Sabbath. You must really excuse me, Jools, it's again' conscience, you know."

"Ah!" said St.-Ange, *"c'est* very true. For you it would be a sin, *mais* for me it is only 'abit. Rilligion is a very strange; I know a man one time, he thing it was wrong to go to cock-fight Sunday evening. I thing it is all 'abit. *Mais,* come, Posson Jone'; I have got one friend, Miguel; led us go at his house and ged some coffee. Come; Miguel have no familie; only him and Joe—always like to see friend; *allons,* led us come yonder."

"Why, Jools, my dear friend, you know," said the shamefaced parson, "I never visit on Sundays."

"Never w'at?" asked the astounded Creole.

"No," said Jones, smiling awkwardly.

"Never visite?"

"Exceptin' sometimes amongst church-members," said Parson Jones.

"Mais," said the seductive St.-Ange, "Miguel and Joe is church-member'—certainlee! They love to talk about rilligion. Come at Miguel and talk about some rilligion. I am nearly expire for my coffee."

Parson Jones took his hat from beneath his chair and rose up.

"Jools," said the weak giant, "I ought to be in church right now."

"Mais, the church is right yond' at Miguel, yes. Ah!" continued St.-Ange, as they descended the stairs, "I thing every man muz have the rilligion he like the bez—me, I like the *Catholique* rilligion the bez—for me it *is* the bez. Every man will sure go to heaven if he like his rilligion the bez."

"Jools," said the West-Floridian, laying his great hand tenderly upon the Creole's shoulder, as they stepped out upon the *banquette,* "do you think you have any shore hopes of heaven?"

"Yaas!" replied St.-Ange; "I am sure-sure. I thing everybody will go to heaven. I thing you will go, *et* I thing Miguel will go, *et* Joe—everybody, I thing—*mais,* h-of course, not if they not have been christen'. Even I thing some niggers will go."

"Jools," said the parson, stopping in his walk—"Jools, I *don't* want to lose my niggah."

"You will not loose him. With Baptiste he *cannot* ged loose."

But Colossus's master was not reassured.

"Now," said he, still tarrying, "this is jest the way; had I of gone to church—"

"Posson Jone'," said Jules.

"What?"

"I tell you. We goin' to church!"

"Will you?" asked Jones, joyously.

"*Allons,* come along," said Jules, taking his elbow.

They walked down the Rue Chartres, passed several corners, and by and by turned into a cross street. The parson stopped an instant as they were turning, and looked back up the street.

"W'at you lookin'?" asked his companion.

"I thought I saw Colossus," answered the parson, with an anxious face; "I reckon 'twa'n't him, though." And they went on.

The street they now entered was a very quiet one. The eye of any chance passer would have been at once drawn to a broad, heavy, white brick edifice on the lower side of the way, with a flag-pole standing out like a bowsprit from one of its great windows, and a pair of lamps hanging before a large closed entrance. It was a theatre, sub-let to gamblers. At this morning hour all was still, and the only sign of life was a knot of little barefoot girls gathered within its narrow shade and each carrying an infant relative. Into this place the parson and M. St.-Ange entered, the little nurses jumping up from the sills to let them pass in.

A half-hour may have passed. At the end of that time the whole juvenile company were laying alternate eyes and ears to the chinks, to gather what they could of an interesting quarrel going on within.

"I did not, saw! I given you no cause of offence, saw! It's not so, saw! Mister Jools simply mistaken the house, thinkin' it was a Sabbath-school! No such thing, saw; I *ain't* bound to bet! Yes, I kin git out! Yes, without bettin'! I hev a right to my opinion; I reckon I'm *a white man,* saw! No, saw! I on'y said I didn't think you could get the game on them cards. 'Sno such thing, saw! I do *not* know how to play! I wouldn't hev a roscal's money ef I should win it! Shoot, ef you dare! You can kill me, but you can't scare me! No, I shayn't bet! I'll die first! Yes, saw; Mr. Jools can bet for me if he admires to; I ain't his mostah."

Here the speaker seemed to direct his words to St.-Ange.

"Saw, I don't understand you, saw. I never said I'd loan you money to bet on me. I didn't suspicion this from you, saw. No, I won't take any mo' lemonade; it's the most notorious stuff I ever drank, saw!"

M. St.-Ange's replies were in falsetto and not without effect; for presently the parson's indignation and anger began to melt. "Don't ask me, Jools, I can't help you. It's no use; it's a matter of conscience with me, Jools."

"*Mais oui!* 'tis a matt' of conscien' wid me, the same."

"But, Jools, the money's none o' mine, nohow; it belongs to Smyrny, you know."

"If I could make juz *one* bet," said the persuasive St.-Ange, "I would leave this place, fas'-fas', yes. If I had thing—*mais* I did not soupspicion this from you, Posson Jone'—"

"Don't, Jools, don't!"

"No! Posson Jone'."

"You're bound to win?" said the parson, wavering.

"*Mais certainement!* But it is not to win that I want; 'tis my conscien'—my honor!"

"Well, Jools, I hope I'm not a-doin' no wrong. I'll loan you some of this money if you say you'll come right out 'thout takin' your winnin's."

All was still. The peeping children could see the parson as he lifted his hand to his breast pocket. There it paused a moment in bewilderment, then plunged to the bottom. It came back empty, and fell lifelessly at his side. His head dropped upon his breast, his eyes were for a moment closed, his broad palms were lifted and pressed against his forehead, a tremor seized him, and he fell all in a lump to the floor. The children ran off with their infant loads, leaving Jules St.-Ange swearing by all his deceased relatives, first to Miguel and Joe, and then to the lifted parson, that he did not know what had become of the money "except if" the black man had got it.

In the rear of ancient New Orleans, beyond the sites of the old rampart (a trio of Spanish forts), where the town has since sprung

up and grown old, green with all the luxuriance of the wild Creole summer, lay the Congo Plains. Here stretched the canvas of the
historic Cayetano, who Sunday after Sunday sowed the sawdust
for his circus-ring.

But to-day the great showman had fallen short of his printed
promise. The hurricane had come by night, and with one fell swash
had made an irretrievable sop of everything. The circus trailed
away its bedraggled magnificence, and the ring was cleared for the
bull.

Then the sun seemed to come out and work for the people. "See,"
said the Spaniards, looking up at the glorious sky with its great
white fleets drawn off upon the horizon—"see—heaven smiles upon
the bull-fight!"

In the high upper seats of the rude amphitheatre sat the gayly
decked wives and daughters of the Gascons, from the *métairies*
along the Ridge, and the chattering Spanish women of the Market,
their shining hair unbonneted to the sun. Next below were their
husbands and lovers in Sunday blouses, milkmen, butchers, bakers,
black-bearded fishermen, Sicilian fruiterers, swarthy Portuguese
sailors in little woollen caps, and strangers of the graver sort;
mariners of England, Germany, and Holland. The lowest seats
were full of trappers, smugglers, Canadian *voyageurs,* drinking and
singing; *Américains,* too—more's the shame—from the upper rivers
—who will not keep their seats, who ply the bottle, and who will
get home by and by and tell how wicked Sodom is; broad-brimmed,
silver-braided Mexicans, also, with their copper cheeks and bat's
eyes, and their tinkling spurred heels. Yonder, in that quieter section,
are the quadroon women in their black lace shawls—and there is
Baptiste; and below them are the turbaned black women, and there
is—but he vanishes—Colossus.

The afternoon is advancing, yet the sport, though loudly demanded, does not begin. The *Américains* grow derisive and find
pastime in gibes and raillery. They mock the various Latins with
their national inflections, and answer their scowls with laughter.
Some of the more aggressive shout pretty French greetings to the
women of Gascony, and one bargeman, amid peals of applause,
stands on a seat and hurls a kiss to the quadroons. The mariners of

England, Germany, and Holland, as spectators, like the fun, while the Spaniards look back and cast defiant imprecations upon their persecutors. Some Gascons, with timely caution, pick their women out and depart, running a terrible fire of gallantries.

In hope of truce, a new call is raised for the bull: "The bull, the bull!—hush!"

In a tier near the ground a man is standing and calling—standing head and shoulders above the rest—calling in the *Américaine* tongue. Another man, big and red, named Joe, and a handsome little Creole in elegant dress and full of laughter, wish to stop him, but the flat-boatmen, ha-haing and cheering, will not suffer it. Ah, through some shameful knavery of the men into whose hands he has fallen, he is drunk! Even the women can see that; and now he throws his arms wildly and raises his voice until the whole great circle hears it. He is preaching!

Ah! kind Lord, for a special providence now! The men of his own nation—men from the land of the open English Bible and temperance cup and song are cheering him on to mad disgrace. And now another call for the appointed sport is drowned by the flat-boatmen singing the ancient tune of Mear. You can hear the words—

"Old Grimes is dead, that good old soul"

—from ribald lips and throats turned brazen with laughter, from singers who toss their hats aloft and roll in their seats the chorus swells to the accompaniment of a thousand brogans—

"He used to wear an old gray coat
All buttoned down before."

A ribboned man in the arena is trying to be heard, and the Latins raise one mighty cry for silence. The big red man gets a hand over the parson's mouth, and the ribboned man seizes his moment.

"They have been endeavoring for hours," he says, "to draw the terrible animals from their dens, but such is their strength and fierceness, that—"

His voice is drowned. Enough has been heard to warrant the inference that the beasts cannot be whipped out of the storm-drenched

cages to which menagerie life and long starvation have attached
them, and from the roar of indignation the man of ribbons flies. The
noise increases. Men are standing up by hundreds, and women are
imploring to be let out of the turmoil. All at once, like the bursting
of a dam, the whole mass pours down into the ring. They sweep
across the arena and over the showman's barriers. Miguel gets a
frightful trampling. Who cares for gates or doors? They tear the
beasts' houses bar from bar, and, laying hold of the gaunt buffalo,
drag him forth by feet, ears, and tail; and in the midst of the
mêlée, still head and shoulders above all, wilder, with the cup of the
wicked, than any beast, is the man of God from the Florida parishes!

In his arms he bore—and all the people shouted at once when
they saw it—the tiger. He had lifted it high up with its back to his
breast, his arms clasped under its shoulders; the wretched brute
had curled up caterpillar-wise, with its long tail against its belly,
and through its filed teeth grinned a fixed and impotent wrath.
And Parson Jones was shouting:

"The tiger and the buffler *shell* lay down together! You dah to
say they shayn't and I'll comb you with this varmint from head to
foot! The tiger and the buffler *shell* lay down together. They *shell.*
Now, you, Joe! Behold! I am here to see it done. The lion and the
buffler *shell* lay down together!"

Mouthing these words again and again, the parson forced his
way through the surge in the wake of the buffalo. This creature
the Latins had secured by a lariat over his head, and were dragging across the old rampart and into a street of the city.

The northern races were trying to prevent, and there was pom-
melling and knocking down, cursing and knife drawing, until
Jules St.-Ange was quite carried away with the fun, laughed,
clapped his hands, and swore with delight, and ever kept close to
the gallant parson.

Joe, contrariwise, counted all this child's play an interruption. He
had come to find Colossus and the money. In an unlucky moment
he made bold to lay hold of the parson, but a piece of the broken
barriers in the hands of a flat-boatman felled him to the sod, the
terrible crowd swept over him, the lariat was cut, and the giant

parson hurled the tiger upon the buffalo's back. In another instant both brutes were dead at the hands of the mob; Jones was lifted from his feet, and prating of Scripture and the millennium, of Paul at Ephesus and Daniel in the "buffler's" den, was borne aloft upon the shoulders of the huzzaing *Américains*. Half an hour later he was sleeping heavily on the floor of a cell in the *calaboza*.

When Parson Jones awoke, a bell was somewhere tolling for midnight. Somebody was at the door of his cell with a key. The lock grated, the door swung, the turnkey looked in and stepped back, and a ray of moonlight fell upon M. Jules St.-Ange. The prisoner sat upon the empty shackles and ring-bolt in the centre of the floor.

"Misty Posson Jone'," said the visitor, softly.

"O Jools!"

"Mais, w'at de matter, Posson Jone'?"

"My sins, Jools, my sins!"

"Ah! Posson Jone', is that something to cry, because a man get sometime a litt' bit intoxicate? *Mais,* if a man keep *all the time* intoxicate, I think that is again' the conscien'."

"Jools, Jools, your eyes is darkened—oh! Jools, where's my pore old niggah?"

"Posson Jone', never mine; he is wid Baptiste."

"Where?"

"I don' know w'ere—*mais* he is wid Baptiste. Baptiste is a beautiful to take care of somebody."

"Is he as good as you, Jools?" asked Parson Jones, sincerely.

Jules was slightly staggered.

"You know, Posson Jone', you know, a nigger cannot be good as a w'ite man—*mais* Baptiste is a good nigger."

The parson moaned and dropped his chin into his hands.

"I was to of left for home to-morrow, sun up, on the *Isabella* schooner. Pore Smyrny!" He sighed deeply.

"Posson Jone'," said Jules, leaning against the wall and smiling, "I swear you is the moz funny man what I never see. If I was you I would say, me, 'Ah! 'ow I am lucky! the money I los', it was not mine, anyhow!' My faith! shall a man make hisse'f to be the more sorry because the money he los' is not his? Me, I would say, 'it is a specious providence.'"

"Ah! Misty Posson Jone'," he continued, "you make a so droll sermon ad the bull-ring. Ha! ha! I swear I thing you can make money to preach thad sermon many time ad the theatre St. Philippe. Hah! you is the moz brave dat I never see, *mais* ad the same time the moz rilligious man. Where I'm goin' to fin' one priest to make like dat? *Mais,* why you can't cheer up an' be 'appy? Me, if I should be miserabl' like dat I would kill meself."

The countryman only shook his head.

"*Bien,* Posson Jone', I have the so good news for you."

The prisoner looked up with eager inquiry.

"Laz evening when they lock' you, I come right off at M. De Blanc's house to get you let out of the calaboose; M. De Blanc he is the judge. So soon I was entering—'Ah! Jules, my boy, juz the man to make complete the game!' Posson Jone', it was a specious providence! I win in t'ree hours more dan six hundred dollah'! Look." He produced a mass of bank-notes, *bons,* and due-bills.

"And you got the pass?" asked the parson, regarding the money with a strange sadness.

"It is here; it take the effect so soon the daylight."

"Jools, my friend, your kindness is in vain."

The Creole's face became a perfect blank.

"Because," said the parson, "for two reasons: firstly, I have broken the laws, and ought to stand the penalty; and secondly—you must really excuse me, Jools, you know, but the pass has been got on-fairly, I'm afeerd. You told the judge I was innocent; and in neither case it don't become a Christian (which I hope I can still say I am one) to 'do evil that good may come.' I muss stay."

M. St.-Ange stood up aghast, and for a moment speechless, at this exhibition of moral heroism; but an artifice was presently hit upon. "*Mais,* Posson Jone'!"—in his old *falsetto*—"de order—you cannot read it, it is in French—compel you to go h-out, sir!"

"Is that so?" cried the parson, bounding up with radiant face —"is that so, Jools?"

The young man nodded, smiling; but, though he smiled, the fountain of his tenderness was opened. He made the sign of the cross as the parson knelt in prayer, and even whispered "Hail Mary," etc., quite through, twice over.

Morning broke in summer glory upon a cluster of villas behind the city, nestled under live-oaks and magnolias on the banks of a deep bayou, and known as Suburb St. Jean.

With the first beam came the West-Floridian and the Creole out upon the bank below the village. Upon the parson's arm hung a pair of antique saddle-bags. Baptiste limped wearily behind; both his eyes were encircled with broad blue rings, and one cheek-bone bore the official impress of every knuckle of Colossus's left hand. The "beautiful to take care of somebody" had lost his charge. At mention of the negro he became wild, and, half in English, half in "gumbo" dialect, said murderous things. Intimidated by Jules to calmness, he became able to speak confidently on one point; he could, would, and did swear that Colossus had gone home to the Florida parishes; he was almost certain; in fact, he thought so.

There was a clicking of pulleys as the three appeared upon the bayou's margin, and Baptiste pointed out, in the deep shadow of a great oak, the *Isabella,* moored among the bulrushes, and just spreading her sails for departure. Moving down to where she lay, the parson and his friend paused on the bank, loath to say farewell.

"O Jools!" said the parson, "supposin' Colossus ain't gone home! O Jools, if you'll look him out for me, I'll never forget you—I'll never forget you, nohow, Jools. No, Jools, I never will believe he taken that money. Yes, I know all niggahs will steal"—he set foot upon the gangplank—"but Colossus wouldn't steal from me. Good-by."

"Misty Posson Jone'," said St.-Ange, putting his hand on the parson's arm with genuine affection, "hol' on. You see dis money—w'at I win las' night? Well, I win it by a specious providence, ain't it?"

"There's no tellin'," said the humbled Jones. "Providence

> 'Moves in a mysterious way
> His wonders to perform.' "

"Ah!" cried the Creole, "*c'est* very true. I ged dis money in the mysterieuze way. *Mais,* if I keep dis money, you know where it goin' be to-night?"

"I really can't say," replied the parson.

"Goin' to the dev'," said the sweetly smiling young man.

The schooner captain, leaning against the shrouds, and even Baptiste, laughed outright.

"O Jools, you mustn't!"

"Well, den, w'at I shall do wid *it*?"

"Any thing!" answered the parson; "better donate it away to some poor man—"

"Ah! Misty Posson Jone', dat is w'at I want. You los' five hondred dollah'—'twas my fault."

"No, it wa'n't, Jools."

"Mais, it was!"

"No!"

"It *was* my fault! I *swear* it was my fault! *Mais,* here is five hondred dollah'; I wish you shall take it. Here! I don't got no use for money.—Oh, my faith! Posson Jone', you must not begin to cry some more."

Parson Jones was choked with tears. When he found voice he said:

"O Jools, Jools, Jools! my pore, noble, dear, misguidened friend! ef you hed of hed a Christian raisin'! May the Lord show you your errors, better'n I kin, and bless you for your good intentions—oh, no! I cayn't touch that money with a ten-foot pole; it wa'n't rightly got; you must really excuse me, my dear friend, but I cayn't touch it."

St.-Ange was petrified.

"Good-by, dear Jools," continued the parson. "I'm in the Lord's haynds, and he's very merciful, which I hope and trust you'll find it out. Good-by!"—the schooner swung slowly off before the breeze—"good-by!"

St.-Ange roused himself.

"Posson Jone'! make me hany'ow *dis* promise: you never, never, *never* will come back to New Orleans."

"Ah, Jools, the Lord willin', I'll never leave home again!"

"All right!" cried the Creole: "I thing He's willin'. Adieu, Posson Jone'. My faith! you are the so fighting an' moz rilligious man as I never saw! Adieu! Adieu!"

Baptiste uttered a cry and presently ran by his master toward the schooner, his hands full of clods.

St.-Ange looked just in time to see the sable form of Colossus of Rhodes emerge from the vessel's hold, and the pastor of Smyrna and Bethesda seize him in his embrace.

"O Colossus! you outlandish old niggah! Thank the Lord! Thank the Lord!"

The little Creole almost wept. He ran down the tow-path, laughing and swearing, and making confused allusion to the entire *personnel* and furniture of the lower regions.

By odd fortune, at the moment that St.-Ange further demonstrated his delight by tripping his mulatto into a bog, the schooner came brushing along the reedy bank with a graceful curve, the sails flapped, and the crew fell to poling her slowly along.

Parson Jones was on the deck, kneeling once more in prayer. His hat had fallen before him; behind him knelt his slave. In thundering tones he was confessing himself "a plumb fool," from whom "the conceit had been jolted out," and who had been made to see that even his "nigger had the longest head of the two."

Colossus clasped his hands and groaned.

The parson prayed for a contrite heart.

"Oh, yes!" cried Colossus.

The master acknowledged countless mercies.

"Dat's so!" cried the slave.

The master prayed that they might still be "piled on."

"Glory!" cried the black man, clapping his hands; "pile on!"

"An' now," continued the parson, "bring this pore, backslidin' jackace of a parson and this pore old fool niggah back to thar home in peace!"

"Pray fo' de money!" called Colossus.

But the parson prayed for Jules.

"Pray fo' de *money!*" repeated the negro.

"And oh, give thy servant back that there lost money!"

Colossus rose stealthily, and tiptoed by his still shouting master. St.-Ange, the captain, the crew, gazed in silent wonder at the strategist. Pausing but an instant over the master's hat to grin an acknowledgment of his beholders' speechless interest, he softly placed in it the faithfully mourned and honestly prayed-for Smyrna fund; then, saluted by the gesticulative, silent applause of St.-Ange and the schooner men, he resumed his first attitude behind his roaring master.

"Amen!" cried Colossus, meaning to bring him to a close.

"Onworthy though I be—" cried Jones.

"*Amen!*" reiterated the negro.

"A-a-amen!" said Parson Jones.

He rose to his feet, and, stooping to take up his hat, beheld the well-known roll. As one stunned he gazed for a moment upon his slave, who still knelt with clasped hands and rolling eyeballs; but when he became aware of the laughter and cheers that greeted him from both deck and shore, he lifted eyes and hands to heaven, and cried like the veriest babe. And when he looked at the roll again, and hugged and kissed it, St.-Ange tried to raise a second shout, but choked, and the crew fell to their poles.

And now up runs Baptiste, covered with slime, and prepares to cast his projectiles. The first one fell wide of the mark; the schooner swung round into a long reach of water, where the breeze was in her favor; another shout of laughter drowned the maledictions of the muddy man; the sails filled; Colossus of Rhodes, smiling and bowing as hero of the moment, ducked as the main boom swept round, and the schooner, leaning slightly to the pleasant influence, rustled a moment over the bulrushes, and then sped far away down the rippling bayou.

M. Jules St.-Ange stood long, gazing at the receding vessel as it now disappeared, now reappeared beyond the tops of the high undergrowth; but, when an arm of the forest hid it finally from sight, he turned townward, followed by that fagged-out spaniel, his servant, saying, as he turned, "Baptiste."

"*Miché?*"

"You know w'at I goin' do wid dis money?"

"*Non, miché.*"

"Well, you can strike me dead if I don't goin' to pay hall my debts! *Allons!*"

He began a merry little song to the effect that his sweetheart was a wine-bottle, and master and man, leaving care behind, returned to the picturesque Rue Royale. The ways of Providence are indeed strange. In all Parson Jones's after life, amid the many painful reminiscences of his visit to the City of the Plain, the sweet knowledge was withheld from him that by the light of the Christian virtue that shone from him even in his great fall, Jules St.-Ange arose, and went to his father an honest man.

FRESCOES FROM THE PAST

———

Mark Twain

[SAMUEL LANGHORNE CLEMENS]

From the third chapter of *Life on the Mississippi* by Mark Twain (1883); first intended to be included in *Huckleberry Finn*.

Born to parents having roots in Virginia, Kentucky, and Tennessee, Samuel Langhorne Clemens (1835-1910) grew up in the Mississippi River town of Hannibal, Missouri, and afterward was a pilot on the river. For the reflection of these early experiences in *Tom Sawyer* (1876), *Life on the Mississippi* (1883), and *The Adventures of Huckleberry Finn* (1884), see Dixon Wecter, *Sam Clemens of Hannibal* (1952) and Minnie M. Brashear, *Mark Twain, Son of Missouri* (1934). For Mark Twain's indebtedness to the humorous tradition lying back of him, see especially Bernard DeVoto, *Mark Twain's America* (1932). A balanced narrative of his full life is DeLancey Ferguson, *Mark Twain: Man and Legend* (1943).

Mark Twain introduces the episode below by saying that in the book for which it is intended Huck Finn needs to know how far he and his rafting companion, Jim, the runaway slave, have drifted down the river. He decides to swim one night to a huge raft and listen to the talk he can overhear from its crew.

I stood up and shook my rags off and jumped into the river, and struck out for the raft's light. By and by, when I got down nearly to her, I eased up and went slow and cautious. But everything was all right—nobody at the sweeps. So I swum down along the raft till I was most abreast the campfire in the middle, then I crawled aboard and inched along and got in among some bundles of shingles on the weather side of the fire. There was thirteen men there—they was the watch on deck of course. And a mighty rough-looking lot, too. They had a jug, and tin cups, and they kept the jug moving. One man was singing—roaring, you may say; and it wasn't a nice song— for a parlor, anyway. He roared through his nose, and strung out the last word of every line very long. When he was done they all fetched a kind of Injun war-whoop, and then another was sung. It begun:

> "There was a woman in our towdn,
>   In our towdn did dwed'l [dwell],
> She loved her husband dear-i-lee,
>   But another man twyste as wed'l.
>
> Singing too, riloo, riloo, riloo,
>   Ri-too, riloo, rilay - - - e,
> She loved her husband dear-i-lee,
>   But another man twyste as wed'l."

And so on—fourteen verses. It was kind of poor, and when he was going to start on the next verse one of them said it was the tune the old cow died on; and another one said: "Oh, give us a rest!" And another one told him to take a walk. They made fun of him till he got mad and jumped up and begun to cuss the crowd, and said he could lam any thief in the lot.

They was all about to make a break for him, but the biggest man there jumped up and says:

"Set whar you are, gentlemen. Leave him to me; he's my meat."

Then he jumped up in the air three times, and cracked his heels together every time. He flung off a buckskin coat that was all hung with fringes, and says, "You lay thar tell the chawin-up's done"; and flung his hat down, which was all over ribbons, and says, "You lay thar tell his sufferin's is over."

Then he jumped up in the air and cracked his heels together again, and shouted out:

"Whoo-oop! I'm the old original iron-jawed, brass-mounted, cop-per-bellied corpse-maker from the wilds of Arkansaw! Look at me! I'm the man they call Sudden Death and General Desolation! Sired by a hurricane, dam'd by an earthquake, half-brother to the cholera, nearly related to the smallpox on the mother's side! Look at me! I take nineteen alligators and a bar'l of whisky for breakfast when I'm in robust health, and a bushel of rattlesnakes and a dead body when I'm ailing. I split the everlasting rocks with my glance, and I squench the thunder when I speak! Whoo-oop! Stand back and give me room according to my strength! Blood's my natural drink, and the wails of the dying is music to my ear! Cast your eye on me, gentlemen! and lay low and hold your breath, for I'm 'bout to turn myself loose!"

All the time he was getting this off, he was shaking his head and looking fierce, and kind of swelling around in a little circle, tucking up his wristbands, and now and then straightening up and beating his breast with his fist, saying, "Look at me, gentlemen!" When he got through, he jumped up and cracked his heels together three times, and let off a roaring "Whoo-oop! I'm the bloodiest son of a wildcat that lives!"

Then the man that had started the row tilted his old slouch hat down over his right eye; then he bent stooping forward, with his back sagged and his south end sticking out far, and his fists a-shoving out and drawing in in front of him, and so went around in a little circle about three times, swelling himself up and breathing hard. Then he straightened, and jumped up and cracked his heels together three times before he lit again (that made them cheer), and he began to shout like this:

"Whoo-oop! bow your neck and spread, for the kingdom of sorrow's a-coming! Hold me down to the earth, for I feel my powers a-working! whoo-oop! I'm a child of sin, *don't* let me get a start! Smoked glass, here, for all! Don't attempt to look at me with the naked eye, gentlemen! When I'm playful I use the meridians of longitude and parallels of latitude for a seine, and drag the Atlantic Ocean for whales! I scratch my head with the lightning and purr myself to sleep with the thunder! When I'm cold, I bile the Gulf of Mexico and bathe in it; when I'm hot I fan myself with an equinoctial storm; when I'm thirsty I reach up and suck a cloud dry like a sponge; when I range the earth hungry, famine follows in my tracks! Whoo-oop! Bow your neck and spread! I put my hand on the sun's face and make it night in the earth; I bite a piece out of the moon and hurry the seasons; I shake myself and crumble the mountains! Contemplate me through leather—*don't* use the naked eye! I'm the man with a petrified heart and biler-iron bowels! The massacre of isolated communities is the pastime of my idle moments, the destruction of nationalities the serious business of my life! The boundless vastness of the great American desert is my inclosed property, and I bury my dead on my own premises!" He jumped up and cracked his heels together three times before he lit (they cheered him again), and as he come down he shouted out: "Whoo-oop! bow your neck and spread, for the Pet Child of Calamity's a-coming!"

Then the other one went to swelling around and blowing again —the first one—the one they called Bob; next, the Child of Calamity chipped in again, bigger than ever; then they both got at it at the same time, swelling round and round each other and punching their fists most into each other's faces, and whooping and jawing like Injuns; then Bob called the Child names, and the Child called him names back again; next, Bob called him a heap rougher names, and the Child come back at him with the very worst kind of language; next, Bob knocked the Child's hat off, and the Child picked it up and kicked Bob's ribbony hat about six foot; Bob went and got it and said never mind, this warn't going to be the last of this thing, because he was a man that never forgot and never forgive, and so the Child better look out, for there was a time a-coming, just as sure as he was a living man, that he would have to answer to him with the best blood in his body. The Child said no man was will-inger than he for that time to come, and he would give Bob fair warning, *now,* never to cross his path again, for he could never rest till he had waded in his blood, for such was his nature, though he was sparing him now on account of his family, if he had one.

Both of them was edging away in different directions, growling and shaking their heads and going on about what they was going to do; but a little black-whiskered chap skipped up and says:

"Come back here, you couple of chicken-livered cowards, and I'll thrash the two of ye!"

And he done it, too. He snatched them, he jerked them this way and that, he booted them around, he knocked them sprawling faster than they could get up. Why, it warn't two minutes till they begged like dogs—and how the other lot did yell and laugh and clap their hands all the way through, and shout, "Sail in, Corpse-Maker!" "Hi! at him again, Child of Calamity!" "Bully for you, little Davy!" Well, it was a perfect pow-wow for a while. Bob and the Child had red noses and black eyes when they got through. Little Davy made them own up that they was sneaks and cowards and not fit to eat with a dog or drink with a nigger; then Bob and the Child shook hands with each other, very solemn, and said they had always respected each other and was willing to let bygones be bygones. So then they washed their faces in the river; and just then there was a loud order to stand by for a crossing, and some of them went forward to man the sweeps there, and the rest went aft to handle the after sweeps.

MR. TERRAPIN SHOWS
HIS STRENGTH

————

Joel Chandler Harris

From *Uncle Remus: His Songs and His Sayings* by Joel Chandler Harris, 1880.

After growing up in rural Georgia, Joel Chandler Harris (1848-1908) became a journalist and in 1879 began writing for the Atlanta *Constitution* the tales of Uncle Remus which at intervals he collected in half a dozen volumes. In novels and in the stories which make up the volumes *Mingo, and Other Sketches in Black and White* (1884) and *Free Joe, and Other Georgian Sketches* (1887), Harris reflected his observations on the plantations and among the mountaineers of his time. The fullest biographical account is in Julia C. Harris, *The Life and Letters of Joel Chandler Harris* (1918). For general evaluations of Harris's work, see F. L. Pattee, *A History of American Literature Since 1870* (1915), pages 301-306; and Jay B. Hubbell, *The South in American Literature, 1607-1900* (1954), pages 782-795, 934-935.

"Brer Tarrypin wuz de out'nes' man," said Uncle Remus, rubbing his hands together contemplatively, and chuckling to himself in a very significant manner; "he wuz de out'nes' man er de whole gang. He wuz dat."

The little boy sat perfectly quiet, betraying no impatience when Uncle Remus paused to hunt, first in one pocket and then in another, for enough crumbs of tobacco to replenish his pipe. Presently the old man proceeded:

"One night Miss Meadows en de gals dey gun a candy-pullin', en so many er de nabers come in 'sponse ter de invite dat day hatter put

de 'lasses in de wash pot en b'il' de fier in de yard. Brer B'ar, he holp
Miss Meadows bring de wood, Brer Fox, he men' de fier, Brer Wolf,
he kep' de dogs off, Brer Rabbit, he grease de bottom er de plates
fer ter keep de candy fum stickin', en Brer Tarrypin, he klum up
in a cheer, en say he'd watch en see dat de 'lasses didn't bile over.
Dey wuz all dere, en dey wern't cuttin' up no didos, nudder, kaze
Miss Meadows, she doen put her foot down, she did, en say dat w'en
dey come ter her place dey hatter hang up a flag er truce at de front
gate en 'bide by it.

"Well, den, w'iles dey wuz all a settin' dar en de 'lasses wuz a
bilin' en a blubberin', dey got ter runnin' on talkin' mighty biggity.
Brer Rabbit, he say he de swiffes'; but Brer Tarrypin, he rock 'long
in de cheer en watch de 'lasses. Brer Fox, he say he de sharpes',
but Brer Tarrypin he rock 'long. Brer Wolf, he say he de mos'
suvvigus, but Brer Tarrypin, he rock en he rock 'long. Brer B'ar, he
say he do mos' stronges', but Brer Tarrypin he rock, en he keep on
rockin'. Bimeby he sorter shet one eye, en say, sezee:

"'Hit look like 'periently dat de old hardshell ain't nowhars
'longside er dis crowd, yit yer I is, en I'm de same man w'at show
Brer Rabbit dat he ain't de swiffes'; en I'm de same man w'at kin
show Brer B'ar dat he ain't de stronges',' sezee.

"Den dey all laff en holler, kaze it look like Brer B'ar mo' stronger
dan a steer. Bimeby, Miss Meadows, she up'n ax, she did, how he
gwine do it.

"'Gimme a good strong rope,' sez Brer Tarrypin, sezee, 'en
lemme git in er puddle er water, en den let Brer B'ar see ef he kin
pull me out,' sezee.

"Den dey all laff g'in, en Brer B'ar, he ups en sez, sezee: 'We
ain't got no rope,' sezee.

"'No,' sez Brer Tarrypin, sezee, 'den needer is you got de strenk,'
sezee, en den Brer Tarrypin, he rock en rock 'long, en watch de
'lasses a bilin' en a blubberin'.

"Atter w'ile Miss Meadows, she up en say, she did, dat she'd take'n
loan de young men her bed-cord, en w'iles de candy wuz a coolin'
in de plates, dey could all go ter de branch en see Brer Tarrypin
kyar out his projick. Brer Tarrypin," continued Uncle Remus, in a
tone at once confidential and argumentative, "wern't much bigger'n

de pa'm er my han', en it look mighty funny fer ter year 'im braggin'
'bout how he kin out-pull Brer B'ar. But dey got de bed-cord atter
w'ile, en den dey all put out ter de branch. W'en Brer Tarrypin fine
de place he wanter, he tuck one een' er de bed-cord, en gun de
yuther een' to Brer B'ar.

"'Now den, ladies en gents,' sez Brer Tarrypin, sezee, 'you all
go wid Brer B'ar up dar in de woods en I'll stay yer, en w'en you
year me holler, den's de time fer Brer B'ar fer ter see ef he kin haul
in de slack er de rope. You all take keer er dat ar een',' sezee, 'en I'll
take keer er dish yer een',' sezee.

"Den dey all put out en lef' Brer Tarrypin at de branch, en w'en
dey got good en gone, he dove down inter de water, he did, en tie
de bed-cord hard en fas' ter wunner deze yer big clay-roots, en den
he riz up en gin a whoop.

"Brer B'ar, he wrop de bed-cord roun' his han', en wink at de
gals, en wid dat he gin a big juk, but Brer Tarrypin ain't budge.
Den he take bofe han's en gin a big pull, but, all de same, Brer Tarrypin ain't budge. Den he tu'n 'roun', he did, en put de rope cross
his shoulders en try ter walk off wid Brer Tarrypin, but Brer Tarrypin look like he don't feel like walkin'. Den Brer Wolf he put in en
holp Brer B'ar pull, but des like he didn't, en den dey all holp 'im, en,
bless grashus! w'iles dey wuz all a pullin', Brer Tarrypin, he holler,
en ax um w'y dey don't take up de slack. Den w'en Brer Tarrypin
feel um quit pullin', he dove down, he did, en ontie de rope, en by de
time dey got ter de branch, Brer Tarrypin, he wuz settin' in de
aidge er de water dez ez natchul ez de nex' un, en he up'n say,
sezee:

"'Dat las' pull er yone wuz a mighty stiff un, en a leetle mo'n
you'd er had me,' sezee. 'You er monstus stout, Brer B'ar,' sezee,
'en you pulls like a yoke er steers, but I sorter had de purchis on
you,' sezee.

"Den Brer B'ar, bein's his mouf 'gun ter water atter de sweetin',
he up'n say he speck de candy's ripe, en off dey put atter it!"

"It's a wonder," said the little boy, after a while, "that the rope
didn't break."

"Break who?" exclaimed Uncle Remus, with a touch of indignation in his tone—"break who? In dem days, Miss Meadow's bed-cord would a hilt a mule."

This put an end to whatever doubts the child might have entertained.

OLD MR. RABBIT, HE'S A GOOD FISHERMAN

Joel Chandler Harris

From *Uncle Remus: His Songs and His Sayings* by Joel Chandler Harris, 1880.

"Brer Rabbit en Brer Fox wuz like some chilluns w'at I knows un," said Uncle Remus, regarding the little boy, who had come to hear another story, with an affectation of great solemnity. "Bofe un um wuz allers atter wunner nudder, a prankin' en a pester'n 'roun', but Brer Rabbit did had some peace, kaze Brer Fox done got skittish 'bout puttin' de clamps on Brer Rabbit.

"One day, w'en Brer Rabbit, en Brer Fox, en Brer Coon, en Brer B'ar, en a whole lot un um wuz clearin' up a new groun' fer ter plant a roas'n'year patch, de sun 'gun ter git sorter hot, en Brer Rabbit he got tired; but de didn't let on, kaze he 'fear'd de balance un um'd call 'im lazy, en he keep on totin' off trash en pilin' up bresh, twel bimeby he holler out dat he gotter brier in his han', en den he take'n slip off, en hunt fer cool place fer ter res'. Atter w'ile he come 'crosst a well wid a bucket hangin' in it.

"'Dat look cool,' sez Brer Rabbit, sezee, 'en cool I speck she is. I'll des 'bout git in dar en take a nap,' en wid dat in he jump, he did, en he ain't no sooner fix hisse'f dan de bucket 'gun ter go down."

"Wasn't the Rabbit scared, Uncle Remus?" asked the little boy.

"Honey, dey ain't no wusser skeer'd beas' sence de worril begin dan dish yer same Brer Rabbit. He fa'rly had a ager. He know whar he cum fum, but he dunner whar he gwine. Dreckly he feel de bucket hit de water, en dar she sot, but Brer Rabbit he keep mighty still, kaze he dunner w'at minnit gwineter be de nex'. He des lay dar en shuck en shiver.

"Brer Fox allers got one eye on Brer Rabbit, en w'en he slip off fum de new groun', Brer Fox he sneak atter 'im. He know Brer Rabbit wuz atter some projick er nudder, en he tuck'n crope off, he did, en watch 'im. Brer Fox see Brer Rabbit come to de well en stop, en den he see 'im jump in de bucket, en den, lo en beholes, he see 'im go down outer sight. Brer Fox wuz de mos' 'stonish Fox dat you ever laid eyes on. He sot off dar in de bushes en study en study, but he don't make no head ner tails ter dis kinder bizness. Den he say ter hisse'f, sezee:

" 'Well, ef dis don't bang my times,' sezee, 'den Joe's dead en Sal's a widder. Right down dar in dat well Brer Rabbit keep his money hid, en ef 'tain't dat den he done gone en 'skiver'd a gole-mine, en ef 'tain't dat, den I'm a gwineter see w'at's in dar,' sezee.

"Brer Fox crope up a little nigher, he did, en lissen, but he don't year no fuss, en he keep on gittin' nigher, en yit he don't year nuthin'. Bimeby he git up close en peep down, but he don't see nuthin' en he don't year nuthin'. All dis time Brer Rabbit mighty nigh skeer'd outen his skin, en he fear'd fer ter move kaze de bucket might keel over en spill him out in de water. W'ile he sayin' his pra'rs over like a train er kyars runnin', old Brer Fox holler out:

" 'Heyo, Brer Rabbit! Who you wizzitin' down dar?' sezee.

" 'Who? Me? Oh, I'm des a fishin', Brer Fox,' sez Brer Rabbit, sezee. 'I des sayter myse'f dat I'd sorter sprize you all wid a mess er fishes fer dinner, en so here I is, en dar's de fishes. I'm a fishin' fer suckers, Brer Fox,' sez Brer Rabbit, sezee.

" 'Is dey many un um down dar, Brer Rabbit?' sez Brer Fox, sezee.

" 'Lots un um, Brer Fox; scoze en scoze un um. De water is natally live wid um. Come down en he'p me haul um in, Brer Fox,' sez Brer Rabbit, sezee.

" 'How I gwineter git down, Brer Rabbit?'

" 'Jump inter de bucket, Brer Fox. Hit'll fetch you down all safe en soun'.'

"Brer Rabbit talk so happy en talk so sweet dat Brer Fox he jump in de bucket, he did, en, ez he went down, co'se his weight pull Brer Rabbit up. W'en dey pass one nudder on de half-way groun', Brer Rabbit he sing out:

> 'Good-by, Brer Fox, take keer yo' cloze,
> Fer dis is de way de worril goes;
> Some goes up en some goes down,
> You'll git ter der bottom all safe en soun'.' *

"W'en Brer Rabbit got out, he gallop off en tole de fokes w'at de well b'long ter dat Brer Fox wuz down in dar muddyin' up de drinkin' water, en den he gallop back ter de well, en holler down ter Brer Fox:

> 'Yer come a man wid a great big gun—
> W'en he haul you up, you jump en run.' "

"What then, Uncle Remus?" asked the little boy, as the old man paused.

"In des 'bout half n'our, honey, bofe un um wuz back in de new groun' wukkin des like dey never heer'd er no well, ceppin' dat eve'y now'n den Brer Rabbit'd bust out in er laff, en old Brer Fox, he'd git a spell er de dry grins."

---

* As a Northern friend suggests that this story may be somewhat obscure, it may be as well to state that the well is supposed to be supplied with a rope over a wheel, or pulley, with a bucket at each end. [Harris's note.]

MADAME CÉLESTIN'S DIVORCE

Kate Chopin

From *Bayou Folk* by Kate Chopin, 1894, in which the story was first published.

Kate Chopin (1851-1904) was a native of St. Louis who married a Louisiana Creole and lived on a plantation in the Cane River region of Louisiana and in New Orleans. Her best work is in the stories of rural Cajuns and New Orleans Creoles which she collected in two books, *Bayou Folk* (1894) and *A Night in Acadie* (1897). Daniel S. Rankin's *Kate Chopin and Her Creole Stories* (1932) contains an account of her life and work and also several tales of hers previously unpublished or uncollected. For an evaluation of her work see F. L. Pattee, *A History of American Literature Since 1870* (1915), pages 364-365.

Madame Célestin always wore a neat and snugly fitting calico wrapper when she went out in the morning to sweep her small gallery. Lawyer Paxton thought she looked very pretty in the gray one that was made with a graceful Watteau fold at the back: and with which she invariably wore a bow of pink ribbon at the throat. She was always sweeping her gallery when lawyer Paxton passed by in the morning on his way to his office in St. Denis Street.

Sometimes he stopped and leaned over the fence to say good-morning at his ease; to criticize or admire her rosebushes; or, when he had time enough, to hear what she had to say. Madame Célestin usually had a good deal to say. She would gather up the train of her calico wrapper in one hand, and balancing the broom gracefully in the other, would go tripping down to where the lawyer leaned, as comfortably as he could, over her picket fence.

Of course she had talked to him of her troubles. Every one knew Madame Célestin's troubles.

"Really, madame," he told her once, in his deliberate, calculating, lawyer-tone, "it's more than human nature—woman's nature—should be called upon to endure. Here you are, working your fingers off"—she glanced down at two rosy finger-tips that showed through the rents in her baggy doe-skin gloves—"taking in sewing; giving music lessons; doing God knows what in the way of manual labor to support yourself and those two little ones"—Madame Célestin's pretty face beamed with satisfaction at this enumeration of her trials.

"You right, Judge. Not a picayune, not one, not one, have I lay my eyes on in the pas' fo' months that I can say Célestin give it to me or sen' it to me."

"The scoundrel!" muttered lawyer Paxton in his beard.

"An' *pourtant,*" she resumed, "they say he's making money down roun' Alexandria w'en he wants to work."

"I dare say you haven't seen him for months?" suggested the lawyer.

"It's good six month' since I see a sight of Célestin," she admitted.

"That's it, that's what I say; he has practically deserted you; fails to support you. It wouldn't surprise me a bit to learn that he has ill treated you."

"Well, you know, Judge," with an evasive cough, "a man that drinks—w'at can you expec'? An' if you would know the promises he has made me! Ah, if I had as manny dolla' as I had promise from Célestin, I would n' have to work, *je vous garantis.*"

"And in my opinion, madame, you would be a foolish woman to endure it longer, when the divorce court is there to offer you redress."

"You spoke about that befo', Judge; I'm goin' think about that divo'ce. I believe you right."

Madame Célestin thought about the divorce and talked about it, too; and lawyer Paxton grew deeply interested in the theme.

"You know, about that divo'ce, Judge," Madame Célestin was waiting for him that morning, "I been talking to my family an' my frien's, an' it's me that tells you, they all plumb agains' that divo'ce."

"Certainly, to be sure; that's to be expected, madame, in this community of Creoles. I warned you that you would meet with opposition, and would have to face it and brave it."

"Oh, don't fear, I'm going to face it! Maman says it's a disgrace like it's neva been in the family. But it's good for Maman to talk, her. W'at trouble she ever had? She says I mus' go by all means consult with Père Duchéron—it's my confessor, you undastan'— Well, I'll go, Judge, to please Maman. But all the confessor' in the worl' ent goin' make me put up with that conduc' of Célestin any longa."

A day or two later, she was there waiting for him again. "You know, Judge, about that divo'ce."

"Yes, yes," responded the lawyer, well pleased to trace a new determination in her brown eyes and in the curves of her pretty mouth. "I suppose you saw Père Duchéron and had to brave it out with him, too."

"Oh, fo' that, a perfec' sermon, I assho you. A talk of giving scandal an' bad example that I thought would neva en'! He says, fo' him, he wash' his hands; I mus' go see the bishop."

"You won't let the bishop dissuade you, I trust," stammered the lawyer more anxiously than he could well understand.

"You don't know me yet, Judge," laughed Madame Célestin with a turn of the head and a flirt of the broom which indicated that the interview was at an end.

"Well, Madame Célestin! And the bishop!" Lawyer Paxton was standing there holding to a couple of the shaky pickets. She had not seen him. "Oh, it's you, Judge?" and she hastened towards him with an *empressement* that could not but have been flattering.

"Yes, I saw Monseigneur," she began. The lawyer had already gathered from her expressive countenance that she had not wavered in her determination. "Ah, he's a eloquent man. It's not a mo' eloquent man in Natchitoches parish. I was fo'ced to cry, the way he talked to me about my troubles; how he understan's them, an' feels for me. It would move even you, Judge, to hear how he talk' about that step I want to take; its danga, its temptation. How it is the duty of a Catholic to stan' everything till the las' extreme. An' that life of retirement an' self-denial I would have to lead,—he tole me all that."

"But he has n't turned you from your resolve, I see," laughed the lawyer complacently.

"For that, no," she returned emphatically. "The bishop don't know w'at it is to be married to a man like Célestin, an' have to endu' that conduc' like I have to endu' it. The Pope himse'f can't make me stan' that any longer, if you say I got the right in the law to sen' Célestin sailing."

A noticeable change had come over lawyer Paxton. He discarded his work-day coat and began to wear his Sunday one to the office. He grew solicitous as to the shine of his boots, his collar, and the set of his tie. He brushed and trimmed his whiskers with a care that had not before been apparent. Then he fell into a stupid habit of dreaming as he walked the streets of the old town. It would be very good to take unto himself a wife, he dreamed. And he could dream of no other than pretty Madame Célestin filling that sweet and sacred office as she filled his thoughts, now. Old Natchitoches would not hold them comfortably, perhaps; but the world was surely wide enough to live in, outside of Natchitoches town.

His heart beat in a strangely irregular manner as he neared Madame Célestin's house one morning, and discovered her behind the rosebushes, as usual plying her broom. She had finished the gallery and steps and was sweeping the little brick walk along the edge of the violet border.

"Good-morning, Madame Célestin."

"Ah, it's you, Judge? Good-morning." He waited. She seemed to be doing the same. Then she ventured, with some hesitancy, "You know, Judge, about that divo'ce. I been thinking,—I reckon you betta neva mine about that divo'ce." She was making deep rings in the palm of her gloved hand with the end of the broom-handle, and looking at them critically. Her face seemed to the lawyer to be unusually rosy; but maybe it was only the reflection of the pink bow at the throat. "Yes, I reckon you need n' mine. You see, Judge, Célestin came home las' night. An' he's promise me on his word an' honor he's going to turn ova a new leaf."

A DELICATE AFFAIR

Grace King

From *Balcony Stories* by Grace King, 1893; first published in the *Century Magazine*, XLVI (October, 1893), 884-889.

A Creole and native of New Orleans, Grace King (1851-1932) did her best work in the stories and sketches which she collected in *Tales of a Time and Place* (1892) and *Balcony Stories* (1893). She wrote novels also, and in her later years she turned to history and biography. See F. L. Pattee, *A History of American Literature Since 1870* (1915), pages 362-364, and J. S. Kendall, "A New Orleans Lady of Letters," *Louisiana Historical Quarterly*, XIX (April, 1936), 436-465.

"But what does this extraordinary display of light mean?" ejaculated my aunt, the moment she entered the parlor from the dining-room. "It looks like the kingdom of heaven in here! Jules! Jules!" she called, "come and put out some of the light!"

Jules was at the front door letting in the usual Wednesday-evening visitor, but now he came running in immediately with his own invention in the way of a gas-stick,—a piece of broom-handle notched at the end,—and began turning one tap after the other, until the room was reduced to complete darkness.

"But what do you mean now, Jules?" screamed the old lady again.

"Pardon, madame," answered Jules, with dignity; "it is an accident. I thought there was one still lighted."

"An accident! An accident! Do you think I hire you to perform accidents for me? You are just through telling me that it was accident made you give me both soup and gumbo for dinner to-day."

"But accidents can always happen, madame," persisted Jules, adhering to his position.

The chandelier, a design of originality in its day, gave light by what purported to be wax candles standing each in a circlet of pendent crystals. The usual smile of ecstatic admiration spread over Jules's features as he touched the match to the simulated wicks, and lighted into life the rainbows in the prisms underneath. It was a smile that did not heighten the intelligence of his features, revealing as it did the toothless condition of his gums.

"What will madame have for her dinner to-morrow," looking benignantly at his mistress, and still standing under his aureole.

"Do I ever give orders for one dinner, with the other one still on my lips?"

"I only asked madame; there is no harm in asking." He walked away, his long stiff white apron rattling like a petticoat about him. Catching sight of the visitor still standing at the threshold: "Oh, madame, here is Mr. Horace. Shall I let him in?"

"Idiot! Every Wednesday you ask me that question, and every Wednesday I answer the same way. Don't you think I could tell you when not to let him in without your asking?"

"Oh, well, madame, one never knows; it is always safe to ask."

The appearance of the gentleman started a fresh subject of excitement.

"Jules! Jules! You have left that front door unlocked again!"

"Excuse me," said Mr. Horace; "Jules did not leave the front door unlocked. It was locked when I rang, and he locked it again most carefully after letting me in. I have been standing outside all the while the gas was being extinguished and relighted."

"Ah, very well, then. And what is the news?" She sank into her arm-chair, pulled her little card-table closer, and began shuffling the cards upon it for her game of solitaire. "I never hear any news, you know. She [nodding toward me] goes out, but she never learns anything. She is as stupid to-night as an empty bottle."

After a few passes her hands, which were slightly tremulous, regained some of their wonted steadiness and brilliancy of movement, and the cards dropped rapidly on the table. Mr. Horace, as he had got into the habit of doing, watched her mechanically, rather absentmindedly retailing what he imagined would interest her, from his week's observation and hearsay. And madame's little world revolved, complete for her, in time, place, and personality.

It was an old-fashioned square room with long ceiling, and broad, low windows heavily curtained with stiff silk brocade, faded by time into mellowness. The tall white-painted mantel carried its obligation of ornaments well: a gilt clock which under a glass case related some brilliant poetical idyl, and told the hours only in an insignificant aside, according to the delicate politeness of bygone French taste; flanked by duplicate continuations of the same idyl in companion candelabra, also under glass; Sèvres, or imitation Sèvres vases, and a crowd of smaller objects to which age and rarity were slowly contributing an artistic value. An oval mirror behind threw replicas of them into another mirror, receiving in exchange the reflected portrait of madame in her youth, and in the partial nudity in which innocence was limned in madame's youth. There were besides mirrors on the other three walls of the room, all hung with such careful intent for the exercise of their vocation that the apartment, in spots, extended indefinitely; the brilliant chandelier was thereby quadrupled, and the furniture and ornaments multiplied everywhere and most unexpectedly into twins and triplets, producing such sociabilities among them, and forcing such correspondences between inanimate objects with such hospitable insistence, that the effect was full of gaiety and life, although the interchange in reality was the mere repetition of one original, a kind of phonographic echo.

The portrait of monsieur, madame's handsome young husband, hung out of the circle of radiance, in the isolation that, wherever they hang, always seems to surround the portraits of the dead.

Old as the parlors appeared, madame antedated them by the sixteen years she had lived before her marriage, which had been the occasion of their furnishment. She had traveled a considerable distance over the sands of time since the epoch commemorated by the portrait. Indeed, it would require almost documentary evidence to prove that she, who now was arriving at eighty, was the same Atalanta that had started out so buoyantly at sixteen.

Instead of a cap, she wore black lace over her head, pinned with gold brooches. Her white hair curled naturally over a low forehead. Her complexion showed care—and powder. Her eyes were still bright, not with the effete intelligence of old age, but with actual potency. She wore a loose black sack flowered in purple, and over that a black lace mantle, fastened with more gold brooches.

She played her game of solitaire rapidly, impatiently, and always won; for she never hesitated to cheat to get out of a tight place, or into a favorable one, cheating with the quickness of a flash, and forgetting it the moment afterward.

Mr. Horace was as old as she, but he looked much younger, although his dress and appearance betrayed no evidence of an effort in that direction. Whenever his friend cheated, he would invariably call her attention to it; and as usual she would shrug her shoulders, and say, "Bah! lose a game for a card!" and pursue the conversation.

He happened to mention mushrooms—fresh mushrooms. She threw down her cards before the words were out of his mouth, and began to call, "Jules! Jules!" Mr. Horace pulled the bell-cord, but madame was too excitable for that means of communication. She ran into the antechamber, and put her head over the banisters, calling, "Jules! Jules!" louder and louder. She might have heard Jules's slippered feet running from the street into the corridor and up-stairs, had she not been so deaf. He appeared at the door.

"But where have you been? Here I have been raising the house a half-hour, calling you. You have been in the street. I am sure you have been in the street."

"Madame is very much mistaken," answered Jules, with resentful dignity. He had taken off his white apron of waiter, and was disreputable in all the shabbiness of his attire as cook. "When madame forbids me to go into the street, I do not go into the street. I was in the kitchen; I had fallen asleep. What does madame desire?" smiling benevolently.

"What is this I hear? Fresh mushrooms in the market!"

"Eh madame?"

"Fresh mushrooms in the market, and you have not brought me any!"

"Madame, there are fresh mushrooms everywhere in the market," waving his hand to show their universality.

"Everybody is eating them—"

"Old Pomponnette," Jules continued, "only this morning offered me a plate, piled up high, for ten cents."

"Idiot! Why did you not buy them?"

"If madame had said so; but madame did not say so. Madame said, 'Soup, Jules; carrots, rice,'" counting on his fingers.

"And the gumbo?"

"I have explained that that was an accident. Madame said 'Soup,'" enumerating his menu again; "madame never once said mushrooms."

"But how could I know there were mushrooms in the market? Do I go to market?"

"That is it!" and Jules smiled at the question thus settled.

"If you had told me there were mushrooms in the market—" pursued madame, persisting in treating Jules as a reasonable being.

"Why did not madame ask me? If madame had asked me, surely I would have told madame. Yesterday Caesar brought them to the door—a whole bucketful for twenty-five cents. I had to shut the door in his face to get rid of him," triumphantly.

"And you brought me yesterday those detestable peas!"

"Ah," shrugging his shoulders, "madame told me to buy what I saw. I saw peas. I bought them."

"Well, understand now, once for all: whenever you see mushrooms, no matter what I ordered, you buy them. Do you hear?"

"No, madame. Surely I cannot buy mushrooms unless madame orders them. Madame's disposition is too quick."

"But I do order them. Stupid! I do order them. I tell you to buy them every day."

"And if there are none in the market every day?"

"Go away! Get out of my sight! I do not want to see you. Ah, it is unendurable! I must—I must get rid of him!" This last was not a threat, as Jules knew only too well. It was merely a habitual exclamation.

During the colloquy Mr. Horace, leaning back in his arm-chair, raised his eyes, and caught the reflected portrait of madame in the mirror before him—the reflection so much softer and prettier, so much more ethereal, than the original painting. Indeed, seen in the mirror, that way, the portrait was as refreshing as the most charming memory. He pointed to it when madame, with considerable loss of temper, regained her seat.

"It is as beautiful as the past," he explained most unnaturally, for he and his friend had a horror of looking at the long, long past, which could not fail to remind them of—what no one cares to contemplate out of church. Making an effort toward some determination which a subtle observer might have noticed weighing upon him all the evening, he added: "And, apropos of the past—"

"*Hein?*" interrogated the old lady, impatiently, still under the influence of her irascibility about the mushrooms.

He moved his chair closer, and bent forward, as if his communication were to be confidential.

"Ah, bah! Speak louder!" she cried. "One would suppose you had some secret to tell. What secrets can there be at our age?" She took up her cards and began to play. There could be no one who bothered herself less about the forms of politeness.

"Yes, yes," answered Mr. Horace, throwing himself back into his chair; "what secrets can there be at our age?"

The remark seemed a pregnant one to him; he gave himself up to it. One must evidently be the age of one's thoughts. Mr. Horace's thoughts revealed him the old man he was. The lines in his face deepened into wrinkles; his white mustache could not pretend to conceal his mouth, worsened by the loss of a tooth or two; and the long, thin hand that propped his head was crossed with blue, distended veins. "At the last judgment"—it was a favorite quotation with him—"the book of our conscience will be read aloud before the whole company."

But the old lady, deep in her game, paid no more heed to his quotation than to him. He made a gesture toward her portrait.

"When that was painted, Josephine—"

Madame threw a glance after the gesture. The time was so long ago, the mythology of Greece hardly more distant! At eighty the golden age of youth must indeed appear an evanescent myth. Madame's ideas seemed to take that direction.

"Ah, at that time we were all nymphs, and you all demigods."

"Demigods and nymphs, yes; but there was one among us who was a god with you all."

The allusion—a frequent one with Mr. Horace—was to madame's husband, who in his day, it is said, had indeed played the god in the little Arcadia of society. She shrugged her shoulders. The truth is so little of a compliment. The old gentleman sighed in an abstracted way, and madame, although apparently absorbed in her game, lent her ear. It is safe to say that a woman is never too old to hear a sigh wafted in her direction.

"Josephine, do you remember—in your memory—"

She pretended not to hear. Remember? Who ever heard of her forgetting? But she was not the woman to say, at a moment's notice, what she remembered or what she forgot.

"A woman's memory! When I think of a woman's memory—in fact, I do not like to think of a woman's memory. One can intrude in imagination into many places; but a woman's memory—"

Mr. Horace seemed to lose his thread. It had been said of him in his youth that he wrote poetry—and it was said against him. It was evidently such lapses as these that had given rise to the accusation. And as there was no one less impatient under sentiment or poetry than madame, her feet began to agitate themselves as if Jules were perorating some of his culinary inanities before her.

"And a man's memory!" totally misunderstanding him. "It is not there that I either would penetrate, my friend. A man—"

When madame began to talk about men she was prompted by imagination just as much as was Mr. Horace when he talked about women. But what a difference in their sentiments! And yet he had received so little, and she so much, from the subjects of their inspiration. But that seems to be the way in life—or in imagination.

"That you should"—he paused with the curious shyness of the old before the word "love"—"that you two should—marry—seemed natural, inevitable, at the time."

Tradition records exactly the same comment by society at the time on the marriage in question. Society is ever fatalistic in its comments.

"But the natural—the inevitable—do we not sometimes, I wonder, perform them as Jules does his accidents?"

"Ah, do not talk about that idiot! An idiot born and bred! I won't have him about me! He is a monstrosity! I tell his grandmother that every day when she comes to comb me. What a farce—what a ridiculous farce comfortable existence has become with us! Fresh mushrooms in market, and bring me carrots!"

The old gentleman, partly from long knowledge of her habit, or from an equally persistent bend of his own, quietly held on to his idea.

"One cannot tell. It seems so at the time. We like to think it so; it makes it easier. And yet, looking back on our future as we once looked forward to it—"

"Eh! but who wants to look back on it, my friend? Who in the world wants to look back on it?" One could not doubt madame's energy of opinion on that question to hear her voice. "We have done our future, we have performed it, if you will. Our future! It is like the dinners we have eaten; of course we cannot remember the good without becoming exasperated over the bad: but—" shrugging her shoulders—"since we cannot beat the cooks, we must submit to fate," forcing a queen that she needed at the critical point of her game.

"At sixteen and twenty-one it is hard to realize that one is arranging one's life to last until sixty, seventy, forever," correcting himself as he thought of his friend, the dead husband. If madame had ever possessed the art of self-control, it was many a long day since she had exercised it; now she frankly began to show ennui.

"When I look back to that time,"—Mr. Horace leaned back in his chair and half closed his eyes, perhaps to avoid the expression of her face,—"I see nothing but lights and flowers, I hear nothing but music and laughter; and all—lights and flowers and music and laughter—seem to meet in this room, where we met so often to arrange our—inevitabilities." The word appeared to attract him. "Josephine,"—with a sudden change of voice and manner,—"Josephine, how beautiful you were!"

The old lady nodded her head without looking from her cards.

"They used to say," with sad conviction of the truth of his testimony—"the men used to say that your beauty was irresistible. None ever withstood you. None ever could."

That, after all, was Mr. Horace's great charm with madame; he was so faithful to the illusions of his youth. As he looked now at her, one could almost feel the irresistibility of which he spoke.

"It was only their excuse, perhaps; we could not tell at the time; we cannot tell even now when we think about it. They said then, talking as men talk over such things, that you were the only one who could remain yourself under the circumstances; you were the only one who could know, who could will, under the circumstances. It was their theory; men can have only theories about such things." His voice dropped, and he seemed to drop too, into some abysm of thought.

Madame looked into the mirror, where she could see the face of the one who alone could retain her presence of mind under the circumstances suggested by Mr. Horace. She could also have seen, had she wished it, among the reflected bric-à-brac of the mantel, the corner of the frame that held the picture of her husband, but peradventure, classing it with the past which held so many unavenged bad dinners, she never thought to link it even by a look with her emotions of the present. Indeed, it had been said of her that in past, present, and future there had ever been but the one picture to interest her eyes—the one she was looking at now. This, however, was the remark of the uninitiated, for the true passion of a beautiful woman is never so much for her beauty as for its booty; as the passion of a gamester is for his game, not for his luck.

"How beautiful *she* was!"

It was apparently down in the depths of his abysm that he found the connection between this phrase and his last, and it was evidently to himself he said it. Madame, however, heard and understood too; in fact, traced back to a certain period, her thoughts and Mr. Horace's must have been fed by pretty much the same subjects. But she had so carefully barricaded certain issues in her memory as almost to obstruct their flow into her life; if she were a cook, one would say that it was her bad dinners which she was trying to keep out of remembrance.

"You there, he there, she there, I there." He pointed to the places on the carpet, under the chandelier; he could have touched them with a walking-stick, and the recollection seemed just as close.

"She was, in truth, what we men called her then; it was her eyes that first suggested it—Myosotis, the little blue flower, the for-get-me-not. It suited her better than her own name. We always called her that among ourselves. How beautiful she was!" He leaned his head on his hand and looked where he had seen her last—so long, such an eternity, ago.

It must be explained for the benefit of those who do not live in the little world where an allusion is all that is necessary to put one in full possession of any drama, domestic or social, that Mr. Horace was speaking of the wedding-night of madame, when the bridal party stood as he described under the chandelier; the bride and groom, with each one's best friend. It may be said that it was the last night or time that madame had a best friend of her own sex. Social gossip, with characteristic kindness, had furnished reasons to suit all tastes, why madame had ceased that night to have a best friend of her own sex. If gossip had not done so, society would still be left to its imagination for information, for madame never tolerated the smallest appeal to her for enlightenment. What the general taste seemed most to relish as a version was that madame in her marriage had triumphed, not conquered; and that the night of her wedding she had realized the fact, and, to be frank, had realized it ever since. In short, madame had played then to gain at love, as she played now to gain at solitaire; and hearts were no more than cards to her—and, "Bah! Lose a game for a card!" must have been always her motto. It is hard to explain it delicately enough, for these are the most delicate affairs in life; but the image of Myosotis had passed through monsieur's heart, and Myosotis does mean "forget me not." And madame well knew that to love monsieur once was to love him always, in spite of jealousy, doubt, distrust, nay, unhappiness (for to love him meant all this and more). He was that kind of man, they said, whom women could love even against conscience. Madame never forgave that moment. Her friend, at least, she could put aside out of her intercourse; unfortunately, we cannot put people out of our lives. God alone can do that, and so far he had interfered in the matter only by removing monsieur. It was known to notoriety that since her wedding madame had abandoned, destroyed, all knowledge of her friend. And the friend? She had disappeared as much as is possible for one in her position and with her duties.

"What there is in blue eyes, light hair, and a fragile form to impress one, I cannot tell; but for us men it seems to me it is blue-eyed, light-haired, and fragile-formed women that are the hardest to forget."

"The less easy to forget," corrected madame; but he paid no attention to the remark.

"They are the women that attach themselves in one's memory. If necessary to keep from being forgotten, they come back into one's dreams. And as life rolls on, one wonders about them,—'Is she happy? Is she miserable? Goes life well or ill with her?'"

Madame played her cards slowly, one would say, for her, prosaically.

"And there is always a pang when, as one is so wondering, the response comes,—that is, the certainty in one's heart responds,—'She is miserable, and life goes ill with her.' Then, if ever, men envy the power of God."

Madame threw over the game she was in, and began a new one.

"Such women should not be unhappy; they are too fragile, too sensitive, too trusting. I could never understand the infliction of misery upon them. I could send death to them, but not—not misfortune."

Madame, forgetting again to cheat in time, and losing her game, began impatiently to shuffle her cards for a new deal.

"And yet, do you know, Josephine, those women are the unhappy ones of life. They seem predestined to it, as others"—looking at madame's full-charmed portrait—"are predestined to triumph and victory. They"—unconscious, in his abstraction, of the personal nature of his simile—"never know how to handle their cards, and they always play a losing game."

"Ha!" came from madame, startled into an irate ejaculation.

"It is their love always that is sacrificed, their hearts always that are bruised. One might say that God himself favors the black-haired ones!"

As his voice sank lower and lower, the room seemed to become stiller and stiller. A passing vehicle in the street, however, now and then drew a shiver of sound from the pendent prisms of the chandelier.

"She was so slight, so fragile, and always in white, with blue in her hair to match her eyes—and—God knows what in her heart, all the time. And yet they stand it, they bear it, they do not die, they live along with the strongest, the happiest, the most fortunate of us," bitterly; "and"—raising his eyes to his old friend, who thereupon immediately began to fumble her cards—"whenever in the street I see a poor, bent, broken woman's figure, I know, without verifying it any more by a glance, that it is the wreck of a fair woman's figure; whenever I hear of a bent, broken existence, I know, without asking any more, that it is the wreck of a fair woman's life."

Poor Mr. Horace spoke with the unreason of a superstitious bigot.

"I have often thought, since, in large assemblies, particularly in weddings, Josephine, of what was going on in the women's hearts there, and I have felt sorry for them; and when I think of God's knowing what is in their hearts, I have felt sorry for the men. And I often think now, Josephine,—I think oftener and oftener of it,—that if the resurrection trumpet of our childhood should sound some day, no matter when, out there, over the old St. Louis cemetery, and we should all have to rise from our long rest of oblivion, what would be the first thing we should do? And though there were a God and a heaven awaiting us,—by that same God, Josephine, I believe that our first thought in awakening would be the last in dying,—confession,—and that our first rush would be to the feet of one another for forgiveness. For there are some offenses that must outlast the longest oblivion, and a forgiveness that will be more necessary than God's own. Then our hearts will be bared to one another; for if, as you say, there are no secrets at our age, there can still be less cause for them after death."

His voice ended in the faintest whisper. The table crashed over, and the cards flew wide-spread on the floor. Before we could recover, madame was in the antechamber, screaming for Jules.

One would have said that, from her face, the old lady had witnessed the resurrection described by Mr. Horace, the rush of the spirits with their burdens of remorse, the one to the feet of the other; and she must have seen herself and her husband, with a unanimity of purpose never apparent in their short married life, rising from their common tomb and hastening to that other tomb at the end of the alley, and falling at the feet of the one to whom in life he had been recreant in love, she in friendship.

Of course Jules answered through the wrong door, rushing in with his gas-stick, and turning off the gas. In a moment we were involved in darkness and dispute.

"But what does he mean? What does the idiot mean? He—" It was impossible for her to find a word to do justice to him and to her exasperation at the same time.

"Pardon, madame; it is not I. It is the cathedral bell; it is ringing nine o'clock."

"But—"

"Madame can hear it herself. Listen!" We could not see it, but we were conscious of the benign, toothless smile spreading over his face as the bell-tones fell in the room.

"But it is not the gas. I—"

"Pardon, madame; but it is the gas. Madame said, 'Jules, put out the gas every night when the bell rings.' Madame told me that only last night. The bell rings: I put out the gas."

"Will you be silent? Will you listen?"

"If madame wishes; just as madame says."

But the old lady had turned to Mr. Horace. "Horace, you have seen—you know—" and it was a question now of overcoming emotion. "I—I—I—a carriage, my friend, a carriage."

"Madame—" Jules interrupted his smile to interrupt her.

She was walking around the room, picking up a shawl here, a lace there; for she was always prepared against draughts.

"Madame—" continued Jules, pursuing her.

"A carriage."

"If madame would only listen, I was going to say—but madame is too quick in her disposition—the carriage has been waiting since a long hour ago. Mr. Horace said to have it there in a half hour."

It was then she saw for the first time that it had all been prepared by Mr. Horace. The rest was easy enough: getting into the carriage, and finding the place of which Mr. Horace had heard, as he said, only that afternoon. In it, on her bed of illness, poverty, and suffering, lay the patient, wasted form of the beautiful fair one whom men had called in her youth Myosotis.

But she did not call her Myosotis.

"Mon Amour!" The old pet name, although it had to be fetched across more than half a century of disuse, flashed like lightning from madame's heart into the dim chamber.

"Ma Divine!" came in counter-flash from the curtained bed.

In the old days women, or at least young girls, could hazard such pet names one upon the other. These—think of it!—dated from the first communion class, the dating period of so much of friendship.

"My poor Amour!"

"My poor, poor Divine!"

The voices were together, close beside the pillow.

"I—I—" began Divine.

"It could not have happened if God had not wished it," interrupted poor Amour, with the resignation that comes, alas! only with the last drop of the bitter cup.

And that was about all. If Mr. Horace had not slipped away, he might have noticed the curious absence of monsieur's name, and of his own name, in the murmuring that followed. It would have given him some more ideas on the subject of woman.

At any rate, the good God must thank him for having one affair the less to arrange when the trumpet sounds out there over the old St. Louis cemetery. And he was none too premature; for the old St. Louis cemetery, as was shortly enough proved, was a near reach for all three of the old friends.

"UNC' EDINBURG'S DROWNDIN'"

A PLANTATION ECHO

Thomas Nelson Page

From *In Ole Virginia* by Thomas Nelson Page, 1887; first published in *Harper's Magazine*, LXXII (January, 1886), 304-315.

Heir to the plantation tradition of Virginia, Thomas Nelson Page (1853-1922) stands foremost among those who shaped and popularized that tradition in literature. He is best known for the stories of the collection *In Ole Virginia* (1887), and his most characteristic stories, like "Unc' Edinburg's Drowndin'," employ an ancient darky telling with fond unreality how things were "befo' de war." Page's novels include *The Old Gentleman of the Black Stock* (1897), *Red Rock* (1898), *Gordon Keith* (1903), and *John Marvel, Assistant* (1909). He published also three volumes of essays, *The Old South* (1892), *Social Life in Old Virginia* (1897), and *The Old Dominion* (1908). See F. L. Pattee, *A History of American Literature Since 1870* (1915), pages 265-269; and Jay B. Hubbell, *The South in American Literature, 1607-1900* (1954), pages 795-804, 952. *Thomas Nelson Page: A Memoir of a Virginia Gentleman* (1923) was written by Page's brother, Rosewell Page.

"Well, suh, dat's a fac—dat's what Marse George al'ays said. 'Tis hard to spile Christmas anyways."

The speaker was "Unc' Edinburg," the driver from Werrowcoke, where I was going to spend Christmas; the time was Christmas

Eve, and the place the muddiest road in eastern Virginia—a measure which, I feel sure, will, to those who have any experience, establish its claim to distinction.

A half-hour before he had met me at the station, the queerest-looking, raggedest old darky conceivable, brandishing a cedar-staffed whip of enormous proportions in one hand, and clutching a calico letter-bag with a twisted string in the other; and with the exception of a brief interval of temporary suspicion on his part, due to the unfortunate fact that my luggage consisted of only a hand-satchel instead of a trunk, we had been steadily progressing in mutual esteem.

"Dee's a boy standin' by my mules; I got de ker'idge heah for you," had been his first remark on my making myself known to him. "Mistis say as how you might bring a trunk."

I at once saw my danger, and muttered something about "a short visit," but this only made matters worse.

"Dee don' nobody nuver pay short visits dyah," he said, decisively, and I fell to other tactics.

"You couldn' spile Christmas den noways," he repeated, reflectingly, while his little mules trudged knee-deep through the mud. " 'Twuz Christmas den, sho' 'nough," he added, the fires of memory smouldering, and then, as they blazed into sudden flame, he asserted, positively: "Dese heah free-issue niggers don' know what Christmas is. Hawg meat an' pop crackers don' meck Christmas. Hit tecks ole times to meck a sho'-'nough, tyahin'-down Christmas. Gord! I's seen 'em! But de wuss Christmas I ever seed tunned out de best in de een," he added, with sudden warmth, "an' dat wuz de Christmas me an' Marse George an' Reveller all got drownded down at Braxton's Creek. You's hearn 'bout dat?"

As he was sitting beside me in solid flesh and blood, and looked as little ethereal in his old hat and patched clothes as an old oak stump would have done, and as Colonel Staunton had made a world-wide reputation when he led his regiment through the Chickahominy thickets against McClellan's intrenchments, I was forced to confess that I had never been so favored, but would like to hear about it now; and with a hitch of the lap blanket under his outside knee, and a supererogatory jerk of the reins, he began:

"Well, you know, Marse George was jes' eighteen when he went to college. I went wid him, 'cause me an' him wuz de same age; I was born like on a Sat'day in de Christmas, an' he wuz born in de new year on a Chuesday, an' my mammy nussed us bofe at one breast. Dat's de reason maybe huccome we took so to one nurr. He sutney set a heap o' sto' by me; an' I 'ain' nuver see nobody yit wuz good to me as Marse George."

The old fellow, after a short reverie, went on:

"Well, we growed up togerr, jes as to say two stalks in one hill. We cotch ole hyahs togerr, an' we hunted 'possums togerr, an' 'coons. Lord! he wuz a climber! I 'member a fight he had one night up in de ve'y top of a big poplar tree wid a 'coon, whar he done gone up after, an' he flung he hat over he head; an' do' de varmint leetle mo' tyah him all to pieces, he fotch him down dat tree 'live; an' me an' him had him at Christmas. 'Coon meat mighty good when dee fat, you know?"

As this was a direct request for my judgment, I did not have the moral courage to raise an issue, although my views on the subject of 'coon meat are well known to my family; so I grunted something which I doubt not he took for assent, and he proceeded:

"Dee warn' nuttin he didn' lead de row in; he wuz de bes' swimmer I ever see, an' he handled a skiff same as a fish handle heself. An' I wuz wid him constant; wherever you see Marse George, dyah Edinburg sho', jes' like he shadow. So twuz, when he went to de university; 'twarn' nuttin would do but I got to go too. Marster he didn' teck much to de notion, but Marse George wouldn' have it no urr way, an' co'se mistis she teck he side. So I went 'long as he body-servant to teck keer on him an' help meck him a gent'man. An' he wuz, too. From time he got dyah tell he cum 'way he wuz de head man.

"Dee wan' but one man dyah didn' compliment him, an' dat wuz Mr. Darker. But he warn' nuttin! not dat he didn' come o' right good fambly—'cep' dee politics; but he wuz sutney pitted, jes' like sometimes you see a weevly runty pig in a right good litter. Well, Mr. Darker he al'ays 'ginst Marse George; he hate me an him bofe, an' he sutney act mischeevous todes us; 'cause he know he warn' as we all. De Stauntons dee wuz de popularitiest folks in Virginia;

an' dee wuz high-larnt besides. So when Marse George run for de medal, an' wuz to meck he gret speech, Mr. Darker he speak 'ginst him. Dat's what Marse George whip him 'bout. Ain' nobody nuver told you 'bout dat?"

I again avowed my misfortune; and although it manifestly aroused new doubts, he worked it off on the mules, and once more took up his story:

"Well, you know, dee had been speakin' 'ginst one nurr ev'y Sat'dy night; and ev'ybody knowed Marse George wuz de bes' speaker, but dee give him one mo' sho', an' dee was bofe gwine spread dee-selves, an' dee wuz two urr gent'mens also gwine speak. An' dat night when Mr. Darker got up he meck sich a fine speech ev'ybody wuz s'prised; an' some on 'em say Mr. Darker done beat Marse George. But shuh! I know better'n dat; an' Marse George face look so curious; but, suh, when he riz I knowed der wuz somen gwine happen—I wuz leanin' in de winder. He jes step out in front an' throwed up he head like a horse wid a rank kyurb on him, and den he begin; an' twuz jes like de river when hit gits out he bank. He swep' ev'ything. When he fust open he mouf I knowed twuz comin'; he face wuz pale, an' he wuds tremble like a fiddle-string, but he eyes wuz blazin', an' in a minute he wuz jes reshin'. He voice soun' like a bell; an' he jes wallered dat turr man, an' wared him out; an' when he set down dee all yelled an' hollered so you couldn' heah you' ears. Gent'mans, twuz royal!

"Den dee tuck de vote, an' Marse George got it munanimous, an' dee all hollered agin, all 'cep' a few o' Mr. Darker's friends. An' Mr. Darker he wuz de second. An' den dee broke up. An' jes den Marse George walked thoo the crowd straight up to him, an' lookin' him right in de eyes, says to him, 'You stole dat speech you made to-night.' Well, suh, you ought to 'a hearn 'em; hit soun' like a mill-dam. You couldn' heah nuttin' 'cep' roarin', an' you couldn' see nuttin 'cep' shovin'; but, big as he wuz, Marse George beat him; an' when dee pull him off, do' he face wuz mighty pale, he stan' out befo' 'em all, dem whar wuz 'ginst him, an' all, an' as straight as an arrow, an' say: 'Dat speech wuz written an' printed years ago by somebody or nurr in Congress, an' this man stole it; had he beat me only, I should not have said one word; but as he has beaten

others, I shall show him up!' Gord, suh, he voice wuz clear as a
game rooster. I sutney wuz proud on him.

"He did show him up, too, but Mr. Darker ain' wait to see it; he
lef' dat night. An' Marse George he wuz de popularest gent'man
at dat university. He could handle dem students dyah same as a man
handle a hoe.

"Well, twuz de next Christmas we meet Miss Charlotte an' Nancy.
Mr. Braxton invite we all to go down to spen' Christmas wid him at
he home. An' sich a time as we had!

"We got dyah Christmas Eve night—dis very night—jes befo'
supper, an' jes natchelly froze to death," he pursued, dealing in his
wonted hyperbole, "an' we jes had time to git a apple toddy or two
when supper was ready, an' wud come dat dee wuz waitin' in de
hall. I had done fix Marse George up gorgeousome, I tell you; and
when he walk down dem stairs in dat swaller-tail coat, an' dem
paten'-leather pumps on, dee warn nay one dyah could tetch him;
he looked like he own 'em all. I jes rest my mind. I seen him when
he shake hands wid 'em all roun', an' I say, 'Um-m-m! he got 'em.'

"But he ain' teck noticement o' none much tell Miss Charlotte
come. She didn' live dyah, had jes come over de river dat evenin'
from her home, 'bout ten miles off, to spen' Christmas like we all,
an' she come down de stairs jes as Marse George finish shakin'
hands. I seen he eye light on her as she come down de steps
smilin', wid her dim blue dress trainin' behind her, an' her little
blue foots peepin' out so pretty, an' holdin' a little hankcher, lookin'
like a spider-web, in one hand, an' a gret blue fan in turr, spread
out like a peacock tail, an' jes her roun' arms an' th'oat white,
an' her gret dark eyes lightin' up her face. I say, 'Dyah 'tis!'
and when de old Cun'l stan' aside an' interduce 'em, an' Marse
George step for'ard an' meck he grand bow, an' she sort o' swing
back an' gin her curtchy, wid her dress sort o' dammed up 'ginst
her, an' her arms so white, an' her face sort o' sunsetty, I say,
'Yes, Lord! Edinburg, dyah you mistis.' Marse George look like he
think she done come down right from de top o' de blue sky an'
bring piece on it wid her. He ain' nuver took he eyes from her dat
night. Dee glued to her, mun! an' she—well, do' she mighty rosy,
an' look mighty unconsarned, she sutney ain' hender him. Hit look

like kyarn nobody else tote dat fan an' pick up dat hankcher skusin o' him; an' after supper, when dee all playin' blindman's-buff in de hall—I don' know how twuz—but do' she jes as nimble as a filly, an' her ankle jes as clean, an' she kin git up her dress an' dodge out de way o' ev'ybody else, somehow or nurr she kyarn help him ketchin' her to save her life; he al'ays got her corndered; an' when dee'd git fur apart, dat ain' nuttin, dee jes as sure to come togerr agin as water is whar you done run you hand thoo. An' do' he kiss ev'ybody else under de mistletow, 'cause dee be sort o' cousins, he ain' nuver kiss her, nor nobody else nurr, 'cep' de ole Cun'l. I wuz standin' down at de een de hall wid de black folks, an' I notice it 'tic'lar, 'cause I done meck de 'quaintance o' Nancy; she wuz Miss Charlotte's maid; a mighty likely young gal she wuz den, an' jes as impident as a fly. She see it too, do' she ain' 'low it.

"Fust thing I know I seen a mighty likely light-skinned gal standin' dyah by me, wid her hyah mos' straight as white folks, an' a mighty good frock on, an' a clean apron, an' her hand mos' like a lady, only it brown, an' she keep on 'vidin' her eyes twix me an' Miss Charlotte; when I watchin' Miss Charlotte she watchin' me, an' when I steal my eye 'roun' on her she noticin' Miss Charlotte; an' presney I sort o' sidle 'longside her, an' I say, 'Lady, you mighty sprightly to-night.' An' she says she 'bleeged to be sprightly, her mistis look so good; an' I ax her which one twuz, an' she tell me, 'Dat queen one over dyah,' an' I tell her dee's a king dyah too, she got her eye set for; an' when I say her mistis tryin' to set her cap for Marse George, she fly up, an' say she an' her mistis don' have to set de cap for nobody; *dee* got to set dee cap an' all de clo'es for dem, an' den dee ain' gwine cotch 'em, 'cause dee ain' studyin' 'bout no up-country folks whar dee ain' nobody know nuttin 'bout.

"Well, dat oudaciousness so aggrivate me, I lite into dat nigger right dyah. I tell her she ain' been nowhar 'tall ef she don' know we all; dat we wuz de bes' of quality, de ve'y top de pot; an' den I tell her 'bout how gret we wuz; how de ker'idges wuz al'ays hitched up night an' day, an' niggers jes thick as weeds; an' how Unc' Torm he wared he swaller-tail ev'y day when he wait on de table; and Marse George he won' wyah a coat mo'n once or twice anyways, to save you life. Oh! I sutney 'stonish dat nigger, 'cause

me! He play de fiddle for he pastime, but he fotched up in de saddle —dat he cradle!

"De fust day dee went out I heah Nancy quoilin 'bout de tail layin' on Miss Charlotte dressin'-table gittin' hyars over ev'ything.

"One day de ladies went out too, Miss Charlotte 'mongst 'em, on Miss Lucy gray myah Switchity, an' Marse George he rid Mr. Braxton's chestnut Willful.

"Well, suh, he stick so close to dat gray myah, he leetle mo' los' dat fox; but, Lord! he know what he 'bout—he monsus 'ceivin' 'bout dat—he know de way de fox gwine jes as well as he know heself; an' all de time he leadin' Miss Charlotte whar she kin heah de music, but he watchin' him too, jes as narrow as a ole hound. So, when de fox tun de head o' de creek, Marse George had Miss Charlotte on de aidge o' de flat, an' he de fust man see de fox tun down on turr side wid de hounds right rank after him. Dat sort o' set him back, 'cause by rights de fox ought to 'a double an' come back dis side: he kyarn git out dat way; an' two or three gent'mens dee had see it too, an' wuz jes layin de horses to do groun' to git roun' fust, 'cause de creek wuz heap too wide to jump, an' wuz 'way over you head, an hit cold as Christmas, sho 'nough; well, suh, when dee tunned, Mr. Clarke he wuz in de lead (he wuz ridin' for Miss Charlotte too), an' hit fyah set Marse George on fire; hé ain' said but one wud, 'Wait,' an' jes set de chestnut's head straight for de creek, whar de fox comin' wid he hyah up on he back, an' de dogs ravlin mos' on him.

"De ladies screamed, an' some de gent'mens hollered for him to come back, but he ain' mind; he went 'cross dat flat like a wild-duck; an' when he retch de water he horse try to flinch, but dat hand on de bridle, an' dem rowels in he side, an' he 'bleeged to teck it.

"Lord! suh, sich a screech as dee set up! But he wuz swimmin' for life, an' he wuz up de bank an' in de middle o' de dogs time dee tetched ole Gray Jacket; an' when Mr. Clarke got dyah Marse George wuz sta'in' holdin' up de tail for Miss Charlotte to see, turr side de creek, an' de hounds wuz wallerin' all over de body, an' I don' think Mr. Clarke done got up wid 'em yit.

"He cotch de fox, an' he cotch some'n' else besides, in my 'pinion, 'cause when de ladies went up-stairs dat night Miss Charlotte had to wait on de steps for a glass o' water, an' couldn' nobody git it but Marse George; an' den when she tell him good-night over de banisters, he couldn' say it good enough; he got to kiss her hand; an' she ain' do nuttin but jes peep upstairs ef anybody dyah lookin'; an' when I come thoo de do' she juck her hand 'way an' ran upstairs jes as farst as she could. Marse George look at me sort o' laughin', an' say: 'Confound you! Nancy couldn' been very good to you.' An' I say, 'She le' me squench my thirst kissin' her hand'; an' he sort o' laugh an' tell me to keep my mouf shet.

"But dat ain' de on'y time I come on 'em. Dee al'ays gittin' cordered; an' de evenin' befo' we come 'way I wuz gwine in thoo de conservity, an' dyah dee wuz sort o' hide 'way. Miss Charlotte she wuz settin' down, an' Marse George he wuz leanin' over her, got her hand to he face, talkin' right low an' lookin' right sweet, an' she ain' say nuttin; an' presney he drapt on one knee by her, an' slip he arm roun' her, an' try to look in her eyes, an' she so 'shamed to look at him she got to hide her face on he shoulder, an' I slipt out.

"We come 'way next mornin'. When marster heah 'bout it he didn' teck to de notion at all, 'cause her pa—dat is, he warn' her own pa, 'cause he had married her ma when she wuz a widder after Miss Charlotte pa died—an' he politics warn' same as ourn. 'Why, you kin never stand him, suh,' he said to Marse George. 'We won't mix any mo'n fire and water; you ought to have found that out at college; dat fellow Darker is his son.'

"Marse George he say he know dat; but he on'y de step-brurr of de young lady, an' ain' got a drap o' her blood in he veins, an' he didn' know it when he meet her, an' anyhow hit wouldn' meck any diffence; an' when de mistis see how sot Marse George is on it she teck he side, an' dat fix it; 'cause when ole mistis warn marster to do a thing, hit jes good as done. I don' keer how much he rar roun' an' say he ain' gwine do it, you jes well go 'long an' put on you hat; you gwine see him presney doin' it jes peaceable as a lamb. She tun him jes like she got bline-bridle on him, an' he ain' nuver know it.

"So she got him jes straight as a string. An' when de time come for Marse George to go, marster he mo' consarned 'bout it 'n Marse

George; he ain' say nuttin 'bout it befo'; but now he walkin' roun' an' roun' axin mistis mo' questions 'bout he cloes an' he horse an' all; an' dat mornin' he gi' him he two Sunday razors, an' gi' me a pyah o' boots an' a beaver hat, 'cause I wuz gwine wid him to kyar he portmanteau, an' git he shavin' water, sence marster say ef he wuz gwine marry a Locofoco, he at least must go like a gent'man; an' me an' Marse George had done settle it 'twixt us, cause we al'ays set bofe we traps on de same hyah parf.

"Well, we got 'em, an' when I ax dat gal out on de wood-pile dat night, she say bein' as her mistis gwine own me, an' we bofe got to be in de same estate, she reckon she ain' nuver gwine to be able to git shet o' me; an' den I clamp her. Oh, she wuz a beauty!"

A gesture and guffaw completed the recital of his conquest.

"Yes, suh, we got 'em sho!" he said, presently. "Dee couldn' persist us; we crowd 'em into de fence an' run 'em off dee foots.

"Den come de 'gagement; an' ev'ything wuz smooth as silk. Marse George an' me wuz ridin' over dyah constant, on'y we nuver did git over bein' skeered when we wuz ridin' up dat turpentine road facin' all dem winders. Hit 'pear like ev'ybody in de wull 'mos' wuz lookin' at us.

"One evenin' Marse George say, 'Edinburg, d'you ever see as many winders p'intin' one way in you' life? When I git a house,' he say, 'I gwine have all de winders lookin' turr way.'

"But dat evenin', when I see Miss Charlotte come walkin' out de gret parlor wid her hyah sort o' rumpled over her face, an' some yaller roses on her bres, an' her gret eyes so soft an' sweet, an' Marse George walkin' 'long hinst her, so peaceable, like she got chain roun' him, I say, 'Winders ain' nuttin.'

"Oh, twuz jes like holiday all de time! An' den Miss Charlotte come over to see mistis, an' of co'se she bring her maid wid her, 'cause she 'bleeged to have her maid, you know, an' dat wuz de bes' of all.

"Dat evenin', 'bout sunset, dee come drivin' up in de big ker'idge, wid de gret hyah trunk stropped on de seat behind, an' Nancy she settin' by Billy, an' Marse George settin' inside by he rose-bud, 'cause he had done gone down to bring her up; an' marster he done been drest in he blue coat an' yallow westket ever sence dinner, an' walkin' roun', watchin' up de road all de time, an' tellin' de mistis he reckon dee ain' comin', an' ole mistis she try to pacify him, an' she come out presney drest, an' rustlin' in her stiff black silk an' all; an' when de ker'idge come in sight, ev'ybody wuz runnin'; an' when dee draw up to de do', Marse George he help her out an' 'duce her to marster an' ole mistis; an' marster he start to meck her a gret bow, an' she jes put up her mouf like a little gal to be kissed, an' dat got him. An' mistis teck her right in her arms an' kiss her twice, an' de servants dee wuz all peepin' an' grinnin'.

"Ev'ywhar you tun you see a nigger teef, 'cause dee all warn see de young mistis whar good 'nough for Marse George. Dee ain' gwine be married tell de next fall, 'count o' Miss Charlotte bein' so young; but she jes good as b'longst to we all now; an' ole marster an' mistis dee jes as much in love wid her as Marse George. Hi! dee warn pull de house down an' buil' it over for her! An' ev'y han' on de place he peepin' to try to git a look at he young mistis whar he gwine b'longst to. One evenin' dee all on 'em come roun' de porch an' send for Marse George, an' when he come out, Charley Brown (he al'ays de speaker, 'cause he got so much mouf, kin' talk pretty as white folks), he say dee warn interduce to de young mistis, an' pay dee bespects to her; an' presney Marse George lead her out on de porch laughin' at her, wid her face jes rosy as a wine-sap apple, an' she meck 'em a beautiful bow, an' speak to 'em ev'y one, Marse George namin' de names; an' Charley Brown he meck her a pretty speech, an' tell her we mighty proud to own her; an' one o' dem impident gals ax her to gin her dat white frock when she git married; an' when she say, 'Well, what am I goin' wear?' Sally say, 'Lord, honey, Marse George gwine dress you in pure gol'!' an' she look up at him wid sparks flashin' out her eyes, while he look like dat ain' good 'nough for her. An' so twuz, when she went 'way, Sally Marshall got dat frock, an' proud on it I tell you.

"Oh, yes; he sutney mindin' her tender. Hi! when she go to ride in evenin' wid him, de ain' no horse-block good 'nough for her! Marse George got to have her step in he hand; an' when dee out walkin' he got de umbreller holdin' 't over her all de time, he so feared de sun 'll kiss her; an' dee walk so slow down dem walks in de shade you got to sight 'em by a tree to tell ef dee movin' 'tall. She use' to look like she used to it too, I tell you, 'cause she wuz quality, one de white-skinned ones; an' she 'd set in dem big cheers, wid her little foots on de cricket whar Marse George al'ays set for her, he so feared dee 'd tetch de groun', jes like she on her throne; an' ole marster he 'd watch her 'mos' edmirin as Marse George; an' when she went 'way hit sutney was lonesome. Hit look like daylight gone wid her. I don' know which I miss mos', Miss Charlotte or Nancy.

"Den Marse George was 'lected to de Legislature, an' ole Jedge Darker run for de Senator, an' Marse George vote gin him and beat him. An' dat commence de fuss; an' den dat man gi' me de whuppin, an' dat breck 'tup an' breck he heart.

"You see, after Marse George wuz 'lected ('lections wuz 'lections dem days; dee warn' no bait-gode 'lections, wid ev'y sort o' worms squirmin' up 'ginst one nurr, wid piece o' paper d' ain' know what on, drappin' in a chink; didn' nuttin but gent'mens vote den, an' dee took dee dram, an' vote out loud, like gent'mens)—well, arter Marse George wuz 'lected, de parties wuz jes as even balanced as stilyuds, an' wen dee ax Marse George who wuz to be de Senator, he vote for de Whig, 'ginst de old jedge, an' dat beat him, of co'se. An' dee ain' got sense to know he 'bleeged to vote wid he politics. Dat he sprinciple; he kyarn vote for Locofoco, I don' keer ef he is Miss Charlotte pa, much less her step-pa. Of co'se de old jedge ain' speak to him arter dat, nur is Marse George ax him to. But who dat gwine s'pose women-folks got to put dee mouf in too? Miss Charlotte she write Marse George a letter dat pester him mightily; he set up all night answerin' dat letter, an' he mighty solemn, I tell you. An' I wuz gittin' right grewsome myself, 'cause I studyin' 'bout dat gal down dyah whar I done gi' my wud to, an' when dee ain' no letters come torectly hit hard to tell which one de anxiouser, me or Marse George. Den presney I so 'straughted 'long o' it I ax Aunt Haly 'bouten it: she know all sich things, 'cause she 'mos' a hundred years ole, an' seed evil sperits, an' got skoripins up her chimley, an' knowed conjure; an' she ax me what wuz de signication, an' I tell her I ain' able nuther to eat nor to sleep, an' dat gal come foolin' 'long me when I sleep jes like as natchel as ef I see her sho 'nough. An' she say I done conjured; dat de gal done tricked me.

"Oh, Gord! dat skeered me!

"You white folks, marster, don' b'lieve nuttin like dat; y'all got too much sense, 'cause y' all kin read; but niggers dee ain' know no better, an' I sutney wuz skeered, 'cause Aunt Haly say my coffin done seasoned, de planks up de chimley.

"Well, I got so bad Marse George ax me 'bout it, an' he sort o' laugh an' sort o' cuss, an' he tell Aunt Haly ef she don' stop dat foolishness skeerin' me he'll sell her an' tyah her ole skoripin house down. Well, co'se he jes talkin', an' he ax me next day how'd I like to go an' see my sweetheart. Gord! suh, I got well torectly. So I set off next evenin', feelin' jes big as ole marster, wid my pass in my pocket, which I warn' to show nobody 'douten I 'bleeged to, 'cause Marse George didn't warn nobody to know he le' me go. An' den dat rascallion teck de shut off my back. But ef Marse George didn' pay him de wuth o' it!

"I done git 'long so good, too.

"When Nancy see me she sutney was 'stonished. She come roun' de cornder in de back yard whar I settin' in Nat's do' (he wuz de gardener), wid her hyah all done untwist, an' breshed out mighty fine, an' a clean ap'on wid fringe on it, meckin' out she so s'prised to see me (whar wuz all a lie, 'cause some on 'em done notify her I dyah), an' she say, 'Hi! what dis black nigger doin' heah?'

"An' I say, 'Who you callin' nigger, you impident, kercumber-faced thing you?' Den we shake hands, an' I tell her Marse George done set me free—dat I done buy myself; dat's de lie I done lay off to tell her.

"An' when I tole her dat, she bust out laughin', an' say, well, I better go 'long 'way, den, dat she don' warn no free nigger to be comp'ny for her. Dat sort o' set me back, an' I tell her she kickin' 'fo' she spurred, dat I ain' got her in my mine; I got a nurr gal at home whar grievin' 'bout me dat ve'y minute. An' after I tell her all sich lies as dat presney she ax me ain' I hongry; an' ef dat nigger didn' git her mammy to gi' me de bes' supter! Umm-m! I kin mos' tas'e it now. Wheat bread off de table, an' zerves, an' fat bacon, tell I couldn'

put a nurr moufful nowhar sep'n I 'd teck my hat. Dat night I
tote Nancy water for her, an' I tell her all 'bout ev'ything, an' she jes
sweet as honey. Next mornin', do', she done sort o' tunned some,
an' ain' so sweet. You know how milk gits sort o' bonny-clabberish?
An' when she see me she 'gin to 'buse me—say I jes tryin' to fool
her, an' all de time got nurr wife at home, or gittin' ready to git one,
for all she know, an' she ain' know wherr Marse George ain' jes
'ceivin' as I is; an' nem mine, she got plenty warn marry her; an'
as to Miss Charlotte, she got de whole wull; Mr. Darker he ain' got
nobody in he way now, dat he deah all de time, an' ain' gwine West
no mo'. Well, dat aggrivate me so I tell her ef she say dat 'bout Marse
George I gwine knock her; an' wid dat she got so oudacious I
meck out I gwine 'way, an' lef' her, an' went up todes de barn; an'
up dyah, fust thing I know, I come across dat ar man Mr. Darker.
Soon as he see me he begin to cuss me, an' he ax me what I doin' on
dat land, an' I tell him nuttin. An' he say, well, he gwine gi' me
some'n; he gwine teach me to come prowlin' round gent'men's
houses. An' he meck me go in de barn an' teck off my shut, an' he
beat me wid he whup tell de blood run out my back. He sutney did
beat me scandalous, 'cause he done hate me an' Marse George ever
since we wuz at college togurr. An' den he say: 'Now you git right
off dis land. Ef either you or you marster ever put you foot on it,
you'll git de same thing agin.' An' I tell you, Edinburg he come
way, 'cause he sutney had worry me. I ain' stop to see Nancy or nobody; I jes come 'long, shakin' de dust, I tell you. An' as I come 'long
de road I pass Miss Charlotte walkin' on de lawn by herself, an'
she call me: 'Why, hi! ain' dat Edinburg?'

"She look so sweet, an' her voice soun' so cool, I say, 'Yes'm; how
you do, missis?' An' she say, she ve'y well, an' how I been, an' whar
I gwine? I tell her I ain' feelin' so well, dat I gwine home. 'Hi!' she
say, 'is anybody treat you bad?' An' I tell her, 'Yes'm.' An' she say,
'Oh! Nancy don' mean nuttin by dat; dat you mus'n mine what
womens say, an' do, 'cause dee feel sorry for it next minute; an'
sometimes dee kyarn help it, or maybe hit you fault; an' anyhow,
you ought to be willin' to overlook it; an' I better go back an'
wait till to-morrow—ef—ef I ain' 'bleeged to git home today.'

"She got mighty mixed up in de een part o' dat, an' she looked mighty anxious 'bout me an' Nancy; an' I tell her, 'No'm, I 'bleeged to git home.'

"Well, when I got home Marse George he warn know all dat gwine on; but I mighty sick—dat man done beat me so; an' he ax me what de marter, an' I upped an' tell him.

"Gord! I nuver see a man in sich a rage. He call me in de office an' meck me teck off my shut, an' he fyah bust out cryin'. He walked up an' down dat office like a caged lion. Ef he had got he hand on Mr. Darker den, he'd 'a' kilt him, sho!

"He wuz most 'stracted. I don't know what he'd been ef I'd tell him what Nancy tell me. He call for Peter to git he horse torectly, an' he tell me to go an' git some'n' from mammy to put on my back, an' to go to bed torectly, an' not to say nuttin to nobody, but to tell he pa he'd be away for two days, maybe; an' den he got on Reveller an' galloped 'way hard as he could, wid he jaw set farst, an' he heaviest whup clamped in he hand. Gord! I wuz most hopin' he wouldn' meet dat man, 'cause I feared ef he did he'd kill him; an' he would, sho, ef he had meet him right den; dee say he leetle mo' did when he fine him next day, an' he had done been ridin' den all night; he cotch him at a sto' on de road, an' dee say he leetle mo' cut him all to pieces; he drawed a weepin on Marse George, but Marse George wrench it out he hand an' flung it over de fence; an' when dee got him 'way he had weared he whup out on him; an' he got dem whelps on him now, ef he ain' dead. Yes, suh, he ain' let nobody else do dat he ain' do heself, sho!

"Dat done de business!

"He sont Marse George a challenge, but Marse George sont him wud he'll cowhide him again ef he ever heah any mo' from him, an' he 'ain't. Dat perrify him, so he shet he mouf. Den come he ring an' all he pictures an' things back—a gret box on 'em, and not a wud wid 'em. Marse George, I think he know'd dee wuz comin', but dat ain' keep it from huttin him, 'cause he done been 'gaged to Miss Charlotte, an' got he mine riveted to her; an' do' befo' dat dee had stop writin', an' a riff done git twixt 'em, he ain' satisfied in he mine dat she ain't gwine 'pologizee—I know by Nancy; but now he got de confirmation dat he done for good, an' dat de gret gulf fixed 'twix him an' Aberham bosom. An', Gord, suh, twuz torment, sho 'nough! He ain' say nuttin 'bout it, but I see de light done pass from him, an' de darkness done wrap him up in it. In a leetle while you wouldn' 'a' knowed him. Den ole mistis died.

"B'lieve me, ole marster he 'most much hut by Miss Charlotte as Marse George. He meck a 'tempt to buy Nancy for me, so I find out arterward, an' write Jedge Darker he'll pay him anything he'll ax for her, but he letter wuz sont back 'dout any answer. He sutney was mad 'bout it—he say he'd horsewhip him as Marse George did dat urr young puppy, but ole mistis wouldn' le' him do nuttin, and den he grieve heself to death. You see he mighty ole, anyways. He nuver got over ole mistis' death. She had been failin' a long time, an' he ain' tarry long 'hinst her; hit sort o' like breckin up a holler—de ole 'coon goes 'way soon arter dat; an' marster nuver could pin he own collar or buckle he own stock—mistis she al'ays do dat; an' do' Marse George do de bes' he kin, an' mighty willin', he kyarn handle pin like a woman; he hand tremble like a p'inter dog; an' anyways he ain' ole mistis. So ole marster foller her dat next fall, when dee wuz gittin in de corn, an' Marse George he ain' got nobody in de wull left; he all alone in dat gret house, an' I wonder sometimes he ain' die too, 'cause he sutney wuz fond o' ole marster.

"When ole mistis wuz dyin', she tell him to be good to ole marster, an' patient wid him, 'cause he ain' got nobody but him now (ole marster he had jes step out de room to cry); an' Marse George he lean over her an' kiss her an' promise her faithful he would. An' he sutney wuz tender wid him as a woman; an' when ole marster die, he set by him an' hol' he hand an' kiss him sorf, like he wuz ole mistis.

"But, Gord! twuz lonesome arter dat, an' Marse George eyes look wistful, like he al'ays lookin' far 'way; an' Aunt Haly say he see harnts whar walk 'bout in de gret house. She say dee walk dyah constant of nights sence ole marster done alterate de rooms from what dee wuz when he gran'pa buil' 'em, an' dat dee huntin' for dee ole chambers an' kyarn git no rest 'cause dee kyarn fine 'em. I don't know how dat wuz. I know Marse George *he* used to walk about heself mightily of nights. All night long, all night long, I'd heah him tell de chickens crowin' dee second crow, an' some mornin's

I'd go dyah an' he ain' even rumple de bed. I thought sho he wuz gwine die, but I suppose he done 'arn he days to be long in de land, an' dat save him. But hit sutney wuz lonesome, an' he nuver went off de plantation, an' he got older an' older, tell we all thought he wuz gwine die.

"An' one day come jes befo' Christmas, 'bout nigh two year after marster die, Mr. Braxton ride up to de do'. He had done come to teck Marse George home to spen' Christmas wid him. Marse George warn git out it, but Mr. Braxton won' teck no disapp'intment; he say he gwine baptize he boy, an' he done name him after Marse George (he had marry Marse George cousin, Miss Peggy Carter, an' he vite Marse George to de weddin', but he wouldn't go, do' I sutney did want him to go, 'cause I heah Miss Charlotte was nominated to marry Mr. Darker, an' I warn know what done 'come o' dat bright-skinned nigger gal whar I used to know down dyah); an' he say Marse George got to come an' stan' for him, an' gi' him a silver cup an' a gol' rattle. So Marse George he finally promise to come an' spend Christmas Day, an' Mr. Braxton went 'way next mornin', an' den hit tun in an' rain so I feared we couldn' go, but hit cler off de day befo' Christmas Eve an' tun cold. Well, suh, we ain' been nowhar for so long I wuz skittish as a young filly; an' den you know twuz de same ole place.

"We didn' git dyah till supper-time, an' twuz a good one too, 'cause seventy miles dat cold a weather hit whet a man's honger jes like a whetstone.

"Dee sutney wuz glad to see we all. We rid roun' by de back yard to gi' Billy de horses, an' we see dee wuz havin' gret fixin's; an' den we went to de house, jest as some o' de folks run in an' tell 'em we wuz come. When Marse George stept in de hall, dee all clustered roun' him like dee gwine hug him, dee faces fyah dimplin' wid pleasure, an' Miss Peggy she jes reched up an' teck him in her arms an' hug him.

"Dee tell me in de kitchen dat dee wuz been 'spectin' of Miss Charlotte over to spend Christmas too, but de river wuz so high dee s'pose dee couldn' git 'cross. Chile, dat sutney disapp'int me!

"Well, after supper de niggers had a dance. Hit wuz down in de wash-house, an' de table wuz set in de carpenter shop jes' by. Oh,

hit sutney wuz beautiful! Miss Lucy an' Miss Ailsy dee had superin-
tend ev'ything wid dee own hands. So dee wuz down dyah wid
dee ap'ons up to dee chins, an' dee had de big silver strandeliers out
de house, two on each table, an' some o' ole mistis's best damas'
table-clothes, an' ole marster's gret bowl full o' egg-nog; hit look
big as a mill-pond settin' dyah in de cornder; an' dee had flowers
out de greenhouse on de table, an' some o' de chany out de gret
house, an' de dinin'-room cheers set roun' de room. Oh! oh! nuttin
warn too good for niggers dem times; an' de little niggers wuz runnin' roun' right 'stracted, squealin' an' peepin' an' gittin' in de way
onder you foots; an' de mens dee wuz totin' in de wood—gret hickory logs, look like stock whar you gwine saw—an' de fire so big hit
look like you gwine kill hawgs, 'cause hit sutney wuz cold dat
night. Dis nigger ain' nuver gwine forgit it! Jack Forester he had
come 'cross de river to lead de fiddlers, an' he say he had to put de
fiddle onder he coat an' poke he bow in he breeches leg to keep de
strings from poppin', an' dat de river would freeze over sho ef
twarn so high; but twuz jes snortin', an' he had hard wuck to git
over in he skiff, an' Unc' Jeems say he ain' gwine come out he boat-
house no mo' dat night—he done tempt Providence often 'nough dat
day.

"Den ev'ything wuz ready, an' de fiddlers got dee dram an'
chuned up, an' twuz lively, I tell you! Twuz jes as thick in dyah as
blackberries on de blackberry bush, 'cause ev'y gal on de plantation
wuz dyah shakin' her foot for some young buck, an' back-steppin'
for to go 'long. Dem ole sleepers wuz jes a-rockin', an' Jack Forester he wuz callin' de figgers for to wake 'em up. I warn' dancin',
'cause I done got 'ligion an' longst to de chutch since de trouble done
tetch us up so rank; but I tell you my foots wuz pintedly eechchin
for a leetle sop on it, an' I had to come out to keep from crossin' 'em
onst, anyways. Den, too, I had a tetch o' misery in my back, an' I lay
off to git a tas'e o' dat egg-nog out dat big bowl, wid snow-drift
on it, from Miss Lucy—she al'ays mighty fond o' Marse George; so
I slip into de carpenter shop, an' ax her kyarn I do nuttin for her,
an' she laugh an' say, yes, I kin drink her health, an' gi' me a gret
gobletful, an' jes den de white folks come in to 'spec' de tables,
Marse George in de lead, an' dee all fill up dee glasses an' pledge

dee health, an' all de servants', an' a merry Christmas; an' den dee
went in de wash-house to see de dancin', an' maybe to teck a hand
deeself, 'cause white folks' 'ligion ain' like niggers', you know; dee
got so much larnin dee kin dance, an' fool de devil too. An' I stay
roun' a little while, an' den went in de kitchen to see how supper
gittin on, 'cause I wuz so hongry when I got dyah I ain' able to
eat 'nough at one time to 'commodate it, an' de smell o' de tuckeys
an' de gret saddlers o' mutton in de tin-kitchens wuz mos' 'nough
by deeself to feed a right hongry man; an' dyah wuz a whole parcel
o' niggers cookin' an' tunnin 'bout for life, an' dee faces jes as shiny
as ef dee done bas'e 'em wid gravy; an' dyah, settin' back in a cheer
out de way, wid her clean frock up off de flo', wuz dat gal! I sutney
did feel curious.

"I say, 'Hi! name o' Gord! whar'd you come from?' She say, 'Oh,
Marster! ef heah ain' dat free nigger agin!' An' ev'ybody laughed.

"Well, presny we come out, 'cause Nancy warn see de dancin', an'
we stop a leetle while 'hind de cornder out de wind while she tell
me 'bout ev'ything. An' she say dat's all a lie she tell me dat day
'bout Mr. Darker an' Miss Charlotte; an' he done gone 'way now
for good 'cause he so low down an' wuthless dee kyarn nobody
stand him; an' all he warn marry Miss Charlotte for is to git her
niggers. But Nancy say Miss Charlotte nuver could abide him; he
so 'sateful, 'spressly sence she fine out what a lie he told 'bout Marse
George. You know, Mr. Darker he done meck 'em think Marse
George sont me dyah to fine out ef he done come home, an' den
dat he fall on him wid he weepin when he ain' noticin' him, an'
sort o' out de way too, an' git two urr mens to hold him while he
beat him, all 'cause he in love wid Miss Charlotte. D'you ever, ever
heah sich a lie? An' Nancy say, do' Miss Charlotte ain' b'lieve it all
togerr, hit look so reasonable she done le' de ole jedge an' her ma,
who wuz 'pending on what she heah, 'duce her to send back he
things; an' dee ain' know no better not tell after de old jedge die;
den dee fine out 'bout de whuppin me, an' all; an' den Miss Charlotte know huccome I ain' gwine stay dat day; an' she say dee was
sutney outdone 'bout it, but it too late den; an' Miss Charlotte
kyarn do nuttin but cry 'bout it, an' dat she did, pintedly, 'cause she
done lost Marse George, an' done 'stroy he life; an' she nuver keer

'bout nobody else sep Marse George, Nancy say. Mr. Clarke he
hangin' on, but Miss Charlotte she done tell him pintedly she ain'
nuver gwine marry nobody. An' dee jes done come, she say, 'cause
dee had to go 'way round by de rope ferry 'long o' de river bein' so
high, an' dee ain' know tell dee done git out de ker'idge an' in de
house dat we all wuz heah; an' Nancy say she glad dee ain', 'cause
she 'feared ef dee had, Miss Charlotte wouldn' 'a come.

"Den I tell her all 'bout Marse George, cause I know she 'bleeged
to tell Miss Charlotte. Twuz powerful cold out dyah, but I ain' mine
dat, chile. Nancy she done had to wrop her arms up in her ap'on
an' she kyarn meck no zistance 'tall, an' dis nigger ain' keerin nuttin
'bout cold den.

"An' jes den two ladies come out de carpenter shop an' went 'long
to de wash-house, an' Nancy say, 'Dyah Miss Charlotte now'; an'
twuz Miss Lucy an' Miss Charlotte; an' we heah Miss Lucy coaxin'
Miss Charlotte to go, tellin' her she kin come right out; an' jes den
dee wuz a gret shout, an' we went in hinst 'em. Twuz Marse
George had done teck de fiddle, an' ef he warn' natchelly layin' hit
down! he wuz up at de urr een o' de room, 'way from we all, 'cause
we wuz at de do', nigh Miss Charlotte whar she wuz standin' 'hind
some on 'em, wid her eyes on him mighty timid, like she hidin' from
him, an' ev'y nigger in de room wuz on dat flo'. Gord! suh, dee wuz
grinnin' so dee warn' a toof in dat room you couldn' git you tweez-
ers on; an' you couldn' heah a wud, dee so proud o' Marse George
playin' for 'em.

"Well, dee danced tell you couldn' tell which wuz de clappers an'
which de back-steppers; de whole house look like it wuz rockin';
an' presney somebody say supper, an' dat stop 'em, an' dee wuz a
spell for a minute, an' Marse George standin' dyah wid de fiddle in
he hand. He face wuz tunned away, an' he wuz studyin'—studyin'
'bout dat urr Christmas so long ago—an' sudney he face drapt down
on de fiddle, an' he drawed he bow 'cross de strings, an' dat chune
begin to whisper right sorf. Hit begin so low ev'ybody had to stop
talkin' an' hold dee mouf to heah it; an' Marse George he ain' know
nuttin 'bout it, he done gone back, an' standin' dyah in de gret hall
playin' it for Miss Charlotte, whar done come down de steps wid
her little blue foots an' gret fan, an' standin' dyah in her dim blue

dress an' her fyah arms, an' her gret eyes lookin' in he face so earnest, whar he ain' gwine nuver speak to no mo'. I see it by de way he look—an' de fiddle wuz jes pleadin'. He drawed it out jes as fine as a stran' o' Miss Charlotte's hyah.

"Hit so sweet, Miss Charlotte, mun, she couldn' stan' it; she made to de do'; an' jes while she watchin' Marse George to keep him from seein' her he look dat way, an' he eyes fall right into hern.

"Well, suh, de fiddle drapt down on de flo'—perlang!—an' he face wuz white as a sycamore limb.

"Dee say twuz a swimmin' in de head he had; an' Jack say de whole fiddle warn' wuff de five dollars.

"Me an' Nancy followed 'em tell dee went in de house, an' den we come back to de shop whar de supper wuz gwine on, an' got we all supper an' a leetle sop o' dat yaller gravy out dat big bowl, an' den we all rejourned to de wash-house agin, an' got onder de big bush o' misseltow whar hangin' from de jice, an' ef you ever see scufflin' dat's de time.

"Well, me an' she had jes done lay off de whole Christmas, when wud come dat Marse George want he horses.

"I went, but it sutney breck me up; an' I wonder whar de name o' Gord Marse George gwine sen' me dat cold night, an' jes as I got to de do' Marse George an' Mr. Braxton come out, an' I know tor-ectly Marse George wuz gwine home. I seen he face by de light o' de lantern, an' twuz set jes rigid as a rock.

"Mr. Braxton he wuz beggin' him to stay; he tell him he ruinin' he life, dat he sho dee's some mistake, an' twill be all right. An' all de answer Marse George meck wuz to swing heself up in de saddle, an' Reveller he look like he gwine fyah 'stracted. He al'ays mighty fool anyways when he git cold, dat horse wuz.

"Well, we come 'long 'way, an' Mr. Braxton an' two mens come down to de river wid lanterns to see us cross, 'cause twuz dark as pitch, sho 'nough.

"An' jes 'fo' I started I got one o' de mens to hol' my horses, an' I went in de kitchen to git warm, an' dyah Nancy wuz. An' she say Miss Charlotte upsteairs cryin' right now, 'cause she think Marse George gwine cross de river 'count o' her, an' she whimper a little herself when I tell her good-by. But twuz too late den.

"Well, de river wuz jes natchelly b'ilin', an' hit soun' like a mill-dam roarin' by; an' when we got dyah Marse George tunned to me an' tell me he reckon I better go back. I ax him whar he gwine, an' he say, 'Home.' 'Den I gwine wid you,' I says. I wuz mighty skeered, but me an' Marse George wuz boys togerr; an' he plunged right in, an' I after him.

"Gord! twuz cold as ice; an' we hadn't got in befo' bofe horses wuz swimmin' for life. He holler to me to byah de myah head up de stream; an' I did try, but what's a nigger to dat water! Hit jes pick me up an' dash me down like I ain' no mo'n a chip, an' de fust thing I know I gwine down de stream like a piece of bark, an' water washin' all over me. I knowed den I gone, an' I hollered for Marse George for help. I heah him answer me not to git skeered, but to hold on; but de myah wuz lungin' an' de water wuz all over me like ice, an' den I washed off de myah back, an' got drownded.

"I 'member comin' up an' hollerin' agin for help, but I know den 'tain' no use, dee ain' no help den, an' I got to pray to Gord, an' den some'n hit me an' I went down agin, an'—de next thing I know I wuz in de bed, an' I heah 'em talkin' 'bout wherr I dead or not, an' I ain' know myself tell I taste de whiskey dee po'rin' down my jugular.

"An' den dee tell me 'bout how when I hollered Marse George tun back an' struck out for me for life, an' how jes as I went down de last time he cotch me an' helt on to me tell we wash down to whar de bank curve, an' dyah de current wuz so rapid hit yuck him off Reveller back, but he helt on to de reins tell de horse lunge so he hit him wid he fo' foot an' breck he collar-bone, an' den he had to let him go, an' jes helt on to me; an' jes den we wash up agin de bank an' cotch in a tree, an' de mens got dyah quick as dee could, an' when dee retched us Marse George wuz holdin' on to me, an' had he arm wropped roun' a limb, an' we wuz lodged in de crotch, an' bofe jes as dead as a nail; an' de myah she got out, but Reveller he wuz drownded, wid his foot cotch in de rein an' de saddle tunned onder he side; an' dee ain' know wherr Marse George ain' dead too, 'cause he not only drownded, but he lef' arm broke up nigh de shoulder.

"An' dee say Miss Charlotte she 'mos' 'stracted; dat de fust thing anybody know 'bout it wuz when some de servants bust in de hall an' holler, an' say Marse George an' me done bofe washed 'way an' drownded, an' dat she drapt down dead on de flo', an' when dee bring her to she 'low to Miss Lucy dat she de 'casion on he death; an' dee say dat when de mens wuz totin' him in de house, an' wuz shufflin' de feets not to meck no noige, an' a little piece o' blue silk drapt out he breast whar somebody picked up an' gin Miss Lucy, Miss Charlotte breck right down agin; an' some on 'em say she sutney did keer for him; an' now when he layin' upstairs dyah dead, hit too late for him ever to know it.

"Well, suh, I couldn' teck it in dat Marse George and Reveller wuz dead, an' jes den somebody say Marse George done comin' to an' dee gi' me so much whiskey I went to sleep.

"An' next mornin' I got up an' went to Marse George room, an' see him layin' dyah in de bed, wid he face so white an' he eyes so tired-lookin', an' he ain' know me no mo' 'n ef he nuver see me, an' I couldn' stan' it; I jes drap down on de flo' an' bust out cryin'. Gord! suh, I couldn' help it, 'cause Reveller wuz drownded, an' Marse George he wuz mos' gone.

"An' he came nigher goin' yit, 'cause he had sich a strain, an' been so long in de water, he heart done got numbed, an' he got 'lirium, an' all de time he thought he tryin' to git 'cross de river to see Miss Charlotte, an' hit so high he kyarn git dyah.

"Hit sutney wuz pitiful to see him layin' dyah tossin' an' pitchin' not knowin' whar he wuz, tell it teck all Mr. Braxton an' me could do to keep him in de bed, an' de doctors say he kyarn hol' out much longer.

"An' all dis time Miss Charlotte she wuz gwine 'bout de house wid her face right white, an' Nancy say she don' do nuttin all day long in her room but cry an' say her pra'rs, prayin' for Marse George whar dyin' upsteairs by 'count o' not knowin' she love him, an' I tell Nancy how he honin' all de time to see her, an' how he constant callin' her name.

"Well, so twuz, tell he mos' done wyah heself out; an' jes lay dyah wid his face white as de pillow, an' he gret pitiful eyes rollin' 'bout so restless, like he still lookin' for her whar he all de time callin' her name, an' kyarn git 'cross dat river to see.

"An' one evenin 'bout sunset he 'peared to be gwine; he weaker 'n he been at all, he ain' able to scuffle no mo', an' jes layin' dyah so quiet, an' presney he say, lookin' mighty wistful,

" 'Edinburg, I'm going' to-night; ef I don' git 'cross dis time, I'll gin't up.'

"Mr. Braxton was standin' nigh de head o' de bed, an' he say, 'Well, by Gord! he *shall* see her!'—jes so. An' he went out de room, an' to Miss Charlotte do', an' call her, an' tell her she got to come, ef she don't, he'll die dat night; an' fust thing I know, Miss Lucy bring Miss Charlotte in, wid her face right white, but jes as tender as a angel's, an' she come an' stan' by de side de bed, an' lean down over him, an' call he name, 'George!'—jes so.

"An' Marse George he ain' answer; he jes look at her study for a minute, an' den he forehead got smooth, an' he tun he eyes to me, an' say, 'Edinburg, I'm 'cross.' "

A BLACKJACK BARGAINER

O. Henry

[WILLIAM SYDNEY PORTER]

From *Whirligigs* by O. Henry (William Sydney Porter), 1910; first published in *Munsey's Magazine,* XXV (August, 1901), 620-627, where a subtitle was added, "The Story of the Strange Ending of the Goree-Coltrane Feud."

William Sydney Porter (1862-1910) grew up in his native state of North Carolina and went afterward to Texas, where he began journalistic writing while engaged in various other activities. Convicted of embezzlement at the bank in Austin where he worked, he served three years in prison and there began writing the stories which he was to produce steadily until his death. Though he often employed Southern settings, his most characteristic stories picture the inhabitants of New York, his "Bagdad on the Subway," at some minor and ironic crisis in life. Among his books of stories are *Cabbages and Kings* (1904), *The Four Million* (1906), *Heart of the West* (1907), *The Gentle Grafter* (1908), and *Roads of Destiny* (1909). For O. Henry's life see E. Hudson Long, *O. Henry: The Man and His Work* (1949) and Gerald Langford, *Alias O. Henry: A Biography of William Sydney Porter* (1957).

The most disreputable thing in Yancey Goree's law office was Goree himself, sprawled in his creaky old armchair. The rickety little office, built of red brick, was set flush with the street—the main street of the town of Bethel.

Bethel rested upon the foot-hills of the Blue Ridge. Above it the mountains were piled to the sky. Far below it the turbid Catawba gleamed yellow along its disconsolate valley.

The June day was at its sultriest hour. Bethel dozed in the tepid shade. Trade was not. It was so still that Goree, reclining in his chair, distinctly heard the clicking of the chips in the grand-jury room, where the "court-house gang" was playing poker. From the open back door of the office a well-worn path meandered across the grassy lot to the court-house. The treading out of that path had cost Goree all he ever had—first inheritance of a few thousand dollars, next the old family home, and latterly the last shreds of his self-respect and manhood. The "gang" had cleaned him out. The broken gambler had turned drunkard and parasite; he had lived to see this day come when the men who had stripped him denied him a seat at the game. His word was no longer to be taken. The daily bout at cards had arranged itself accordingly, and to him was assigned the ignoble part of the onlooker. The sheriff, the county clerk, a sportive deputy, a gay attorney, and a chalk-faced man hailing "from the valley," sat at table, and the sheared one was thus tacitly advised to go and grow more wool.

Soon wearying of his ostracism, Goree had departed for his office, muttering to himself as he unsteadily traversed the unlucky pathway. After a drink of corn whiskey from a demijohn under the table, he had flung himself into the chair, staring, in a sort of maudlin apathy, out at the mountains immersed in the summer haze. The little white patch he saw away up on the side of Blackjack was Laurel, the village near which he had been born and bred. There, also, was the birthplace of the feud between the Gorees and the Coltranes. Now no direct heir of the Gorees survived except this plucked and singed bird of misfortune. To the Coltranes, also, but one male supporter was left—Colonel Abner Coltrane, a man of substance and standing, a member of the State Legislature, and a contemporary with Goree's father. The feud had been a typical one of the region; it had left a red record of hate, wrong and slaughter.

But Yancey Goree was not thinking of feuds. His befuddled brain was hopelessly attacking the problem of the future maintenance of himself and his favorite follies. Of late, old friends of the family had seen to it that he had whereof to eat and a place to sleep, but whiskey they would not buy for him, and he must have whiskey. His law business was extinct; no case had been intrusted to him in two years. He had been a borrower and a sponge, and it seemed that if he fell no lower it would be from lack of opportunity. One more chance—he was saying to himself—if he had one more stake at the game, he thought he could win; but he had nothing left to sell, and his credit was more than exhausted.

He could not help smiling, even in his misery, as he thought of the man to whom, six months before, he had sold the old Goree homestead. There had come from "back yan'" in the mountains two of the strangest creatures, a man named Pike Garvey and his wife. "Back yan'," with a wave of the hand toward the hills, was understood among the mountaineers to designate the remotest fast-nesses, the unplumbed gorges, the haunts of lawbreakers, the wolf's den, and the boudoir of the bear. In the cabin far up on Black-jack's shoulder, in the wildest part of these retreats, this odd couple had lived for twenty years. They had neither dog nor children to mitigate the heavy silence of the hills. Pike Garvey was little known in the settlements, but all who had dealt with him pronounced him "crazy as a loon." He acknowledged no occupation save that of a squirrel hunter, but he "moonshined" occasionally by way of diversion. Once the "revenues" had dragged him from his lair, fighting silently and desperately like a terrier, and he had been sent to state's prison for two years. Released, he popped back into his hole like an angry weasel.

Fortune, passing over many anxious wooers, made a freakish flight into Blackjack's bosky pockets to smile upon Pike and his faithful partner.

One day a party of spectacled, knickerbockered, and altogether absurd prospectors invaded the vicinity of the Garveys' cabin. Pike lifted his squirrel rifle off the hooks and took a shot at them at long range on the chance of their being revenues. Happily he missed, and the unconscious agents of good luck drew nearer, disclosing their innocence of anything resembling law or justice. Later on, they offered the Garveys an enormous quantity of ready, green, crisp money for their thirty-acre patch of cleared land, mentioning, as an excuse for such a mad action, some irrelevant and inadequate nonsense about a bed of mica underlying the said property.

When the Garveys became possessed of so many dollars that they faltered in computing them, the deficiencies of life on Blackjack began to grow prominent. Pike began to talk of new shoes, a hogshead of tobacco to set in the corner, a new lock to his rifle; and, leading Martella to a certain spot on the mountain-side, he pointed out to her how a small cannon—doubtless a thing not beyond the scope of their fortune in price—might be planted so as to command and defend the sole accessible trail to the cabin, to the confusion of revenues and meddling strangers forever.

But Adam reckoned without his Eve. These things represented to him the applied power of wealth, but there slumbered in his dingy cabin an ambition that soared far above his primitive wants. Somewhere in Mrs. Garvey's bosom still survived a spot of femininity unstarved by twenty years of Blackjack. For so long a time the sounds in her ears had been the scaly-barks dropping in the woods at noon, and the wolves singing among the rocks at night, and it was enough to have purged her vanities. She had grown fat and sad and yellow and dull. But when the means came, she felt a rekindled desire to assume the perquisites of her sex—to sit at tea tables; to buy inutile things; to whitewash the hideous veracity of life with a little form and ceremony. So she coldly vetoed Pike's proposed system of fortifications, and announced that they would descend upon the world, and gyrate socially.

And thus, at length, it was decided, and the thing done. The village of Laurel was their compromise between Mrs. Garvey's preference for one of the large valley towns and Pike's hankering for primeval solitudes. Laurel yielded a halting round of feeble social distractions comportable with Martella's ambitions, and was not entirely without recommendation to Pike, its contiguity to the mountains presenting advantages for sudden retreat in case fashionable society should make it advisable.

Their descent upon Laurel had been coincident with Yancey Goree's feverish desire to convert property into cash, and they bought the old Goree homestead, paying four thousand dollars ready money into the spendthrift's shaking hands.

Thus it happened that while the disreputable last of the Gorees sprawled in his disreputable office, at the end of his row, spurned by the cronies whom he had gorged, strangers dwelt in the halls of his fathers.

A cloud of dust was rolling slowly up the parched street, with something travelling in the midst of it. A little breeze wafted the cloud to one side, and a new, brightly painted carryall, drawn by a slothful gray horse, became visible. The vehicle deflected from the middle of the street as it neared Goree's office, and stopped in the gutter directly in front of his door.

On the front seat sat a gaunt, tall man, dressed in black broadcloth, his rigid hands incarcerated in yellow kid gloves. On the back seat was a lady who triumphed over the June heat. Her stout form was armoured in a skin-tight silk dress of the description known as "changeable," being a gorgeous combination of shifting hues. She sat erect, waving a much-ornamented fan, with her eyes fixed stonily far down the street. However Martella Garvey's heart might be rejoicing at the pleasures of her new life, Blackjack had done his work with her exterior. He had carved her countenance to the image of emptiness and inanity; had imbued her with the stolidity of his crags, and the reserve of his hushed interiors. She always seemed to hear, whatever her surroundings were, the scaly-barks falling and pattering down the mountainside. She could always hear the awful silence of Blackjack sounding through the stillest of nights.

Goree watched this solemn equipage, as it drove to his door, with only faint interest; but when the lank driver wrapped the reins about his whip, and awkwardly descended, and stepped into the office, he rose unsteadily to receive him, recognizing Pike Garvey, the new, the transformed, the recently civilized.

The mountaineer took the chair Goree offered him. They who cast doubts upon Garvey's soundness of mind had a strong witness in the man's countenance. His face was too long, a dull saffron in hue, and immobile as a statue's. Pale-blue, unwinking round eyes without lashes added to the singularity of his gruesome visage. Goree was at a loss to account for the visit.

"Everything all right at Laurel, Mr. Garvey?" he inquired.

"Everything all right, sir, and mighty pleased is Missis Garvey and me with the property. Missis Garvey likes yo' old place, and she likes the neighbourhood. Society is what she 'lows she wants, and she is gettin' of it. The Rogerses, the Hapgoods, the Pratts, and the Troys hev been to see Missis Garvey, and she hev et meals to most of thar houses. The best folks hev axed her to differ'nt kinds of doin's. I cyan't say, Mr. Goree, that sech things suits me—fur me, give me them thar." Garvey's huge, yellow-gloved hand flourished in the direction of the mountains. "That's whar I b'long, 'mongst the wild honey bees and the b'ars. But that ain't what I come fur to say, Mr. Goree. Thar's somethin' you got what me and Missis Garvey wants to buy."

"Buy!" echoed Goree. "From me?" Then he laughed harshly. "I reckon you are mistaken about that. I reckon you are mistaken about that. I sold out to you, as you yourself expressed it, 'lock, stock and barrel.' There isn't even a ramrod left to sell."

"You've got it; and we 'uns want it. 'Take the money,' says Missis Garvey, 'and buy it fa'r and squar'.'"

Goree shook his head. "The cupboard's bare," he said.

"We've riz," pursued the mountaineer, undeflected from his object, "a heap. We was pore as possums, and now we could hev folks to dinner every day. We been reco'nized, Missis Garvey says, by the best society. But there's somethin' we need we ain't got. She says it ought to been put in the 'ventory ov the sale, but it tain't thar. 'Take the money, then,' she says, 'and buy it fa'r and squar'.'"

"Out with it," said Goree, his racked nerves growing impatient.

Garvey threw his slouch hat upon the table, and leaned forward, fixing his unblinking eyes upon Goree's.

"There's a old feud," he said distinctly and slowly, "'tween you 'uns and the Coltranes."

Goree frowned ominously. To speak of his feud to a feudist is a serious breach of the mountain etiquette. The man from "back yan'" knew it as well as the lawyer did.

"Na offense," he went on, "but purely in the way of business. Missis Garvey hev studied all about feuds. Most of the quality folks in the mountains hev 'em. The Settles and the Goforths, the Rankins and the Boyds, the Silers and the Galloways, hev all been cyarin' on feuds f'om twenty to a hundred year. The last man to drap was when yo' uncle, Jedge Paisley Goree, 'journed co't and shot Len Coltrane f'om the bench. Missis Garvey and me we come f'om the po' white trash. Nobody wouldn't pick a feud with we 'uns, no mo'n with a fam'ly of tree-toads. Quality people everywhar, says Missis

Garvey, has feuds. We 'uns ain't quality, but we're buyin' into it as fur as we can. 'Take the money, then,' says Missis Garvey, 'and buy Mr. Goree's feud, fa'r and squar'.'"

The squirrel hunter straightened a leg half across the room, drew a roll of bills from his pocket, and threw them on the table.

"Thar's two hundred dollars, Mr. Goree; what you would call a fa'r price for a feud that's been 'lowed to run down like yourn hev. Thar's only you left to cyar' on yo' side of it, and you'd make mighty po' killin'. I'll take it off yo' hands, and it'll set me and Missis Garvey up among the quality. Thar's the money."

The little roll of currency on the table slowly untwisted itself, writhing and jumping as its folds relaxed. In the silence that followed Garvey's last speech the rattling of the poker chips in the court-house could be plainly heard. Goree knew that the sheriff had just won a pot, for the subdued whoop with which he always greeted a victory floated across the square upon the crinkly heat waves. Beads of moisture stood on Goree's brow. Stooping, he drew the wicker-covered demijohn from under the table, and filled a tumbler from it.

"A little corn liquor, Mr. Garvey? Of course you are joking about —what you spoke of? Opens quite a new market, doesn't it? Feuds, prime, two-fifty to three. Feuds, slightly damaged—two hundred, I believe you said, Mr. Garvey?"

Goree laughed self-consciously.

The mountaineer took the glass Goree handed him, and drank the whiskey without a tremor of the lids of his staring eyes. The lawyer applauded the feat by a look of envious admiration. He poured his own drink, and took it like a drunkard, by gulps, and with shudders at the smell and taste.

"Two hundred," repeated Garvey. "Thar's the money."

A sudden passion flared up in Goree's brain. He struck the table with his fist. One of the bills flipped over and touched his hand. He flinched as if something had stung him.

"Do you come to me," he shouted, "seriously with such a ridiculous, insulting, darned-fool proposition?"

"It's fa'r and squar'," said the squirrel hunter, but he reached out his hand as if to take back the money; and then Goree knew that his own flurry of rage had not been from pride or resentment, but from anger at himself, knowing that he would set foot in the deeper depths that were being opened to him. He turned in an instant from an outraged gentleman to an anxious chafferer recommending his goods.

"Don't be in a hurry, Garvey," he said, his face crimson and his speech thick. "I accept your p-p-proposition, though it's dirt cheap at two hundred. A t-trade's all right when both p-purchaser and b-buyer are s-satisfied. Shall I w-wrap it up for you, Mr. Garvey?"

Garvey rose, and shook out his broadcloth. "Missis Garvey will be pleased. You air out of it, and it stands Coltrane and Garvey. Just a scrap ov writin', Mr. Goree, you bein' a lawyer, to show we traded."

Goree seized a sheet of paper and a pen. The money was clutched in his moist hand. Everything else suddenly seemed to grow trivial and light.

"Bill of sale, by all means. 'Right, title, and interest in and to' . . . 'forever warrant and——' No, Garvey, we'll have to leave out that 'defend,' " said Goree with a loud laugh. "You'll have to defend this title yourself."

The mountaineer received the amazing screed that the lawyer handed him, folded it with immense labour, and placed it carefully in his pocket.

Goree was standing near the window. "Step here," he said, raising his finger, "and I'll show you your recently purchased enemy. There he goes, down the other side of the street."

The mountaineer crooked his long frame to look through the window in the direction indicated by the other. Colonel Abner Coltrane, an erect, portly gentleman of about fifty, wearing the inevitable long, double-breasted frock coat of the Southern lawmaker, and an old high silk hat, was passing on the opposite sidewalk. As Garvey looked, Goree glanced at his face. If there be such a thing as yellow wolf, here was its counterpart. Garvey snarled as his unhuman eyes followed the moving figure, disclosing long, amber-coloured fangs.

"Is that him? Why, that's the man who sent me to the pen'tentiary once!"

"He used to be district attorney," said Goree carelessly. "And, by the way, he's a first-class shot."

"I kin hit a squirrel's eye at a hundred yard," said Garvey. "So that thar's Coltrane! I made a better trade than I was thinkin'. I'll take keer ov this feud, Mr. Goree, better'n you ever did!"

He moved toward the door, but lingered there, betraying a slight perplexity.

"Anything else to-day?" inquired Goree with frothy sarcasm. "Any family traditions, ancestral ghosts, or skeletons in the closet? Prices as low as the lowest."

"Thar was another thing," replied the unmoved squirrel hunter, "that Missis Garvey was thinkin' of. 'Tain't so much in my line as t'other, but she wanted partic'lar that I should inquire, and ef you was willin', 'pay fur it,' she says, 'fa'r and squar'.' Thar's a buryin' groun', as you know, Mr. Goree, in the yard of yo' old place, under the cedars. Them that lies thar is yo' folks what was killed by the Coltranes. The monyments has the names on 'em. Missis Garvey says a fam'ly buryin' groun' is a sho' sign of quality. She says ef we git the feud, thar's somethin' else ought to go with it. The names on them monyments is 'Goree,' but they can be changed to ourn by——"

"Go! Go!" screamed Goree, his face turning purple. He stretched out both hands toward the mountaineer, his fingers hooked and shaking. "Go, you ghoul! Even a Ch-Chinaman protects the g-graves of his ancestors—go!"

The squirrel hunter slouched out of the door to his carryall. While he was climbing over the wheel Goree was collecting, with feverish celerity, the money that had fallen from his hand to the floor. As the vehicle slowly turned about, the sheep, with a coat of newly grown wool, was hurrying, in indecent haste, along the path to the court-house.

At three o'clock in the morning they brought him back to his office, shorn and unconscious. The sheriff, the sportive deputy, the county clerk, and the gay attorney carried him, the chalk-faced man "from the valley" acting as escort.

"On the table," said one of them, and they deposited him there among the litter of his unprofitable books and papers.

"Yance thinks a lot of a pair of deuces when he's liquored up," sighed the sheriff reflectively.

"Too much," said the gay attorney. "A man has no business to play poker who drinks as much as he does. I wonder how much he dropped to-night."

"Close to two hundred. What I wonder is whar he got it. Yance ain't had a cent fur over a month, I know."

"Struck a client, maybe. Well, let's get home before daylight. He'll be all right when he wakes up, except for a sort of beehive about the cranium."

The gang slipped away through the early morning twilight. The next eye to gaze upon the miserable Goree was the orb of day. He peered through the uncurtained window, first deluging the sleeper in a flood of faint gold, but soon pouring upon the mottled red of his flesh a searching, white, summer heat. Goree stirred, half unconsciously, among the table's débris, and turned his face from the window. His movement dislodged a heavy law book, which crashed upon the floor. Opening his eyes, he saw, bending over him, a man in a black frock coat. Looking higher, he discovered a well-worn silk hat, and beneath it the kindly, smooth face of Colonel Abner Coltrane.

A little uncertain of the outcome, the colonel waited for the other to make some sign of recognition. Not in twenty years had male members of these two families faced each other in peace. Goree's eyelids puckered as he strained his blurred sight toward this visitor, and then he smiled serenely.

"Have you brought Stella and Lucy over to play?" he said calmly.

"Do you know me, Yancey?" asked Coltrane.

"Of course I do. You brought me a whip with a whistle in the end."

So he had—twenty-four years ago; when Yancey's father was his best friend.

Goree's eyes wandered about the room. The colonel understood. "Lie still, and I'll bring you some," said he. There was a pump in the yard at the rear, and Goree closed his eyes, listening with rapture to the click of its handle, and the bubbling of the falling stream. Coltrane brought a pitcher of the cool water, and held it for him to drink. Presently Goree sat up—a most forlorn object, his summer suit of flax soiled and crumpled, his discreditable head tousled and unsteady. He tried to wave one of his hands toward the colonel.

"Ex-excuse—everything, will you?" he said. "I must have drunk too much whiskey last night, and gone to bed on the table." His brows knitted into a puzzled frown.

"Out with the boys a while?" asked Coltrane kindly.

"No, I went nowhere. I haven't had a dollar to spend in the last two months. Struck the demijohn too often, I reckon, as usual."

Colonel Coltrane touched him on the shoulder.

"A little while ago, Yancey," he began, "you asked me if I had brought Stella and Lucy over to play. You weren't quite awake then, and must have been dreaming you were a boy again. You are awake now, and I want you to listen to me. I have come from Stella and Lucy to their old playmate, and to my old friend's son. They know that I am going to bring you home with me, and you will find them as ready with a welcome as they were in the old days. I want you to come to my house and stay until you are yourself again, and as much longer as you will. We heard of your being down in the world, and in the midst of temptation, and we agreed that you should come over and play at our house once more. Will you come, my boy? Will you drop our old family trouble and come with me?"

"Trouble!" said Goree, opening his eyes wide. "There was never any trouble between us that I know of. I'm sure we've always been the best friends. But, good Lord, Colonel, how could I go to your home as I am—a drunken wretch, a miserable, degraded spendthrift and gambler——"

He lurched from the table into his armchair, and began to weep maudlin tears, mingled with genuine drops of remorse and shame. Coltrane talked to him persistently and reasonably, reminding him of the simple mountain pleasures of which he had once been so fond, and insisting upon the genuineness of the invitation.

Finally he landed Goree by telling him he was counting upon his help in the engineering and transportation of a large amount of felled timber from a high mountainside to a waterway. He knew that Goree had once invented a device for this purpose—a series of slides and chutes—upon which he had justly prided himself. In an instant the poor fellow, delighted at the idea of his being of use to any one, had paper spread upon the table, and was drawing rapid but pitifully shaky lines in demonstration of what he could and would do.

The man was sickened of the husks; his prodigal heart was turning again toward the mountains. His mind was yet strangely clogged, and his thoughts and memories were returning to his brain one by one, like carrier pigeons over a stormy sea. But Coltrane was satisfied with the progress he had made.

Bethel received the surprise of its existence that afternoon when a Coltrane and a Goree rode amicably together through the town. Side by side they rode, out from the dusty streets and gaping towns-people, down across the creek bridge, and up toward the mountain. The prodigal had brushed and washed and combed himself to a more decent figure, but he was unsteady in the saddle, and he seemed to be deep in the contemplation of some vexing problem. Coltrane left him in his mood, relying upon the influence of changed surroundings to restore his equilibrium.

Once Goree was seized with a shaking fit, and almost came to a collapse. He had to dismount and rest at the side of the road. The colonel, foreseeing such a condition, had provided a small flask of whiskey for the journey but when it was offered to him Goree refused it almost with violence, declaring he would never touch it again. By and by he was recovered, and went quietly enough for a mile or two. Then he pulled up his horse suddenly, and said:

"I lost two hundred dollars last night, playing poker. Now, where did I get that money?"

"Take it easy, Yancey. The mountain air will soon clear it up. We'll go fishing, first thing, at the Pinnacle Falls. The trout are jumping there like bullfrogs. We'll take Stella and Lucy along, and have a picnic on Eagle Rock. Have you forgotten how a hickory-cured-ham sandwich tastes, Yancey, to a hungry fisherman?"

Evidently the colonel did not believe the story of his lost wealth; so Goree retired again into brooding silence.

By late afternoon they had travelled ten of the twelve miles between Bethel and Laurel. Half a mile this side of Laurel lay the old Goree place; a mile or two beyond the village lived the Coltranes.

The road was now steep and laborious, but the compensations were many. The tilted aisles of the forest were opulent with leaf and bird and bloom. The tonic air put to shame the pharmacopœia. The glades were dark with mossy shade, and bright with shy rivulets winking from the ferns and laurels. On the lower side they viewed, framed in the near foliage, exquisite sketches of the far valley swooning in its opal haze.

Coltrane was pleased to see that his companion was yielding to the spell of the hills and woods. For now they had but to skirt the base of Painter's Cliff; to cross Elder Branch and mount the hill beyond, and Goree would have to face the squandered home of his fathers. Every rock he passed, every tree, every foot of the roadway, was familiar to him. Though he had forgotten the woods, they thrilled him like the music of *"Home, Sweet Home."*

They rounded the cliff, descended into Elder Branch, and paused there to let the horses drink and splash in the swift water. On the right was a rail fence that cornered there, and followed the road and stream. Inclosed by it was the old apple orchard of the home place; the house was yet concealed by the brow of the steep hill. Inside and along the fence, pokeberries, elders, sassafras, and sumac grew high and dense. At a rustle of their branches, both Goree and Coltrane glanced up, and saw a long, yellow, wolfish face above the fence, staring at them with pale, unwinking eyes. The head quickly disappeared; there was a violent swaying of the bushes, and an ungainly figure ran up through the apple orchard in the direction of the house, zig-zagging among the trees.

"That's Garvey," said Coltrane; "the man you sold out to. There's no doubt but he's considerably cracked. I had to send him up for moonshining once, several years ago, in spite of the fact that I believed him irresponsible. Why, what's the matter, Yancey?"

Goree was wiping his forehead, and his face had lost its colour. "Do I look queer, too?" he asked, trying to smile. "I'm just remembering a few more things." Some of the alcohol had evaporated from his brain. "I recollect now where I got that two hundred dollars."

"Don't think of it," said Coltrane cheerfully. "Later on we'll figure it all out together."

They rode out of the branch, and when they reached the foot of the hill Goree stopped again.

"Did you ever suspect I was a very vain kind of fellow, Colonel?" he asked. "Sort of foolish proud about appearances?"

The colonel's eyes refused to wander to the soiled, sagging suit of flax and the faded slouch hat.

"It seems to me," he replied, mystified, but humouring him, "I remember a young buck about twenty, with the tightest coat, the sleekest hair, and the prancingest saddle horse in the Blue Ridge."

"Right you are," said Goree eagerly. "And it's in me yet, though it don't show. Oh, I'm as vain as a turkey gobbler, and as proud as Lucifer. I'm going to ask you to indulge this weakness of mine in a little matter."

"Speak out, Yancey. We'll create you Duke of Laurel and Baron of Blue Ridge, if you choose; and you shall have a feather out of Stella's peacock's tail to wear in your hat."

"I'm in earnest. In a few minutes we'll pass the house up there on the hill where I was born, and where my people have lived for nearly a century. Strangers live there now—and look at me! I am about to show myself to them ragged and poverty-stricken, a wastrel and a beggar. Colonel Coltrane, I'm ashamed to do it. I want you to let me wear your coat and hat until we are out of sight beyond. I know you think it a foolish pride, but I want to make as good a showing as I can when I pass the old place."

"Now, what does this mean?" said Coltrane to himself, as he compared his companion's sane looks and quiet demeanour with his strange request. But he was already unbuttoning the coat, assenting readily, as if the fancy were in no wise to be considered strange.

The coat and hat fitted Goree well. He buttoned the former about him with a look of satisfaction and dignity. He and Coltrane were nearly the same size—rather tall, portly, and erect. Twenty-five years were between them, but in appearance they might have been brothers. Goree looked older than his age; his face was puffy and lined; the colonel had the smooth, fresh complexion of a temperate liver. He put on Goree's disreputable old flax coat and faded slouch hat.

"Now," said Goree, taking up the reins, "I'm all right. I want you to ride about ten feet in the rear as we go by, Colonel, so that they can get a good look at me. They'll see I'm no back number yet, by any means. I guess I'll show up pretty well to them once more, anyhow. Let's ride on."

He set out up the hill at a smart trot, the colonel following, as he had been requested.

Goree sat straight in the saddle, with head erect, but his eyes were turned to the right, sharply scanning every shrub and fence and hiding-place in the old homestead yard. Once he muttered to himself, "Will the crazy fool try it, or did I dream half of it?"

It was when he came opposite the little family burying ground that he saw what he had been looking for—a puff of white smoke, coming from the thick cedars in one corner. He toppled so slowly to the left that Coltrane had time to urge his horse to that side, and catch him with one arm.

The squirrel hunter had not overpraised his aim. He had sent the bullet where he intended, and where Goree had expected that it would pass—through the breast of Colonel Abner Coltrane's black frock coat.

Goree leaned heavily against Coltrane, but he did not fall. The horses kept pace, side by side, and the Colonel's arm kept him steady. The little white houses of Laurel shone through the trees, half a mile away. Goree reached out one hand and groped until it rested upon Coltrane's fingers, which held his bridle.

"Good friend," he said, and that was all.

Thus did Yancey Goree, as he rode past his old home, make, considering all things, the best showing that was in his power.

REDBONE

———

Ada Jack Carver

From *Harper's Magazine,* CL (February, 1925), 257-270.

Ada Jack Carver (Mrs. John Snell of Minden, Louisiana) published short stories in magazines during the 1920's. "Redbone" won the Harper Short-Story Prize in 1925.

It is lazy and sweet along the Côte Joyeuse and on into the piney red-clay hills—a land which for nearly four hundred years has been held enthralled by a river. And here among the whites and blacks there dwell in ecstatic squalor a people whom, in the intricate social system of the South, strangers find it difficult to place. For although they may be bartered with, jested with, enjoyed, despised, made friends and enemies of—yet in the eyes of those born to the subtle distinction they are forever beyond the pale.

They are a mixture of Spanish, French, and Indian, and God only knows what besides; and along the Côte Joyeuse, a region given to phrase and to fable, they are dubbed "redbones" because of their dusky skins so oddly, transparently tinted. They are shiftless and slovenly, childlike and treacherous; and yet from somewhere, like a benediction, they have been touched with something precious.

Of this hybrid and tragic tribe was Baptiste Grabbo, planter, and his the story of a man who desired and obtained a son.

One summer morn at a peep-o-day hour this Baptiste set out for Natchitoches, riding his little red pony. His mission was three-fold: first, of course, to get drunk; second, to make a thank-offering to his patron saint, whose business it was to look after him and who did it rather well, all things considered; third, in accordance with a custom that still prevails, to purchase in tribute a gift for his wife, who had been delivered of a fine and lusty son—a man-child born in the crook of a horned moon and destined for great good fortune.

Baptiste rode hard, like a centaur. Above him the frail enchantment of budding clematis filled the woods with light and, reflecting on his fortune, he recalled complacently the insults and insinuations with which since his marriage his relatives had derided his childless estate. Bah! He would make 'em swallow their words, the yellow chinquapin-eaters! He accursed of Heaven?

The glory of fatherhood gave him a heart a-tune to the tumult of summer. There were flowers purple with adoration praying in the grass; wings brushed his cheek; and Baptiste, his mind still full of the night's travail, thought of birth. He thought of The Birth, and an immense and terrible holiness shook him as with an ague. Why, God was right up in that tree. God—benignant, amused. He could talk with God if he cared to. He spread his hands in a little prayer, like a child that laughs and prays. He was shaken and spent with rapture.

Conceive of Baptiste if you can: an uncouth, oafish little man, thin and pointed and sly; but with something about him grotesque and delightful, for all the world like a clown—something of quaint buffoonery that charmed little children, even the little boys and girls who lived in the fine old houses along the river front and walked abroad so sweetly with their nurses.

"Hi, Baptiste!" they would squeal when they saw him; "Howdy, *Mister* Baptiste!"

And then they would laugh with an elfin delight as if they shared some wanton secret with him. And their nurses—respectable, coalblack "mammies"—would pull them away, disgruntled; "Lawd, white chillun, come along. Dat triflin', low-down redbone—"

But this heaven-lent quality, whatever it was, that endeared him to children caused the women of his race to stick out their tongues at him. His love tale, how for a fabulous sum he bought from her father the prettiest maid in all the Indian pinewoods, was the talk of a region already famous far and wide for its romance. Baptiste—through no effort of his own, of course—was rich, as occasionally redbones get to be when their luscious acres fringe the winding

Cane; and the slim and blossomy Clorinda had pleased him mightily. She was a lovely thing with sea-green eyes and the chiseled beauty her women possess for a season; and Baptiste thought of babies when he looked at her—he who could pipe to children and trill like a bird in a tree. They would come one right after the other, of course, as was right for babies to come: brown little stairsteps of children.

He had even gone so far as to hail old Granny Loon one time as she hobbled past the courthouse; Granny who brought her babies in baskets (white ones and black ones and yellow and red ones!) and charged a fortune a day.

"Hey, Granny, what you got in there?" he wheedled in a voice that had the drawling music of the sluggish old witch-river. "You give him to me for my wife, old Granny. Yessir, we need us a son."

But Granny, disdainful, made no reply; and shifting her mysterious basket, passed with dignity down the shaded street. She could be high-and-mighty when it pleased her and, "blue-gummed" African though she was—and proud of her pure descent—she was by virtue of her calling above and beyond all race distinction. Granny Loon was dedicated, consecrated, sacred. But the greasy old mulatto women around their coffee stalls, who were shrewdly informed as to Granny's comings and goings, broke out into ribald laughter, shaking their fat gingham sides.

"Huh!" they snorted, "dat chile Granny got ain't fo' no ornery redbone. Dat chile is fo' white folks, yessir. Baptiste, he better go find his se'f one in de briar-patch."

He had swaggered away, Baptiste, pretending not to hear; but his face had burned and his heart had ached. Ah, but now he would show them. . . .

Baptiste, whose thoughts were prayerful if he but stumped his toe, had that very day taken up the matter with High Heaven. You slipped into the dim cathedral where God was all about you and your bony knees sank richly down into passionate crimson velvet.

"A son, sweet Saint. A lil' son. Send us a son, sweet Mother—"

And then to make assurance doubly sure, on emerging he had crossed two sticks to fling at a chance stray cat.

The creed of the redbone is past understanding: things vaguely heard and remembered; things felt and but dimly divined; super-stitions drilled into him by the wrinkled old crones of his race. His religion is compounded of Catholic altars where candles burn through the thick dim smoke from the swinging incense bowls; of pinewoods tremulous like a sounding organ; of forest fires and thunders and winds; of fetishes against the powers of darkness; of a moon that comes up red from the swamp; of a wilful river that doles out life and death.

Sometimes when Baptiste lay prone on a hillside things came to him, ancient things, and he knew what people had known when the earth was young—something stirring in him that had swung a papoose in the treetops. Sometimes when the moon was thin and the cotton greening in the fields was beginning to square, something lifted his soul that had strummed a guitar under a lady's window. Sometimes when that same young moon had grown sullen with orange fire, sometimes when he lay on the hot black earth and heard the negroes singing, something ached within him like the curse of a voodoo witch.

His patron saint he had chosen for reasons best known to himself, not the least significant of which was the little saint's unobtrusive-ness; for he was an ecstatic little blue fellow who lived in a niche of the church, in so dim and distant a corner that one might pray to him without exciting comment. The redbone, you must know, is secretive in matters religious; and pagan as he is at heart, is chary of dogma and fixed belief—his erratic worship being tolerated rather than condoned by the priesthood.

To this adopted saint, then, Baptiste told his beads, beseeching intercession: three masses a week, so many "Hail Marys," the Way of the Cross for a baby. Since he always returned from his orisons uplifted and slightly unsteady, Baptiste's mysterious pilgrimages had provoked his relatives to what was to them an obvious and foregone conclusion: Baptiste was drinking and gambling *awful!* He had better stay home with his wife.

Baptiste, jogging the deep-rutted roads, suddenly laughed and smacked at his pony. Now that a son had been born to him he would pour the shining dollars into his little saint's outstretched paws, the little saint who had moved Heaven and earth in his, Baptiste's, behalf. And then across the young day's joy a wavering shadow passed, and then another. Bats! From the swamp near by. The creatures came flickering, velvet-black and crazy, with the uncertain, chittering, sweezy sound that their wings make in the air; and when Baptiste struck out to fend them off, one of the gibbety things fell to the earth, stricken. Aghast that he had unwittingly wounded the devil's own, Baptiste turned straight about, although fully two miles from home. The sweet havoc in his heart had chilled into dreadful foreboding—for what man in his senses would flaunt such disaster?

Could it mean that his child was ill, perhaps at this moment dead?

When he rode into the back yard he saw his wife's pink petticoat a-hanging in the sun. His throat was dry and parched as he opened the kitchen door.

Granny was in the kitchen, crouching over the stove and stirring a viscous substance in a kettle. Her sacred basket hung above her on a nail. Her snowy white head was bound with a red bandanna, and she wore a spotless apron in the pocket of which was a buckeye to ward off the dread swamp fever. From a cord around her neck hung a curious carved African stone that dangled against her breasts. She turned and squinted at him as he entered.

"The lil' feller . . . is he . . . do he still breathe? Answer me, old woman."

Granny shrugged her shoulders. Her scorn of men was instinctive, she who assisted them into the world and first clothed their nakedness. There was not a midwife in all that neck of the woods who could hold a candle to her. When not "waiting" on a woman she lived alone on the edge of the Indian pinewoods in a shack half hidden with splashy sunflowers. There was a rail fence around it and toadstools at the door; and in the back yard an iron pot that looked like a cauldron. She was age-old and deathless, and all her movements were soft as if timed to the sleeping of children.

She gave Baptiste a mystic look; and then from above, down the rickety stairs, there sounded a thin little wail. Baptiste listened, woe in his eyes. It sounded so strange and so young.

"*Mon Dieu!*" he implored, "what was that?"

"De good Lawd he'p us," Granny answered, stirring and tasting,

tasting and stirring. "Fo' shame, Mister Baptiste Grabbo. Dat up dere's yo' son, man, a-cryin' fo' his dinner."

"And her? Is she well?—Clorinda—"

His agonized eyes searched the old woman's face, but Granny was muttering incantations over her ill-smelling brew: runes for the newborn babe and his mother; spells against milk-leg and childbed-fever. It was a full minute before she turned to him her sybil face, wrinkled with a thousand tragedies.

"Gawd-a-mighty!" she grumbled, "how many time yo' come runnin' back to ask 'bout dat wife an' dat chile? How come yo' don't go an' git outer my way? I done brung a many a baby, to white folks an' niggers an' mixed blood too. But I ain't nebber seen no daddy take on like dat befo'. Nussir, not since I been bo'n."

She looked at him and relented. "Heylaw—wait, I go make yo' a cup—"

Baptiste sat down, still shaking, and Granny poured for him hot black comforting coffee. Behind her somewhere in the dim old house she heard a door open and close. But her gaze held Baptiste's eye.

"Now, go long wid yo' se'f, Mister Grabbo," she said when he had drained the last drop. "A fine strappin' son yo' got, an' yo' all a-tremblin' and shakin'. I oughter brung yo' a lil' ole puny gal. Now yo' go on to town an' git drunk like a man."

Baptiste stumbled out into the sunlight, his heart mounting again with the joy-giving warmth of the coffee. *Mon Dieu!* What a fool he was indeed! Well . . . It was broad daylight now, and in the brick courtyard he saw Olaf, his overseer, puttering around. Olaf was blond and giantlike, and although he had been but a tramp two years before when Baptiste picked him up in town to help with a big cotton crop, he had gradually taken the reins in his hands; and of late he flaunted a bullying, insolent manner that was like a slap in the face.

To-day, however, although Olaf's sullen bigness oppressed Baptiste as usual, his heart at sight of the younger man turned over with pride of possession; and Baptiste felt suddenly sorry for Olaf. Olaf had no little son, no pretty wife and child.

"Hey, Olaf boy!" he called with gayety, "what you think of that baby, huh? You go and you tell that old granny in there to let you look at that child. You kiss him, Olaf—just once, mind. You go and tell 'em I sent you."

Baptiste passed through lanes that were dense with Cherokee roses, on down the road through the frenzied bloom of blackeyed Susan and bitterweed. And where the sinuous river begins to work its magic he saw the town, already asleep with summer. On the edge of the commons the breath of sweet-olive rushed at his lips like a kiss; and it is here that the road grows into a street, with quaint little sociable houses that squat on the sidewalk like children. The morning was lavish of sunlight that looked as if you could peel it up in thick yellow flakes, and as Baptiste jogged on into town his feeling of holiness grew, the feeling of brooding infinity.

He considered: Court was in session; along the narrow streets ox-teams were crawling and creaking, filled with niggers and country people "passing" the time of day; now and then some fine old carriage, drawn by satin bays, would permit him a glimpse of ravishing ladies in gay little flowered bonnets; around the hitching-posts on the river bank, where umbrella-chinas made pools of shade and the flies circled, drunken and sleepy, the planters had left their horses and mules; and bits of blue and orange and red flashed abroad in the streets. Baptiste sighed with a deep satisfaction. It was, indeed, a gala day in tune with his heart's own joy.

He left his pony in the shade and started afoot for the courthouse in search of his dear friend, Toni La Salle. For Baptiste had wisely decided that before he could quench his thirst his news must be told; and some one other than himself must be the bearer of it, to give it due weight and importance. Toni, who loved to gossip and whose mind was the mind of a child, must go and tell those women around their coffee stalls that Heaven had blessed Baptiste's marriage and had sent him a little son.

Baptiste, as he had expected, found Toni hanging about the courthouse, grabbing at stray tamales and running everyone's business. He enticed the boy to the shade of a magnolia tree and stuck a hand in his pocket.

"Toni, my love, my son," Baptiste said, "I got great news for you. Out to my house we got us a baby—now what you think about that?"

Toni seemed unimpressed, but his shallow eyes wavered to the money in Baptiste's hand.

"A *son,* Toni. A man-child, mind, what Granny Loon bring in her basket. Now listen to me: you go spread the news and I give you this dollar. You tell all those women, and this money is yours. A son, remember, and not no girl. And listen to me: his mama's eyes, maybe, but a head like his papa's, Toni. Yessir, you tell 'em that my baby's his daddy's son from his head clear down to his heels."

Toni departed, enraptured; but he had gone only a few steps when Baptiste ran after him. "Wait, Toni, my boy. Not so fast, not so fast. Now listen: my son he ain't no puny child. He'll make a big strappin' man. You tell all those meddlesome women my son he weigh ten pound."

As Toni made his announcements, Baptiste behind the screen of magnolias witnessed the incredulous excitement along the coffee stalls; noted with joy the uplifted arms and rolling eyes of the gossipers. Well, by the time he had had a drink or two, he calculated, the news would be abroad and he could saunter forth to receive congratulations and the jests which the occasion demanded. "Papa" his friends would call him. "Papa Grabbo." How sweet, how delicious, how holy!

Baptiste ambled gaily through a swinging door and had a drink across a slick green counter; and then another and yet another. Like wine in your very soul it was to be a father, the father of a son. He wiped his mouth on a greasy sleeve and smiled. It was the practiced smile of aloof indifference that he'd seen upon the lips of younger papas. He felt waggish and tipsy. Bah—a son? It was two little sons that he had.

He emerged into the sunlight comfortably drunk, so that the world remained a crushed-strawberry pink.

The merchants down the street were lying in wait for him. There was something in the thought of Baptiste's being a papa that tickled their funny-bones—Baptiste a day-old papa and drunk, with money burning his pocket! A boat had come up the river from New Orleans only the week before, and they had consignments to show him: displays of magnificent silks and shawls and fans and plumes from the East. But although Baptiste's eyes warmed to the sheen of the cloth, he refrained from buying. Nothing suited his mood. Silks and shawls were as dust—*Mon Dieu*—for would not moths corrupt them and thieves break through and steal? A jewel, the merchants advised him. A ruby, glowing with passion in the deep rich heart of itself. But Baptiste waved their gleaming trays away. Bah! A jewel he had given Clorinda the time his mare had a colt!

The merchants, shrugging their shoulders, fell in with his mood. A rosary, then, of amethysts, to kiss the holy hours into Heaven. Or a statue—see?—of the Virgin. A pretty gilded thing with the Child in blue, such a fat little kissable Christ. Surely this, this out of them all to commemorate Clorinda's motherhood.

But even this did not please Baptiste, although his fingers, tapered like a woman's, lingered adoringly on the Child's sweet china curls. Gold and frankincense and myrrh he would have laid at Clorinda's feet, mother of his son. He felt uplifted, eternal. A necklace of stars should encircle her throat and the moon she should wear for a halo.

He hunched his shoulders, inarticulate, he who could talk one language with his tongue and fifteen with his hands and eyes.

"Something . . . not to break," he besought them. "Something to set up in the parlor, maybe, like a what-you-call-'em. Something what my son can say: 'Look here, this here my papa he bought one time when I was born.'"

They brought forth glittering prismed lamps and carpets splashed with huge roses. They brought forth a hand-carved "press"; they brought forth imposing family albums of elegant crimson velvet. But Baptiste gestured and shook his head.

"Something nobody ain't had," he insisted. "Something big and grand, like a organ, maybe."

"Huh, go buy her the church, Baptiste," one of the merchants suggested.

Baptiste's eyes, wishful and strange, turned to the ivied cathedral. His thoughts were still rapturous. Across the street, two by two, the nuns were pacing to prayers, and Baptiste's joy was tinged with melancholy for their pale, frustrated womanhood. By all the saints in Heaven, sweet women like that weren't made to spend their days down on their knees!

And then somebody waved to him from across the way. It was Zuboff, of course, a distant kinsman, his thin little body in slim silhouette against a background of marble.

Baptiste gestured the clamoring merchants away and started across the street, swaying a little.

There had been an epidemic of yellow fever in Natchitoches that spring, a crawling, devastating thing that had licked up the high and the low; and for old Zuboff, the monument man, business was thriving and good. Baptiste saw that he was engraving cunning little names and dates on the surface of cold marble: "So and So; *Mort* such-and-such-a-date: Thy Will Be Done." To-day Baptiste was oddly aroused. Old Zuboff, his tongue in his cheek, wielded the mallet and chisel adroitly with tender caressing fingers. He looked up at Baptiste's approach and nodded hospitably.

"Sit down, Cousin, sit down," he invited, "right there on *Tante* Lisa's tombstone. Ah, Mister Papa Grabbo, well . . . what about that baby?" His tone changed and a craftiness caught in his hard little eyes. "Ah, Baptiste, sorrow we've had . . . trouble and tribulation. The Catholic graveyard is full."

Baptiste belched and spat at a date, 1852. "My son is a big fine child—" he began. But Zuboff cut him short, Zuboff the father of ten.

"Two dozen order for tombstone I got," he imparted, seeking without success to look lugubrious; "and all for the rich white folks. A new lot on hand last week too, Baptiste, what come on the boat from the city. Such beautiful granite, exquisite marble! Come with me, Baptiste, come, come."

In the rear of his shop, his holy of holies, Zuboff parted a curtain and with an air of solemn pride motioned Baptiste to enter. Within he displayed his masterpieces—two shafts with wreaths of lilies and with beautiful wide-winged angels. Passionately Zuboff ran his fingers over the hard white bodies. "Superb, Baptiste," he muttered, wetting his lips; "Cherubim, Cousin, and seraphim—" His voice sank to a whisper. "You hear 'bout them two nun what is sick at the convent? Well, then, who know . . . 'Tis good to be prepare. And only last night the priest he say—"

Baptiste's heart had turned over. He breathed heavy and hard in his throat. Cherubim and seraphim . . . they fell on his soul like music; they sounded like the glad hosannas that children sing at Christmas; they sounded like the holy joy of his little newborn babe. He thought he had never seen anything so beautiful as those angels. He gulped and aimed tobacco juice at 1852. Those po' sick nun at the convent—well, he was powerful sorry for them. But no, they could never sleep beneath these majestic wings. Not so long as he, Baptiste, had money in his pocket.

"Zuboff, I want them tombstone," he declared. He caught at the angels to steady himself, his throat burning, his eyes bloodshot. "I want 'em both, for me and my wife. Yessir, we got to die some day, same as them nun at the convent. 'Tis good to be ready, yessir, just like what you say. And you listen to me, Cousin Zuboff; you put this on one, like a poetry: *Clorinda, the Wife of Baptiste Grabbo, and Mother of his Son."*

Baptiste, having emptied his pockets at the shrine of his patron saint, jogged out of town in the late evening sunlight. His babe's little cry, thin and strange, still echoed in his heart: and he felt that if he could sing it the sound would be like those young pale leaves on the quivering cottonwood trees. On the edge of the commons the Angelus caught him, dropping the Holy Trinity soft into the waiting stillness. Baptiste bowed his head and crooned a prayer. It was a prayer that was half a lullaby to the wife and the child of his heart, a plaintive maudlin lullaby as sick with love as the moon. . . .

His horse, head down, tail swinging, rocked him home. Sometimes—swaying and riding, riding and swaying—Baptiste would feel again the damp, velvet kiss of the bats. But he was too drowsy to care. When his pony finally nosed down the bars of the gate and wandered into the lot, it was nearly midnight. The moon had set and myriads of stars swam out into the heavens. The sky looked billowy, as if you could catch the corners of it and toss the stars around as in a net. Mosquitoes, thin and fierce, whined keen in his ear.

Baptiste slumped down from his horse and did not see the figure that slipped out the door through the shadows. He felt for the gate and stumbled toward the steps. Old Granny, according to custom, was waiting to receive him and assist him to bed. She loomed before him, a shapeless thing smelling of paregoric. She helped him into the house and up the rickety stairs; and instinctively, her haughtiness gone, this mother of a race began to croon as she pulled off his shoes. A man, bah! They never grew up. They were all helpless babes in the cradle, to be comforted, petted, and nursed.

Granny lifted, half-dragged Baptiste to a featherbed in the corner and she paused at the door to look back at him—a little amusing toy of a man like she'd seen in Christmas stockings. He was muttering in his drunken sleep, something concerning angels and stars and cradles high in the treetops.

"De Lawd hab mussy on our souls!" she said as she closed the door. She stood there a moment—motionless, sad, peering before her.

Old Zuboff worked industriously on Baptiste's beautiful gravestones, concealed behind the curtain in the little back room of his shop: for Baptiste had insisted that his gift be kept a secret; only Zuboff was to know, and Zuboff's sons, until the monuments were erected and he could reveal them to Clorinda. Faithfully, zealously Zuboff worked, for even without the discount in courtesy due a kinsman, they would bring him nine hundred dollars in gold. Late every night old Zuboff worked, sawing and scraping and filing and chiseling until "Clorinda" took shape from the marble. *"Clorinda, the Wife of Baptiste Grabbo, and Mother of his Son."*

Three weeks it took to engrave them, and during this time Baptiste went back and forth from house to town like a shuttle, riding his runty red pony. He liked to loaf around Zuboff's shop and watch the old man at work. *"Clorinda, the Wife of Baptiste Grabbo, and Mother of his Son."* In truth, a poem in marble. He knew every stroke of the mallet, every delicate curve of the chisel. And as their beauty and dignity took hold of his very soul, he hinted to Zuboff, wistfully, that he would like to set the gravestones up as statues in his house. But Zuboff made fun of him:

"Bah! A graveyard Baptiste wants in his parlor! Look what a cousin I got!"

Often as Baptiste sat and watched old Zuboff work he would talk of his son, of the changed and changing ways of his household, of the growing demands of Clorinda. This and the other thing she must have—lace for that infant, yessir, made by the nuns at the convent; a baby-buggy with canopied top, all silk and velvet and tassels, to wheel that child around in the yard same as if he was big-folks. Baptiste would grunt and throw out his hands, but in his heart he was pleased.

"Bah!" he complained, "a prince we got. Nothing ain't good enough. That baby he ruin me, Zuboff. He got to live just like a king."

The goings-on of Baptiste's family were, indeed, the talk of the countryside; living like big-folks, yessir, just because, with children as common as pig tracks, old Granny Loon had fetched 'em one po' lil' baby.

"Well, now, for suppose we do that way whenever *we* get us a baby!" women said to their husbands, rolling their eyes.

Baptiste's old adobe house, with its sagging roof and its paved courtyard in the rear, was hilarious night and day with relatives come to take potluck—like a party that would go on forever. And when at home, four times a day Baptiste made coffee and four times passed it around. Always wine a-flowing too, to pledge the young child's health. His male relatives began to view Baptiste with heightened respect and to ask his advice about corn and cotton and the raising of young pigs. But the female ones, as was the custom, ignored him pleasantly; and this, too, enchanted Baptiste.

"Howdy, Papa!" they would call, impudently. "Howdy, Papa Grabbo!"

And away they would bustle to talk with Granny of broths and brews and teas; of the merits of sassafras root boiled down to make the milk come fast; of this, that, and the other thing that women have always known.

Impossible to work. Out in the fields the darkies sang all day and half the night. And the place, despite its joyousness, was going to wrack and ruin because Olaf, the sullen young fool, was always a-fishing under a tree, seduced by the old witch-river. Time and again Baptiste made up his mind to bring Olaf to task; but he himself was filled with exquisite lassitude. And on those rare occasions when there were no petticoats about, the lure of the cradle drew him to sit and gaze at the baby, or sing his queer little lullabies, always about the moon—the great big yellow nigger-moon that rose up out of the swamp. . . .

Three weeks of this while Zuboff worked: and then of a sudden, putting an end to festivity, August had come like a smothering blanket; and all the breath and bloom of summer had rotted to a stench.

On a certain morning during this month a log wagon drawn by three yoke of oxen set out from Natchitoches, toiling painfully over the rutted roadways where the weeds were rank and heavy with dust. Propped upright in the wagon were Baptiste's beautiful monuments, the lovely spreading angel-wings bulging in fantastic fashion under layers of cotton sacking. There were cloud shadows running far and sweet across the fields that morning, but no rain; and at noon, as the oxen grunted under a blazing sun, buzzards wheeled and floated against a sky that showed through the trees in splotches of hot hard blue. It was late afternoon when the wagon reached the Grabbo burying-ground.

Here Baptiste and Zuboff and Zuboff's sons got out and erected the shafts—the one on the left for Clorinda, the one on the right for Baptiste. "Like when you lay in bed," Baptiste insisted. For this would be their marriage-bed, eternal in the heavens.

The burying-ground of the Grabbos is nearly a mile from the house in a secluded spot that the negroes shun on the edge of the Indian pinewoods: six bayberry bushes, three cedars; and among the tangled grasses many a Spanish cross. When Zuboff and his sons had gone, Baptiste spent an hour gathering branches of leaves and flowers and trailing honeysuckle. He found some old, old roses too, and masses of golden lovebine; and he made them into garlands and draped them over the stones so that they covered the wreaths and the angels and Zuboff's so-beautiful verses.

Finally, having looked upon his labor and seen that it was good, he sat down on a stump to make his plans. That night when the moon rode high, he decided, he would put Clorinda on the back of his pony and lead her across the cotton fields and up to the edge of the woods. And there he would unveil his shining tributes, unveil them of leaves and of flowers. It would be her first excursion since the baby came, and she would laugh in the mocking way he loved. And because she could not read, he, who knew them by heart, would recite the verses to her while she traced them with her finger: *"Clorinda, the Wife of Baptiste Grabbo, and Mother of his Son."* He knew how her eyes would look, strange eyes that eluded you so that you had to search for them like flowers in the grass. . . . The moon would spill white magic. Who could tell but that here amid the dead she would give him of her love, she so stingy with kisses! She would be all in white; and as he looked at her he would see her head, Madonna-wise, hallowed against the moon. . . .

And later, of course—Baptiste chuckled—in a day or so, perhaps, he would have all the relatives out to a gumbo-supper or something; and maybe he'd make 'em a speech!

Baptiste felt the need of coffee, thick and strong and black. He straggled to his feet and trailed along through the fields toward home. The sun had gone, raw and flaming; and already mosquitoes were stirring—great, filmy, floating things as they get to be in August. The canebrake looked snaky and the bilious breath of cotton blooms hung low like a sickly incense. Baptiste walked slowly, dragging his feet. It was the season of three-day chills. When he reached home it was good dusk.

Old Granny was sitting on the gallery, alone with the baby. She seemed surprised to see him and a little anxious.

"How come yo' done come back fum town?" she wanted to know. "How come yo' don't stay all night at Zuboff's like yo' say?" She squinted at him suspiciously and puffed on her corncob pipe. "How come yo' ain't gone an' git drunk, same as always?"

Baptiste smiled. One corner of his mouth turned up and the other down. "Where is the lil' mama?" he inquired. "What you got her a-doing now, old woman, with your hoodoo tricks and such?"

Old Granny looked at him, then veiled her eyes. She seemed withdrawn and mystic. Suddenly she spoke out, something indignant and venomous in her drawling, cool old voice. "Hit been mos' four week since dat baby come," she recited; "an' all dat time she a-pesterin' me to let her take a walk. Jest down by de gate. An' all in good time, I keep tellin' her. De ladies in town, *dey* minds what I say. Six week, an' *den* take a walk. But to-night . . . out she go. Jest like wild hosses was pullin' her."

Baptiste mopped his streaming face. The baby, naked but for a swab of flannel about his belly, lay on a pallet and stared at the moon. Now and then he squirmed, with a quick little wrench as of pain. Baptiste regarded him anxiously. "The lil' feller . . . is he sick?" he asked, the ever-present fear tight at his heart.

"Colic," old Granny grumbled. "Dey all has de colic. Dem dat is hearty."

A surge of pride, intense, unreasonable, poured into Baptiste's heart: a nice healthy baby with colic. Well . . . he liked it that his baby was just as other babies. And then a hot resentment flamed within him, a primitive ache to hear his mate a-crooning over a cradle. "The lil' feller got colic," he grunted, "well, why ain't she a-singing, then? She belong here, where the baby got colic."

Granny grunted behind the cypress-vines and slapped at the flies with her fan. She looked like one of the fates sitting there, the old tragic one with the shears. She pulled herself up and suggested coffee, and creaked across the floor in her flat bare feet. But Baptiste shook his head. "I b'lieve I go find Clorinda," he said, dispiritedly. "I go find that baby's mama. He need her a-singing."

Down by the gate he looked. But no mutinous wife was walking in the shadows. The front yard was matted and rank with weeds, and the stench of the cotton blooms hung sickly sweet, head high. A plume of lilac brushed his face as if she had just passed; the pale mist of crêpe-myrtle trees closed languidly about him.

And then, suddenly, Baptiste saw her through some bushes. She was stealing, gliding soundlessly (blood of an Indian squaw!). She wore something bright in her hair, something bright and festive like a star. She had on shoes and stockings. . . .

He opened his mouth to call her, but as he did he saw that she was taking the path which led through the fields to the burying-ground; and a terrible thought came to him: had one of the niggers been spying? Did she know about the gravestones?

She began to run—Granny was right—as if wild horses were pulling her. Baptiste, keeping to the trees along the river, followed draggingly. In places the river was choked with scum and pinkish water-hyacinths, as if—with death in its heart—it had woven a shroud for itself and had strewn it with flowers. Above it hung an evil moon, a yellow witch in a mist that drew the cotton blooms unto itself and spilled them back to the earth. From remote and outlying cabins Baptiste could hear low snatches of song, and he knew that the niggers about the place were sitting in their doorways—half naked, and half asleep, and half crazy with the heat and the cotton scent. . . . Now and then there was chanting . . . and stealing shapes in the fields; for there is a night life that goes on among negroes as it does among beasts and insects—creatures that see in the dark and prowl and flit. . . .

Baptiste now saw Clorinda flash through the sugar-cane patch on the edge of the burying-ground. He stole after her. Her slim arms, out-straying to the brambles, had a soft expectancy about them —Madonna-arms, rocking. There was hidden joy in her swift sure flight.

And now, ten feet away, white against the cedars, white against the bayberry bushes, white against the roses of the dead—Baptiste saw her go into Olaf's arms. The moon was a lover's moon by now, beginning to float and run; and in its path they stood with the soft breast of a pine tree pushed against them. They were just in front of the garlanded monuments, standing on the place that would yawn some day to receive unto itself sweet human flesh. . . . And it seemed to Baptiste's fevered gaze that one of the terrible angels was holding a flaming sword above their heads. . . .

He sank down presently upon the trunk of a fallen cedar, a movement that made a swishing sound like a wood creature stirring. He felt cold under his shirt, benumbed. He didn't know how long he had been sitting there when Clorinda stole away. . . . Once he had heard Olaf say, "To-morrow night . . . if he goes to town, you come to me. Get away from that old hag of a granny. I'll be waiting, girl, same as always." The sullen insolent voice of Olaf the tramp!

Baptiste got to his feet and straggled back to the house.

The following day Baptiste spent off in the woods and fields, making arrangements, perfecting his plans, a terrible woe in his eyes so that he had to return to the house at intervals and drink coffee, heavy and strong and black. During these intervals he avoided the baby—the little son that his saint had sent. And whenever it cried, Baptiste in agony would put his trembling fingers in his ears. 'Cose now, he conceded, the little saint had managed as well as he could; the little blue saint in the grotto whose business it was to look after him and who did it rather well, all things considered. Take those gravestones, for example: they, or one of them, would come in pretty handy; and who but his saint, with foresight rare, had let him to erect them? . . . But now, of course, there was business to do. And he alone must do it; a duty inevitable, according to his code.

Clorinda? . . . He shrugged his shoulders and dismissed her. She was after all a woman, a young woman and a fool. A few drinks and a few "Hail Marys" and he could in time forgive her. He even felt a certain sorrow for her, so radiant she had been. Well, she would say (she and Granny) that the river had swallowed Olaf— he was always slipping his evil body deep in its bilious slime. And Granny would remind them of what people have always said: that when a stranger drinks of the waters of the Cane he can never leave the land of Natchitoches. Yes, when they went to look for Olaf they would cross themselves and lament that the river had swallowed him up.

At twilight the heat was intense; and the big sullen moon, shoving a dusky shoulder over the edge of the swamp, brought with it a desperate booming of bullfrogs. The baby was fretful again, but now Clorinda sat on the gallery and held it in her arms, her eyes brooding dark in the gloom.

Baptiste got up presently and yawned, and moved off into the shadows. He slipped through the fields and was first at the tryst. And when he saw Olaf coming he stepped out into the moonlight with something hoofed and horned and forked about him. . . .

The Indian in Baptiste performed the deed with neatness and despatch, so that Olaf for an instant knew only a face before him— high cheek bones, thin straight lips, and comic eyes that were sad. The Spanish in Baptiste dug the grave and the French tossed a rose upon it.

But the something unaccounted for that made him what he was sent him dragging back to the house, his face the color of leaves. Clorinda had gone to bed and had taken the baby with her. But old Granny was waiting for him behind the cypress-vines. She peered at him out of the darkness. "Lawd-a-mighty, man," she said, "I 'spec' I go make yo' some coffee."

Baptiste gave her a faint smile and his familiar hunch of the shoulders. But his voice when he spoke had lost its music. It was the old flat voice of despair.

"I thank you, Granny Loon," he said; "but me, I b'lieve not tonight. Not nothing, if you will excuse me. I feel—" He touched his stomach—"I feel . . . moved inside myself."

Above him down the rickety stairs there sounded a little wail—thin and strange and very, very young.

It is lazy and sweet along the Côte Joyeuse and on into the piney red-clay hills; for Time has been kind to Natchitoches. At the Resurrection season every year an Art Colony descends upon it with pallet and brush to paint its decaying witchery against the glory of massed crêpe-myrtles. There are little shops along St. Denis Street where you can buy flamboyant postcards, stating in wreaths of roses "This is the land God remembers."

How beautifully, indeed, He remembers! . . . A church still reaching its golden domes to the blue, wide summer sky; a river no longer willful since the Chamber of Commerce, smugly entrenched behind wrought-iron balustrades, has diverted its meanderings and confined it into a lake. "The Beautiful and Dammed," as the young artists call it.

The town itself looks on at all this pleasant exploitation like a little old high-born exquisite lady laughing up her sleeve. . . . At certain seasons of the year the breath of sweet-olive still blows delicately.

On a dewy summer morning the great bell in the domed cathedral, having just come back from Rome, began to toll. There were numbers of cars parked along St. Denis Street and in front of the courthouse where, if you be so minded, you can still loaf and invite your soul. And people drawled to one another, "Well, I wonder who's dead."

A few of the idly curious about the coffee stalls began to count the strokes of the bell: "Thirteen . . . fourteen . . . fifteen—"

Now it is said that for each of these mellow golden dropping balls of sound (you can count up to twenty between them) you must pay one good dollar bill. Take a rich man, now: when he dies, say the wise ones, the tolling is greatly prolonged. Occasionally, if the deceased be poor, a hat will be passed around among his relatives, who contribute to the tolling-fund according to their pockets, the generosity of their hearts, and the amount of family pride they possess.

"Twenty-two . . . twenty-three . . . twenty-four—"

The loafers around the coffee stalls were becoming elated now. They began to speculate, "What you bet? I bet you the Mayor's dead."

To one side of the courthouse, in the shade of a giant magnolia, there was a little group of boys sitting astride a barrel and being cleverly painted by three young ladies in knickers. They were stunted, tragic-eyed little fellows, and curiously apathetic. But when the bell stopped tolling they crossed themselves and looked at one another in awe. "Heylaw, well . . . she's gone," they said. "Old lady Grabbo's dead."

Old Baptiste had passed on in the same manner many years before.

Up in the lazy red-clay hills the relatives had been gathering for hours to the bedside of Madame Clorinda (such was her title among them!). They came, some of them, driving shiny new Fords; others, whole families together, creaked along in wagons behind undersized scrawny old horses. Out at the Grabbo house everybody kissed everybody else and whispered in mournful eagerness: "She's sinking. Yessir, the doc he say that she can't last out the night."

But the bloated old creature was three days a-dying, a death like that of a princess. And during this time of her soul's travail she talked incessantly of the monument which, it seemed, had been erected for her long ago in the family burying-ground. Her dim thoughts, fitful and already strange with eternity, were full of it: how that her husband, himself asleep this many a year, had bought it with his own in Natchitoches; how handsome it was, so that people used to journey miles to see it; how that every fine Sabbath afternoon she had walked through the fields with bouquets of waxy cape jasmine to lay among the grasses and the blowing buttercups—one for Baptiste and one for herself, in the place that would yawn wide for her.

Three days of this, and then she lay ponderous in death; and according to her dying wish, word was dispatched to town to have the bell tolled sixty times, once for each of her years. Two at her head and two at her feet the tall white candles burned, while outside in the soft air that was languid and sweet with summer the negroes began to sway and rock; and her relatives, standing about in store-bought clothes as if bid to a marriage feast, drank coffee and said among themselves it had been a most beautiful passing.

And then something happened. There came riding a man on horseback. He was a distant cousin and he was one of the gravediggers, it seemed. His clothes were caked with mud, and buttercups stuck weirdly in his hair. He looked frightened (Holy Mother preserve us!) and he said that in digging the grave of the deceased beside that of her husband, in the Grabbo burying-ground, they had come upon a human skeleton cradled in what remained of a hastily-constructed old yellow-pine box.

EVE AND THAT SNAKE

———

Roark Bradford

From *Ol' Man Adam an' His Chillun* by Roark Bradford, 1928.

Roark Bradford (1896-1948) was steeped in the lore of the Negroes living in New Orleans and on the plantations of the lower Mississippi River valley. *Ol' Man Adam an' His Chillun* (1928), from which the play *Green Pastures* was adapted, and *Ol' King David an' the Philistine Boys* (1930) continue the method first employed effectively by Irwin Russell in the late 1870's of telling Biblical stories through the mind and through the speech of the simple darky. Other books by Bradford are *This Side of Jordan* (1929), *John Henry* (1931), and *The Green Roller* (1949).

Well, a long time ago things was diffrunt. Hit wa'n't nothin' on de yearth 'cause hit wa'n't no yearth. And hit wa'n't nothin' nowheres and ev'y day was Sunday. Wid de Lawd r'ared back preachin' all day long ev'y day. 'Ceptin' on Sadday, and den ev'ybody went to de fish fry.

So one day ev'ybody was out to de fish fry, eatin' fish and b'iled custard and carryin' on, to all at once de Lawd swallowed some b'iled custard which didn't suit his tas'e.

"Dis custard," say de Lawd, "ain't seasoned right. Hit's too thick."

"Hit's got a heap of sugar and aigs and milk and things in hit, Lawd," say Gabriel.

"I know," say de Lawd, "but hit tas'es like hit needs jest a little bit more firmament in hit."

"Us ain't got no more firmament, Lawd," say Gabriel. "Us ain't got a drap in de jug."

"You been usin' a heap of firmament," say de Lawd. "Seem like ev'y time I come to a fish fry I got to create some more firmament. I bet I'm gonter make enough dis time to last a month of Sundays. I'm sick and tired of passin' a miracle ev'y time I wants some firmament."

So de Lawd r'ared back and passed a miracle and say, "Let hit be some firmament. And when I say let hit be some firmament, I mean let hit be a whole heap of firmament. I'm sick and tired of lettin' hit be jest a little bitty dab of firmament when I pass a miracle."

And you jest ought to see de firmament! Hit jest sloshed all over ev'ything so de angels and cherubs couldn't hardly fly, and ev'ybody was standin' round, knee deep, shiverin' and chatterin' and squirmin' round.

"Well," say de mammy angel, "I guess I better git my cherubs and git on home and dry 'em out. They's shiverin' like they got a buck aguer, right now."

"Don't go bustin' up de fish fry jest 'cause de cherubs is wet," say de Lawd. "I'll dry 'em out."

So de Lawd passed another miracle and say, "Let hit be de sun to dry out deseyar cherubs." And dar was de sun. And de cherubs got dried, but quick as they got dried they got wet again, 'cause hit was so much firmament.

"Dis ain't gittin' us nowheres," say de Lawd. "Gabriel, maybe us men-folks better git out and ditch around some and dreen some of disyar firmament off."

"Good idea," say Gabriel, "only hit ain't no 'count, 'cause hit ain't no place to dreen hit off to."

"Well," say de Lawd, "I guess I got to pass another miracle and make a place to dreen hit off to. Hit look like when I git started passin' miracles hit's always somethin' else." So he r'ared back and passed a miracle and said, "Let hit be de yearth to hold dis firmament." And dar was de yearth.

Well, de firmament runned on de yearth, and hit runned in de rivers and creeks and ditches—'cause firmament wa'n't nothin' but a fancy name for water—and dar was de yearth wid de firmament dreened off and a heap of dry land left.

"Now looky what you done done, Lawd," say Gabriel. "Cou'se hit ain't none of my business, 'cause I got to practice on my hawn all time. But somebody got to go work dat land, 'cause you know good as me dat de land ain't gonter work hitself."

Well, de Lawd looked round to see who he gonter send to work his land, and all de angels was mighty busy. "Well," he say, "I guess I got pass one more miracle to git somebody to work dat land. And I bet de next time I pass a miracle for some firmament I bet I won't git so brash about hit."

So de Lawd got a handful of dirt and made hit in a ball and passed a miracle over hit and say, "Let dis dirt be mankind." And de dirt turn to a man.

De Lawd looked at de man and say, "What's yo' name, man?"

"Adam," say de man.

"Adam—which?" say de Lawd.

"Jest plain Adam," say de man.

"What's you' family name?" say de Lawd.

"Ain't got no family," say Adam.

"Well," say de Lawd, "I got to change dat. I ain't gonter have none of deseyar single mens workin' on my farm. They runs around wid de women all night and come de next day they's too sleepy to work."

"I don't run around wid no women," say Adam. "I ain't studdin' de women."

"Yeah?" say de Lawd. "But I ain't gonter take no chances. Yo' heart might be all right now, but de first good-lookin' woman come along she gonter change yo' mind. So I'm jest gonter put you to sleep again."

So de Lawd put Adam to sleep and tuck out a rib and turned de rib into a woman name Eve. So when Adam woke up again, dar was Eve, stretched out by his side, wid her haid on his pillow.

"Where'd you come from, gal?" say Adam.

"No mind whar I come from," say Eve, "I's yar, ain't I?"

So Adam and Eve got married and settle down to raise a crop for de Lawd.

So ev'ything went along all right to summertime. Eve was out pickin' blackberries, and de Lawd come wawkin' down de road.

"Good mawnin', Sister Eve," say de Lawd. "Pickin' a few blackberries?"

"A few, Lawd," say Eve. "Adam 'lowed he'd like to has some for preserves next winter."

"Help yo'self," say de Lawd. "Put up all de blackberries you want. And peaches too. And plums, ef'n you and Adam likes 'em. Hit ain't but one thing which I don't want you to tech, and dat's de apple orchard. 'Cause from de news I yars, apples is kind of scarce and they ought to bring a good price next fall. So help yo'self to de berries and de peaches and things, but jest stay out of de apples.

Well, hit jest goes to show you. Eve didn't like apples and Adam didn't too. But no quicker do de Lawd wawk on down de road to Eve see a great big highland moccasin crawlin' long twarg her.

"Look at dat scound'el," says Eve, and she pick up a rock. "I'm gonter mash his old haid quick as I gits a shot at him." So de snake crawls through de apple orchard fence, and Eve climbs over hit.

Well, Eve and dat snake went round and round. Eve was chunkin' at him and de snake was dodgin' to finally Eve got a clear shot at him and she r'ared back and let de big rock go.

Eve was all right, but she was a woman. And hit ain't never yit been a woman which could throw straight. So Eve missed de snake and hit de apple tree. And down come a big red apple, right in front of her.

"Well, I be doggone!" she say. "Look at dat apple!" So she stood and looked at hit a long time. "I didn't aim to knock hit down," she say, "but hit's down, now, and I can't put hit back. And does I let hit lay, de hawgs is gonter eat hit and hit's too purty for de hawgs to eat." So she tuck a bite.

"Don't taste like much," she say. "I wonder do Adam want to eat hit?" So she tuck de apple out to whar Adam was plowin' de cawn, and give hit to him.

"I don't like apples, gal," say Adam. "Whyn't you give me somethin' I like?"

"Cou'se you don't like apples," say Eve. "You don't never like nothin' I gives you. You got to think of hit yo'self before you likes hit," and Eve blubbers up and commences to cry.

"Aw, don't cry, sugar," say Adam. "I was jest funnin' wid you. I likes apples. Give me a bite."

"Nawp," say Eve. "You's jest mean, dat's what you is. You treats me mean 'cause I ain't nothin' but a poor little weak woman and you's a big, stout man. I ain't gonter give you nothin'."

"Aw, honey, don't tawk like dat," say Adam. "Dat ain't de way hit is, a-tall. I was jest playin' wid you. Give me a bite of apple and I buys you a new dress."

Well, when a man go to tawkin' new dresses to a woman he gonter git some action. So Eve dry up her cryin' and Adam et de apple and got her de dress. But dat wa'n't all.

De Lawd seed Eve's new dress and he found out all about hit. And he got mad, 'cause he didn't aim to have nobody on his place which stole his apples. So he bailed old Adam's trover and leveled on his crop and mule, and put Adam and Eve off'n de place. And de next news anybody yared of old Adam, he was down on de levee tryin' to git a job at six bits a day.

THE JILTING OF
GRANNY WEATHERALL

―――――

Katherine Anne Porter

From *Flowering Judas* by Katherine Anne Porter, 1930. First published in *transition*, XV (February, 1929), 139-146.

Katherine Anne Porter (1894-   ), a native of Texas, has lived also in Europe, Mexico, and other parts of the United States. An author primarily of short stories and novelettes, she has set many of them in the Southwest and in Mexico. Besides the stories collected under the title *Flowering Judas* (1930, and 1935 with four additional stories), others have appeared in *Pale Horse, Pale Rider* (1939), and *The Leaning Tower and Other Stories* (1944). See Edmund Wilson, *Classics and Commercials* (1950), pages 219-223; Robert Penn Warren, "Katherine Anne Porter: Irony with a Center," *The Kenyon Review,* IV (Winter, 1942), 29-42; V. A. Young, "The Art of Katherine Anne Porter," *The New Mexico Quarterly Review,* XV (August, 1945), 326-341; and Harry John Mooney, Jr., *The Fiction and Criticism of Katherine Anne Porter* (1957).

She flicked her wrist neatly out of Doctor Harry's pudgy careful fingers and pulled the sheet up to her chin. The brat ought to be in knee breeches. Doctoring around the country with spectacles on his nose! "Get along now, take your school-books and go. There's nothing wrong with me."

Doctor Harry spread a warm paw like a cushion on her forehead where the forked green vein danced and made her eyelids twitch. "Now, now, be a good girl, and we'll have you up in no time."

"That's no way to speak to a woman nearly eighty years old just because she's down. I'd have you respect your elders, young man."

"Well, Missy, excuse me." Doctor Harry patted her cheek. "But I've got to warn you, haven't I? You're a marvel, but you must be careful or you're going to be good and sorry."

"Don't tell me what I'm going to be. I'm on my feet now, morally speaking. It's Cornelia. I had to go to bed to get rid of her."

Her bones felt loose, and floated around in her skin, and Doctor Harry floated like a balloon around the foot of the bed. He floated and pulled down his waistcoat and swung his glasses on a cord. "Well, stay where you are, it certainly can't hurt you."

"Get along and doctor your sick," said Granny Weatherall. "Leave a well woman alone. I'll call for you when I want you. . . . Where were you forty years ago when I pulled through milk-leg and double pneumonia? You weren't even born. Don't let Cornelia lead you on," she shouted, because Doctor Harry appeared to float up to the ceiling and out. "I pay my own bills, and I don't throw my money away on nonsense!"

She meant to wave good-by, but it was too much trouble. Her eyes closed of themselves, it was like a dark curtain drawn around the bed. The pillow rose and floated under her, pleasant as a hammock in a light wind. She listened to the leaves rustling outside the window. No, somebody was swishing newspapers: no, Cornelia and Doctor Harry were whispering together. She leaped broad awake, thinking they whispered in her ear.

"She was never like this, *never* like this!" "Well, what can we expect?" "Yes, eighty years old. . . ."

Well, and what if she was? She still had ears. It was like Cornelia to whisper around doors. She always kept things secret in such a public way. She was always being tactful and kind. Cornelia was dutiful; that was the trouble with her. Dutiful and good: "So good and dutiful," said Granny, "that I'd like to spank her." She saw herself spanking Cornelia and making a fine job of it.

"What'd you say, Mother?"

Granny felt her face tying up in hard knots.

"Can't a body think, I'd like to know?"

"I thought you might want something."

"I do. I want a lot of things. First off, go away and don't whisper."

She lay and drowsed, hoping in her sleep that the children would keep out and let her rest a minute. It had been a long day. Not that she was tired. It was always pleasant to snatch a minute now and then. There was always so much to be done, let me see: tomorrow.

Tomorrow was far away and there was nothing to trouble about. Things were finished somehow when the time came; thank God there was always a little margin over for peace: then a person could spread out the plan of life and tuck in the edges orderly. It was good to have everything clean and folded away, with the hair brushes and tonic bottles sitting straight on the white embroidered linen: the day started without fuss and the pantry shelves laid out with rows of jelly glasses and brown jugs and white stone-china jars with blue whirligigs and words painted on them: coffee, tea, sugar, ginger, cinnamon, allspice: and the bronze clock with the lion on top nicely dusted off. The dust that lion could collect in twenty-four hours! The box in the attic with all those letters tied up, well, she'd have to go through that tomorrow. All those letters—George's letters and John's letters and her letters to them both—lying around for the children to find afterwards made her uneasy. Yes, that would be tomorrow's business. No use to let them know how silly she had been once.

While she was rummaging around she found death in her mind and it felt clammy and unfamiliar. She had spent so much time preparing for death there was no need for bringing it up again. Let it take care of itself now. When she was sixty she had felt very old, finished, and went around making farewell trips to see her children and grandchildren, with a secret in her mind: This is the very last of your mother, children! Then she made her will and came down with a long fever. That was all just a notion like a lot of other things, but it was lucky too, for she had once for all got over the idea of dying for a long time. Now she couldn't be worried. She hoped she had better sense now. Her father had lived to be one hundred and two years old and had drunk a noggin of strong hot toddy on his last birthday. He told the reporters it was his daily habit, and he owed his long life to that. He had made quite a scandal and was very pleased about it. She believed she'd just plague Cornelia a little.

"Cornelia! Cornelia!" No footsteps, but a sudden hand on her cheek. "Bless you, where have you been?"

"Here, mother."

"Well, Cornelia, I want a noggin of hot toddy."

"Are you cold, darling?"

"I'm chilly, Cornelia. Lying in bed stops the circulation. I must have told you that a thousand times."

Well, she could just hear Cornelia telling her husband that Mother was getting a little childish and they'd have to humor her. The thing that most annoyed her was that Cornelia thought she was deaf, dumb, and blind. Little hasty glances and tiny gestures tossed around her and over her head saying, "Don't cross her, let her have her way, she's eighty years old," and she sitting there as if she lived in a thin glass cage. Sometimes Granny almost made up her mind to pack up and move back to her own house where nobody could remind her every minute that she was old. Wait, wait, Cornelia, till your own children whisper behind your back!

In her day she had kept a better house and had got more work done. She wasn't too old yet for Lydia to be driving eighty miles for advice when one of the children jumped the track, and Jimmy still dropped in and talked things over: "Now, Mammy, you've a good business head, I want to know what you think of this? . . ." Old. Cornelia couldn't change the furniture around without asking. Little things, little things! They had been so sweet when they were little. Granny wished the old days were back again with the children young and everything to be done over. It had been a hard pull, but not too much for her. When she thought of all the food she had cooked, and all the clothes she had cut and sewed, and all the gardens she had made—well, the children showed it. There they were, made out of her, and they couldn't get away from that. Sometimes she wanted to see John again and point to them and say, Well, I didn't do so badly, did I? But that would have to wait. That was for tomorrow. She used to think of him as a man, but now all the

children were older than their father, and he would be a child
beside her if she saw him now. It seemed strange and there was
something wrong in the idea. Why, he couldn't possibly recognize
her. She had fenced in a hundred acres once, digging the post
holes herself and clamping the wires with just a negro boy to
help. That changed a woman. John would be looking for a young
woman with the peaked Spanish comb in her hair and the painted
fan. Digging post holes changed a woman. Riding country roads in
the winter when women had their babies was another thing: sitting
up nights with sick horses and sick negroes and sick children and
hardly ever losing one. John, I hardly ever lost one of them! John
would see that in a minute, that would be something he could understand, she wouldn't have to explain anything!

It made her feel like rolling up her sleeves and putting the whole
place to rights again. No matter if Cornelia was determined to be
everywhere at once, there were a great many things left undone on
this place. She would start tomorrow and do them. It was good to
be strong enough for everything, even if all you made melted and
changed and slipped under your hands, so that by the time you
finished you almost forgot what you were working for. What was it
I set out to do? she asked herself intently, but she could not remember. A fog rose over the valley, she saw it marching across the
creek swallowing the trees and moving up the hill like an army of
ghosts. Soon it would be at the near edge of the orchard, and then it
was time to go in and light the lamps. Come in, children, don't
stay out in the night air.

Lighting the lamps had been beautiful. The children huddled up
to her and breathed like little calves waiting at the bars in the twilight. Their eyes followed the match and watched the flame rise
and settle in a blue curve, then they moved away from her. The
lamp was lit, they didn't have to be scared and hang on to mother
any more. Never, never, never more. God, for all my life I thank
Thee. Without Thee, my God, I could never have done it. Hail,
Mary, full of grace.

I want you to pick all the fruit this year and see that nothing is
wasted. There's always someone who can use it. Don't let good
things rot for want of using. You waste life when you waste good

food. Don't let things get lost. It's bitter to lose things. Now, don't let me get to thinking, not when I am tired and taking a little nap before supper. . . .

The pillow rose about her shoulders and pressed against her heart and the memory was being squeezed out of it: oh, push down the pillow, somebody: it would smother her if she tried to hold it. Such a fresh breeze blowing and such a green day with no threats in it. But he had not come, just the same. What does a woman do when she has put on the white veil and set out the white cake for a man and he doesn't come? She tried to remember. No, I swear he never harmed me but in that. He never harmed me but in that . . . and what if he did? There was the day, the day, but a whirl of dark smoke rose and covered it, crept up and over into the bright field where everything was planted so carefully in orderly rows. That was hell, she knew hell when she saw it. For sixty years she had prayed against remembering him and against losing her soul in the deep pit of hell, and now the two things were mingled in one and the thought of him was a smoky cloud from hell that moved and crept in her head when she had just got rid of Doctor Harry and was trying to rest a minute. Wounded vanity, Ellen, said a sharp voice in the top of her mind. Don't let your wounded vanity get the upper hand of you. Plenty of girls get jilted. You were jilted, weren't you? Then stand up to it. Her eyelids wavered and let in streamers of blue-gray light like tissue paper over her eyes. She must get up and pull the shades down or she'd never sleep. She was in bed again and the shades were not down. How could that happen? Better turn over, hide from the light, sleeping in the light gave you nightmares. "Mother, how do you feel now?" and a stinging wetness on her forehead. But I don't like having my face washed in cold water!

Hapsy? George? Lydia? Jimmy? No, Cornelia, and her features were swollen and full of little puddles. "They're coming, darling, they'll all be here soon." Go wash your face, child, you look funny.

Instead of obeying, Cornelia knelt down and put her head on the pillow. She seemed to be talking but there was no sound.

"Well, are you tongue-tied? Whose birthday is it? Are you going to give a party?"

Cornelia's mouth moved urgently in strange shapes. "Don't do that, you bother me, daughter."

"Oh, no, Mother. Oh, no. . . ."

Nonsense. It was strange about children. They disputed your every word. "No what, Cornelia?"

"Here's Doctor Harry."

"I won't see that boy again. He just left five minutes ago."

"That was this morning, Mother. It's night now. Here's the nurse."

"This is Doctor Harry, Mrs. Weatherall. I never saw you look so young and happy!"

"Ah, I'll never be young again—but I'd be happy if they'd let me lie in peace and get rested."

She thought she spoke up loudly, but no one answered. A warm weight on her forehead, a warm bracelet on her wrist, and a breeze went on whispering, trying to tell her something. A shuffle of leaves in the everlasting hand of God, He blew on them and they danced and rattled. "Mother, don't mind, we're going to give you a little hypodermic." "Look here, daughter, how do ants get in this bed? I saw sugar ants yesterday." Did you send for Hapsy too?

It was Hapsy she really wanted. She had to go a long way back through a great many rooms to find Hapsy standing with a baby on her arm. She seemed to herself to be Hapsy also, and the baby on Hapsy's arm was Hapsy and himself and herself, all at once, and there was no surprise in the meeting. Then Hapsy melted from within and turned flimsy as gray gauze and the baby was a gauzy shadow, and Hapsy came up close and said, "I thought you'd never come," and looked at her very searchingly and said, "You haven't changed a bit!" They leaned forward to kiss, when Cornelia began whispering from a long way off, "Oh, is there anything you want to tell me? Is there anything I can do for you?"

Yes, she had changed her mind after sixty years and she would like to see George. I want you to find George. Find him and be sure to tell him I forgot him. I want him to know I had my husband just the same and my children and my house like any other woman. A good house too and a good husband that I loved and fine children out of him. Better than I hoped for even. Tell him I was given back everything he took away and more. Oh, no, oh, God, no, there was something else besides the house and the man and the children. Oh, surely they were not all? What was it? Something not given back. . . . Her breath crowded down under her ribs and grew into a monstrous frightening shape with cutting edges; it bored up into her head, and the agony was unbelievable: Yes, John, get the Doctor now, no more talk, my time has come.

When this one was born it should be the last. The last. It should have been born first, for it was the one she had truly wanted. Everything came in good time. Nothing left out, left over. She was strong, in three days she would be as well as ever. Better. A woman needed milk in her to have her full health.

"Mother, do you hear me?"

"I've been telling you—"

"Mother, Father Connolly's here."

"I went to Holy Communion only last week. Tell him I'm not so sinful as all that."

"Father just wants to speak to you."

He could speak as much as he pleased. It was like him to drop in and inquire about her soul as if it were a teething baby, and then stay on for a cup of tea and a round of cards and gossip. He always had a funny story of some sort, usually about an Irishman who made his little mistakes and confessed them, and the point lay in some absurd thing he would blurt out in the confessional showing his struggles between native piety and original sin. Granny felt easy about her soul. Cornelia, where are your manners? Give Father Connolly a chair. She had her secret comfortable understanding with a few favorite saints who cleared a straight road to God for her. All as surely signed and sealed as the papers for the new Forty Acres. Forever . . . heirs and assigns forever. Since the day the wedding cake was not cut, but thrown out and wasted. The whole bottom dropped out of the world, and there she was blind and sweating with nothing under her feet and the walls falling away. His hand had caught her under the breast, she had not fallen, there was the freshly polished floor with the green rug on it, just as before. He had cursed like a sailor's parrot and said, "I'll kill him for you." Don't lay a hand on him, for my sake leave something to God. "Now, Ellen, you must believe what I tell you. . . ."

So there was nothing, nothing to worry about any more, except sometimes in the night one of the children screamed in a nightmare, and they both hustled out shaking and hunting for the matches and calling, "There, wait a minute, here we are!" John, get the doctor now, Hapsy's time has come. But there was Hapsy standing by the bed in a white cap. "Cornelia, tell Hapsy to take off her cap. I can't see her plain."

Her eyes opened very wide and the room stood out like a picture she had seen somewhere. Dark colors with the shadows rising towards the ceiling in long angles. The tall black dresser gleamed with nothing on it but John's picture, enlarged from a little one, with John's eyes very black when they should have been blue. You never saw him, so how do you know how he looked? But the man insisted the copy was perfect, it was very rich and handsome. For a picture, yes, but it's not my husband. The table by the bed had a linen cover and a candle and a crucifix. The light was blue from Cornelia's silk lampshades. No sort of light at all, just frippery. You had to live forty years with kerosene lamps to appreciate honest electricity. She felt very strong and she saw Doctor Harry with a rosy nimbus around him.

"You look like a saint, Doctor Harry, and I vow that's as near as you'll ever come to it."

"She's saying something."

"I heard you, Cornelia. What's all this carrying-on?"

"Father Connolly's saying—"

Cornelia's voice staggered and bumped like a cart in a bad road. It rounded corners and turned back again and arrived nowhere. Granny stepped up in the cart very lightly and reached for the reins, but a man sat beside her and she knew him by his hands, driving the cart. She did not look in his face, for she knew without seeing, but looked instead down the road where the trees leaned over and bowed to each other and a thousand birds were singing a Mass. She felt like singing too, but she put her hand in the bosom of her dress and pulled out a rosary, and Father Connolly murmured Latin in a very solemn voice and tickled her feet. My God, will you stop that nonsense? I'm a married woman. What if he did run away and leave me to face the priest by myself? I found another a whole world better. I wouldn't have exchanged my husband for anybody except St. Michael himself, and you may tell him that for me with a thank you in the bargain.

Light flashed on her closed eyelids, and a deep roaring shook her. Cornelia, is that lightning? I hear thunder. There's going to be a storm. Close all the windows. Call the children in. . . . "Mother, here we are, all of us." "Is that you, Hapsy?" "Oh, no, I'm Lydia. We drove as fast as we could." Their faces drifted above her, drifted away. The rosary fell out of her hands and Lydia put it back. Jimmy tried to help, their hands fumbled together, and Granny closed two fingers around Jimmy's thumb. Beads wouldn't do, it must be something alive. She was so amazed her thoughts ran round and round. So, my dear Lord, this is my death and I wasn't even thinking about it. My children have come to see me die. But I can't, it's not time. Oh, I always hated surprises. I wanted to give Cornelia the amethyst set—Cornelia, you're to have the amethyst set, but Hapsy's to wear it when she wants, and, Doctor Harry, do shut up. Nobody sent for you. Oh, my dear Lord, do wait a minute. I meant to do something about the Forty Acres, Jimmy doesn't need it and Lydia will later on, with that worthless husband of hers. I meant to finish the altar cloth and send six bottles of wine to Sister Borgia for her dyspepsia. I want to send six bottles of wine to Sister Borgia, Father Connolly, now don't let me forget.

Cornelia's voice made short turns and tilted over and crashed. "Oh, Mother, oh, Mother, oh, Mother. . . ."

"I'm not going, Cornelia. I'm taken by surprise. I can't go."

You'll see Hapsy again. What about her? "I thought you'd never come." Granny made a long journey outward, looking for Hapsy. What if I don't find her? What then? Her heart sank down and down, there was no bottom to death, she couldn't come to the end of it. The blue light from Cornelia's lampshade drew into a tiny point in the center of her brain, it flickered and winked like an eye, quietly it fluttered and dwindled. Granny lay curled down within herself, amazed and watchful, staring at the point of light that was herself; her body was now only a deeper mass of shadow in an endless darkness and this darkness would curl around the light and swallow it up. God, give a sign!

For the second time there was no sign. Again no bridegroom and the priest in the house. She could not remember any other sorrow because this grief wiped them all away. Oh, no, there's nothing more cruel than this—I'll never forgive it. She stretched herself with a deep breath and blew out the light.

SATURDAY AFTERNOON

————

Erskine Caldwell

From *The Complete Stories of Erskine Caldwell,* 1941. Published in *American Earth,* 1931.

Erskine Caldwell (1903-   ) was born in Georgia and in his early years had varied employment at different places in the South. His first success came with *Tobacco Road* (1932) which was dramatized and had a long run on the stage. The novel exploits the earthiness of folk humor at the same time that it pleads the case of degraded sharecroppers such as the Jeter Lester of this book. *God's Little Acre* (1933), which has been fabulously popular, is cut to much the same pattern. Others of his novels dealing with Southern problems are *Trouble in July* (1940), *A House in the Uplands* (1946), and *Episode in Palmetta* (1950). In short stories such as those collected in the volume *Kneel to the Rising Son* (1935) Caldwell has probably done his best work. His book *Call It Experience* (1951) is a sort of literary autobiography. See W. M. Frohock, "Erskine Caldwell—The Dangers of Ambiguity," in *The Novel of Violence in America* (Second Edition, 1957), pages 106-123.

Tom Denny shoved the hunk of meat out of his way and stretched out on the meat block. He wanted to lie on his back and rest. The meat block was the only comfortable place in the butcher shop where a man could stretch out and Tom just had to rest every once in a while. He could prop his foot on the edge of the block, swing the other leg across his knee and be fairly comfortable with a hunk of rump steak under his head. The meat was nice and cool just after it came from the icehouse. Tom did that. He wanted to rest himself a while and he had to be comfortable on the meat block. He kicked off his shoes so he could wiggle his toes.

Tom's butcher shop did not have a very pleasant smell.

Strangers who went in to buy Tom's meat for the first time were always asking him what it was that had died between the walls. The smell got worse and worse year after year.

Tom bit off a chew of tobacco and made himself comfortable on the meat block.

There was a swarm of flies buzzing around the place; those lazy, stinging, fat and greasy flies that lived in Tom's butcher shop. A screen door at the front kept out some of them that tried to get inside, but if they were used to coming in and filling up on the fresh blood on the meat block they knew how to fly around to the back door where there had never been a screen.

Everybody ate Tom's meat, and liked it. There was no other butcher shop in town. You walked in and said, "Hello, Tom. How's everything today?" "Everything's slick as a whistle with me, but my old woman's got the chills and fever again." Then after Tom had finished telling how it felt to have chills and fever, you said, "I want a pound of pork chops, Tom." And Tom said, "By gosh, I'll git it for you right away." While you stood around waiting for the chops Tom turned the hunk of beef over two or three times businesslike and hacked off a pound of pork for you. If you wanted veal it was all the same to Tom. He slammed the hunk of beef around several times making a great to-do, and got the veal for you. He pleased everybody. Ask Tom for any kind of meat you could name, and Tom had it right there on the meat block waiting to be cut off and weighed.

Tom brushed the flies off his face and took a little snooze. It was midday. The country people had not yet got to town. It was laying-by season and everybody was working right up to twelve o'clock sun time, which was half an hour slower than railroad time. There was hardly anybody in town at this time of day, even though it was Saturday. All the town people who had wanted some of Tom's meat for Saturday dinner had already got what they needed, and it was too early in the day to buy Sunday meat. The best time of day to get meat from Tom if it was to be kept over until Sunday was about ten o'clock Saturday night. Then you could take it home and be fairly certain that it would not turn bad before noon the next day—if the weather was not too hot.

The flies buzzed and lit on Tom's mouth and nose and Tom knocked them away with his hand and tried to sleep on the meat block with the cool hunk of rump steak under his head. The tobacco juice kept trying to trickle down his throat and Tom had to keep spitting it out. There was a cigar box half full of sawdust in the corner behind the showcase where livers and brains were kept for display, but he could not quite spit that far from the position he was in. The tobacco juice splattered on the floor midway between the meat block and cigar box. What little of it dripped on the piece of rump steak did not really matter: most people cleaned their meat before they cooked and ate it, and it would all wash off.

But the danged flies! They kept on buzzing and stinging as mean as ever, and there is nothing any meaner than a lazy, well-fed, butcher-shop fly in the summertime, anyway. Tom knocked them off his face and spat them off his mouth the best he could without having to move too much. After a while he let them alone.

Tom was enjoying a good little snooze when Jim Baxter came running through the back door from the barbershop on the corner. Jim was Tom's partner and he came in sometimes on busy days to help out. He was a great big man, almost twice as large as Tom. He always wore a big wide-brimmed black hat and a blue shirt with the sleeves rolled up above his elbows. He had a large egg-shaped belly over which his breeches were always slipping down. When he walked he tugged at his breeches all the time, pulling them up over the top of his belly. But they were always working down until it looked as if they were ready to drop to the ground any minute and trip him. Jim would not wear suspenders. A belt was more sporty-looking.

Tom was snoozing away when Jim ran in the back door and grabbed him by the shoulders. A big handful of flies had gone to sleep on Tom's mouth. Jim shooed them off.

"Hey, Tom, Tom!" Jim shouted breathlessly. "Wake up, Tom! Wake up quick!"

Tom jumped to the floor and pulled on his shoes. He had become so accustomed to people coming in and waking him up to buy a quarter's worth of steak or a quarter's worth of ham that he had mistaken Jim for a customer. He rubbed the back of his hands over his mouth to take away the fly stings.

"What the hell!" he sputtered, looking up and seeing Jim standing there beside him. "What you want?"

"Come on, Tom! Git your gun! We're going after a nigger down the creek a ways."

"God Almighty, Jim!" Tom shouted, now fully awake. He clutched Jim's arm and begged: "You going to git a nigger, sure enough?"

"You're damn right, Tom. You know that gingerbread nigger what used to work on the railroad a long time back? Him's the nigger we're going to git. And we're going to git him good and proper, the yellow-face coon. He said something to Fred Jackson's oldest gal down the road yonder about an hour ago. Fred told us all about it over at the barbershop. Come on, Tom. We got to hurry. I expect we'll jerk him up pretty soon now."

Tom tied on his shoes and ran across the street behind Jim. Tom had his shotgun under his arm, and Jim had pulled the cleaver out of the meat block. They'd get the God-damn nigger all right—God damn his yellow hide to hell!

Tom climbed into an automobile with some other men. Jim jumped on the running board of another car just as it was leaving. There were thirty or forty cars headed for the creek bottom already and more getting ready to start.

They had a place already picked out at the creek. There was a clearing in the woods by the road and there was just enough room to do the job like it should be done. Plenty of dry brushwood nearby and a good-sized sweet-gum tree in the middle of the clearing. The automobiles stopped and the men jumped out in a hurry. Some others had gone for Will Maxie. Will was the gingerbread Negro. They would probably find him at home laying his cotton by. Will could grow good cotton. He cut out all the grass first, and then he banked his rows with earth. Everybody else laid his cotton by without going to the trouble of taking out the grass. But Will was a pretty smart Negro. And he could raise a lot of corn too, to the acre. He always cut out the grass before he laid his corn by.

But nobody liked Will. He made too much money by taking out the grass before laying by his cotton and corn. He made more money than Tom and Jim made in the butcher shop selling people meat.

Doc Cromer had sent his boy down from the drugstore with half a dozen cases of Coca-Cola and a piece of ice in a wash tub. The tub had some muddy water put in it from the creek, then the chunk of ice, and then three cases of Coca-Cola. When they were gone the boy would put the other three cases in the tub and give the dopes a chance to cool. Everybody likes to drink a lot of dopes when they are nice and cold.

Tom went out in the woods to take a drink of corn with Jim and Hubert Wells. Hubert always carried a jug of corn with him wherever he happened to be going. He made the whisky himself at his own still and got a fairly good living by selling it around the courthouse and the barbershop. Hubert made the best corn in the county.

Will Maxie was coming up the big road in a hurry. A couple of dozen men were behind him poking him with sticks. Will was getting old. He had a wife and three grown daughters, all married and settled. Will was a pretty good Negro too, minding his own business, stepping out of the road when he met a white man, and otherwise behaving himself. But nobody liked Will. He made too much money by taking the grass out of his cotton before it was laid by.

Will came running up the road and the men steered him into the clearing. It was all fixed. There was a big pile of brushwood and a trace chain for his neck and one for his feet. That would hold him. There were two or three cans of gasoline, too.

Doc Cromer's boy was doing a good business with his Coca-Colas. Only five or six bottles of the first three cases were left in the wash tub. He was getting ready to put the other cases in now and give the dopes a chance to get nice and cool. Everybody likes to have a dope every once in a while.

The Cromer boy would probably sell out and have to go back to town and bring back several more cases. And yet there was not such a big crowd today, either. It was the hot weather that made people have to drink a lot of dopes to stay cool. There were only a hundred and fifty or seventy-five there today. There had not been enough time for the word to get passed around. Tom would have missed it if Jim had not run in and told him about it while he was taking a nap on the meat block.

Will Maxie did not drink Coca-Cola. Will never spent his money on anything like that. That was what was wrong with him. He was too damn good for a Negro. He did not drink corn whisky, nor make it; he did not carry a knife, nor a razor; he bared his head when he met a white man, and he lived with his own wife. But they had him now! God damn his gingerbread hide to hell! They had him where he could not take any more grass out of his cotton before laying it by. They had him tied to a sweet-gum tree in the clearing at the creek with a trace chain around his neck and another around his knees. Yes, sir, they had Will Maxie now, the yellow-face coon! He would not take any more grass out of his cotton before laying it by!

Tom was feeling good. Hubert gave him another drink in the woods. Hubert was all right. He made good corn whisky. Tom liked him for that. And Hubert always took his wife a big piece of meat Saturday night to use over Sunday. Nice meat, too. Tom cut off the meat and Hubert took it home and made a present of it to his wife.

Will Maxie was going up in smoke. When he was just about gone they gave him the lead. Tom stood back and took good aim and fired away at Will with his shotgun as fast as he could breech it and put in a new load. About forty or more of the other men had shotguns too. They filled him so full of lead that his body sagged from his neck where the trace chain held him up.

The Cromer boy had sold completely out. All of his ice and dopes were gone. Doc Cromer would feel pretty good when his boy brought back all that money. Six whole cases he sold, at a dime a bottle. If he had brought along another case or two he could have sold them easily enough. Everybody likes Coca-Cola. There is nothing better to drink on a hot day, if the dopes are nice and cool.

After a while the men got ready to draw the body up in the tree and tie it to a limb so it could hang there, but Tom and Jim could not wait and they went back to town the first chance they got to ride. They were in a big hurry. They had been gone several hours and it was almost four o'clock. A lot of people came downtown early Saturday afternoon to get their Sunday meat before it was picked over by the country people. Tom and Jim had to hurry back and open up the meat market and get to work slicing steaks and chopping soupbones with the cleaver on the meat block. Tom was the butcher. He did all the work with the meat. He went out and killed a cow and quartered her. Then he hauled the meat to the butcher shop and hung it on the hooks in the icehouse. When somebody wanted to buy some meat, he took one of the quarters from the hook and threw it on the meat block and cut what you asked for. You told Tom what you wanted and he gave it to you, no matter what it was you asked for.

Then you stepped over to the counter and paid Jim the money for it. Jim was the cashier. He did all the talking, too. Tom had to do the cutting and weighing. Jim's egg-shaped belly was too big for him to work around the meat block. It got in his way when he tried to slice you a piece of tenderloin steak, so Tom did that and Jim took the money and put it into the cashbox under the counter.

Tom and Jim got back to town just in time. There was a big crowd standing around on the street getting ready to do their weekly trading, and they had to have some meat. You went in the butcher shop and said, "Hello, Tom. I want two pounds and a half of pork chops." Tom said, "Hello, I'll get it for you right away." While you were waiting for Tom to cut the meat off the hunk of rump steak you asked him how was everything.

"Everything's slick as a whistle," he said, "except my old woman's got the chills and fever pretty bad again."

Tom weigned the pork chops and wrapped them up for you and then you stepped over to Jim and paid him the money. Jim was the cashier. His egg-shaped belly was too big for him to work around the meat block. Tom did that part, and Jim took the money and put it into the cashbox under the counter.

THE LOST BOY

———

Thomas Wolfe

From *The Hills Beyond,* by Thomas Wolfe, 1941; first published in *Redbook,* November, 1937.

Thomas Wolfe (1900-1938) grew up in Asheville, North Carolina, and attended the state university; and though he afterward studied at Harvard, taught at New York University, and traveled in Europe, the impressions of his youthful experiences in his family and in Asheville appear on virtually every page that he wrote. The two novels which he published himself, *Look Homeward, Angel* (1929) and *Of Time and the River* (1935), deal with the autobiographical character, Eugene Gant. A parallel character, George Webber, appears in the two novels published after Wolfe's death, *The Web and the Rock* (1939) and *You Can't Go Home Again* (1940). A one-volume selection of Wolfe's letters has been published (1958) by Elizabeth Nowell. Louis D. Rubin's *Thomas Wolfe: The Weather of His Youth* (1955) is an interpretative study. In a book entitled *Thomas Wolfe's Characters: Portraits from Life* (1957) Floyd C. Watkins treats mainly Wolfe's characters drawn from his acquaintances in Asheville. See also W. M. Frohock, "Thomas Wolfe—Time and the National Neurosis," in *The Novel of Violence in America* (Second Edition, 1957), pages 52-68; also the chapters on Wolfe in Alfred Kazin, *On Native Grounds* (1942), and Maxwell Geismar, *Writers in Crisis* (1942).

I

Light came and went and came again, the booming strokes of three o'clock beat out across the town in thronging bronze from the courthouse bell, light winds of April blew the fountain out in rainbow sheets, until the plume returned and pulsed, as Grover turned into the Square. He was a child, dark-eyed and grave, birthmarked upon his neck—a berry of warm brown—and with a gentle face, too quiet and too listening for his years. The scuffed boy's shoes, the thick-ribbed stockings gartered at the knees, the short knee pants cut straight with three small useless buttons at the side, the sailor blouse, the old cap battered out of shape, perched sideways up on top of the raven head, the old soiled canvas bag slung from the shoulder, empty now, but waiting for the crisp sheets of the afternoon—these friendly, shabby garments, shaped by Grover, uttered him. He turned and passed along the north side of the Square and in that moment saw the union of Forever and of Now.

Light came and went and came again, the great plume of the fountain pulsed and winds of April sheeted it across the Square in a rainbow gossamer of spray. The fire department horses drummed on the floors with wooden stomp, most casually, and with dry whiskings of their clean, coarse tails. The street cars ground into the Square from every portion of the compass and halted briefly like wound toys in their familiar quarter-hourly formula. A dray, hauled by a boneyard nag, rattled across the cobbles on the other side before his father's shop. The courthouse bell boomed out its solemn warning of immediate three, and everything was just the same as it had always been.

He saw that haggis of vexed shapes with quiet eyes—that hodge-podge of ill-sorted architectures that made up the Square, and he did not feel lost. For "Here," thought Grover, "here is the Square as it has always been—and papa's shop, the fire department and the City Hall, the fountain pulsing with its plume, the street cars coming in and halting at the quarter hour, the hardware store on the corner there, the row of old brick buildings on this side of the street, the people passing and the light that comes and changes and that always will come back again, and everything that comes and goes and changes in the Square, and yet will be the same again. And here," the boy thought, "is Grover with his paper bag. Here is old Grover, almost twelve years old. Here is the month of April, 1904. Here is the courthouse bell and three o'clock. Here is

Grover on the Square that never changes. Here is Grover, caught upon this point of time."

It seemed to him that the Square, itself the accidental masonry of many years, the chance agglomeration of time and of disrupted strivings, was the center of the universe. It was for him, in his soul's picture, the earth's pivot, the granite core of changelessness, the eternal place where all things came and passed, and yet abode forever and would never change.

He passed the old shack on the corner—the wooden fire-trap where S. Goldberg ran his wiener stand. Then he passed the Singer place next door, with its gleaming display of new machines. He saw them and admired them, but he felt no joy. They brought back to him the busy hum of housework and of women sewing, the intricacy of stitch and weave, the mystery of style and pattern, the memory of women bending over flashing needles, the pedaled tread, the busy whir. It was women's work: it filled him with unknown associations of dullness and of vague depression. And always, also, with a moment's twinge of horror, for his dark eye would always travel toward that needle stitching up and down so fast the eye could never follow it. And then he would remember how his mother once had told him she had driven the needle through her finger, and always, when he passed this place, he would remember it and for a moment crane his neck and turn his head away.

He passed on then, but had to stop again next door before the music store. He always had to stop by places that had shining perfect things in them. He loved hardware stores and windows full of accurate geometric tools. He loved windows full of hammers, saws, and planing boards. He liked windows full of strong new rakes and hoes, with unworn handles, of white perfect wood, stamped hard and vivid with the maker's seal. He loved to see such things as these in the windows of hardware stores. And he would fairly gloat upon them and think that some day he would own a set himself.

Also, he always stopped before the music and piano store. It was a splendid store. And in the window was a small white dog upon his haunches, with head cocked gravely to one side, a small white dog that never moved, that never barked, that listened attentively at the flaring funnel of a horn to hear "His Master's Voice"—a horn forever silent, and a voice that never spoke. And within were many rich and shining shapes of great pianos, an air of splendor and of wealth.

And now, indeed, he *was* caught, held suspended. A waft of air, warm, chocolate-laden, filled his nostrils. He tried to pass the white front of the little eight-foot shop; he paused, struggling with conscience; he could not go on. It was the little candy shop run by old Crocker and his wife. And Grover could not pass.

"Old stingy Crockers!" he thought scornfully. "I'll not go there any more. But—" as the maddening fragrance of rich cooking chocolate touched him once again—"I'll just look in the window and see what they've got." He paused a moment, looking with his dark and quiet eyes into the window of the little candy shop. The window, spotlessly clean, was filled with trays of fresh-made candy. His eyes rested on a tray of chocolate drops. Unconsciously he licked his lips. Put one of them upon your tongue and it just melted there, like honeydew. And then the trays full of rich home-made fudge. He gazed longingly at the deep body of the chocolate fudge, reflectively at maple walnut, more critically, yet with longing, at the mints, the nougatines, and all the other dainties.

"Old stingy Crockers!" Grover muttered once again, and turned to go. "I wouldn't go in *there* again."

And yet he did not go away. "Old stingy Crockers" they might be; still, they did make the best candy in town, the best, in fact, that he had ever tasted.

He looked through the window back into the little shop and saw Mrs. Crocker there. A customer had gone in and had made a purchase, and as Grover looked he saw Mrs. Crocker, with her little wrenny face, her pinched features, lean over and peer primly at the scales. She had a piece of fudge in her clean, bony, little fingers, and as Grover looked, she broke it, primly, in her little bony hands. She dropped a morsel down into the scales. They weighted down alarmingly, and her thin lips tightened. She snatched the piece of fudge out of the scales and broke it carefully once again. This time the scales wavered, went down very slowly, and came back again. Mrs. Crocker carefully put the reclaimed piece of fudge back in the tray, dumped the remainder in a paper bag, folded it and gave it to the customer, counted the money carefully and doled it out into the till, the pennies in one place, the nickels in another.

Grover stood there, looking scornfully. "Old stingy Crocker—afraid that she might give a crumb away!"

He grunted scornfully and again he turned to go. But now Mr. Crocker came out from the little partitioned place where they made all their candy, bearing a tray of fresh-made fudge in his skinny hands. Old Man Crocker rocked along the counter to the front and put it down. He really rocked along. He was a cripple. And like his wife, he was a wrenny, wizened little creature, with bony hands, thin lips, a pinched and meager face. One leg was inches shorter than the other, and on this leg there was an enormous thick-soled boot, with a kind of wooden, rocker-like arrangement, six inches high at least, to make up for the deficiency. On this wooden cradle Mr. Crocker rocked along, with a prim and apprehensive little smile, as if he were afraid he was going to lose something.

"Old stingy Crocker!" muttered Grover. "Humph! He wouldn't give you anything!"

And yet—he did not go away. He hung there curiously, peering through the window, with his dark and gentle face now focused and intent, alert and curious, flattening his nose against the glass. Unconsciously he scratched the thick-ribbed fabric of one stockinged leg with the scuffed and worn toe of his old shoe. The fresh, warm odor of the new-made fudge was delicious. It was a little maddening. Half consciously he began to fumble in one trouser pocket, and pulled out his purse, a shabby worn old black one with a twisted clasp. He opened it and prowled about inside.

What he found was not inspiring—a nickel and two pennies and —he had forgotten them—the stamps. He took the stamps out and unfolded them. There were five twos, eight ones, all that remained of the dollar-sixty-cents' worth which Reed, the pharmacist, had given him for running errands a week or two before.

"Old Crocker," Grover thought, and looked somberly at the grotesque little form as it rocked back into the shop again, around the counter, and up the other side. "Well—" again he looked indefinitely at the stamps in his hand—"he's had all the rest of them. He might as well take these."

So, soothing conscience with this sop of scorn, he went into the shop and stood looking at the trays in the glass case and finally decided. Pointing with a slightly grimy finger at the fresh-made tray of chocolate fudge, he said, "I'll take fifteen cents' worth of this, Mr. Crocker." He paused a moment, fighting with embarrassment, then he lifted his dark face and said quietly, "And please, I'll have to give you stamps again."

Mr. Crocker made no answer. He did not look at Grover. He pressed his lips together primly. He went rocking away and got the candy scoop, came back, slid open the door of the glass case, put fudge into the scoop, and, rocking to the scales, began to weigh the candy out. Grover watched him as he peered and squinted, he watched him purse and press his lips together, he saw him take a piece of fudge and break it in two parts. And then old Crocker broke two parts in two again. He weighed, he squinted, and he hovered, until it seemed to Grover that by calling *Mrs.* Crocker stingy he had been guilty of a rank injustice. But finally, to his vast relief, the job was over, the scales hung there, quivering apprehensively, upon the very hair-line of nervous balance, as if even the scales were afraid that one more move from Old Man Crocker and they would be undone.

Mr. Crocker took the candy then and dumped it in a paper bag and, rocking back along the counter toward the boy, he dryly said: "Where are the stamps?" Grover gave them to him. Mr. Crocker relinquished his clawlike hold upon the bag and set it down upon the counter. Grover took the bag and dropped it in his canvas sack, and then remembered. "Mr. Crocker—" again he felt the old embarrassment that was almost like strong pain—"I gave you too much," Grover said. "There were eighteen cents in stamps. You —you can just give me three ones back."

Mr. Crocker did not answer. He was busy with his bony little hands, unfolding the stamps and flattening them out on top of the glass counter. When he had done so, he peered at them sharply for a moment, thrusting his scrawny neck forward and running his eye up and down, like a bookkeeper who totes up rows of figures.

When he had finished, he said tartly: "I don't like this kind of business. If you want candy, you should have the money for it. I'm not a post office. The next time you come in here and want anything, you'll have to pay me money for it."

Hot anger rose in Grover's throat. His olive face suffused with angry color. His tarry eyes got black and bright. He was on the verge of saying: "Then why did you take my other stamps? Why do you tell me now, when you have taken all the stamps I had, that you don't want them?"

But he was a boy, a boy of eleven years, a quiet, gentle, gravely thoughtful boy, and he had been taught how to respect his elders. So he just stood there looking with his tar-black eyes. Old Man Crocker, pursing at the mouth a little, without meeting Grover's gaze, took the stamps up in his thin, parched fingers and, turning, rocked away with them down to the till.

He took the twos and folded them and laid them in one rounded scallop, then took the ones and folded them and put them in the one next to it. Then he closed the till and started to rock off, down toward the other end. Grover, his face now quiet and grave, kept looking at him, but Mr. Crocker did not look at Grover. Instead he began to take some stamped cardboard shapes and fold them into boxes.

In a moment Grover said, "Mr. Crocker, will you give me the three ones, please?"

Mr. Crocker did not answer. He kept folding boxes, and he compressed his thin lips quickly as he did so. But Mrs. Crocker, back turned to her spouse, also folding boxes with her birdlike hands, muttered tartly: "Hm! *I'd* give him nothing!"

Mr. Crocker looked up, looked at Grover, said, "What are you waiting for?"

"Will you give me the three ones, please?" Grover said.

"I'll give you nothing," Mr. Crocker said.

He left his work and came rocking forward along the counter. "Now you get out of here! Don't you come in here with any more of those stamps," said Mr. Crocker.

"I should like to know where he gets them—that's what *I* should like to know," said Mrs. Crocker.

She did not look up as she said these words. She inclined her head a little to the side, in Mr. Crocker's direction, and continued to fold the boxes with her bony fingers.

"You get out of here!" said Mr. Crocker. "And don't you come back here with any stamps. . . . Where did you get those stamps?" he said.

"That's just what *I've* been thinking," Mrs. Crocker said. *"I've* been thinking all along."

"You've been coming in here for the last two weeks with those stamps," said Mr. Crocker. "I don't like the look of it. Where did you get those stamps?" he said.

"That's what *I've* been thinking," said Mrs. Crocker, for a second time.

Grover had got white underneath his olive skin. His eyes had lost their luster. They looked like dull, stunned balls of tar. "From Mr. Reed," he said. "I got the stamps from Mr. Reed." Then he burst out desperately: "Mr. Crocker—Mr. Reed will tell you how I got the stamps. I did some work for Mr. Reed, he gave me those stamps two weeks ago."

"Mr. Reed," said Mrs. Crocker acidly. She did not turn her head. "I call it mighty funny."

"Mr. Crocker," Grover said, "if you'll just let me have three ones——"

"You get out of here!" cried Mr. Crocker, and he began rocking forward toward Grover. "Now don't you come in here again, boy! There's something funny about this whole business! I don't like the look of it," said Mr. Crocker. "If you can't pay as other people do, then I don't want your trade."

"Mr. Crocker," Grover said again, and underneath the olive skin his face was gray, "if you'll just let me have those three——"

"You get out of here!" Mr. Crocker cried, rocking down toward the counter's end. "If you don't get out, boy——"

"*I'd* call a policeman, that's what I'd do," Mrs. Crocker said.

Mr. Crocker rocked around the lower end of the counter. He came rocking up to Grover. "You get out," he said.

He took the boy and pushed him with his bony little hands, and Grover was sick and gray down to the hollow pit of his stomach. "You've got to give me those three ones," he said.

"You get out of here!" shrilled Mr. Crocker. He seized the screen door, pulled it open, and pushed Grover out. "Don't you come back in here," he said, pausing for a moment, and working thinly at the lips. He turned and rocked back in the shop again. The screen door slammed behind him. Grover stood there on the pavement. And light came and went and came again into the Square.

The boy stood there, and a wagon rattled past. There were some people passing by, but Grover did not notice them. He stood there blindly, in the watches of the sun, feeling this was Time, this was the center of the universe, the granite core of changelessness, and feeling, this is Grover, this the Square, this is Now.

But something had gone out of day. He felt the overwhelming, soul-sickening guilt that all the children, all the good men of the earth, have felt since Time began. And even anger had died down, had been drowned out, in this swelling tide of guilt, and "This is the Square"—thought Grover as before—"This is Now. There is my father's shop. And all of it is as it has always been—save I."

And the Square reeled drunkenly around him, light went in blind gray motes before his eyes, the fountain sheeted out to rainbow iridescence and returned to its proud, pulsing plume again. But all the brightness had gone out of day, and "Here is the Square, and here is permanence, and here is Time—and all of it the same as it has always been, save I."

The scuffed boots of the lost boy moved and stumbled blindly. The numb feet crossed the pavement—reached the cobbled street, reached the plotted central square—the grass plots, and the flower beds, so soon to be packed with red geraniums.

"I want to be alone," thought Grover, "where I cannot go near him. . . . Oh God, I hope he never hears, that no one ever tells him——"

The plume blew out, the iridescent sheet of spray blew over him.

He passed through, found the other side and crossed the street, and —"Oh God, if papa ever hears!" thought Grover, as his numb feet started up the steps into his father's shop.

He found and felt the steps—the width and thickness of old lumber twenty feet in length. He saw it all—the iron columns on his father's porch, painted with the dull anomalous black-green that all such columns in this land and weather come to; two angels, flyspecked, and the waiting stones. Beyond and all around, in the stonecutter's shop, cold shapes of white and marble, rounded stone, the languid angel with strong marble hands of love.

He went on down the aisle, the white shapes stood around him. He went on to the back of the workroom. This he knew—the little cast-iron stove in the left-hand corner, caked, brown, heat-blistered, and the elbow of the long stack running out across the shop; the high and dirty window looking down across the Market Square toward Niggertown; the rude old shelves, plank-boarded, thick, the wood not smooth but pulpy, like the strong hair of an animal; upon the shelves the chisels of all sizes and a layer of stone dust; an emery wheel with pump tread; and a door that let out on the alleyway, yet the alleyway twelve feet below. Here in the room, two trestles of this coarse spiked wood upon which rested gravestones, and at one, his father at work.

The boy looked, saw the name was Creasman: saw the carved analysis of John, the symmetry of the s, the fine sentiment that was being polished off beneath the name and date: "John Creasman, November 7, 1903."

Gant looked up. He was a man of fifty-three, gaunt-visaged, mustache cropped, immensely long and tall and gaunt. He wore good dark clothes—heavy, massive—save he had no coat. He worked in shirt-sleeves with his vest on, a strong watch chain stretching across his vest, wing collar and black tie, Adam's apple, bony forehead, bony nose, light eyes, gray-green, undeep and cold, and, somehow, lonely-looking, a striped apron going up around his shoulders, and starched cuffs. And in one hand a tremendous rounded wooden mallet like a butcher's bole; and in his other hand, a strong cold chisel.

"How are you, son?"

He did not look up as he spoke. He spoke quietly, absently. He worked upon the chisel and the wooden mallet, as a jeweler might work on a watch, except that in the man and in the wooden mallet there was power too.

"What is it, son?" he said.

He moved around the table from the head, started up on "J" once again.

"Papa, I never stole the stamps," said Grover.

Gant put down the mallet, laid the chisel down. He came around the trestle.

"What?" he said.

As Grover winked his tar-black eyes, they brightened, the hot tears shot out. "I never stole the stamps," he said.

"Hey? What is this?" his father said. "What stamps?"

"That Mr. Reed gave me, when the other boy was sick and I worked there for three days. . . . And Old Man Crocker," Grover said, "he took all the stamps. And I told him Mr. Reed had given them to me. And now he owes me three ones—and Old Man Crocker says he don't believe that they were mine. He says—he says—that I must have taken them somewhere," Grover blurted out.

"The stamps that Reed gave you—hey?" the stonecutter said. "The stamps you had—" He wet his thumb upon his lips, threw back his head and slowly swung his gaze around the ceiling, then turned and strode quickly from his workshop out into the store-room.

Almost at once he came back again, and as he passed the old gray painted-board partition of his office he cleared his throat and wet his thumb and said, "Now, I tell you——"

Then he turned and strode up toward the front again and cleared his throat and said, "I tell you now—" He wheeled about and started back, and as he came along the aisle between the mar-shaled rows of gravestones he said beneath his breath, "By God, now——"

He took Grover by the hand and they went out flying. Down the aisle they went by all the gravestones, past the fly-specked angels waiting there, and down the wooden steps and across the Square. The fountain pulsed, the plume blew out in sheeted iridescence, and it swept across them; an old gray horse, with a peaceful look about his torn lips, swucked up the cool mountain water from the trough as Grover and his father went across the Square, but they did not notice it.

They crossed swiftly to the other side in a direct line to the candy shop. Gant was still dressed in his long striped apron, and he was still holding Grover by the hand. He opened the screen door and stepped inside.

"Give him the stamps," Gant said.

Mr. Crocker came rocking forward behind the counter, with the prim and careful look that now was somewhat like a smile. "It was just—" he said.

"Give him the stamps," Gant said, and threw some coins down on the counter.

Mr. Crocker rocked away and got the stamps. He came rocking back. "I just didn't know—" he said.

The stonecutter took the stamps and gave them to the boy. And Mr. Crocker took the coins.

"It was just that—" Mr. Crocker began again, and smiled.

Gant cleared his throat: "You never were a father," he said. "You never knew the feelings of a father, or understood the feelings of a child; and that is why you acted as you did. But a judgment is upon you. God has cursed you. He has afflicted you. He has made you lame and childless as you are—and lame and childless, miserable as you are, you will go to your grave and be forgotten!"

And Crocker's wife kept kneading her bony little hands and said imploringly, "Oh, no—oh don't say that, please don't say that."

The stonecutter, the breath still hoarse in him, left the store, still holding the boy tightly by the hand. Light came again into the day.

"Well, son," he said, and laid his hand on the boy's back. "Well, son," he said, "now don't you mind."

They walked across the Square, the sheeted spray of iridescent light swept out on them, the horse swizzled at the water-trough, and "Well, son," the stonecutter said.

And the old horse sloped down, ringing with his hoofs upon the cobblestones.

"Well, son," said the stonecutter once again, "Be a good boy."

And he trod his own steps then with his great stride and went back again into his shop.

The lost boy stood upon the Square, hard by the porch of his father's shop.

"This is Time," thought Grover. "Here is the Square, here is my father's shop, and here am I."

And light came and went and came again—but now not quite the same as it had done before. The boy saw the pattern of familiar shapes and knew that they were just the same as they had always been. But something had gone out of day, and something had come in again. Out of the vision of those quiet eyes some brightness had gone, and into their vision had come some deeper color. He could not say, he did not know through what transforming shadows life had passed within that quarter hour. He only knew that something had been lost—something forever gained.

Just then a buggy curved out through the Square, and fastened to the rear end was a poster, and it said "St. Louis" and "Excursion" and "The Fair."

II THE MOTHER

As we went down through Indiana—you were too young, child, to remember it—but I always think of all of you the way you looked that morning, when we went down through Indiana, going to the Fair. All of the apple trees were coming out, and it was April; it was the beginning of spring in southern Indiana and everything was getting green. Of course we don't have farms at home like those in Indiana. The childern had never seen such farms as those, and I reckon, kidlike, they had to take it in.

So all of them kept running up and down the aisle—well, no, except for you and Grover. *You* were too young, Eugene. You were just three, I kept you with me. As for Grover—well, I'm going to tell you about that.

But the rest of them kept running up and down the aisle and from one window to another. They kept calling out and hollering to each other every time they saw something new. They kept try-

ing to look out on all sides, in every way at once, as if they wished
they had eyes at the back of their heads. It was the first time any of
them had ever been in Indiana, and I reckon that it all seemed
strange and new.

And so it seemed they couldn't get enough. It seemed they never
could be still. They kept running up and down and back and forth,
hollering and shouting to each other, until—"I'll vow! You childern! I never saw the beat of you!" I said. "The way that you keep
running up and down and back and forth and never can be quiet
for a minute beats all I ever saw," I said.

You see, they were excited about going to St. Louis, and so
curious over everything they saw. They couldn't help it, and they
wanted to see everything. But—"I'll vow!" I said. "If you childern
don't sit down and rest you'll be worn to a frazzle before we ever
get to see St. Louis and the Fair!"

Except for Grover! He—no, sir! not him. Now, boy, I want to
tell you—I've raised the lot of you—and if I do say so, there wasn't
a numbskull in the lot. But *Grover!* Well, you've all grown up now,
all of you have gone away, and none of you are childern any more.
. . . And of course, I hope that, as the fellow says, you have
reached the dignity of man's estate. I suppose you have the judgment of grown men. . . . But *Grover! Grover* had it even then!

Oh, even as a child, you know—at a time when I was almost
afraid to trust the rest of you out of my sight—I could depend on
Grover. He could go anywhere, I could send him anywhere, and
I'd always know he'd get back safe, and do exactly what I told him
to!

Why, I didn't even have to tell him. You could send that child to
market and tell him what you wanted, and he'd come home with
twice as much as you could get yourself for the same money!

Now you know, I've always been considered a good trader.
But *Grover!*—why, it got so finally that I wouldn't even tell him.
Your papa said to me: "You'd be better off if you'd just tell him
what you want and leave the rest to him. For," your papa says,
"damned if I don't believe he's a better trader than you are. He gets
more for the money than anyone I ever saw."

Well, I had to admit it, you know. I had to own up then.

Grover, even as a child, was a far better trader than I was. . . .
Why, yes, they told it on him all over town, you know. They
said all of the market men, all of the farmers, knew him. They'd
begin to laugh when they saw him coming—they'd say: "Look out!
Here's Grover! Here's one trader you're not going to fool!"

And they were right! *That* child! I'd say, "Grover, suppose you
run uptown and see if they've got anything good to *eat* today"—
and I'd just wink at him, you know, but he'd know what I meant. I
wouldn't let on that I *wanted* anything exactly, but I'd say, "Now it
just occurs to me that some good fresh stuff may be coming in
from the country, so suppose you take this dollar and just see what
you can do with it."

Well, sir, that was all that was needed. The minute you told that
child that you depended on his judgment, he'd have gone to the
ends of the earth for you—and, let me tell you something, he
wouldn't *miss,* either!

His eyes would get as black as coals—oh! the way that child
would look at you, the intelligence and sense in his expression. He'd
say: "Yes, *ma'am!* Now don't you worry, mama. You leave it all to
me—and I'll do *good!*" said Grover.

And he'd be off like a streak of lightning and—oh Lord! As your
father said to me, "I've been living in this town for almost thirty
years," he said—"I've seen it grow up from a crossroads village, and
I thought I knew everything there was to know about it—but that
child—." your papa says—"he knows places that I never heard of!"
. . . Oh, he'd go right down there to that place below your papa's
shop where the draymen and the country people used to park their
wagons—or he'd go down there to those old lots on Concord
Street where the farmers used to keep their wagons. And, child
that he was, he'd go right in among them, sir—*Grover* would!—go
right in and barter with them like a grown man!

And he'd come home with things he'd bought that would make
your eyes stick out. . . . Here he comes one time with another boy,
dragging a great bushel basket full of ripe termaters between them.
"Why, Grover!" I says. "How on earth are we ever going to use
them? Why they'll go bad on us before we're half way through
with them." "Well, mama," he says, "I know—" oh, just as solemn

as a judge—"but they were the last the man had," he says, "and he wanted to go home, and so I got them for ten cents," he says. "They were so cheap," said Grover, "I thought it was a shame to let 'em go, and I figgered that what we couldn't eat—why," says Grover, "you could *put up!*" Well, the way he said it—so earnest and so serious—I had to laugh. "But I'll vow!" I said. "If you don't beat all!" . . . But that was *Grover!*—the way he was in *those* days! As everyone said, boy that he was, he had the sense and judgment of a grown man. . . . Child, child, I've seen you all grow up, and all of you were bright enough. There were no half-wits in *my* family. But for all-round intelligence, judgment, and general ability, Grover surpassed the whole crowd. I've never seen his equal, and everyone who knew him as a child will say the same.

So that's what I tell them now when they ask me about all of you. I have to tell the truth. I always said that *you* were smart enough, Eugene—but when they come around and brag to me about you, and about how you have got on and have a kind of name—I don't let on, you know. I just sit there and let them talk. I don't brag on you—if *they* want to brag on you, that's *their* business. I never bragged on one of my own childern in my life. When father raised us up, we were all brought up to believe that it was not good breeding to brag about your kin. "If the others want to do it," father said, "well, let *them* do it. Don't ever let on by a word or sign that you know what they are talking about. Just let *them* do the talking, and say nothing."

So when they come around and tell me all about the things *you've* done—I don't let on to them, I never say a word. Why yes! —why, here, you know—oh, along about a month or so ago, this feller comes—a well-dressed man, you know—he looked intelligent, a good substantial sort of person. He said he came from New Jersey, or somewhere up in that part of the country, and he began to ask me all sorts of questions—what you were like when you were a boy, and all such stuff as that.

I just pretended to study it all over and then I said, "Well, yes"— real serious-like, you know—"well, yes—I reckon I ought to know a little something about him. Eugene was my child, just the same as all the others were. I brought him up just the way I brought up all the others. And," I says—oh, just as solemn as you please—"he wasn't a *bad* sort of a boy. Why," I says, "up to the time that he was twelve years old he was just about the same as any other boy —a good, average, normal sort of fellow."

"Oh," he says. "But didn't you notice something? Wasn't there something kind of strange?" he says—"something different from what you noticed in the other childern?"

I didn't let on, you know—I just took it all in and looked as solemn as an owl—I just pretended to study it all over, just as serious as you please.

"Why no," I says, real slow-like, after I'd studied it all over. "As I remember it, he was a good, ordinary, normal sort of boy, just like all the others."

"Yes," he says—oh, all excited-like, you know—"But didn't you notice how brilliant he was? Eugene must have been more brilliant than the rest!"

"Well, now," I says, and pretended to study that all over too. "Now let me see. . . . Yes," I says—I just looked him in the eye, as solemn as you please—"he did pretty well. . . . Well, yes," I says, "I guess he was a fairly bright sort of a boy. I never had no complaints to make of him on that score. He was bright enough," I says. "The only trouble with him was that he was lazy."

"Lazy!" he says—oh, you should have seen the look upon his face, you know—he jumped like someone had stuck a pin in him. "Lazy!" he says. "Why, you don't mean to tell me——"

"Yes," I says—oh, I never cracked a smile—"I was telling him the same thing myself the last time that I saw him. I told him it was a mighty lucky thing for him that he had the gift of gab. Of course, he went off to college and read a lot of books, and I reckon that's where he got this flow of language they say he has. But as I said to him the last time that I saw him: 'Now look a-here,' I said. 'If you can earn your living doing a light, easy class of work like this you do,' I says, 'you're mighty lucky, because none of the rest of your people,' I says, 'had any such luck as that. They had to work hard for a living.' "

Oh, I told him, you know. I came right out with it. I made no bones about it. And I tell you what—I wish you could have seen his face. It was a study.

"Well," he says, at last, "you've got to admit this, haven't you— he was the brightest boy you had, now wasn't he?"

I just looked at him a moment. I had to tell the truth. I couldn't fool him any longer. "No," I says. "He was a good, bright boy— I got no complaint to make about him on that score—but the brightest boy I had, the one that surpassed all the rest of them in sense, and understanding, and in judgment—the best boy I had—the smartest boy I ever saw—was—well, it wasn't Eugene," I said. "It was another one."

He looked at me a moment, then he said, "Which boy was that?"

Well, I just looked at him, and smiled. I shook my head, you know. I wouldn't tell him. "I never brag about my own," I said. "You'll have to find out for yourself."

But—I'll have to tell *you*—and you know yourself, I brought the whole crowd up, I knew you all. And you can take my word for it —the best one of the lot was—*Grover!*

And when I think of Grover as he was along about that time, I always see him sitting there, so grave and earnest-like, with his nose pressed to the window, as we went down through Indiana in the morning, to the Fair.

All through that morning we were going down along beside the Wabash River—the Wabash River flows through Indiana, it is the river that they wrote the song about—so all that morning we were going down along the river. And I sat with all you childern gathered about me as we went down through Indiana, going to St. Louis, to the Fair.

And Grover sat there, so still and earnest-like, looking out the window, and he didn't move. He sat there like a man. He was just eleven and a half years old, but he had more sense, more judgment, and more understanding than any child I ever saw.

So here he sat beside this gentleman and looked out the window. I never knew the man—I never asked his name—but I tell you what! He was certainly a fine-looking, well-dressed, good, substantial sort of man, and I could see that he had taken a great liking to

Grover. And Grover sat there looking out, and then turned to this gentleman, as grave and earnest as a grown-up man, and says, "What kind of crops grow here, sir?" Well, this gentleman threw his head back and just hah-hahed. "Well, I'll see if I can tell you," says this gentleman, and then, you know, he talked to him, they talked together, and Grover took it all in, as solemn as you please, and asked this gentleman every sort of question—what the trees were, what was growing there, how big the farms were—all sorts of questions, which this gentleman would answer, until I said: "Why, I'll vow, Grover! You shouldn't ask so many questions. You'll bother the very life out of this gentleman."

The gentleman threw his head back and laughed right out. "Now you leave that boy alone. He's all right," he said. "He doesn't bother me a bit, and if I know the answers to his questions I will answer him. And if I don't know, why, then, I'll tell him so. But he's *all right*," he said, and put his arm round Grover's shoulders. "You leave him alone. He doesn't bother me a bit."

And I can still remember how he looked that morning, with his black eyes, his black hair, and with the birthmark on his neck—so grave, so serious, so earnest-like—as he sat by the train window and watched the apple trees, the farms, the barns, the houses, and the orchards, taking it all in, I reckon, because it was strange and new to him.

It was so long ago, but when I think of it, it all comes back, as if it happened yesterday. Now all of you have either died or grown up and gone away, and nothing is the same as it was then. But all of you were there with me that morning and I guess I should remember how the others looked, but somehow I don't. Yet I can still see Grover just the way he was, the way he looked that morning when we went down through Indiana, by the river, to the Fair.

III THE SISTER

Can you remember, Eugene, how Grover used to look? I mean the birthmark, the black eyes, the olive skin. The birthmark always showed because of those open sailor blouses kids used to wear. But I guess you must have been too young when Grover died. . . . I was looking at that old photograph the other day. You know the one I mean—that picture showing mama and papa and all of us children before the house on Woodson Street. *You* weren't there, Eugene. *You* didn't get in. *You* hadn't arrived when that was taken. . . . You remember how mad you used to get when we'd tell you that you were only a dishrag hanging out in Heaven when something happened?

You were the baby. That's what you get for being the baby. You don't get in the picture, do you? . . . I was looking at that old picture just the other day. There we were. And, my God, what is it all about? I mean, when you see the way we were—Daisy and Ben and Grover, Steve and all of us—and then how everyone either dies or grows up and goes away—and then—look at us now! Do you ever get to feeling funny? You know what I mean—do you ever get to feeling *queer*—when you try to figure these things out? You've been to college and you ought to know the answer—and I wish you'd tell me if you know.

My Lord, when I think sometimes of the way I used to be—the dreams I used to have. Playing the piano, practicing seven hours a day, thinking that some day I would be a great pianist. Taking singing lessons from Aunt Nell because I felt that some day I was going to have a great career in opera. . . . Can you beat it now? Can you imagine it? *Me!* In grand opera! . . . Now I want to ask you. I'd like to know.

My Lord! When I go uptown and walk down the street and see all these funny-looking little boys and girls hanging around the drug store—do you suppose any of them have ambitions the way we did? Do you suppose any of these funny-looking little girls are thinking about a big career in opera? . . . Didn't you ever see that picture of us? I was looking at it just the other day. It was made before the old house down on Woodson Street, with papa standing there in his swallow-tail, and mama there beside him—and Grover, and Ben, and Steve, and Daisy, and myself, with our feet upon our bicycles. Luke, poor kid, was only four or five. *He* didn't have a bicycle like us. But there he was. And there were all of us together.

Well, there I was, and my poor old skinny legs and long white dress, and two pigtails hanging down my back. And all the funny·

looking clothes we wore, with the doo-lolley business on them. . . .
But I guess you can't remember. You weren't born.

But, well, we were a right nice-looking set of people, if I do say
so. And there was "86" the way it used to be, with the front porch,
the grape vines, and the flower beds before the house—and "Miss
Eliza" standing there by papa, with a watch charm pinned upon
her waist. . . . I shouldn't laugh, but "Miss Eliza"—well, mama
was a pretty woman then. Do you know what I mean? "Miss
Eliza" was a right good-looking woman, and papa in his swallow-
tail was a good-looking man. Do you remember how he used to
get dressed up on Sunday? And how grand we thought he was?
And how he let me take his money out and count it? And how
rich we all thought he was? And how wonderful that dinkey little
shop on the Square looked to us? . . . Can you beat it, now? Why
we thought that papa was the biggest man in town and—oh, you
can't tell me! You can't tell me! He had his faults, but papa was a
wonderful man. You know he was!

And there was Steve and Ben and Grover, Daisy, Luke, and me
lined up there before the house with one foot on our bicycles. And
I got to thinking back about it all. It all came back.

Do you remember anything about St. Louis? You were only
three or four years old then, but you must remember something.
. . . Do you remember how you used to bawl when I would scrub
you? How you'd bawl for Grover? Poor kid, you used to yell for
Grover every time I'd get you in the tub. . . . He was a sweet kid
and he was crazy about you—he almost brought you up.

That year Grover was working at the Inside Inn out on the Fair
Grounds. Do you remember the old Inside Inn? That big old
wooden thing inside the Fair? And how I used to take you there to
wait for Grover when he got through working? And old fat Billy
Pelham at the newsstand—how he always used to give you a stick of
chewing gum?

They were all crazy about Grover. Everybody liked him. . . .
And how proud Grover was of you! Don't you remember how he
used to show you off? How he used to take you around and make
you talk to Billy Pelham? And Mr. Curtis at the desk? And how
Grover would try to make you talk and get you to say "Grover"?

And you couldn't say it—you couldn't pronounce the "r." You'd say "Gova." Have you forgotten that? You shouldn't forget *that*, because—you were a *cute* kid, then—Ho-ho-ho-ho-ho—I don't know where it's gone to, but you were a big hit in those days. . . . I tell you, boy, you were Somebody back in those days.

And I was thinking of it all the other day when I was looking at that photograph. How we used to go and meet Grover there, and how he'd take us to the Midway. Do you remember the Midway? The Snake-Eater and the Living Skeleton, the Fat Woman and the Chute-the-chute, the Scenic Railway and the Ferris Wheel? How you bawled the night we took you up on the Ferris Wheel? You yelled your head off—I tried to laugh it off, but I tell you, I was scared myself. Back in those days, that was Something. And how Grover laughed at us and told us there was no danger. . . . My Lord! poor little Grover. He wasn't quite twelve years old at the time, but he seemed so grown up to us. I was two years older, but I thought he knew it all.

It was always that way with him. Looking back now, it sometimes seems that it was Grover who brought us up. He was always looking after us, telling us what to do, bringing us something— some ice cream or some candy, something he had bought out of the poor little money he'd gotten at the Inn.

Then I got to thinking of the afternoon we sneaked away from home. Mama had gone out somewhere. And Grover and I got on the street car and went downtown. And my Lord, we thought that we were going Somewhere. In those days, that was what we called a *trip*. A ride in the street car was something to write home about in those days. . . . I hear that it's all built up around there now.

So we got on the car and rode the whole way down into the business section of St. Louis. We got out on Washington Street and walked up and down. And I tell you, boy, we thought that that was Something. Grover took me into a drug store and set me up to soda water. Then we came out and walked around some more, down to the Union Station and clear over to the river. And both of us half scared to death at what we'd done and wondering what mama would say if she found out.

We stayed down there till it was getting dark, and we passed by a lunchroom—an old one-armed joint with one-armed chairs and people sitting on stools and eating at the counter. We read all the signs to see what they had to eat and how much it cost, and I guess nothing on the menu was more than fifteen cents, but it couldn't have looked grander to us if it had been Delmonico's. So we stood there with our noses pressed against the window, looking in. Two skinny little kids, both of us scared half to death, getting the thrill of a lifetime out of it. You know what I mean? And smelling everything with all our might and thinking how good it all smelled. . . . Then Grover turned to me and whispered: "Come on, Helen. Let's go in. It says fifteen cents for pork and beans. And I've got the money," Grover said. "I've got sixty cents."

I was so scared I couldn't speak. I'd never been in a place like that before. But I kept thinking, "Oh Lord, if mama should find out!" I felt as if we were committing some big crime. . . . Don't you know how it is when you're a kid? It was the thrill of a lifetime. . . . I couldn't resist. So we both went in and sat down on those high stools before the counter and ordered pork and beans and a cup of coffee. I suppose we were too frightened at what we'd done really to enjoy anything. We just gobbled it all up in a hurry, and gulped our coffee down. And I don't know whether it was the excitement—I guess the poor kid was already sick when we came in there and didn't know it. But I turned and looked at him, and he was white as death. . . . And when I asked him what was the matter, he wouldn't tell me. He was too proud. He said he was all right, but I could see that he was sick as a dog. . . . So he paid the bill. It came to forty cents—I'll never forget *that* as long as I live. . . . And sure enough, we no more than got out the door—he hardly had time to reach the curb—before it all came up.

And the poor kid was so scared and so ashamed. And what scared him so was not that he had gotten sick, but that he had spent all that money and it had come to nothing. And mama would find out. . . . Poor kid, he just stood there looking at me and he whispered: "Oh Helen, don't tell mama. She'll be mad if she finds out." Then we hurried home, and he was still white as a sheet when we got there.

Mama was waiting for us. She looked at us—you know how

"Miss Eliza" looks at you when she thinks you've been doing something that you shouldn't. Mama said, "Why, where on earth have you two children been?" I guess she was all set to lay us out. Then she took one look at Grover's face. That was enough for her. She said, "Why, child, what in the world!" She was white as a sheet herself. . . . And all that Grover said was—"Mama, I feel sick."

He was sick as a dog. He fell over on the bed, and we undressed him and mama put her hand upon his forehead and came out in the hall—she was so white you could have made a black mark on her face with chalk—and whispered to me, "Go get the doctor quick, he's burning up."

And I went chasing up the street, my pigtails flying, to Dr. Packer's house. I brought him back with me. When he came out of Grover's room he told mama what to do but I don't know if she even heard him.

Her face was white as a sheet. She looked at me and looked right through me. She never saw me. And oh, my Lord, I'll never forget the way she looked, the way my heart stopped and came up in my throat. I was only a skinny little kid of fourteen. But she looked as if she was dying right before my eyes. And I knew that if anything happened to him, she'd never get over it if she lived to be a hundred.

Poor old mama. You know, he always was her eyeballs—you know that, don't you?—not the rest of us!—no, sir! I know what I'm talking about. It always has been Grover—she always thought more of him than she did of any of the others. And—poor kid!— he was a sweet kid. I can still see him lying there, and remember how sick he was, and how scared I was! I don't know why I was so scared. All we'd done had been to sneak away from home and go into a lunchroom—but I felt guilty about the whole thing, as if it was my fault.

It all came back to me the other day when I was looking at that picture, and I thought, my God, we were two kids together, and I was only two years older than Grover was, and now I'm forty-six. . . . Can you believe it? Can you figure it out—the way we grow up and change and go away? . . . And my Lord, Grover seemed so grown-up to me. He was such a quiet kid—I guess that's why he seemed older than the rest of us.

I wonder what Grover would say now if he could see that picture. All my hopes and dreams and big ambitions have come to nothing, and it's all so long ago, as if it happened in another world. Then it comes back, as if it happened yesterday. . . . Sometimes I lie awake at night and think of all the people who have come and gone, and how everything is different from the way we thought that it would be. Then I go out on the street next day and see the faces of the people that I pass. . . . Don't they look strange to you? Don't you see something funny in people's eyes, as if all of them were puzzled about something? As if they were wondering what had happened to them since they were kids? Wondering what it is that they have lost? . . . Now am I crazy, or do you know what I mean? You've been to college, Gene, and I want you to tell me if you know the answer. Now do they look that way to you? I never noticed that look in people's eyes when I was a kid—did you?

My God, I wish I knew the answer to these things. I'd like to find out what is wrong—what has changed since then—and if we have the same queer look in our eyes, too. Does it happen to us all, to everyone? . . . Grover and Ben, Steve, Daisy, Luke, and me—all standing there before that house on Woodson Street in Altamont—there we are, and you see the way we were—and how it all gets lost. What is it, anyway, that people lose?

How is it that nothing turns out the way we thought it would be? It all gets lost until it seems that it has never happened—that it is something we dreamed somewhere. . . . You see what I mean? . . . It seems that it must be something we heard somewhere—that it happened to someone else. And then it all comes back again.

And suddenly you remember just how it was, and see again those two funny, frightened, skinny little kids with their noses pressed against the dirty window of that lunchroom thirty years ago. You remember the way it felt, the way it smelled, even the strange smell in the old pantry in that house we lived in then. And the steps before the house, the way the rooms looked. And those two little boys in sailor suits who used to ride up and down before the house on tricycles. . . . And the birthmark on Grover's neck. . . . The Inside Inn. . . . St. Louis, and the Fair.

It all comes back as if it happened yesterday. And then it goes away again, and seems farther off and stranger than if it happened in a dream.

IV THE BROTHER

"*This* is King's Highway," the man said.

And then Eugene looked and saw that it was just a street. There were some big new buildings, a large hotel, some restaurants and "bar-grill" places of the modern kind, the livid monotone of neon lights, the ceaseless traffic of motor cars—all this was new, but it was just a street. And he knew that it had always been just a street, and nothing more—but somehow—well, he stood there looking at it, wondering what else he had expected to find.

The man kept looking at him with inquiry in his eyes, and Eugene asked him if the Fair had not been out this way.

"Sure, the Fair was out beyond here," the man said. "Out where the park is now. But this street you're looking for—don't you remember the name of it or nothing?" the man said.

Eugene said he thought the name of the street was Edgemont, but that he wasn't sure. Anyhow it was something like that. And he said the house was on the corner of that street and of another street.

Then the man said: "What was that other street?"

Eugene said he did not know, but that King's Highway was a block or so away, and that an interurban line ran past about half a block from where he once had lived.

"What line was this?" the man said, and stared at him.

"The interurban line," Eugene said.

Then the man stared at him again, and finally, "I don't know no interurban line," he said.

Eugene said it was a line that ran behind some houses, and that there were board fences there and grass beside the tracks. But some-how he could not say that it was summer in those days and that you could smell the ties, a wooden, tarry smell, and feel a kind of absence in the afternoon after the car had gone. He only said the interurban line was back behind somewhere between the backyards of some houses and some old board fences, and that King's Highway was a block or two away.

He did not say that King's Highway had not been a street in those days but a kind of road that wound from magic out of some dim and haunted land, and that along the way it had got mixed in with Tom the Piper's son, with hot cross buns, with all the light that came and went, and with coming down through Indiana in the morning, and the smell of engine smoke, the Union Station, and most of all with voices lost and far and long ago that said "King's Highway."

He did not say these things about King's Highway because he looked about him and he saw what King's Highway was. All he could say was that the street was near King's Highway, and was on the corner, and that the interurban trolley line was close to there. He said it was a stone house, and that there were stone steps before it, and a strip of grass. He said he thought the house had had a turret at one corner, he could not be sure.

The man looked at him again, and said, "This is King's Highway, but I never heard of any street like that."

Eugene left him then, and went on till he found the place. And so at last he turned into the street, finding the place where the two corners met, the huddled block, the turret, and the steps, and paused a moment, looking back, as if the street were Time.

For a moment he stood there, waiting—for a word, and for a door to open, for the child to come. He waited, but no words were spoken; no one came.

Yet all of it was just as it had always been, except that the steps were lower, the porch less high, the strip of grass less wide, than he had thought. All the rest of it was as he had known it would be. A graystone front, three-storied, with a slant slate roof, the side red brick and windowed, still with the old arched entrance in the center for the doctor's use.

There was a tree in front, and a lamp post; and behind and to the side, more trees than he had known there would be. And all the slatey turret gables, all the slatey window gables, going into points, and the two arched windows, in strong stone, in the front room.

It was all so strong, so solid, and so ugly—and all so enduring and so good, the way he had remembered it, except he did not smell the tar, the hot and caulky dryness of the old cracked ties, the boards of backyard fences and the coarse and sultry grass, and absence in the afternoon when the street car had gone, and the twins, sharp-visaged in their sailor suits, pumping with furious shrillness on tricycles up and down before the house, and the feel of the hot afternoon, and the sense that everyone was absent at the Fair.

Except for this, it all was just the same; except for this and for King's Highway, which was now a street; except for this, and for the child that did not come.

It was a hot day. Darkness had come. The heat rose up and hung and sweltered like a sodden blanket in St. Louis. It was wet heat, and one knew that there would be no relief or coolness in the night. And when one tried to think of the time when the heat would go away, one said: "It cannot last. It's bound to go away," as we always say it in America. But one did not believe it when he said it. The heat soaked down and men sweltered in it; the faces of the people were pale and greasy with the heat. And in their faces was a patient wretchedness, and one felt the kind of desolation that one feels at the end of a hot day in a great city in America—when one's home is far away, across the continent, and he thinks of all that distance, all that heat, and feels, "Oh God! but it's a big country!"

And he feels nothing but absence, absence, and the desolation of America, the loneliness and sadness of the high, hot skies, and evening coming on across the Middle West, across the sweltering and heat-sunken land, across all the lonely little towns, the farms, the fields, the oven swelter of Ohio, Kansas, Iowa, and Indiana at the close of day, and voices, casual in the heat, voices at the little stations, quiet, casual, somehow faded into that enormous vacancy and weariness of heat, of space, and of the immense, the sorrowful, the most high and awful skies.

Then he hears the engine and the wheel again, the wailing whistle and the bell, the sound of shifting in the sweltering yard, and walks the street, and walks the street, beneath the clusters of hard lights, and by the people with sagged faces, and is drowned in desolation and in no belief.

He feels the way one feels when one comes back, and knows that he should not have come, and when he sees that, after all, King's Highway is—a street; and St. Louis—the enchanted name—a big, hot, common town upon the river, sweltering in wet, dreary heat, and not quite South, and nothing else enough to make it better.

It had not been like this before. He could remember how it would get hot, and how good the heat was, and how he would lie out in the backyard on an airing mattress, and how the mattress would get hot and dry and smell like a hot mattress full of sun, and how the sun would make him want to sleep, and how, sometimes, he would go down into the basement to feel coolness, and how the cellar smelled as cellars always smell—a cool, stale smell, the smell of cobwebs and of grimy bottles. And he could remember, when you opened the door upstairs, the smell of the cellar would come up to you—cool, musty, stale and dank and dark—and how the thought of the dark cellar always filled him with a kind of numb excitement, a kind of visceral expectancy.

He could remember how it got hot in the afternoons, and how he would feel a sense of absence and vague sadness in the afternoons, when everyone had gone away. The house would seem so lonely, and sometimes he would sit inside, on the second step of the hall stairs, and listen to the sound of silence and of absence in the afternoon. He could smell the oil upon the floor and on the stairs, and see the sliding doors with their brown varnish and the beady chains across the door, and thrust his hands among the beady chains, and gather them together in his arms, and let them clash, and swish with light beady swishings all around him. He could feel darkness, absence, varnished darkness, and stained light within the house, through the stained glass of the window on the stairs, through the small stained glasses by the door, stained light and absence, silence and the smell of floor oil and vague sadness in the house on a hot mid-afternoon. And all these things themselves would have a kind of life: would seem to wait attentively, to be most living and most still.

He would sit there and listen. He could hear the girl next door practice her piano lessons in the afternoon, and hear the street car coming by between the backyard fences, half a block away, and smell the dry and sultry smell of backyard fences, the smell of coarse hot grasses by the car tracks in the afternoon, the smell of tar, of dry caulked ties, the smell of bright worn flanges, and feel the loneliness of backyards in the afternoon and the sense of absence when the car was gone.

Then he would long for evening and return, the slant of light, and feet along the street, the sharp-faced twins in sailor suits upon their tricycles, the smell of supper and the sound of voices in the house again, and Grover coming from the Fair.

That is how it was when he came into the street, and found the place where the two corners met, and turned at last to see if Time was there. He passed the house: some lights were burning, the door was open, and a woman sat upon the porch. And presently he turned, came back, and stopped before the house again. The corner light fell blank upon the house. He stood looking at it, and put his foot upon the step.

Then he said to the woman who was sitting on the porch: "This house—excuse me—but could you tell me, please who lives in this house?"

He knew his words were strange and hollow, and he had not said what he wished to say. She stared at him a moment, puzzled.

Then she said: "I live here. Who are you looking for?"

He said, "Why, I am looking for——"

And then he stopped, because he knew he could not tell her what it was that he was looking for.

"There used to be a house—" he said.

The woman was now staring at him hard.

He said, "I think I used to live here."

She said nothing.

In a moment he continued, "I used to live here in this house," he said, "when I was a little boy."

She was silent, looking at him, then she said: "Oh. Are you sure this was the house? Do you remember the address?"

"I have forgotten the address," he said, "but it was Edgemont Street, and it was on the corner. And I know this is the house."

"This isn't Edgemont Street," the woman said. "The name is Bates."

"Well, then, they changed the name of the street," he said, "but this is the same house. It hasn't changed."

She was silent a moment, then she nodded: "Yes. They did change the name of the street. I remember when I was a child they called it something else," she said. "But that was a long time ago. When was it that you lived here?"

"In 1904."

Again she was silent, looking at him. Then presently: "Oh. That was the year of the Fair. You were here then?"

"Yes." He now spoke rapidly, with more confidence. "My mother had the house, and we were here for seven months. And the house belonged to Dr. Packer," he went on. "We rented it from him."

"Yes," the woman said, and nodded, "this was Dr. Packer's house. He's dead now, he's been dead for many years. But this was the Packer house, all right."

"That entrance on the side," he said, "where the steps go up, that was for Dr. Packer's patients. That was the entrance to his office."

"Oh," the woman said, "I didn't know that. I've often wondered what it was. I didn't know what it was for."

"And this big room in front here," he continued, "that was the office. And there were sliding doors, and next to it, a kind of alcove for his patients——"

"Yes, the alcove is still there, only all of it has been made into one room now—and I never knew just what the alcove was for."

"And there were sliding doors on this side, too, that opened on the hall—and a stairway going up upon this side. And half-way up the stairway, at the landing, a little window of colored glass—and across the sliding doors here in the hall, a kind of curtain made of strings of beads."

She nodded, smiling. "Yes, it's just the same—we still have the sliding doors and the stained glass window on the stairs. There's no bead curtain any more," she said, "but I remember when people had them. I know what you mean."

"When we were here," he said, "we used the doctor's office for a parlor—except later on—the last month or two—and then we used it for—a bedroom."

"It is a bedroom now," she said. "I run the house—I rent rooms—all of the rooms upstairs are rented—but I have two brothers and they sleep in this front room."

Both of them were silent for a moment, then Eugene said, "My brother stayed there too."

"In the front room?" the woman said.

He answered, "Yes."

She paused, then said: "Won't you come in? I don't believe it's changed much. Would you like to see?"

He thanked her and said he would, and he went up the steps. She opened the screen door to let him in.

Inside it was just the same—the stairs, the hallway, the sliding doors, the window of stained glass upon the stairs. And all of it was just the same, except for absence, the stained light of absence in the afternoon, and the child who once had sat there, waiting on the stairs.

It was all the same except that as a child he had sat there feeling things were *Somewhere*—and now he *knew*. He had sat there feeling that a vast and sultry river was somewhere—and now he knew! He had sat there wondering what King's Highway was, where it began, and where it ended—now he knew! He had sat there haunted by the magic word "downtown"—now he knew!—and by the street car, after it had gone—and by all things that came and went and came again, like the cloud shadows passing in a wood, that never could be captured.

And he felt that if he could only sit there on the stairs once more, in solitude and absence in the afternoon, he would be able to get it back again. Then would he be able to remember all that he had seen and been—the brief sum of himself, the universe of his four years, with all the light of Time upon it—that universe which was so short to measure, and yet so far, so endless, to remember. Then would he be able to see his own small face again, pooled in the dark mirror of the hall, and peer once more into the grave eyes of the child that he had been, and discover there in his quiet three-years' self the lone integrity of "I," knowing: "Here is the House, and here House listening; here is Absence, Absence in the afternoon; and here in this House, this Absence, is my core, my kernel —here am I!"

But as he thought it, he knew that even if he could sit here alone and get it back again, it would be gone as soon as seized, just as it had been then—first coming like the vast and drowsy rumors of the distant and enchanted Fair, then fading like cloud shadows on a hill, going like faces in a dream—coming, going, coming, possessed and held but never captured, like lost voices in the mountains long ago—and like the dark eyes and quiet face of the dark, lost boy, his brother, who, in the mysterious rhythms of his life and work, used to come into this house, then go, and then return again.

The woman took Eugene back into the house and through the hall. He told her of the pantry, told her where it was and pointed to the place, but now it was no longer there. And he told her of the backyard, and of the old board fence around the yard. But the old board fence was gone. And he told her of the carriage house, and told her it was painted red. But now there was a small garage. And the backyard was still there, but smaller than he thought, and now there was a tree.

"I did not know there was a tree," he said. "I do not remember any tree."

"Perhaps it was not there," she said. "A tree could grow in thirty years." And then they came back through the house again and paused at the sliding doors.

"And could I see this room?" he said.

She slid the doors back. They slid open smoothly, with a rolling heaviness, as they used to do. And then he saw the room again. It was the same. There was a window at the side, the two arched windows at the front, the alcove and the sliding doors, the fireplace with the tiles of mottled green, the mantle of dark mission wood, the mantel posts, a dresser and a bed, just where the dresser and the bed had been so long ago.

"Is this the room?" the woman said. "It hasn't changed?"

He told her that it was the same.

"And your brother slept here where my brothers sleep?"

"This is his room," he said.

They were silent. He turned to go, and said, "Well, thank you. I appreciate your showing me."

She said that she was glad and that it was no trouble. "And when you see your family, you can tell them that you saw the house," she said. "My name is Mrs. Bell. You can tell your mother that a Mrs. Bell has the house now. And when you see your brother, you can tell him that you saw the room he slept in, and that you found it just the same."

He told her then that his brother was dead.

The woman was silent for a moment. Then she looked at him and said: "He died here, didn't he? In this room?"

He told her that it was so.

"Well, then," she said, "I knew it. I don't know how. But when you told me he was here, I knew it."

He said nothing. In a moment the woman said, "What did he die of?"

"Typhoid."

She looked shocked and troubled, and said involuntarily, "My two brothers——"

"That was a long time ago," he said. "I don't think you need to worry now."

"Oh, I wasn't thinking about that," she said. "It was just hearing that a little boy—your brother—was—was in this room that my two brothers sleep in now——"

"Well, maybe I shouldn't have told you then. But he was a good boy—and if you'd known him you wouldn't mind."

She said nothing, and he added quickly: "Besides, he didn't stay here long. This wasn't really his room—but the night he came back with my sister he was so sick—they didn't move him."

"Oh," the woman said, "I see." And then: "Are you going to tell your mother you were here?"

"I don't think so."

"I—I wonder how she feels about this room."

"I don't know. She never speaks of it."

"Oh. . . . How old was he?"

"He was twelve."

"You must have been pretty young yourself."

"I was not quite four."

"And—you just wanted to see the room, didn't you? That's why you came back."

"Yes."

"Well—" indefinitely—"I guess you've seen it now."

"Yes, thank you."

"I guess you don't remember much about him, do you? I shouldn't think you would."

"No, not much."

The years dropped off like fallen leaves: the face came back again—the soft dark oval, the dark eyes, the soft brown berry on the neck, the raven hair, all bending down, approaching—the whole appearing to him ghost-wise, intent and instant.

"Now say it—*Grover!*"

"Gova."

"No—not Gova—*Grover!* . . . Say it!"

"Gova."

"Ah-h—you didn't say it. You said Gova. *Grover*—now say it!"

"Gova."

"Look, I tell you what I'll do if you say it right. Would you like to go down to King's Highway? Would you like Grover to set you up? All right, then. If you say Grover and say it right, I'll take you to King's Highway and set you up to ice cream. Now say it right—*Grover!*"

"Gova."

"Ah-h, you-u. You're the craziest little old boy I ever did see. Can't you even say Grover?"

"Gova."

"Ah-h, you-u. Old Tongue-Tie, that's what you are. . . . Well, come on, then, I'll set you up anyway."

It all came back, and faded, and was lost again. Eugene turned to go, and thanked the woman and said good-bye.

"Well, then, good-bye," the woman said, and they shook hands. "I'm glad if I could show you. I'm glad if—" She did not finish, and at length she said: "Well, then, that was a long time ago. You'll find everything changed now, I guess. It's all built up around here now—and way out beyond here, out beyond where the Fair Grounds used to be. I guess you'll find it changed."

They had nothing more to say. They just stood there for a moment on the steps, and then shook hands once more.

"Well, good-bye."

And again he was in the street, and found the place where the corners met, and for the last time turned to see where Time had gone.

And he knew that he would never come again, and that lost magic would not come again. Lost now was all of it—the street, the heat, King's Highway, and Tom the Piper's son, all mixed in with the vast and drowsy murmur of the Fair, and with the sense of absence in the afternoon, and the house that waited, and the child that dreamed. And out of the enchanted wood, that thicket of man's memory, Eugene knew that the dark eye and the quiet face of his friend and brother—poor child, life's stranger, and life's exile, lost like all of us, a cipher in blind mazes, long ago—the lost boy was gone forever, and would not return.

MULE IN THE YARD

———

William Faulkner

From *The Collected Stories of William Faulkner,* 1950; first published in *Scribner's Magazine,* XCVI (August, 1934), 65-70.

William Faulkner (1897-   ) has lived most of his life at Oxford, Mississippi, and has set his most characteristic fiction in the town of Jefferson and the county of Yoknapatawpha, which are Oxford and the surrounding region thinly disguised. In such novels as *The Sound and the Fury* (1929), *Sartoris* (1929), *As I Lay Dying* (1930), *Sanctuary* (1931), *Absalom, Absalom!* (1936), and *Intruder in the Dust* (1948), and in such stories and sketches as those collected in *The Unvanquished* (1938), *Go Down, Moses and Other Stories* (1942), *The Hamlet* (1940), *The Town* (1957), and *The Mansion* (1959), he includes the kind of people, often both realistic and symbolic in presentation, who have lived in the South during the past several generations. See Ward L. Miner, *The World of William Faulkner* (1952). Useful essays on Faulkner appear in Maxwell Geismar, *Writers in Crisis* (1942), pages 141-184; Harry Hartwick, *The Foreground of American Fiction* (1934), pages 160-166; and William M. Frohock, *Violence in the American Novel* (Second Edition, 1958), pages 144-165. See also Harry M. Campbell and Ruel E. Foster, *William Faulkner: A Critical Appraisal* (1951), Frederick J. Hoffman and Olga W. Vickery, eds., *William Faulkner: Two Decades of Criticism* (1951), and Robert Penn Warren's essay in *Forms of Modern Fiction,* ed. William Van O'Connor (1948).

It was a gray day in late January, though not cold because of the fog. Old Het, just walked in from the poorhouse, ran down the hall toward the kitchen, shouting in a strong, bright, happy voice. She was about seventy probably, though by her own counting, calculated from the ages of various housewives in the town from brides to grandmothers whom she claimed to have nursed in infancy, she would have to be around a hundred and at least triplets. Tall, lean, fog-beaded, in tennis shoes and a long rat-colored cloak trimmed with what forty or fifty years ago had been fur, a modish though not new purple toque set upon her headrag and carrying (time was when she made her weekly rounds from kitchen to kitchen carrying a brocaded carpetbag though since the advent of the ten-cent stores the carpetbag became an endless succession of the convenient paper receptacles with which they supply their customers for a few cents) the shopping-bag, she ran into the kitchen and shouted with strong and childlike pleasure: "Miss Mannie! Mule in de yard!"

Mrs. Hait, stooping to the stove, in the act of drawing from it a scuttle of live ashes, jerked upright; clutching the scuttle, she glared at old Het, then she too spoke at once, strong too, immediate. "Them sons of bitches," she said. She left the kitchen, not running exactly, yet with a kind of outraged celerity, carrying the scuttle—a compact woman of forty-odd, with an air of indomitable yet relieved bereavement, as though that which had relicted her had been a woman and a not particularly valuable one at that. She wore a calico wrapper and a sweater coat, and a man's felt hat which they in the town knew had belonged to her ten years' dead husband. But the man's shoes had not belonged to him. They were high shoes which buttoned, with toes like small tulip bulbs, and in the town they knew that she had bought them new for herself. She and old Het ran down the kitchen steps and into the fog. That's why it was not cold: as though there lay supine and prisoned between earth and mist the long winter night's suspiration of the sleeping town in dark, close rooms—the slumber and the rousing; the stale waking thermostatic, by re-heating heat-engendered: it lay like a scum of cold grease upon the steps and the wooden entrance to the basement and upon the narrow plank walk which led to a shed building in the corner of the yard: upon these planks, running and still carrying the scuttle of live ashes, Mrs. Hait skated viciously.

"Watch out!" old Het, footed securely by her rubber soles, cried happily. "Dey in de front!" Mrs. Hait did not fall. She did not even pause. She took in the immediate scene with one cold glare and was running again when there appeared at the corner of the house and

apparently having been born before their eyes of the fog itself, a
mule. It looked taller than a giraffe. Longheaded, with a flying
halter about its scissorlike ears, it rushed down upon them with
violent and apparitionlike suddenness.

"Dar hit!" old Het cried, waving the shopping-bag. "Hoo!" Mrs.
Hait whirled. Again she skidded savagely on the greasy planks as
she and the mule rushed parallel with one another toward the shed
building, from whose open doorway there now projected the static
and astonished face of a cow. To the cow the fog-born mule doubtless looked taller and more incredibly sudden than a giraffe even,
and apparently bent upon charging right through the shed as
though it were made of straw or were purely and simply mirage.
The cow's head likewise had a quality transient and abrupt and
unmundane. It vanished, sucked into invisibility like a match flame,
though the mind knew and the reason insisted that she had withdrawn into the shed, from which, as proof's burden, there came an
indescribable sound of shock and alarm by shed and beast engen-
dered, analogous to a single note from a profoundly struck lyre or
harp. Toward this sound Mrs. Hait sprang, immediately, as if by
pure reflex, as though in invulnerable compact of female with female against a world of mule and man. She and the mule converged upon the shed at top speed, the heavy scuttle poised lightly
in her hand to hurl. Of course it did not take this long, and likewise it was the mule which refused the gambit. Old Het was still
shouting "Dar hit! Dar hit!" when it swerved and rushed at her
where she stood tall as a stove pipe, holding the shopping-bag which
she swung at the beast as it rushed past her and vanished beyond
the other corner of the house as though sucked back into the fog
which had produced it, profound and instantaneous and without
any sound.

With that unhasteful celerity Mrs. Hait turned and set the scuttle
down on the brick coping of the cellar entrance and she and old
Het turned the corner of the house in time to see the now wraithlike mule at the moment when its course converged with that of a
choleric-looking rooster and eight Rhode Island Red hens emerging
from beneath the house. Then for an instant its progress assumed
the appearance and trappings of an apotheosis: hell-born and hell-

returning, in the act of dissolving completely into the fog, it seemed to rise vanishing into a sunless and dimensionless medium borne upon and enclosed by small winged goblins.

"Dey's mo in de front!" old Het cried.

"Them sons of bitches," Mrs. Hait said, again in that grim, prescient voice without rancor or heat. It was not the mules to which she referred; it was not even the owner of them. It was her whole town-dwelling history as dated from that April dawn ten years ago when what was left of Hait had been gathered from the mangled remains of five mules and several feet of new Manila rope on a blind curve of the railroad just out of town; the geographical hap of her very home; the very components of her bereavement—the mules, the defunct husband, and the owner of them. His name was Snopes; in the town they knew about him too—how he bought his stock at the Memphis market and brought it to Jefferson and sold it to farmers and widows and orphans black and white, for whatever he could contrive—down to a certain figure; and about how (usually in the dead season of winter) teams and even small droves of his stock would escape from the fenced pasture where he kept them and, tied one to another with sometimes quite new hemp rope (and which item Snopes included in the subsequent claim), would be annihilated by freight trains on the same blind curve which was to be the scene of Hait's exit from this world; once a town wag sent him through the mail a printed train schedule for the division. A squat, pasty man perennially tieless and with a strained, harried expression, at stated intervals he passed athwart the peaceful and somnolent life of the town in dust and uproar, his advent heralded by shouts and cries, his passing marked by a yellow cloud filled with tossing jug-shaped heads and clattering hooves and the same forlorn and earnest cries of the drovers; and last of all and well back out of the dust, Snopes himself moving at a harried and panting trot, since it was said in the town that he was deathly afraid of the very beasts in which he cleverly dealt.

The path which he must follow from the railroad station to his pasture crossed the edge of town near Hait's home; Hait and Mrs. Hait had not been in the house a week before they waked one morning to find it surrounded by galloping mules and the air filled with the shouts and cries of the drovers. But it was not until that April dawn some years later, when those who reached the scene first found what might be termed foreign matter among the mangled mules and the savage fragments of new rope, that the town suspected that Hait stood in any closer relationship to Snopes and the mules than that of helping at periodical intervals to drive them out of his front yard. After that they believed that they knew; in a three days' recess of interest, surprise, and curiosity they watched to see if Snopes would try to collect on Hait also.

But they learned only that the adjuster appeared and called upon Mrs. Hait and that a few days later she cashed a check for eight thousand five hundred dollars, since this was back in the old halcyon days when even the companies considered their southern branches and divisions the legitimate prey of all who dwelt beside them. She took the cash: she stood in her sweater coat and the hat which Hait had been wearing on the fatal morning a week ago and listened in cold, grim silence while the teller counted the money and the president and the cashier tried to explain to her the virtues of a bond, then of a savings account, then of a checking account, and departed with the money in a salt sack under her apron; after a time she painted her house: that serviceable and time-defying color which the railroad station was painted, as though out of sentiment or (as some said) gratitude.

The adjuster also summoned Snopes into conference, from which he emerged not only more harried-looking than ever, but with his face stamped with a bewildered dismay which it was to wear from then on, and that was the last time his pasture fence was ever to give inexplicably away at dead of night upon mules coupled in threes and fours by adequate rope even though not always new. And then it seemed as though the mules themselves knew this, as if, even while haltered at the Memphis block at his bid, they sensed it somehow as they sensed that he was afraid of them. Now, three or four times a year and as though by fiendish concord and as soon as they were freed of the box car, the entire uproar—the dust cloud filled with shouts earnest, harried, and dismayed, with plunging demoniac shapes—would become translated in a single burst of perverse and uncontrollable violence, without any intervening contact with time, space, or earth, across the peaceful and astonished town and into Mrs. Hait's yard, where, in a certain hapless despair which abrogated for the moment even physical fear, Snopes ducked and dodged among the thundering shapes about the house (for whose very impervious paint the town believed that he felt he had paid and whose inmate lived within it a life of idle and queenlike ease on money which he considered at least partly his own) while gradually that section and neighborhood gathered to look on from behind adjacent window curtains and porches screened and not, and from the sidewalks and even from halted wagons and cars in the street—housewives in the wrappers and boudoir caps of morning, children on the way to school, casual Negroes and casual whites in static and entertained repose.

They were all there when, followed by old Het and carrying the stub of a worn-out broom, Mrs. Hait ran around the next corner and onto the handkerchief-sized plot of earth which she called her front yard. It was small; any creature with a running stride of three feet could have spanned it in two paces, yet at the moment, due perhaps to the myopic and distortive quality of the fog, it seemed to be as incredibly full of mad life as a drop of water beneath the microscope. Yet again she did not falter. With the broom clutched in her hand and apparently with a kind of sublime faith in her own invulnerability, she rushed on after the haltered mule which was still in that arrested and wraithlike process of vanishing furiously into the fog, its wake indicated by the tossing and dispersing shapes of the nine chickens like so many jagged scraps of paper in the dying air blast of an automobile, and the madly dodging figure of a man. The man was Snopes; beaded too with moisture, his wild face gaped with hoarse shouting and the two heavy lines of shaven beard descending from the corners of it as though in alluvial retrospect of years of tobacco, he screamed at her: "Fore God, Miz Hait! I done everything I could!" She didn't even look at him.

"Ketch that big un with the bridle on," she said in her cold, panting voice. "Git that big un outen here."

"Sho!" Snopes shrieked. "Jest let um take their time. Jest don't git um excited now."

"Watch out!" old Het shouted. "He headin fer de back again!"

"Git the rope," Mrs. Hait said, running again. Snopes glared back at old Het.

"Fore God, where is ere rope?" he shouted.

"In de cellar fo God!" old Het shouted, also without pausing. "Go roun de udder way en head um." Again she and Mrs. Hait turned the corner in time to see again the still-vanishing mule with the halter once more in the act of floating lightly onward in its cloud of chickens with which, they being able to pass under the house and so on the chord of a circle while it had to go around on the arc, it had once more coincided. When they turned the next corner they were in the back yard again.

"Fo God!" old Het cried. "He fixin to misuse de cow!" For they had gained on the mule now, since it had stopped. In fact, they came around the corner on a tableau. The cow now stood in the centre of the yard. She and the mule faced one another a few feet apart. Motionless, with lowered heads and braced forelegs, they looked like two book ends from two distinct pairs of a general pattern which some one of amateurly bucolic leanings might have purchased, and which some child had salvaged, brought into idle juxtaposition and then forgotten; and, his head and shoulders projecting above the back-flung slant of the cellar entrance where the scuttle still sat, Snopes standing as though buried to the armpits for a Spanish-Indian-American suttee. Only again it did not take this long. It was less than tableau; it was one of those things which later even memory cannot quite affirm. Now and in turn, man and cow and mule vanished beyond the next corner, Snopes now in the lead, carrying the rope, the cow next with her tail rigid and raked slightly like the stern staff of a boat. Mrs. Hait and old Het ran on, passing the open cellar gaping upon its accumulation of human necessities and widowed womanyears—boxes for kindling wood, old papers and magazines, the broken and outworn furniture and utensils which no woman ever throws away; a pile of coal and another of pitch pine for priming fires—and ran on and turned the next corner to see man and cow and mule all vanishing now in the wild cloud of ubiquitous chickens which had once more crossed beneath the house and emerged. They ran on, Mrs. Hait in grim and unflagging silence, old Het with the eager and happy amazement of a child.

But when they gained the front again they saw only Snopes. He lay flat on his stomach, his head and shoulders upreared by his outstretched arms, his coat tail swept forward by its own arrested momentum about his head so that from beneath it his slack-jawed face mused in wild repose like that of a burlesqued nun.

"Whar'd dey go?" old Het shouted at him. He didn't answer.

"Dey tightenin' on de curves!" she cried. "Dey already in de back again!" That's where they were. The cow made a feint at running into her shed, but deciding perhaps that her speed was too great, she whirled in a final desperation of despair-like valor. But they did not see this, nor see the mule, swerving to pass her, crash and blunder for an instant at the open cellar door before going on. When they arrived, the mule was gone. The scuttle was gone too, but they did not notice it; they saw only the cow standing in the centre of the yard as before, panting, rigid, with braced forelegs and lowered head facing nothing, as if the child had returned and removed one of the book ends for some newer purpose or game. They ran on. Mrs. Hait ran heavily now, her mouth too open, her face putty-colored and one hand pressed to her side. So slow was their progress that the mule in its third circuit of the house overtook them from behind and soared past with undiminished speed, with brief demon thunder and a keen ammonia-sweet reek of sweat sudden and sharp as a jeering cry, and was gone. Yet they ran doggedly on around the next corner in time to see it succeed at last in vanishing into the fog; they heard its hoofs, brief, staccato, and derisive, on the paved street, dying away.

"Well!" old Het said, stopping. She panted, happily. "Gentlemen, hush! Ain't we had—" Then she became stone still; slowly her head turned, high-nosed, her nostrils pulsing; perhaps for the instant she saw the open cellar door as they had last passed it, with no scuttle beside it. "Fo God I smells smoke!" she said. "Chile, run, git yo money."

That was still early, not yet ten o'clock. By noon the house had burned to the ground. There was a farmers' supply store where Snopes could be usually found; more than one had made a point of finding him there by that time. They told him about how when the fire engine and the crowd reached the scene, Mrs. Hait, followed by old Het carrying her shopping-bag in one hand and a framed portrait of Mr. Hait in the other, emerged with an umbrella and wearing a new, dun-colored, mail-order coat, in one pocket of which lay a fruit jar filled with smoothly rolled banknotes and in the other a heavy, nickel-plated pistol, and crossed the street to the house opposite, where with old Het beside her in another rocker, she had been sitting ever since on the veranda, grim, inscrutable, the two of them rocking steadily, while hoarse and tireless men hurled her dishes and furniture and bedding up and down the street.

"What are you telling me for?" Snopes said. "Hit warn't me that set that ere scuttle of live fire where the first thing that passed would knock hit into the cellar."

"It was you that opened the cellar door, though."

"Sho. And for what? To git that rope, her own rope, where she told me to git it."

"To catch your mule with, that was trespassing on her property. You can't get out of it this time, I.O. There ain't a jury in the county that won't find for her."

"Yes. I reckon not. And just because she is a woman. That's why. Because she is a durn woman. All right. Let her go to her durn jury with hit. I can talk too; I reckon hit's a few things I could tell a jury myself about—" He ceased. They were watching him.

"What? Tell a jury about what?"

"Nothing. Because hit ain't going to no jury. A jury between her and me? Me and Mannie Hait? You boys don't know her if you think she's going to make trouble over a pure acci-dent couldn't nobody help. Why, there ain't a fairer, finer woman in the county than Miz Mannie Hait. I just wisht I had a opportunity to tell her so." The opportunity came at once. Old Het was behind her, carrying the shopping-bag. Mrs. Hait looked once, quietly, about at the faces, making no response to the murmur of curious salutation, then not again. She didn't look at Snopes long either, nor talk to him long.

"I come to buy that mule," she said.

"What mule?" They looked at one another. "You'd like to own that mule?" She looked at him. "Hit'll cost you a hundred and fifty, Miz Mannie."

"You mean dollars?"

"I don't mean dimes nor nickels neither, Miz Mannie."

"Dollars," she said. "That's more than mules was in Hait's time."

"Lots of things is different since Hait's time. Including you and me."

"I reckon so," she said. Then she went away. She turned without a word, old Het following.

"Maybe one of them others you looked at this morning would suit you," Snopes said. She didn't answer. Then they were gone.

"I don't know as I would have said that last to her," one said.

"What for?" Snopes said. "If she was aiming to law something outen me about that fire, you reckon she would have come and offered to pay me money for hit?" That was about one o'clock. About four o'clock he was shouldering his way through a throng of Negroes before a cheap grocery store when one called his name. It was old Het, the now bulging shopping-bag on her arm, eating bananas from a paper sack.

"Fo God I wuz jest dis minute huntin fer you," she said. She handed the banana to a woman beside her and delved and fumbled in the shopping-bag and extended a greenback. "Miz Mannie gimme dis to give you; I wuz jest on de way to de sto whar you stay at. Here." He took the bill.

"What's this? From Miz Hait?"

"Fer de mule." The bill was for ten dollars. "You don't need to gimme no receipt. I kin be de witness I give hit to you."

"Ten dollars? For that mule? I told her a hundred and fifty dollars."

"You'll have to fix dat up wid her yo'self. She jest gimme dis to give ter you when she sot out to fetch de mule."

"Set out to fetch— She went out there herself and taken my mule outen my pasture?"

"Lawd, chile," old Het said, "Miz Mannie ain't skeered of no mule. Ain't you done foun dat out?"

And then it became late, what with the yet short winter days; when she came in sight of the two gaunt chimneys against the sunset, evening was already finding itself. But she could smell the ham cooking before she came in sight of the cow shed even, though she could not see it until she came around in front where the fire burned beneath an iron skillet set on bricks and where nearby Mrs. Hait was milking the cow. "Well," old Het said, "you is settled down, ain't you?" She looked into the shed, neated and raked and swept even, and floored now with fresh hay. A clean new lantern burned on a box, beside it a pallet bed was spread neatly on the straw and turned neatly back for the night. "Why, you is fixed up," she said with pleased astonishment. Within the door was a kitchen chair. She drew it out and sat down beside the skillet and laid the bulging shopping-bag beside her.

"I'll tend dis meat whilst you milks. I'd offer to strip dat cow fer you ef I wuzn't so wo out wid all dis excitement we been had." She looked around her. "I don't believe I sees yo new mule, dough." Mrs. Hait grunted, her head against the cow's flank. After a moment she said,

"Did you give him that money?"

"I give um ter him. He ack surprise at first, lak maybe he think you didn't aim to trade dat quick. I tole him to settle de details wid you later. He taken de money, dough. So I reckin dat's offen his mine en yo'n bofe." Again Mrs. Hait grunted. Old Het turned the ham in the skillet. Beside it the coffee pot bubbled and steamed. "Cawfee smell good too," she said. "I ain't had no appetite in years now. A bird couldn't live on de vittles I eats. But jest lemme git a whiff er cawfee en seem lak hit always whets me a little. Now, ef you jest had nudder little piece o dis ham, now— Fo God, you got company aready." But Mrs. Hait did not even look up until she had finished. Then she turned without rising from the box on which she sat.

"I reckon you and me better have a little talk," Snopes said. "I reckon I got something that belongs to you and I hear you got something that belongs to me." He looked about, quickly, ceaselessly, while old Het watched him. He turned to her. "You go away, aunty. I don't reckon you want to set here and listen to us."

"Lawd, honey," old Het said. "Don't you mind me. I done already had so much troubles myself dat I kin set en listen to udder folks' widout hit worryin me a-tall. You gawn talk whut you came ter talk; I jest set here en tend de ham." Snopes looked at Mrs. Hait.

"Ain't you going to make her go away?" he said.

"What for?" Mrs. Hait said. "I reckon she ain't the first critter that ever come on this yard when hit wanted and went or stayed when hit liked." Snopes made a gesture, brief, fretted, restrained.

"Well," he said. "All right. So you taken the mule."

"I paid you for it. She give you the money."

"Ten dollars. For a hundred-and-fifty-dollar mule. Ten dollars."

"I don't know anything about hundred-and-fifty-dollar mules. All I know is what the railroad paid." Now Snopes looked at her for a full moment.

"What do you mean?"

"Them sixty dollars a head the railroad used to pay you for mules back when you and Hait——"

"Hush," Snopes said; he looked about again, quick, ceaseless. "All right. Even call it sixty dollars. But you just sent me ten."

"Yes. I sent you the difference." He looked at her, perfectly still. "Between that mule and what you owed Hait."

"What I owed——"

"For getting them five mules onto the tr——"

"Hush!" he cried. "Hush!" Her voice went on, cold, grim, level. "For helping you. You paid him fifty dollars each time, and the railroad paid you sixty dollars a head for the mules. Ain't that right?" He watched her. "The last time you never paid him. So I taken that mule instead. And I sent you the ten dollars difference."

"Yes," he said in a tone of quiet, swift, profound bemusement; then he cried: "But look! Here's where I got you. Hit was our agreement that I wouldn't never owe him nothing until after the mules was——"

"I reckon you better hush yourself," Mrs. Hait said.

"—until hit was over. And this time, when over had come, I never owed nobody no money because the man hit would have been owed to wasn't nobody," he cried triumphantly. "You see?" Sitting on the box, motionless, downlooking, Mrs. Hait seemed to muse. "So you just take your ten dollars back and tell me where my mule is and we'll just go back good friends to where we started at. Fore God, I'm as sorry as ere a living man about that fire——"

"Fo God!" old Het said, "hit was a blaze, wuzn't it?"

"—but likely with all that ere railroad money you still got, you just been wanting a chance to build new, all along. So here. Take hit." He put the money into her hand. "Where's my mule?" But Mrs. Hait didn't move at once.

"You want to give it back to me?" she said.

"Sho. We been friends all the time; now we'll just go back to where we left off being. I don't hold no hard feelings and don't you hold none. Where you got the mule hid?"

"Up at the end of that ravine ditch behind Spilmer's," she said.

"Sho. I know. A good, sheltered place, since you ain't got nere barn. Only if you'd a just left hit in the pasture, hit would a saved us both trouble. But hit ain't no hard feelings though. And so I'll bid you goodnight. You're all fixed up, I see. I reckon you could save some more money by not building no house a-tall."

"I reckon I could," Mrs. Hait said. But he was gone.

"Whut did you leave de mule dar fer?" old Het said.

"I reckon that's far enough," Mrs. Hait said.

"Fer enough?" But Mrs. Hait came and looked into the skillet, and old Het said, "Wuz hit me er you dat mentioned something erbout er nudder piece o dis ham?" So they were both eating when in the not-quite-yet accomplished twilight Snopes returned. He came up quietly and stood, holding his hands to the blaze as if he were quite cold. He did not look at any one now.

"I reckon I'll take that ere ten dollars," he said.

"What ten dollars?" Mrs. Hait said. He seemed to muse upon the fire. Mrs. Hait and old Het chewed quietly, old Het alone watching him.

"You ain't going to give hit back to me?" he said.

"You was the one that said to let's go back to where we started," Mrs. Hait said.

"Fo God you wuz, en dat's de fack," old Het said. Snopes mused upon the fire; he spoke in a tone of musing and amazed despair:

"I go to the worry and the risk and the agoment for years and years and I get sixty dollars. And you, one time, without no trouble and no risk, without even knowing you are going to git it, git eighty-five hundred dollars. I never begrudged hit to you; can't nere a man say I did, even if hit did seem a little strange that you should git it all when he wasn't working for you and you never even knowed where he was at and what doing; that all you done to git it was to be married to him. And now, after all these ten years of not begrudging you hit, you taken the best mule I had and you ain't even going to pay me ten dollars for hit. Hit ain't right. Hit ain't justice."

"You got de mule back, en you ain't satisfried yit," old Het said. "Whut does you want?" Now Snopes looked at Mrs. Hait.

"For the last time I ask hit," he said. "Will you or won't you give hit back?"

"Give what back?" Mrs. Hait said. Snopes turned. He stumbled over something—it was old Het's shopping-bag—and recovered and went on. They could see him in silhouette, as though framed by the two blackened chimneys against the dying west; they saw him fling up both clenched hands in a gesture almost Gallic, of resignation and impotent despair. Then he was gone. Old Het was watching Mrs. Hait.

"Honey," she said. "Whut did you do wid de mule?" Mrs. Hait leaned forward to the fire. On her plate lay a stale biscuit. She lifted the skillet and poured over the biscuit the grease in which the ham had cooked.

"I shot it," she said.

"You which?" old Het said. Mrs. Hait began to eat the biscuit. "Well," old Het said, happily, "de mule burnt de house en you shot de mule. Dat's whut I calls justice." It was getting dark fast now, and before her was still the three-mile walk to the poorhouse. But the dark would last a long time in January, and the poorhouse too would not move at once. She sighed with weary and happy relaxation. "Gentlemen, hush! Ain't we had a day!"

THE HAUNTED PALACE

Elizabeth Madox Roberts

From *Not by Strange Gods* by Elizabeth Madox Roberts, 1941.

Elizabeth Madox Roberts (1886-1941) was a native of rural Kentucky, and after living in Chicago, where she attended the University of Chicago and began writing, then in New York and California, she returned home and settled down to write. In her poetry and her novels and stories she achieves a fascinating blend of realism and fantasy. Her best known novels are *The Time of Man* (1926), *The Great Meadow* (1930), and *Black Is My Truelove's Hair* (1938). *The Haunted Mirror* (1932) and *Not by Strange Gods* (1941) are collections of stories. A full-scale critical study is Harry M. Campbell and Ruel E. Foster, *Elizabeth Madox Roberts: American Novelist* (1956). See also Mark Van Doren, "Elizabeth Madox Roberts, Her Mind and Style," *The English Journal*, XXI (September, 1932), 521-528.

The House stood at the head of a valley where the hollow melted away into the rolling uplands. The high trees about the place so confined the songs of the birds that on a spring morning the jargoning seemed to emerge from the walls. The birds seemed to be indoors or within the very bricks of the masonry. In winter the winds blew up the hollow from the valley and lashed at the old house that stood square before the storms. The place was called Wickwood. It had been the abode of a family, Wickley, a group that had once clustered about the hearths there or had tramped over the courtyard or ridden through the pastures.

From a road that ran along the top of a ridge two miles to the east, the House could be seen as a succession of rhomboids and squares that flowed together beneath the vague misty reds of the mass. Or from the valley road to the west, looking up the hollow into the melting hills, in winter one could see it as a distant brick wall set with long windows, beneath a gray sloping roof. Sometimes a traveler, allured by the name of the place or by the aloof splendor of the walls as seen vaguely from one or the other of these highways, would cross the farmlands by the way of the uneven roads. He would trundle over the crooked ways and mount through the broken woodland to come at last to the House. Leaving his conveyance, he would cross the wide courtyard on the smooth flag stones, and he would hear the strange report his footfalls made as they disturbed the air that had, but for the birds and the wind, been quiet for so great a length of time that it had assumed stillness. He would wonder at the beauty of the doorways and deplore the waste that let the House stand unused and untended. He would venture up the stone steps at the west front and peer through the glass of the side lights. The strange quality of the familiar fall of his own shoe on stone would trouble his sense of all that he had discovered, so that he would at last come swiftly away.

The country rolled in changing curves and lines and spread toward the river valleys, where it dropped suddenly into a basin. The farms were owned by men and women who had labored to win them. But among these were younger men who worked for hire or as share-owners in the yield.

One of these last, Hubert, lived with Jess, his wife, in a small whitewashed shelter behind a cornfield. Jess spoke more frequently than the man and thus she had more memory. She had been here two years, but before that time she had lived beside a creek, and before that again in another place, while farther back the vista was run together in a fog of forgetting. She had courted Hubert in a cabin close beside a roadway. She remembered another place where there was a plum tree that bore large pink-red fruits, and a place where her father had cut his foot with an ax. Now, as a marker, her own children ran a little way into a cornfield to play. Beyond these peaks in memory, going backward, the life there rested in a formless level out of which only self emerged. She met any demand upon this void with a contempt in which self was sheltered.

Hubert was a share-laborer, but he wanted to be able to rent some land. He wanted to use land as if he were the owner, and yet to be free to go to fresh acres when he had exhausted a tract as he willed. After the first child, Albert, was born, he said to Jess:

"If a person could have ahead, say, four hundred dollars and against the Dean land might come idle. . . ."

His fervor had the power of a threat. He was knotty and bony and his muscles were dry and lean. He had learned at school to write his name and to make a few slow marks that signified numbers or quantities, but later he had used this knowledge so infrequently that most of it was lost to him. He wrote his name painfully and, writing, he drew his fingers together about the pen. His breath would flow hard and fast under the strain, his hand trembling. If there were other men standing about he would, if he were asked to write his name, sometimes say that he could not, preferring to claim complete illiteracy rather than to undergo the ordeal.

"Against the Dean land might come idle. . . ." He had a plan over which he brooded, wanting to get a power over some good land that he might drain money out of it. He was careful, moving forward through the soil, taking from it.

When the second child came they lived at the Dean land, behind the cornfield. Jess would fling a great handful of grain toward her hens and they would come with reaching bills and outthrust necks, their wings spread. She would throw ears of corn to the sow and it would chew away the grains while the sucklings would drag milk, the essence of the corn, from the dark udders.

"We ought, it seems, to build the sow a little shed against winter comes," Jess said to Hubert.

"We might eat the sow. I might fatten up the sow and get me another."

"She always was a no-account sow. Has only five or six to a litter. It's hardly worth while to pester yourself with a lazy hog."

"Fannie Burt asked me what was the name of the sow or to name what kind or breed she was. 'Name?' I says. As if folks would name the food they eat!"

Hubert laughed at the thought of naming the food. Names for the swine, either mother or species, gave him laughter. To write with one's hand the name of a sow in a book seemed useless labor.

Instead of giving her a name he fastened her into a closed pen and gave her all the food he could find. When she was sufficiently fat he stuck her throat with a knife and prepared her body for his own eating.

Jess yielded to the decision Hubert made, being glad to have decisions made for her, and thus she accepted the flesh of the brood sow. Of this she ate heavily. She was large and often of a placid temper, sitting in unbrooding inattention, but often she flamed to sudden anger and thrust about her then with her hands or her fists. She did not sing about the house or the dooryard. Singing came to her from a wooden box that was charged by a small battery. She adjusted the needle of this to a near sending station and let the sound pour over the cabin. Out of the abundant jargon that flowed from the box she did not learn, and before it she did not remember. . . .

Jess had a few friends who came sometimes to see her. They were much like herself in what they knew and in what they liked. She would look curiously at their new clothing.

But one of them, named Fannie Burt, would come shouting to the children as she drove up the lane in a small cart, and her coming filled the day with remembered sayings and finer arrangements. When Fannie came Jess would call Albert, the oldest child, and send him on his hands and knees under the house to rob the hen's nest if there were not enough eggs in the basket, for the day called for a richer pudding. Fannie had no children as yet and she could be light and outflowing. She went here and there and she knew many of the people.

"Miss Anne mended the cover to the big black sofa in the parlor. . . ." She would tell of many things—of tapestry on a wall, blue and gold. Words seemed light when she talked, as being easily made to tell of strange and light matters. Jess was not sure that Fannie knew more of these things than she knew herself, since the words conveyed but an undefined sense. The lightness of bubbles floated about Fannie, things for which Jess had no meanings. Fannie had lived the year before at a farm where the owner had been as a neighbor to her. She often went back to call there, staying all day as a friend.

"Miss Anne mended the cover to the sofa where it was worn." Jess laughed with Fannie, and she scarcely knew whether she laughed at the sofa or at the mended place. She herself could not sew, and thus she could not mend any broken fabric of any kind. She laughed, however, Fannie's call being just begun. She was not yet hostile to it. She tried for the moment to stretch her imaginings to see something desired or some such thing as grace or beauty in the person who leaned over the ancient tapestry to mend it. The effort was spent in wonder and finally in anger. Fannie laughed at the sullenness that came to Jess. The sofa had come from Wickwood, she said. It had been given to Miss Anne at her marriage, for she was somehow related to the Wickleys. Laughing, Fannie tossed the least child and settled to tell again. Her tales would be, all together, a myth of houses and families, of people marrying and settling into new abodes. She was gay and sharp, and her face was often pointed with smiles. Or she would be talking now with the children and telling them the one story she had from a book.

"Then a great ogre lived in the place . . . a Thing that threatens to get you . . . a great Thing . . . destroys . . . eats up Life itself. Drinks the blood out of Life. It came with a club in its hand. . . . It was a fine place, but had a Thing inside it. . . . That would be when little Blue Wing went to the woods to play. She found this place in the woods. . . ."

"What was that?" Jess asked suddenly. "What kind was that you named?"

"A giant. Ogry or ogre. A Thing. Comes to eat up a man and to eat Life itself. . . ."

Fannie would be gone and Jess would be glad to have an end of her. As if too much had been asked of her she would sit now in vague delight, and she would forget to run her radio instrument while she saw Fannie's bright pointed face as something slipping past her. The stories that had been told had become a blend of indistinct mental colorings that would drop out of memory at length, as a spent pleasure no longer wanted. She would reject the visit completely and turn to anger, thrusting Fannie out. Then, complete hostility to the visitor having come to her, she would set roughly upon her tasks. If the children spoke of the stories that had been told she would order them to be quiet.

Some of the farms had lost their former owners. A house here and there was shut and still while the acres were farmed by the shifting men who lived in the cabins or in the town. A man came searching for Hubert at the end of the harvest to offer him a part of the Wickley place to farm.

"It's said fine people once lived there," Hubert said when he told Jess of his offer.

"If they're gone now I wouldn't care."

"It's not like any place ever you saw in life. It's good land, howsoever."

Other tenants would be scattered over the acres, laborers who would farm by sharing the crops. Hubert would rent the acres about the house and he would live there.

"Is there a good well of water?"

"Two wells there are," he answered her.

"I never heard of two wells."

"One has got a little fancy house up over it."

"What would I do with a little fancy house built up over a well? I can't use such a house." As if more might be required of her than she could perform, Jess was uneasy in thinking of the new place to which they would go. She did not want to go there. "It's a place made for some other," she said. She could not see the women of the place going about their labors. She could not discover what they might carry in their hands and what their voices might call from the doorways, or how they would sleep or dress themselves or find themselves food. In her troubled thought, while she came and went about the cabin room where the least child lay, shapes without outline, the women of the Wickleys, went into vague distances where doors that were not defined were opened and closed into an uncomprehended space.

But the next day Fannie Burt came and there was something further to know. The Wickley farm was called Wickwood, she said. Miss Anne's father had gone there in old Wickley's lifetime. Together these two men had made experiments in the growing of fine animals. Sometimes it would be a horse old Wickley wanted. "Egad!" he would say, or "I'm not dead yet!" Another story running into a comic ending, "A good colt she is, but a leetle matter of interference. Look at her hind feet." Fannie had something that Miss Anne had in mind. It was told imperfectly, thrown out in a hint and retained in a gesture, put back upon Miss Anne, who could tell with fluent words and meaning gestures. She would be sitting over the last of the dessert in the old, faded dining room. She would be telling for the pure joy of talking, laughing with the past. "Pappy went over to Wickwood. . . . It was Tuesday . . . . Came Sunday then and we all said, 'Where's Pappy?' Came to find out and he's still over to Wickwood with Cousin Bob. All that time to get the brown mare rightly in foal. And all still on paper."

Fannie would seem to be talking fast, and one thing would seem to be entangled with another, although she spoke with Miss Anne's quiet, slow cadence. In her telling men would be sitting together in a library. One would be making a drawing of a horse, such a horse as he would be devising. A horse would be sketched on paper before it was so much as foaled. This would be old Robert Wickley, a pen between his thumb and his fingers. "What we want after all is a good Kentucky saddle horse, fifteen hands high and two inches over. Take Danbury II, say, over at Newmarket. . . ."

"You take Danbury and you'll plumb get a jackass."

"Pappy laughed over a thing once for a week before he told us," Miss Anne's speaking through Fannie's speaking. "Pappy in a big tellen way one day and he let it be known what he was so amused about."

A man had come in at the door at Wickwood, a hurried man with money in cash saved by. He wanted the Wickley land on which to grow something. He wanted to buy, offering cash.

"Do you think you could live in my house and on my land?" old Wickley asked.

Fannie would be telling as Miss Anne had told and, beyond again, the father who had told in a moment of amusement. Men who came on business were let in at a side door. "Business was a Nobody then," Miss Anne said. Mollie would be off somewhere in the house singing. Carline had run off to get married. Old Wickley, father to Robert, rolling back his shirtsleeves because the day was hot, and walking barefoot out into the cool grass, or he would be standing under the shower in the bath house while somebody pumped the water that sprayed over him. Miss Sallie made the garden with her own hands and designed the sundial. They made things for themselves with their hands. Bob Wickley sketching for himself the horse he wanted on a large sheet of manila paper. His grandmother had, as a bride, set the house twelve feet back of the builder's specifications in order to save a fine oak tree that still grew before the front door. A man wanting to plow his pastures. . . .

"Two hundred dollars an acre for the creek bottom, cash money." Wickley had called him a hog and sent him away.

"Pappy laughed over it for a week. ' "You think you could live in my house? Come back three generations from now." . . . And, egad, he couldn't,' Pappy said."

"Hogs want to root in my pasture," Bob Wickley said. He was angry. . . . Miss Anne speaking through Fannie's speaking, reports fluttering about, intermingled, right and wrong, the present and the past. Fannie could scarcely divide one Wickley from another. One had gathered the books. One had held a high public office. One had married a woman who pinned back her hair with a gold comb. Their children had read plentifully from the books. Justus, William, and Robert had been names among them. Miss Anne now owned the portrait of the lady of the golden comb. There had been farewells and greetings, dimly remembered gifts, trinkets, portraits to be made, children to be born. . . .

In this telling as it came from the telling of Miss Anne, there was one, a Robert, who danced along the great parlor floor with one named Mollie. Mollie was the wife of Andrew. She had come from a neighboring farm. When they danced the music from the piano had crashed and tinkled under the hands of Miss Lizette, Robert's mother, or of Tony Barr, a young man who came to visit at Wickwood. Down would fling the chords on the beat and at the same instant up would fling the dancers, stepping upward on the rhythm and treading the air. Mollie's long slim legs would flash from beneath her flying skirts, or one would lie for an instant outstretched while the pulse of the music beat, then off along the shining floor, gliding and swaying with the gliding of Robert, until it seemed as if the two of them were one, and as if they might float out the window together, locked into the rhythms, and thus dance away across the world.

"Where are they now?" Jess asked.

Fannie did not know. Miss Anne had not told her.

"Where would be Andrew, the one that was her husband?" She was angry and she wanted to settle blame somewhere.

He would be beside the wall. He would look at Mollie with delight. His head would move, or his hands, with the rhythm, and his eyes would be bright. Mollie loved him truly.

Sometimes it would be the old fast waltzes that were danced, and then Miss Lizette and old Bob would come into it. Then they would whirl swiftly about the floor and the music would be "Over the Waves." The young would try it, dizzy and laughing, or they would change the steps to their own.

"What did they do?" Jess asked. "I feel staggered to try to know about such a house."

"They had a wide scope of land," Fannie answered her. "They burned the bricks and made the house. They cut the timber for the beams of the house off their own fields."

The House had become an entity, as including the persons and the legends of it. All the Wickleys were blurred into one, were gathered into one report.

"There was a woman, Mollie Wickley. She was the mother of Andrew, or maybe she was his wife," Fannie said. "I don't recall. It's all one. There was a Sallie Wickley. I don't know whe'r she was his daughter or his wife."

"Iffen he couldn't keep it for his children," Jess called out, "why would he build such a place?"

"He lived in the house *himself*."

Jess and Hubert would be going to the place where these had been. All these were gone now. The land was still good. Hubert would be able to take money out of it. He would hold the plow into the soil and his tongue would hang from the side of his mouth in his fervor to plant more and to have a large yield. The people would be gone. Jess dismissed them with the clicking of her tongue. They seemed, nevertheless, to be coming nearer. In Fannie's presence, while she sat in the chair beside the door, they came nearer, to flit as shapes about her fluttering tongue while Jess fixed her gaze upon the mouth that was speaking or shifted to look at the familiar cups and plates on the table. Shapes fluttered then over the cups. Vague forms, having not the shapes of defined bodies, but the ends of meanings, appeared and went. Fannie knew little beyond the myths she had made, and Jess knew much less, knew nothing beyond the bright tinkle of Fannie's chatter.

"It was the horse then," Fannie said, in part explaining. "Now nobody wants enough horses. . . . Now it's tobacco."

Hubert and Jess came to the place, Wickwood, at sundown of an early winter afternoon. Hubert talked of the land, of the fields, growing talkative as their small truck rolled slowly through the ruts of the old driveway. When they had passed through the woodland, which was now in part denuded of its former growth, they came near to the house. It seemed to Jess that there was a strange wideness about the place, as if space were spent outward without bounds. They went under some tall oaks and maples while Hubert muttered of his plans.

A great wall arose in the dusk. The trees stretched their boughs toward the high wall in the twilight. When it seemed that the truck would drive into the hard darkness of the wall that stood before them as if it went into the sky, Hubert turned toward the left and rounded among the trees. Other walls stood before them. Jess had never before seen a place like this. It seemed to her that it might be a town, but there were no people there. The children began to cry and Albert screamed, "I want to go away!" Jess herself was frightened.

"Hush your fuss," Hubert said. His words were rough. "Get out of the truck," he said to her. She attended to his short angry speech; it jerked her out of her fear and dispersed a part of her dread of the place. It made her know that they, themselves and their goods, their life and their ways of being, would somehow fit into the brick walls, would make over some part of the strangeness for their own use. He had climbed from the vehicle and he walked a little way among the buildings, stalking in the broad courtyard among the flagstones and over the grass. He looked about him. Then he went toward a wing of the largest house and entered a small porch that stood out from one of the walls.

"We'll live here," he said.

She did not know how he had discovered which part of the circle of buildings, of large houses and small rooms, would shelter them. He began to carry their household goods from the truck. Jess found her lantern among her things and she made a light. When the lantern was set on a shelf she could look about the room where they would live.

There were windows opposite the door through which they had entered. Outside, the rain dripped slowly through the great gnarled trees. The rain did not trouble her. A press built into the wall beside the chimney seemed ample to hold many things. Hubert set the cooking stove before the fireplace and fixed the stovepipe into the small opening above the mantel. The children cried at the strangeness, but when the lamp was lighted and food had been cooked they cried no more. When Jess set the food on the table they had begun to live in the new place.

Hubert went away across the courtyard and his step was hollow, amplified among the walls of the building. He came back later, the sound he made enlarged as he walked nearer over the flagstones.

"It's no such place as ever I saw before!" Jess cried out.

She had begun a longer speech but she was hushed by Hubert's hostile look. They would stay here, he said. It was the Wickley place. She closed the door to shut in the space she had claimed for their living, being afraid of the great empty walls that arose outside. The beds were hastily set up and the children fell asleep clutching the familiar pillows and quilts. Her life with Hubert, together with her children and her things for housekeeping, these she gathered mentally about her to protect herself from being obliged to know and to use the large house outside her walls. She began to comfort herself with thoughts of Hubert and to court him with a fine dish of food she had carefully saved.

The morning was clear after the rain. Hubert had gone to bring the fowls from their former abode. Albert had found a sunny nook in which to play and with the second child he was busy there.

"What manner of place is this?" Jess asked herself again and again. Outside the windows toward the south were the great gnarled trees. Outside to the north was the courtyard round which were arranged the buildings, all of them built of red, weathered brick. Toward the west, joined to the small wing in which Hubert had set up their home, arose the great house. There were four rows of windows here, one row above the other.

The buildings about the court were empty. A large bell hung in the middle of the court on the top of a high pole. There was a deep well at the back of the court where the water was drawn by a bucket lifted by a winch. Jess had a great delight in the well, for it seemed to hold water sufficient to last through any drought. Not far from the well stood a large corncrib, holding only a little corn now, but ready for Hubert's filling. She went cautiously about in the strange air.

She had no names for all the buildings that lay about her. She was frightened of the things for which she had no use, as if she might be called upon to know and to use beyond her understanding. She walked toward the west beneath the great wall of the tallest house.

There were birds in the high trees and echoes among the high walls. The singing winter wren was somewhere about, and the cry of the bird was spread widely and repeated in a shadowy call again and again. Jess rounded the wall and looked cautiously at the west side. There were closed shutters at some of the windows, but some of the shutters were opened. In the middle of the great western wall there were steps of stone. They were cut evenly and laid smoothly, one above another, reaching toward a great doorway about which was spread bright glass in straight patterns at the sides, in a high fan-shape above.

Jess went cautiously up the steps, watching for Hubert to come with the fowls, delaying, looking out over the woodland and the fields. Hubert had said again and again that this would be the Wickley place, Wickwood, that they would live there, tilling the soil, renting the land. Jess saw before her, on the great left-hand door, a knocker. She lifted it and tapped heavily, listening to the sound she made, waiting.

There was no sound to answer her rap but a light echo that

seemed to come from the trees. Her own hate of the place forbade her and she dared not tap again. Standing half fearfully, she waited, laying her hands on the smooth door frame, on the fluted pillars and the leading of the glass. A cord hung near her hand and, obeying the suggestion it offered, she closed her fingers about it and pulled it stiffly down. A sound cut the still air where no sound had been for so long a time that every vibration had been stilled. The tone broke the air. The first tone came in unearthly purity, but later the notes joined and overflowed one another.

She waited, not daring to touch the cord again. The stillness that followed after the peal of the bell seemed to float out from the house itself and to hush the birds. She could not think what kind of place this might be or see any use that one might make of the great doorway, of the cord, of the bell. A strange thing stood before her. Strangeness gathered to her own being until it seemed strange that she should be here, on the top of a stair of stone before a great door, waiting for Hubert to come with her hens. It was as if he might never come. As if hens might be gone from the earth.

She saw then that the doors were not locked together, that one throbbed lightly on the other when she touched it with her hand. She pushed the knob and the door spread open wide.

Inside, a great hall reached to a height that was three or four times her own stature. Tall white doors were opened into other great rooms and far back before her a stairway began. She could not comprehend the stair. It lifted, depending from the rail that spread upward like a great ribbon in the air. Her eyes followed it, her breath coming quick and hard. It rose as a light ribbon spreading toward a great window through which came the morning sun. But leaving the window in the air, it arose again and wound back, forward and up, lost from view for a space, to appear again, higher up, at a mythical distance before another great window where the sun spread a broad yellow glow. It went at last into nothingness, and the ceiling and the walls melted together in shadows.

When she had thus, in mind, ascended, her eyes closed and a faint sickness went over her, delight mingled with fear and hate. She was afraid of being called upon to know this strange ribbon of ascent that began as a stair with rail and tread and went up into unbelievable heights, step after step. She opened her eyes to look again, ready to reject the wonder as being past all belief and, therefore, having no reality.

"What place is this?" she asked, speaking in anger. Her voice rang through the empty hall, angry words, her own, crying, "What place is this?"

At one side of the floor there were grains of wheat in streaks, as if someone might have stored sacks of wheat there. Jess thought of her hens, seeing the scattered grain, and she knew that they would pick up the remaining part of it. They would hop from stone to stone, coming cautiously up the steps, and they would stretch their long necks cautiously in at the doorway, seeing the corn. They would not see the great stairway.

A light dust lay on the window ledges. A few old cobwebs hung in fragments from the ceiling. The dust, the webs, and the wheat were a link between things known and unknown, and, seeing them, she walked a little way from the hall, listening, going farther, looking into the rooms, right and left. She was angry and afraid. What she could not bring to her use she wanted to destroy. In the room to her right a large fireplace stood far at the end of a patterned floor. There were shelves set into the white wall beside the large chimney. She left this room quickly and turned toward the room at the left. Here two large rooms melted together and tall doors opened wide. There were white shapes carved beneath the windows and oblong shapes carved again on the wood of the doors, on the pillars that held the mantel. Before her a long mirror was set into a wall. In it were reflected the boughs of the trees outside against a crisscross of the window opposite.

She was confused after she had looked into the mirror, and she looked about hastily to find the door through which she had come. It was a curious, beautiful, fearful place. She wanted to destroy it. Her feet slipped too lightly on the smooth wood of the floor. There was no piece of furniture anywhere, but the spaces seemed full, as filled with their wide dimensions and the carvings on the wood. In the hall she looked again toward the stair and she stood near the doorway looking back. Then suddenly without plan, scarcely knowing that her own lips spoke, she flung out an angry cry, half screaming, "Mollie Wickley! Mollie! Where's she at?" The harsh echoes pattered and knocked among the upper walls after her own voice was done. Turning her back on the place, she went quickly out of the doorway.

In the open air she looked back toward the steps she had ascended, seeing dimly into the vista of the hall and the upward-lifting ribbon of the stair. A sadness lay heavily upon her because she could not know what people might live in the house, what shapes of women and men might fit into the doorway. She hated her sadness and she turned it to anger. She went from the west front and entered the courtyard. Hubert came soon after with the fowls and there was work to do in housing them and getting them corn.

On a cold day in January when his ewes were about to lamb, Hubert brought them into the large house, driving them up the stone steps at the west front, and he prepared to stable them in the rooms there. The sheep cried and their bleating ran up the long ribbon of the stair. They were about thirty in number, and thus the wailing was incessant. Hubert and Jess went among them with lanterns. The ewes turned and drifted about among the large rooms; but as they began to bear their lambs Hubert bedded them here and there, one beneath the stairway and three others in the room to the right where the empty bookshelves spread wide beside the tall fireplace. The night came, dark and cold.

"They are a slow set," Jess said. She wanted to be done and she was out of patience with delaying sheep.

"Whoop, here! Shut fast the door!" Hubert called.

Jess was wrapped in a heavy coat and hooded in a shawl. She went among the sheep and she held a lantern high to search out each beast. If a ewe gave birth to three lambs she took one up quickly and dropped it beside a stout young beast that was giving life to but one and she thus induced it to take the second as her own. She flung out sharp commands and she brought the animals here and there. The halls were filled with the crying of the sheep. Threats came back upon her from her own voice, so that she was displeased with what she did and her displeasure made her voice more high-

pitched and angry. Anger spoke again and again through the room.
She wanted the lambing to be easily done, but the days had been very
cold and the sheep delayed.

"It was a good place to come to lamb the sheep," she called to
Hubert. "I say, a good place." She had a delight in seeing that the
necessities of lambing polluted the wide halls. "A good place to
lamb. . . ."

"Whoop! Bring here the old nanny as soon as you pick up the
dead lamb!" Hubert was shouting above the incessant crying of
the sheep.

The ewes in labor excited her anew so that she wanted to be using her strength and to be moving swiftly forward, but she had no
plan beyond Hubert's. "Whoop, rouse up the young nanny! Don't
let the bitches sleep! Whoop, there!"

He was everywhere with his commands. When the task was more
than half done he called to Jess that he must go to the barn for more
straw for bedding. "Whoop! Shut the door tight after me. Keep
the old ewe there up on her legs." He went away, carrying his lantern.

Jess fastened the outer door and she turned back into the parlors.
Then she saw a dim light at the other end of the long dark space
that lay before her. She saw another shape, a shrouded figure, moving far down the long way. The apparition, the Thing, seemed to be
drifting forward out of the gloom, and it seemed to be coming toward her where she stood among the sheep. Jess drove the laboring
mothers here and there, arranging their places and assisting their
travail with her club. She would not believe that she saw anything
among the sheep at the farther end of the rooms, but as she worked
she glanced now and then toward the way in which she had
glimpsed it. It was there or it was gone entirely. The sheep and the
lambs made a great noise with their crying. Jess went to and fro,
and she forgot that she had seen anything beyond the sheep far
down the room in the moving dusk of white and gray which flowed
in the moving light of her lantern.

All at once, looking up suddenly as she walked forward, she saw
that an apparition was certainly moving there and that it was coming toward her. It carried something in its upraised hand. There

was a dark covering over the head and shoulders that were sunk into the upper darkening gloom. The whole body came forward as a dark thing illuminated by a light the creature carried low at the left side. The creature or the Thing moved among the sheep. It came forward slowly and became a threatening figure, a being holding a club and a light in its hands. Jess screamed at it, a great oath flung high above the crying of the sheep. Fright had seized her and with it came a great strength to curse with her voice and to hurl forward her body.

"God curse you!" she yelled in a scream that went low in scale and cracked in her throat. "God's curse on you!" She lunged forward and lifted her lantern high to see her way among the sheep. "God's damn on you!"

The curse gave strength to her hands and to her limbs. As she hurled forward with uplifted stick the other came forward toward her, lunging and threatening. She herself moved faster. The creature's mouth was open to cry words but no sound came from it.

She dropped the lantern and flung herself upon the approaching figure, and she beat at the creature with her club while it beat at her with identical blows. Herself and the creature then were one. Anger continued, shared, and hurled against a crash of falling glass and plaster. She and the creature had beaten at the mirror from opposite sides.

The din arose above the noise of the sheep, and for an instant the beasts were quiet while the glass continued to fall. Jess stood back from the wreckage to try to understand it. Then slowly she knew that she had broken the great mirror that hung on the rear wall of the room. She took the lamp again into her hand and peered at the breakage on the floor and at the fragments that hung, cracked and crazed, at the sides of the frame.

"God's own curse on you!" She breathed her oath heavily, backing away from the dust that floated in the air.

Hubert was entering with a load of straw on his back. He had not heard the crash of glass nor had he noticed the momentary quiet of the sheep. These were soon at their bleating again, and Jess returned from the farther room where the dust of the plaster still lay on the air. Hubert poured water into deep pans he had placed here and there through the rooms. He directed Jess to make beds of the straw in each room. Their feet slipped in the wet that ran over the polished boards of the floor.

It was near midnight. Jess felt accustomed to the place now and more at ease there, she and Hubert being in possession of it. They walked about through the monstrous defilement. Hubert was muttering the count of the sheep with delight. There were two lambs beside each of the ewes but five and there were but two lambs dead and flung to the cold fireplace where they were out of the way. There were thirty-two ewes, they said, and their fingers pointed to assist and the mouths held to the sums, repeating numbers and counting profits.

Lamb by lamb, they were counted. There were two to each mother but the three in the farther room and the two under the staircase. These had but one each. "Twice thirty-two makes sixty-four," they said to assist themselves, and from this they subtracted one for each of the deficient ewes, but they became confused in this and counted all one by one. Counting with lantern and club, Jess went again through the halls, but she made thus but forty lambs, for she lost the sums and became addled among the words Hubert muttered. At last by taking one from sixty-four and then another, four times more, in the reckoning they counted themselves thirty-two ewes and fifty-nine lambs. The sheep were becoming quiet. Each lamb had nursed milk before they left it. At length they fastened the great front door with a rope tied to a nail in the door frame, and they left the sheep stabled there, being pleased with the number they had counted.

THE WIDE NET

Eudora Welty

From *The Wide Net, and Other Stories* by Eudora Welty, 1943; first published in *Harper's Magazine,* May (CLXXXIV, 582-594), 1942; First Prize Story of the O. Henry Memorial Award, 1942.

Eudora Welty (1909-   ) has kept close ties to her home community, Jackson, Mississippi, and has peopled her fiction with characters drawn minutely from models in that community. She has published a novelette, *The Robber Bridegroom* (1942); two novels, *Delta Wedding* (1946) and *The Ponder Heart* (1954); and five books of stories, *A Curtain of Green* (1941), *The Wide Net, and Other Stories* (1943), *Music from Spain* (1948), *The Golden Apples* (1949), and *The Bride of the Innisfallen* (1955). Katherine Anne Porter supplied a critical appreciation as a preface to *A Curtain of Green,* and Robert Penn Warren wrote a critical essay, "The Love and Separateness in Miss Welty," *The Kenyon Review,* VI (Spring, 1944), 246-259.

William Wallace Jamieson's wife Hazel was going to have a baby. But this was October, and it was six months away, and she acted exactly as though it would be tomorrow. When he came in the room she would not speak to him, but would look as straight at nothing as she could, with her eyes glowing. If he only touched her she stuck out her tongue or ran around the table. So one night he went out with two of the boys down the road and stayed out all night. But that was the worst thing yet, because when he came home in the early morning Hazel had vanished. He went through the house not believing his eyes, balancing with both hands out, his yellow cowlick rising on end, and then he turned the kitchen inside out looking for her, but it did no good. Then when he got back to the front room he saw she had left him a little letter, in an envelope. That was doing something behind someone's back. He took out the letter, pushed it open, held it out at a distance from his eyes. . . . After one look he was scared to read the exact words, and he crushed the whole thing in his hand instantly, but what it had said was that she would not put up with him after that and˙was going to the river to drown herself.

"Drown herself. . . . But she's in mortal fear of the water!"

He ran out front, his face red like the red of the picked cotton field he ran over, and down in the road he gave a loud shout for Virgil Thomas, who was just going in his own house, to come out again. He could just see the edge of Virgil, he had almost got in, he had one foot inside the door.

They met half-way between the farms, under the shade-tree.

"Haven't you had enough of the night?" asked Virgil. There they were, their pants all covered with dust and dew, and they had had to carry the third man home flat between them.

"I've lost Hazel, she's vanished, she went to drown herself."

"Why, that ain't like Hazel," said Virgil.

William Wallace reached out and shook him. "You heard me. Don't you know we have to drag the river?"

"Right this minute?"

"You ain't got nothing to do till spring."

"Let me go set foot inside the house and speak to my mother and tell her a story, and I'll come back."

"This will take the wide net," said William Wallace. His eyebrows gathered, and he was talking to himself.

"How come Hazel to go and do that way?" asked Virgil as they started out.

William Wallace said, "I reckon she got lonesome."

"That don't argue—drown herself for getting lonesome. My mother gets lonesome."

"Well," said William Wallace. "It argues for Hazel."

"How long is it now since you and her was married?"

"Why, it's been a year."

"It don't seem that long to me. A year!"

"It was this time last year. It seems longer," said William Wallace, breaking a stick off a tree in surprise. They walked along, kicking at the flowers on the road's edge. "I remember the day I seen her first, and that seems a long time ago. She was coming along the road holding a little frying-size chicken from her grandma, under her arm, and she had it real quiet. I spoke to her with nice manners. We knowed each other's names, being bound to, just didn't know each other to speak to. I says, 'Where are you taking the fryer?' and she says, 'Mind your manners,' and I kept on till after while she says, 'If you want to walk me home, take littler steps.' So I didn't lose time. It was just four miles across the field and full of blackberries, and from the top of the hill there was Dover below, looking sizeable-like and clean, spread out between the two churches like that. When we got down, I says to her, 'What kind of water's in this well?' and she says, 'The best water in the world.' So I drew a bucket and took out a dipper and she drank and I drank. I didn't think it was that remarkable, but I didn't tell her."

"What happened that night?" asked Virgil.

"We ate the chicken," said William Wallace, "and it was tender. Of course that wasn't all they had. The night I was trying their table out, it sure had good things to eat from one end to the other. Her mama and papa sat at the head and foot and we was face to face with each other across it, with I remember a pat of butter between. They had real sweet butter, with a tree drawed down it, elegant-like. Her mama eats like a man. I had brought her a whole hat-ful of berries and she didn't even pass them to her husband. Hazel, she would leap up and take a pitcher of new milk and fill up the glasses. I had heard how they couldn't have a singing at the church without a fight over her."

"Oh, she's a pretty girl, all right," said Virgil. "It's a pity for the ones like her to grow old, and get like their mothers."

"Another thing will be that her mother will get wind of this and come after me," said William Wallace.

"Her mother will eat you alive," said Virgil.

"She's just been watching her chance," said William Wallace. "Why did I think I could stay out all night."

"Just something come over you."

"First it was just a carnival at Carthage, and I had to let them guess my weight . . . and after that . . ."

"It was nice to be sitting on your neck in a ditch singing," prompted Virgil, "in the moonlight. And playing on the harmonica like you can play."

"Even if Hazel did sit home knowing I was drunk, that wouldn't kill her," said William Wallace. "What she knows ain't ever killed her yet. . . . She's smart, too, for a girl," he said.

"She's a lot smarter than her cousins in Beula," said Virgil. "And especially Edna Earle, that never did get to be what you'd call a heavy thinker. Edna Earle could sit and ponder all day on how the little tail of the 'C' got through the 'L' in a Coca-Cola sign."

"Hazel *is* smart," said William Wallace. They walked on. "You ought to see her pantry shelf, it looks like a hundred jars when you open the door. I don't see how she could turn around and jump in the river."

"It's a woman's trick."

"I always behaved before. Till the one night—last night."

"Yes, but the one night," said Virgil. "And she was waiting to take advantage."

"She jumped in the river because she was scared to death of the water and that was to make it worse," he said. "She remembered how I used to have to pick her up and carry her over the oak-log bridge, how she'd shut her eyes and make a dead-weight and hold me round the neck, just for a little creek. I don't see how she brought herself to jump."

"Jumped backwards," said Virgil. "Didn't look."

When they turned off, it was still early in the pink and green fields. The fumes of morning, sweet and bitter, sprang up where they walked. The insects ticked softly, their strength in reserve; butterflies chopped the air, going to the east, and the birds flew carelessly and sang by fits and starts, not the way they did in the evening in sustained and drowsy songs.

"It's a pretty *day* for sure," said William Wallace. "It's a pretty *day* for it."

"I don't see a sign of her ever going along here," said Virgil.

"Well," said William Wallace. "She wouldn't have dropped anything. I never saw a girl to leave less signs of where she's been."

"Not even a plum seed," said Virgil, kicking the grass.

In the grove it was so quiet that once William Wallace gave a jump, as if he could almost hear a sound of himself wondering where she had gone. A descent of energy came down on him in the thick of the woods and he ran at a rabbit and caught it in his hands.

"Rabbit . . . Rabbit . . ." He acted as if he wanted to take it off to himself and hold it up and talk to it. He laid a palm against its pushing heart. "Now . . . There now . . ."

"Let her go, William Wallace, let her go." Virgil, chewing on an elderberry whistle he had just made, stood at his shoulder: "What do you want with a live rabbit?"

William Wallace squatted down and set the rabbit on the ground but held it under his hand. It was a little, old, brown rabbit. It did not try to move. "See there?"

"Let her go."

"She can go if she wants to, but she don't want to."

Gently he lifted his hand. The round eye was shining at him sideways in the green gloom.

"Anybody can freeze a rabbit, that wants to," said Virgil. Suddenly he gave a far-reaching blast on the whistle, and the rabbit went in a streak. "Was you out catching cotton-tails, or was you out catching your wife?" he said, taking the turn to the open fields. "I come along to keep you on the track."

"Who'll we get, now?" They stood on top of a hill and William Wallace looked critically over the countryside. "Any of the Malones?"

"I was always scared of the Malones," said Virgil. "Too many *of* them."

"This is my day with the net, and they would have to watch out," said William Wallace. "I reckon some Malones, and the Doyles, will be enough. The six Doyles and their dogs, and you and me, and two little nigger boys is enough, with just a few Malones."

"That ought to be enough," said Virgil, "no matter what."

"I'll bring the Malones, and you bring the Doyles," said William Wallace, and they separated at the spring.

When William Wallace came back, with a string of Malones just showing behind him on the hilltop, he found Virgil with the two little Rippen boys waiting behind him, solemn little towheads. As soon as he walked up, Grady, the one in front, lifted his hand to signal silence and caution to his brother Brucie who began panting merrily and untrustworthily behind him.

Brucie bent readily under William Wallace's hand-pat, and gave him a dreamy look out of the tops of his round eyes, which were pure green-and-white like clover tops. William Wallace gave him a nickel. Grady hung his head; his white hair lay in a little tail in the nape of his neck.

"Let's let them come," said Virgil.

"Well, they can come then, but if we keep letting everybody come it is going to be too many," said William Wallace.

"They'll appreciate it, those little-old boys," said Virgil. Brucie held up at arm's length a long red thread with a bent pin tied on the end; and a look of helpless and intense interest gathered Grady's face like a drawstring—his eyes, one bright with a sty, shone pleadingly under his white bangs, and he snapped his jaw and tried to speak. . . . "Their papa was drowned in the Pearl River," said Virgil.

There was a shout from the gully.

"Here come all the Malones," cried William Wallace. "I asked four of them would they come, but the rest of the family invited themselves."

"Did you ever see a time when they didn't," said Virgil. "And yonder from the other direction comes the Doyles, still with biscuit crumbs on their cheeks, I bet, now it's nothing to do but eat as their mother said."

"If two little niggers would come along now, or one big nigger," said William Wallace. And the words were hardly out of his mouth when two little Negro boys came along, going somewhere, one behind the other, stepping high and gay in their overalls, as though they waded in honeydew to the waist.

"Come here, boys. What's your names?"

"Sam and Robbie Bell."

"Come along with us, we're going to drag the river."

"You hear that, Robbie Bell?" said Sam.

They smiled.

The Doyles came noiselessly, their dogs made all the fuss. The Malones, eight giants with great long black eyelashes, were already stamping the ground and pawing each other, ready to go. Everybody went up together to see Doc.

Old Doc owned the wide net. He had a house on top of the hill and he sat and looked out from a rocker on the front porch.

"Climb the hill and come in!" he began to intone across the valley. "Harvest's over . . . slipped up on everybody . . . cotton's picked, gone to the gin . . . hay cut . . . molasses made around here. . . . Big explosion's over, supervisors elected, some pleased, some not. . . . We're hearing talk of war!"

When they got closer, he was saying, "Many's been saved at revival, twenty-two last Sunday including a Doyle, ought to counted two. Hope they'll be a blessing to Dover community besides a shining star in Heaven. Now what?" he asked, for they had arrived and stood gathered in front of the steps.

"If nobody is using your wide net, could we use it?" asked William Wallace.

"You just used it a month ago," said Doc. "It ain't your turn."

Virgil jogged William Wallace's arm and cleared his throat. "This time is kind of special," he said. "We got reason to think William Wallace's wife Hazel is in the river, drowned."

"What reason have you got to think she's in the river drowned?" asked Doc. He took out his old pipe. "I'm asking the husband."

"Because she's not in the house," said William Wallace.

"Vanished?" and he knocked out the pipe.

"Plum vanished."

"Of course a thousand things could have happened to her," said Doc, and he lighted the pipe.

"Hand him up the letter, William Wallace," said Virgil. "We can't wait around till Doomsday for the net while Doc sits back thinkin'."

"I tore it up, right at the first," said William Wallace. "But I know it by heart. It said she was going to jump straight in the Pearl River and that I'd be sorry."

"Where do you come in, Virgil?" asked Doc.

"I was in the same place William Wallace sat on his neck in, all night, and done as much as he done, and come home the same time."

"You-all were out cuttin' up, so Lady Hazel has to jump in the river, is that it? Cause and effect? Anybody want to argue with me? Where do these others come in, Doyles, Malones, and what not?"

"Doc is the smartest man around," said William Wallace, turning to the solidly waiting Doyles, "but it sure takes time."

"These are the ones that's collected to drag the river for her," said Virgil.

"Of course I am not going on record to say so soon that *I* think she's drowned," Doc said, blowing out blue smoke.

"Do you think . . ." William Wallace mounted a step, and his hands both went into fists. "Do you think she was *carried off?*"

"Now that's the way to argue, see it from all sides," said Doc promptly. "But who by?"

Some Malone whistled, but not so you could tell which one.

"There's no booger around the Dover section that goes around carrying off young girls that's married," stated Doc.

"She was always scared of the Gypsies." William Wallace turned scarlet. "She'd sure turn her ring around on her finger if she passed one, and look in the other direction so they couldn't see she was pretty and carry her off. They come in the end of summer."

"Yes, there are the Gypsies, kidnappers since the world began. But was it to be you that would pay the grand ransom?" asked Doc. He pointed his finger. They all laughed then at how clever old Doc was and clapped William Wallace on the back. But that turned into a scuffle and they fell to the ground.

"Stop it, or you can't have the net," said Doc. "You're scaring my wife's chickens."

"It's time we was gone," said William Wallace.

The big barking dogs jumped to lean their front paws on the men's chests.

"My advice remains, Let well enough alone," said Doc. "Whatever this mysterious event will turn out to be, it has kept one woman from talking a while. However, Lady Hazel is the prettiest girl in Mississippi, you've never seen a prettier one and you never will. A golden-haired girl." He got to his feet with the nimbleness that was always his surprise, and said, "I'll come along with you."

The path they always followed was the Old Natchez Trace. It took them through the deep woods and led them out down below on the Pearl River, where they could begin dragging it upstream to a point near Dover. They walked in silence around William Wallace, not letting him carry anything, but the net dragged heavily and the buckets were full of clatter in a place so dim and still.

Once they went through a forest of cucumber trees and came up on a high ridge. Grady and Brucie who were running ahead all the way stopped in their tracks; a whistle had blown and far down and far away a long freight train was passing. It seemed like a little festival procession, moving with the slowness of ignorance or a dream, from distance to distance, the tiny pink and gray cars like secret boxes. Grady was counting the cars to himself, as if he could certainly see each one clearly, and Brucie watched his lips, hushed and cautious, the way he would watch a bird drinking. Tears suddenly came to Grady's eyes, but it could only be because a tiny man walked along the top of the train, walking and moving on top of the moving train.

They went down again and soon the smell of the river spread over the woods, cool and secret. Every step they took among the great walls of vines and among the passion-flowers started up a little life, a little flight.

"We're walking along in the changing-time," said Doc. "Any day now the change will come. It's going to turn from hot to cold, and we can kill the hog that's ripe and have fresh meat to eat. Come one of these nights and we can wander down here and tree a nice possum. Old Jack Frost will be pinching things up. Old Mr. Winter will be standing in the door. Hickory tree there will be yellow. Sweet-gum red, hickory yellow, dogwood red, sycamore yellow." He went along rapping the tree trunks with his knuckle.

"Magnolia and live-oak never die. Remember that. Persimmons will all get fit to eat, and the nuts will be dropping like rain all through the woods here. And run, little quail, run, for we'll be after you too."

They went on and suddenly the woods opened upon light, and they had reached the river. Everyone stopped, but Doc talked on ahead as though nothing had happened. "Only today," he said, "today, in October sun, it's all gold—sky and tree and water. Everything just before it changes looks to be made of gold."

William Wallace looked down, as though he thought of Hazel with the shining eyes, sitting at home and looking straight before her, like a piece of pure gold, too precious to touch.

Below them the river was glimmering, narrow, soft, and skin-colored, and slowed nearly to stillness. The shining willow trees hung round them. The net that was being drawn out, so old and so long-used, it too looked golden, strung and tied with golden threads.

Standing still on the bank, all of a sudden William Wallace, on whose word they were waiting, spoke up in a voice of surprise. "What is the name of this river?"

They looked at him as if he were crazy not to know the name of the river he had fished in all his life. But a deep frown was on his forehead, as if he were compelled to wonder what people had come to call this river, or to think there was a mystery in the name of a river they all knew so well, the same as if it were some great far torrent of waves that dashed through the mountains somewhere, and almost as if it were a river in some dream, for they could not give him the name of that.

"Everybody knows Pearl River is named the Pearl River," said Doc.

A bird note suddenly bold was like a stone thrown into the water to sound it.

"It's deep here," said Virgil, and jogged William Wallace. "Remember?"

William Wallace stood looking down at the river as if it were still a mystery to him. There under his feet which hung over the bank it was transparent and yellow like an old bottle lying in the sun, filling with light.

Doc clattered all his paraphernalia.

Then all of a sudden all the Malones scattered jumping and tumbling down the bank. They gave their loud shout. Little Brucie started after them, and looked back.

"Do you think she jumped?" Virgil asked William Wallace.

II

Since the net was so wide, when it was all stretched it reached from bank to bank of the Pearl River, and the weights would hold it all the way to the bottom. Jug-like sounds filled the air, splashes lifted in the sun, and the party began to move upstream. The Malones with great groans swam and pulled near the shore, the Doyles swam and pushed from behind with Virgil to tell them how to do it best; Grady and Brucie with his thread and pin trotted along the sandbars hauling buckets and lines. Sam and Robbie Bell, naked and bright, guided the old oarless rowboat that always drifted at the shore, and in it, sitting up tall with his hat on, was Doc—he went along without ever touching water and without ever taking his eyes off the net. William Wallace himself did everything but most of the time he was out of sight, swimming about under water or diving, and he had nothing to say any more.

The dogs chased up and down, in and out of the water, and in and out of the woods.

"Don't let her get too heavy, boys," Doc intoned regularly, every few minutes, "and she won't let nothing through."

"She won't let nothing through, she won't let nothing through," chanted Sam and Robbie Bell, one at his front and one at his back.

The sandbars were pink or violet drifts ahead. Where the light fell on the river, in a wandering from shore to shore, it was leaf-shaped spangles that trembled softly, while the dark of the river was calm. The willow trees leaned overhead under muscadine vines, and their trailing leaves hung like waterfalls in the morning air. The thing that seemed like silence must have been the endless cry of all the crickets and locusts in the world, rising and falling.

Every time William Wallace took hold of a big eel that slipped the net, the Malones all yelled, "Rassle with him, son!"

"Don't let her get too heavy, boys," said Doc.

"This is hard on catfish," William Wallace said once.

There were big and little fishes, dark and bright, that they caught, good ones and bad ones, the same old fish.

"This is more shoes than I ever saw got together in any store," said Virgil when they emptied the net to the bottom. "Get going!" he shouted in the next breath.

The little Rippens who had stayed ahead in the woods stayed ahead on the river. Brucie, leading them all, made small jumps and hops as he went, sometimes on one foot, sometimes on the other.

The winding river looked old sometimes, when it ran wrinkled and deep under high banks where the roots of trees hung down, and sometimes it seemed to be only a young creek, shining with the colors of wildflowers. Sometimes sandbars in the shapes of fishes lay nose to nose across, without the track of even a bird.

"Here comes some alligators," said Virgil. "Let's let them by."

They drew out on the shady side of the water, and three big alligators and four middle-sized ones went by, taking their own time.

"Look at their great big old teeth!" called a shrill voice. It was Grady making his only outcry, and the alligators were not showing their teeth at all.

"The better to eat folks with," said Doc from his boat, looking at him severely.

"Doc, you are bound to declare all you know," said Virgil. "Get going!"

When they started off again the first thing they caught in the net was the baby alligator.

"That's just what we wanted!" cried the Malones.

They set the little alligator down on a sandbar and he squatted perfectly still; they could hardly tell when it was he started to move. They watched with set faces his incredible mechanics, while the dogs after one bark stood off in inquisitive humility, until he winked.

"He's ours!" shouted all the Malones. "We're taking him home with us!"

"He ain't nothing but a little-old baby," said William Wallace.

The Malones only scoffed, as if he might be only a baby but he looked like the oldest and worst lizard.

"What are you going to do with him?" asked Virgil.

"Keep him."

"I'd be more careful what I took out of this net," said Doc.

"Tie him up and throw him in the bucket," the Malones were saying to each other, while Doc was saying, "Don't come running to me and ask me what to do when he gets big."

They kept catching more and more fish, as if there was no end in sight.

"Look, a string of lady's beads," said Virgil. "Here, Sam and Robbie Bell."

Sam wore them around his head, with a knot over his forehead and loops around his ears, and Robbie Bell walked behind and stared at them.

In a shadowy place something white flew up. It was a heron, and it went away over the dark treetops. William Wallace followed it with his eyes and Brucie clapped his hands, but Virgil gave a sigh, as if he knew that when you go looking for what is lost, everything is a sign.

An eel slid out of the net.

"Rassle with him, son!" yelled the Malones. They swam like fiends.

"The Malones are in it for the fish," said Virgil.

It was about noon that there was a little rustle on the bank.

"Who is that yonder?" asked Virgil, and he pointed to a little undersized man with short legs and a little straw hat with a band around it, who was following along on the other side of the river.

"Never saw him and don't know his brother," said Doc.

Nobody had ever seen him before.

"Who invited you?" cried Virgil hotly. "Hi . . . !" and he made signs for the little undersized man to look at him, but he would not.

"Looks like a crazy man, from here," said the Malones.

"Just don't pay any attention to him and maybe he'll go away," advised Doc.

But Virgil had already swum across and was up on the other bank. He and the stranger could be seen exchanging a word apiece and then Virgil put out his hand the way he would pat a child and patted the stranger to the ground. The little man got up again just as quickly, lifted his shoulders, turned around, and walked away with his hat tilted over his eyes.

When Virgil came back he said, "Little-old man claimed he was harmless as a baby. I told him to just try horning in on this river and anything in it."

"What did he look like up close?" asked Doc.

"I wasn't studying how he looked," said Virgil. "But I don't like anybody to come looking at me that I am not familiar with." And he shouted, "Get going!"

"Things are moving in too great a rush," said Doc.

Brucie darted ahead and ran looking into all the bushes, lifting up their branches and looking underneath.

"Not one of the Doyles has spoke a word," said Virgil.

"That's because they're not talkers," said Doc.

All day William Wallace kept diving to the bottom. Once he dived down and down into the dark water, where it was so still that nothing stirred, not even a fish, and so dark that it was no longer the muddy world of the upper river but the dark clear world of deepness, and he must have believed this was the deepest place in the whole Pearl River, and if she was not here she would not be anywhere. He was gone such a long time that the others stared hard at the surface of the water, through which the bubbles came from below. So far down and all alone, had he found Hazel? Had he suspected down there, like some secret, the real, the true trouble that Hazel had fallen into, about which words in a letter could not speak . . . how (who knew?) she had been filled to the brim with that elation that they all remembered, like their own secret, the elation that comes of great hopes and changes, sometimes simply of the harvest time, that comes with a little course of its own like a tune to run in the head, and there was nothing she could do about it—they knew—and so it had turned into this? It could be nothing but the old trouble that William Wallace was finding out, reaching and turning in the gloom of such depths.

"Look down yonder," said Grady softly to Brucie.

He pointed to the surface, where their reflections lay colorless and still side by side. He touched his brother gently as though to impress him.

"That's you and me," he said.

Brucie swayed precariously over the edge, and Grady caught him by the seat of his overalls. Brucie looked, but showed no recognition. Instead, he backed away, and seemed all at once unconcerned and spiritless, and pressed the nickel William Wallace had given him into his palm, rubbing it into his skin. Grady's inflamed eyes rested on the brown water. Without warning he saw something . . . perhaps the image in the river seemed to be his father, the drowned man—with arms open, eyes open, mouth open. . . . Grady stared and blinked, again something wrinkled up his face.

And when William Wallace came up it was in an agony from submersion, which seemed an agony of the blood and of the very heart, so woeful he looked. He was staring and glaring around in astonishment, as if a long time had gone by, away from the pale world where the brown light of the sun and the river and the little party watching him trembled before his eyes.

"What did you bring up?" somebody called—was it Virgil?

One of his hands was holding fast to a little green ribbon of plant, root and all. He was surprised, and let it go.

It was afternoon. The trees spread softly, the clouds hung wet and tinted. A buzzard turned a few slow wheels in the sky, and drifted upwards. The dogs promenaded the banks.

"It's time we ate fish," said Virgil.

On a wide sandbar on which seashells lay they dragged up the haul and built a fire.

Then for a long time among clouds of odors and smoke, all half-naked except Doc, they cooked and ate catfish. They ate until the Malones groaned and all the Doyles stretched out on their faces, though for long after, Sam and Robbie Bell sat up to their own little table on a cypress stump and ate on and on. Then they all were silent and still, and one by one fell asleep.

"There ain't a thing better than fish," muttered William Wallace.

He lay stretched on his back in the glimmer and shade of trampled sand. His sunburned forehead and cheeks seemed to glow with fire. His eyelids fell. The shadow of a willow branch dipped and moved over him. "There is nothing in the world as good as . . . fish. The fish of Pearl River." Then slowly he smiled. He was asleep.

But it seemed almost at once that he was leaping up, and one by one up sat the others in their ring and looked at him, for it was impossible to stop and sleep by the river.

"You're feeling as good as you felt last night," said Virgil, setting his head on one side.

"The excursion is the same when you go looking for your sorrow as when you go looking for your joy," said Doc.

But William Wallace answered none of them anything, for he was leaping all over the place and all, over them and the feast and the bones of the feast, trampling the sand, up and down, and doing a dance so crazy that he would die next. He took a big catfish and hooked it to his belt buckle and went up and down so that they all hollered, and the tears of laughter streaming down his cheeks made him put his hand up, and the two days' growth of beard began to jump out, bright red.

But all of a sudden there was an even louder cry, something almost like a cheer, from everybody at once, and all pointed fingers moved from William Wallace to the river. In the center of three light-gold rings across the water was lifted first an old hoary head ("It has whiskers!" a voice cried) and then in an undulation loop after loop and hump after hump of a long dark body, until there were a dozen rings of ripples, one behind the other, stretching all across the river, like a necklace.

"The King of the Snakes!" cried all the Malones at once, in high tenor voices and leaning together.

"The King of the Snakes," intoned old Doc in his profound base. "He looked you in the eye."

William Wallace stared back at the King of the Snakes with all his might.

It was Brucie that darted forward, dangling his little thread with the pin tied to it, going toward the water.

"That's the King of the Snakes!" cried Grady, who always looked after him.

Then the snake went down.

The little boy stopped with one leg in the air, spun around on the other, and sank to the ground.

"Git up," Grady whispered. "It was just the King of the Snakes. He went off whistling. Git up. It wasn't a thing but the King of the Snakes."

Brucie's green eyes opened, his tongue darted out, and he sprang up; his feet were heavy, his head light, and he rose like a bubble coming to the surface.

Then thunder like a stone loosened and rolled down the bank.

They all stood unwilling on the sandbar, holding to the net. In the eastern sky were the familiar castles and the round towers to which they were used, gray, pink, and blue, growing darker and filling with thunder. Lightning flickered in the sun along their thick walls. But in the west the sun shone with such a violence that in an illumination like a long-prolonged glare of lightning the heavens looked black and white; all color left the world, the goldenness of everything was like a memory, and only heat, a kind of glamor and oppression, lay on their heads. The thick heavy trees on the other side of the river were brushed with mile-long streaks of silver, and a wind touched each man on the forehead. At the same time there was a long roll of thunder that began behind them, came up and down mountains and valleys of air, passed over their heads, and left them listening still. With a small, near noise a mocking-bird followed it, the little white bars of its body flashing over the willow trees.

"We are here for a storm now," Virgil said. "We will have to stay till it's over."

They retreated a little, and hard drops fell in the leathery leaves at their shoulders and about their heads.

"Magnolia's the loudest tree there is in a storm," said Doc.

Then the light changed the water, until all about them the woods in the rising wind seemed to grow taller and blow inward together and suddenly turn dark. The rain struck heavily. A huge tail seemed to lash through the air and the river broke in a wound of silver. In silence the party crouched and stooped beside the trunk of the great tree, which in the push of the storm rose full of a fragrance and unyielding weight. Where they all stared, past their tree, was another tree, and beyond that another and another, all the way down the bank of the river, all towering and darkened in the storm.

"The outside world is full of endurance," said Doc. "Full of endurance."

Robbie Bell and Sam squatted down low and embraced each other from the start.

"Runs in our family to get struck by lightnin'," said Robbie Bell. "Lightnin' drawed a pitchfork right on our grandpappy's cheek, stayed till he died. Pappy got struck by some bolts of lightnin' and was dead three days, dead as that-there axe."

There was a succession of glares and crashes.

"This'n's goin' to be either me or you," said Sam. "Here come a little bug. If he go to the left, be me, and to the right, be you."

But at the next flare a big tree on the hill seemed to turn into fire before their eyes, every branch, twig, and leaf, and a purple cloud hung over it.

"Did you hear that crack?" asked Robbie Bell. "That were its bones."

"Why do you little niggers talk so much!" said Doc. "Nobody's profiting by this information."

"We always talks this much," said Sam, "but now everybody so quiet, they hears us."

The great tree, split and on fire, fell roaring to earth. Just at its moment of falling, a tree like it on the opposite bank split wide open and fell in two parts.

"Hope they ain't goin' to be no balls of fire come rollin' over the water and fry all the fishes with they scales on," said Robbie Bell.

The water in the river had turned purple and was filled with sudden currents and whirlpools. The little willow trees bent almost to its surface, bowing one after another down the bank and almost breaking under the storm. A great curtain of wet leaves was borne along before a blast of wind, and every human being was covered.

"Now us got scales," wailed Sam. "Us is the fishes."

"Hush up, little-old colored children," said Virgil. "This isn't the way to act when somebody takes you out to drag a river."

"Poor lady's-ghost, I bet it is scareder than us," said Sam.

"All I hoping is, us don't find her!" screamed Robbie Bell.

William Wallace bent down and knocked their heads together. After that they clung silently in each other's arms, the two black heads resting, with wind-filled cheeks and tight-closed eyes, one upon the other until the storm was over.

"Right over yonder is Dover," said Virgil. "We've come all the way. William Wallace, you have walked on a sharp rock and cut your foot open."

III

In Dover it had rained, and the town looked somehow like new. The wavy heat of late afternoon came down from the watertank and fell over everything like shiny mosquito-netting. At the wide place where the road was paved and patched with tar, it seemed newly embedded with Coca-Cola tops. The old circus posters on the store were nearly gone, only bits, the snowflakes of white horses, clinging to its side. Morning-glory vines started almost visibly to grow over the roofs and cling round the ties of the railroad track, where bluejays lighted on the rails, and umbrella chinaberry trees hung heavily over the whole town, dripping intermittently upon the tin roofs.

Each with his counted fish on a string the members of the river-dragging party walked through the town. They went toward the town well, and there was Hazel's mother's house, but no sign of her yet coming out. They all drank a dipper of the water, and still there was not a soul on the street. Even the bench in front of the store was empty, except for a little corn-shuck doll.

But something told them somebody had come, for after one moment people began to look out of the store and out of the postoffice. All the bird dogs woke up to see the Doyle dogs and such a large number of men and boys materialize suddenly with such a big catch of fish, and they ran out barking. The Doyle dogs joyously barked back. The bluejays flashed up and screeched above the town, whipping through their tunnels in the chinaberry trees. In the café a nickel clattered inside a music box and a love song began to play. The whole town of Dover began to throb in its wood and tin, like an old tired heart, when the men walked through once more, coming around again and going down the street carrying the fish, so drenched, exhausted, and muddy that no one could help but admire them.

William Wallace walked through the town as though he did not see anybody or hear anything. Yet he carried his great string of fish held high where it could be seen by all. Virgil came next, imitating William Wallace exactly, then the modest Doyles crowded by the Malones, who were holding up their alligator, tossing it in the air, even, like a father tossing his child. Following behind and pointing authoritatively at the ones in front strolled Doc, with Sam and Robbie Bell still chanting in his wake. In and out of the whole little line Grady and Brucie jerked about. Grady, with his head ducked, and stiff as a rod, walked with a springy limp; it made him look forever angry and unapproachable. Under his breath he was whispering, "Sty, sty, git out of my eye, and git on somebody passin' by." He traveled on with narrowed shoulders, and kept his eye unerringly upon his little brother, wary and at the same time proud, as though he held a flying June-bug on a string. Brucie, making a twanging noise with his lips, had shot forth again, and he was darting rapidly everywhere at once, delighted and tantalized, running in circles around William Wallace, pointing to his fish. A frown of pleasure like the print of a bird's foot was stamped between his faint brows, and he trotted in some unknown realm of delight.

"Did you ever see so many fish?" said the people in Dover.

"How much are your fish, mister?"

"Would you sell your fish?"

"Is that all the fish in Pearl River?"

"How much you sell them all for? Everybody's?"

"Three dollars," said William Wallace suddenly, and loud.

The Malones were upon him and shouting, but it was too late.

And just as William Wallace was taking the money in his hand,

Hazel's mother walked solidly out of her front door and saw it.

"You can't head her mother off," said Virgil. "Here she comes in full bloom."

But William Wallace turned his back on her, that was all, and on everybody, for that matter, and that was the breaking-up of the party.

Just as the sun went down, Doc climbed his back steps, sat in his chair on the back porch where he sat in the evenings, and lighted his pipe. William Wallace hung out the net and came back and Virgil was waiting for him, so they could say good evening to Doc.

"All in all," said Doc, when they came up, "I've never been on a better river-dragging, or seen better behavior. If it took catching catfish to move the Rock of Gibraltar, I believe this outfit could move it."

"Well, we didn't catch Hazel," said Virgil.

"What did you say?" asked Doc.

"He don't really pay attention," said Virgil. "I said, 'We didn't catch Hazel.'"

"Who says Hazel was to be caught?" asked Doc. "She wasn't in there. Girls don't like the water—remember that. Girls don't just haul off and go jumping in the river to get back at their husbands. They got other ways."

"Didn't you ever think she was in there?" asked William Wallace. "The whole time?"

"Nary once," said Doc.

"He's just smart," said Virgil, putting his hand on William Wallace's arm. "It's only because we didn't find her that he wasn't looking for her."

"I'm beholden to you for the net, anyway," said William Wallace.

"You're welcome to borry it again," said Doc.

On the way home Virgil kept saying, "Calm down, calm down, William Wallace."

"If he wasn't such an old skinny man I'd have wrung his neck for him," said William Wallace. "He had no business coming."

"He's too big for his britches," said Virgil. "Don't nobody know everything. And just because it's his net. Why does it have to be his net?"

"If it wasn't for being polite to old men, I'd have skinned him alive," said William Wallace.

"I guess he don't really know nothing about wives at all, his wife's so deaf," said Virgil.

"He don't know Hazel," said William Wallace. "I'm the only man alive knows Hazel: would she jump in the river or not, and I say she would. She jumped in because I was sitting on the back of my neck in a ditch singing, and that's just what she ought to done. Doc ain't got no right to say one word about it."

"Calm down, calm down, William Wallace," said Virgil.

"If it had been you that talked like that, I'd have broke every bone in your body," said William Wallace. "Just let you talk like that. You're my age and size."

"But I ain't going to talk like that," said Virgil. "What have I done the whole time but keep this river-dragging going straight and running even, without no hitches? You couldn't have drug the river a foot without me."

"What are you talking about! Without who!" cried William Wallace. "This wasn't your river-dragging! It wasn't your wife!" He jumped on Virgil and they began to fight.

"Let me up." Virgil was breathing heavily.

"Say it was my wife. Say it was my river-dragging."

"Yours!" Virgil was on the ground with William Wallace's hand putting dirt in his mouth.

"Say it was my net."

"Your net!"

"Get up then."

They walked along getting their breath, and smelling the honey-suckle in the evening. On a hill William Wallace looked down, and at the same time there went drifting by the sweet sounds of music outdoors. They were having the Sacred Harp Sing on the grounds of an old white church glimmering there at the crossroads, far below. He stared away as if he saw it minutely, as if he could see a lady in white take a flowered cover off the organ, which was set on a little slant in the shade, dust the keys, and start to pump and play. . . . He smiled faintly, as he would at his mother, and at Hazel, and at the singing women in his life, now all one young girl standing up to sing under the trees the oldest and longest ballads there were.

Virgil told him good night and went into his own house and the door shut on him.

When he got to his own house, William Wallace saw to his surprise that it had not rained at all. But there, curved over the roof, was something he had never seen before as long as he could remember, a rainbow at night. In the light of the moon, which had risen again, it looked small and of gauzy material, like a lady's summer dress, a faint veil through which the stars showed.

He went up on the porch and in at the door, and all exhausted he had walked through the front room and through the kitchen when he heard his name called. After a moment, he smiled, as if no matter what he might have hoped for in his wildest heart, it was better than that to hear his name called out in the house. The voice came out of the bedroom.

"What do you want?" he yelled, standing stock-still.

Then she opened the bedroom door with the old complaining creak, and there she stood. She was not changed a bit.

"How do you feel?" he said.

"I feel pretty good. Not too good," Hazel said, looking mysterious.

"I cut my foot," said William Wallace, taking his shoe off so she could see the blood.

"How in the world did you do that?" she cried, with a step back.

"Dragging the river. But it don't hurt any longer."

"You ought to have been more careful," she said. "Supper's ready and I wondered if you would ever come home, or if it would be last night all over again. Go and make yourself fit to be seen," she said, and ran away from him.

After supper they sat on the front steps a while.

"Where were you this morning when I came in?" asked William Wallace when they were ready to go in the house.

"I was hiding," she said. "I was still writing on the letter. And then you tore it up."

"Did you watch me when I was reading it?"

"Yes, and you could have put out your hand and touched me, I was so close."

But he bit his lip, and gave her a little tap and slap, and then turned her up and spanked her.

"Do you think you will do it again?" he asked.

"I'll tell my mother on you for this!"

"Will you do it again?"

"No!" she cried.

"Then pick yourself up off my knee."

It was just as if he had chased her and captured her again. She lay smiling in the crook of his arm. It was the same as any other chase in the end.

"I will do it again if I get ready," she said. "Next time will be different, too."

Then she was ready to go in, and rose up and looked out from the top step, out across their yard where the China tree was and beyond, into the dark fields where the lightning-bugs flickered away. He climbed to his feet too and stood beside her, with the frown on his face, trying to look where she looked. And after a few minutes she took him by the hand and led him into the house, smiling as if she were smiling down on him.

GREENLEAF

Flannery O'Connor

First published in *The Kenyon Review*, XVIII (Summer, 1956), 384-410; O. Henry Memorial Award Prize Story, 1957.

Flannery O'Connor (1925-   ) is a native of Georgia, and she lives today outside Milledgeville. She graduated from the Georgia State College for Women in 1945 and afterward studied writing at the State University of Iowa, where she took the Master of Fine Arts degree in 1947. She published her first story in 1946 and a novel, *Wise Blood,* in 1952. A book of her short stories, *A Good Man Is Hard to Find, and Other Stories,* appeared in 1955.

Mrs. May's bedroom window was low and faced on the east and the bull, silvered in the moonlight, stood under it, his head raised as if he listened—like some patient god come down to woo her—for a stir inside the room. The window was dark and the sound of her breathing too light to be carried outside. Clouds crossing the moon blackened him and in the dark he began to tear at the hedge. Presently they passed and he appeared again in the same spot, chewing steadily, with a hedge-wreath that he had ripped loose for himself caught in the tips of his horns. When the moon drifted into retirement again, there was nothing to mark his place but the sound of steady chewing. Then abruptly a pink glow filled the window. Bars of light slid across him as the venetian blind was slit. He took a step backward and lowered his head as if to show the wreath across his horns.

For almost a minute there was no sound from inside, then as he raised his crowned head again, a woman's voice, guttural as if addressed to a dog, said, "Get away from here, Sir!" and in a second muttered, "Some nigger's scrub bull."

The animal pawed the ground and Mrs. May, standing bent forward behind the blind, closed it quickly lest the light make him charge into the shrubbery. For a second she waited, still bent forward, her nightgown hanging loosely from her narrow shoulders. Green rubber curlers sprouted neatly over her forehead and her face beneath them was smooth as concrete with an egg-white paste that drew the wrinkles out while she slept.

She had been conscious in her sleep of a steady rhythmic chewing as if something were eating one wall of the house. She had been aware that whatever it was had been eating as long as she had had the place and had eaten everything from the beginning of her fence line up to the house and now was eating the house and calmly with the same steady rhythm would continue through the house, eating her and the boys, and then on, eating everything but the Greenleafs, on and on, eating everything until nothing was left but the Greenleafs on a little island all their own in the middle of what had been her place. When the munching reached her elbow, she jumped up and found herself, fully awake, standing in the middle of her room. She identified the sound at once: a cow was tearing at the shrubbery under her window. Mr. Greenleaf had left the lane gate open and she didn't doubt that the entire herd was on her lawn. She turned on the dim pink table lamp and then went to the window and slit the blind. The bull, gaunt and long-legged, was standing about four feet from her, chewing calmly like an uncouth country suitor.

For fifteen years, she thought as she squinted at him fiercely, she had been having shiftless people's hogs root up her oats, their mules wallow on her lawn, their scrub bulls breed her cows. If this one was not put up now, he would be over the fence, ruining her herd before morning—and Mr. Greenleaf was soundly sleeping a half mile down the road in the tenant house. There was no way to get him unless she dressed and got in her car and rode down there and woke him up. He would come but his expression, his whole figure, his every pause, would say: "Hit looks to me like one or both of them boys would not make their maw ride out in the middle of the night thisaway. If hit was my boys, they would have got thet bull up theirself."

The bull lowered his head and shook it and the wreath slipped down to the base of his horns where it looked like a menacing pricky crown. She had closed the blind then; in a few seconds she heard him move off heavily.

Mr. Greenleaf would say, "If hit was my boys they would never have allowed their maw to go after hired help in the middle of the night. They would have did it theirself."

Weighing it, she decided not to bother Mr. Greenleaf. She returned to bed thinking that if the Greenleaf boys had risen in the world it was because she had given their father employment when no one else would have him. She had had Mr. Greenleaf fifteen years but no one else would have had him five minutes. Just the way he approached an object was enough to tell anybody with eyes what kind of a worker he was. He walked with a high-shouldered creep and he never appeared to come directly forward. He walked on the perimeter of some invisible circle and if you wanted to look him in the face, you had to move and get in front of him. She had not fired him because she had always doubted she could do better. He was too shiftless to go out and look for another job; he didn't have the initiative to steal, and after she had told him three or four times to do a thing, he did it; but he never told her about a sick cow until it was too late to call the veterinarian and if her barn had caught on fire, he would have called his wife to see the flames before he began to put them out. And of the wife, she didn't even like to think. Beside the wife, Mr. Greenleaf was an aristocrat.

"If it had been my boys," he would have said, "they would have cut off their right arm before they would have allowed their maw to. . . ."

"If your boys had any pride, Mr. Greenleaf," she would like to say to him some day, "there are many things that they would not *allow* their mother to do."

The next morning as soon as Mr. Greenleaf came to the back door, she told him there was a stray bull on the place and that she wanted him penned up at once.

"Done already been here three days," he said, addressing his right foot which he held forward, turned slightly as if he were trying to look at the sole. He was standing at the bottom of the three back steps while she leaned out the kitchen door, a small woman with pale nearsighted eyes and grey hair that rose on top like the crest of some disturbed bird.

"Three days!" she said in the restrained screech that had become habitual with her.

Mr. Greenleaf, looking into the distance over the near pasture, removed a package of cigarets from his shirt pocket and let one fall into his hand. He put the package back and stood for a while looking at the cigaret. "I put him in the bull pen but he torn out of there," he said presently. "I didn't see him none after that." He bent over the cigaret and lit it and then turned his head briefly in her direction. The upper part of his face sloped gradually into the lower which was long and narrow, shaped like a rough chalice. He had deep-set fox-colored eyes shadowed under a grey felt hat that he wore slanted forward following the line of his nose. His build was insignificant.

"Mr. Greenleaf," she said, "get that bull up this morning before you do anything else. You know he'll ruin the breeding schedule. Get him up and keep him up and the next time there's a stray bull on this place, tell me at once. Do you understand?"

"Where do you want him put at?" Mr. Greenleaf asked.

"I don't care where you put him," she said. "You are supposed to have some sense. Put him where he can't get out. Whose bull is he?"

For a moment Mr. Greenleaf seemed to hesitate between silence and speech. He studied the air to the left of him. "He must be some-body's bull," he said after a while.

"Yes, he must!" she said and shut the door with a precise little slam.

She went into the dining room where the two boys were eating breakfast and sat down on the edge of her chair at the head of the table. She never ate breakfast but she sat with them to see that they had what they wanted. "Honestly!" she said, and began to tell about the bull, aping Mr. Greenleaf saying, "It must be *somebody's* bull."

Wesley continued to read the newspaper folded beside his plate but Scofield interrupted his eating from time to time to look at her and laugh. The two boys never had the same reaction to anything. They were as different, she said, as night and day. The only thing they did have in common was that neither of them cared what happened on the place. Scofield was a business type and Wesley was an intellectual.

Wesley, the younger child, had had rheumatic fever when he was seven and Mrs. May thought that this was what had caused him to be an intellectual. Scofield, who had never had a day's sickness in his life, was an insurance salesman. She would not have minded his selling insurance if he had sold a nicer kind but he sold the kind that only negroes buy. He was what negroes call a "policy man." He said there was more money in nigger-insurance than any other kind, and before company, he was very loud about it. He would shout, "Mamma don't like to hear me say it but I'm the best nigger-insurance salesman in this county!"

Scofield was thirty-six and he had a broad pleasant smiling face but he was not married. "Yes," Mrs. May would say, "and if you sold decent insurance, some *nice* girl would be willing to marry you. What nice girl wants to marry a nigger-insurance man? You'll wake up some day and it'll be too late."

And at this Scofield would yodle and say, "Why Mamma, I'm not going to marry until you're dead and gone and then I'm going to marry me some nice fat farm girl that can take over this place!" And once he had added, "—some nice lady like Mrs. Greenleaf." When he had said this, Mrs. May had risen from her chair, her back stiff as a rake handle, and had gone to her room. There she had sat down on the edge of her bed for some time with her small face drawn. Finally she had whispered, "I work and slave, I struggle and sweat to keep this place for them and as soon as I'm dead, they'll marry trash and bring it in here and ruin everything. They'll marry trash and ruin everything I've done," and she had made up her mind at that moment to change her will. The next day she had gone to her lawyer and had had the property entailed so that if they married, they could not leave it to their wives.

The idea that one of them might marry a woman even remotely like Mrs. Greenleaf was enough to make her ill. She had put up with Mr. Greenleaf for fifteen years, but the only way she had endured his wife had been by keeping entirely out of her sight. Mrs. Greenleaf was large and loose. The yard around her house looked like a dump and her five girls were always filthy; even the youngest one dipped snuff. Instead of making a garden or washing their clothes, her preoccupation was what she called "prayer healing."

Every day she cut all the morbid stories out of the newspaper— the accounts of women who had been raped and criminals who had escaped and children who had been burned and of train wrecks and plane crashes and the divorces of movie stars. She took these to the woods and dug a hole and buried them and then she fell on the ground over them and mumbled and groaned for an hour or so, moving her huge arms back and forth under her and out again and finally just lying down flat and, Mrs. May suspected, going to sleep in the dirt.

She had not found out about this until the Greenleafs had been with her a few months. One morning she had been out to inspect a field that she had wanted planted in rye but that had come up in clover because Mr. Greenleaf had used the wrong seeds in the grain drill. She was returning through a wooded path that separated two pastures, muttering to herself and hitting the ground methodically with a long stick she carried in case she saw a snake. "Mr. Greenleaf," she was saying in a low voice, "I cannot afford to pay for your mistakes. I am a poor woman and this place is all I have. I have two boys to educate. I cannot. . . ."

Out of nowhere a guttural agonized voice groaned, "Jesus! Jesus!" In a second it came again with a terrible urgency. "Jesus! Jesus!"

Mrs. May stopped still, one hand lifted to her throat. The sound was so piercing that she felt as if some violent unleashed force had broken out of the ground and was charging toward her. Her second thought was more reasonable: somebody had been hurt on the place and would sue her for everything she had. She had no insurance. She rushed forward and turning a bend in the path, she saw Mrs. Greenleaf sprawled on her hands and knees off the side of the road, her head down.

"Mrs. Greenleaf!" she shrilled, "what's happened!"

Mrs. Greenleaf raised her head. Her face was a patchwork of dirt and tears and her small eyes, the color of two field peas, were red-rimmed and swollen, but her expression was as composed as a bulldog's. She swayed back and forth on her hands and knees and groaned, "Jesus, Jesus."

Mrs. May winced. She thought the word, Jesus, should be kept inside the church building like other words inside the bedroom. She was a good Christian woman with a large respect for religion, though she did not, of course, believe any of it was true. "What is the matter with you?" she asked sharply.

"You broken my healing," Mrs. Greenleaf said, waving her aside. "I can't talk to you until I finish."

Mrs. May stood, bent forward, her mouth open and her stick raised off the ground as if she were not sure what she wanted to strike with it.

"Oh Jesus, stab me in the heart!" Mrs. Greenleaf shrieked. "Jesus, stab me in the heart!" and she fell back flat in the dirt, a huge human mound, her legs and arms spread out as if she were trying to wrap them around the earth.

Mrs. May felt as furious and helpless as if she had been insulted by a child. "Jesus," she said, drawing herself back, "would be *ashamed* of you. He would tell you to get up from there this instant and go wash your children's clothes!" and she had turned and walked off as fast as she could.

Whenever she thought of how the Greenleaf boys had advanced in the world, she had only to think of Mrs. Greenleaf sprawled obscenely on the ground, and say to herself, "Well, no matter how far they *go*, they *came* from that."

She would like to have been able to put in her will that when she died, Wesley and Scofield were not to continue to employ Mr. Greenleaf. She was capable of handling Mr. Greenleaf; they were not. Mr. Greenleaf had pointed out to her once that her boys didn't know hay from silage. She had pointed out to him that they had other talents, that Scofield was a successful business man and Wesley a successful intellectual. Mr. Greenleaf did not comment, but he never lost an opportunity of letting her see, by his expression or some simple gesture, that he held the two of them in infinite contempt. As scrub-human as the Greenleafs were, he never hesitated to let her know that in any like circumstance in which his own boys might have been involved, they—O. T. and E. T. Greenleaf—would have acted to better advantage.

The Greenleaf boys were two or three years younger than the May boys. They were twins and you never knew when you spoke to one of them whether you were speaking to O.T. or E.T., and they never had the politeness to enlighten you. They were long-legged and raw-boned and red-skinned, with bright grasping fox-colored eyes like their father's. Mr. Greenleaf's pride in them began with the fact that they were twins. He acted, Mrs. May said, as if this were something smart they had thought of themselves. They were energetic and hard-working and she would admit to anyone that they had come a long way—and that the Second World War was responsible for it.

They had both joined the service and, disguised in their uniforms, they could not be told from other people's children. You could tell, of course, when they opened their mouths but they did that seldom. The smartest thing they had done was to get sent overseas and there to marry French wives. They hadn't married French trash either. They had married nice girls who naturally couldn't tell that they murdered the king's English or that the Greenleafs were who they were.

Wesley's heart condition had not permitted him to serve his country but Scofield had been in the army for two years. He had not cared for it and at the end of his military service, he was only a Private First Class. The Greenleaf boys were both some kind of sergeants, and Mr. Greenleaf, in those days, had never lost an opportunity of referring to them by their rank. They had both managed to get wounded and now they both had pensions. Further, as soon as they were released from the army, they took advantage of all the benefits and went to the school of agriculture at the university—the taxpayers meanwhile supporting their French wives. The two of them were living now about two miles down the highway on a piece of land that the government had helped them to buy and in a brick duplex bungalow that the government had helped to build and pay for. If the war had made anyone, Mrs. May said, it had made the Greenleaf boys. They each had three little children apiece, who spoke Greenleaf English and French, and who, on account of their mothers' background, would be sent to the convent school and brought up with manners. "And in twenty years," Mrs. May asked Scofield and Wesley, "do you know what those people will be?

"Society," she said blackly.

She had spent fifteen years coping with Mr. Greenleaf and, by now, handling him had become second nature with her. His disposition on any particular day was as much a factor in what she could and couldn't do as the weather was, and she had learned to read his face the way real country people read the sunrise and sunset.

She was a country woman only by persuasion. The late Mr. May, a business man, had bought the place when land was down, and when he died it was all he had to leave her. The boys had not been happy to move to the country to a broken-down farm, but there was nothing else for her to do. She had the timber on the place cut and with the proceeds had set herself up in the dairy business after Mr. Greenleaf had answered her ad. "i seen yor add and i will come have 2 boys," was all his letter said, but he arrived the next day in a pieced-together truck, his wife and five daughters sitting on the floor in the back, himself, and the two boys in the cab.

Over the years they had been on her place, Mr. and Mrs. Greenleaf had aged hardly at all. They had no worries, no responsibilities. They lived like the lilies of the field, off the fat that she struggled to put into the land. When she was dead and gone from overwork and worry, the Greenleafs, healthy and thriving, would be just ready to begin draining Scofield and Wesley.

Wesley said the reason Mrs. Greenleaf had not aged was because she released all her emotions in prayer healing. "You ought to start praying, Sweetheart," he had said in the voice that, poor boy, he could not help making deliberately nasty.

Scofield only exasperated her beyond endurance but Wesley caused her real anxiety. He was thin and nervous and bald and being an intellectual was a terrible strain on his disposition. She doubted if he would marry until she died but she was certain that then the wrong woman would get him. Nice girls didn't like Scofield but Wesley didn't like nice girls. He didn't like anything. He drove twenty miles every day to the university where he taught and twenty miles back every night, but he said he hated the twenty-mile drive

322 • Flannery O'Connor

and he hated the second-rate university and he hated the morons who attended it. He hated the country and he hated the life he lived; he hated living with his mother and his idiot brother and he hated hearing about the damn dairy and the damn help and the damn broken machinery. But in spite of all he said, he never made any move to leave. He talked about Paris and Rome but he never went even to Atlanta.

"You'd go to those places and you'd get sick," Mrs. May would say. "Who in Paris is going to see that you get a salt-free diet? And do you think if you married one of those odd numbers you take out that *she* would cook a salt-free diet for you? No indeed, she would not!" When she took this line, Wesley would turn himself roughly around in his chair and ignore her. Once when she had kept it up too long, he had snarled, "Well, why don't you do something practical, Woman? Why don't you pray for me like Mrs. Greenleaf would?"

"I don't like to hear you boys make jokes about religion," she had said. "If you would go to church, you would meet some nice girls."

But it was impossible to tell them anything. When she looked at the two of them now, sitting on either side of the table, neither one caring the least if a stray bull ruined her herd—which was their herd, their future—when she looked at the two of them, one hunched over a paper and the other teetering back in his chair, grinning at her like an idiot, she wanted to jump up and beat her fist on the table and shout, "You'll find out one of these days, you'll find out what *Reality* is when it's too late!"

"Mamma," Scofield said, "don't you get excited now but I'll tell you whose bull that is." He was looking at her wickedly. He let his chair drop forward and he got up. Then with his shoulders bent and his hands held up to cover his head, he tiptoed to the door. He backed into the hall and pulled the door almost to so that it hid all of him but his face. "You want to know, Sugar-pie?" he asked.

Mrs. May sat looking at him coldly.

"That's O.T. and E.T.'s bull," he said. "I collected from their nigger yesterday and he told me they were missing it," and he showed her an exaggerated expanse of teeth and disappeared silently.

Wesley looked up and laughed.

Mrs. May turned her head forward again, her expression unaltered. "I am the only *adult* on this place," she said. She leaned across the table and pulled the paper from the side of his plate. "Do you see how it's going to be when I die and you boys have to handle him?" she began. "Do you see why he didn't know whose bull that was? Because it was theirs. Do you see what I have to put up with? Do you see that if I hadn't kept my foot on his neck all these years, you boys might be milking cows every morning at four o'clock?"

Wesley pulled the paper back toward his plate and staring at her full in the face, he murmured, "I wouldn't milk a cow to save your soul from hell."

"I know you wouldn't," she said in a brittle voice. She sat back and began rapidly turning her knife over at the side of her plate. "O.T. and E.T. are fine boys," she said. "They ought to have been my sons." The thought of this was so horrible that her vision of Wesley was blurred at once by a wall of tears. All she saw was his dark shape, rising quickly from the table. "And you two," she cried, "you two should have belonged to that woman!"

He was heading for the door.

"When I die," she said in a thin voice, "I don't know what's going to become of you."

"You're always yapping about when-you-die," he growled as he rushed out, "but you look pretty healthy to me."

For some time she sat where she was, looking straight ahead through the window across the room into a scene of indistinct greys and greens. She stretched her face and her neck muscles and drew in a long breath but the scene in front of her flowed together anyway into a watery grey mass. "They needn't think I'm going to die any time soon," she muttered, and some more defiant voice in her added: I'll die when I get good and ready.

She wiped her eyes with the table napkin and got up and went to the window and gazed at the scene in front of her. The cows were grazing on two pale green pastures across the road and behind them, fencing them in, was a black wall of trees with a sharp sawtooth edge that held off the indifferent sky. The pastures were enough to calm her. When she looked out any window in her house, she saw the reflection of her own character. Her city friends said she was the most remarkable woman they knew, to go, practically penniless and with no experience, out to a rundown farm and make a success of it. "Everything is against you," she would say, "the weather is against you and the dirt is against you and the help is against you. They're all in league against you. There's nothing for it but an iron hand!"

"Look at Mamma's iron hand!" Scofield would yell and grab her arm and hold it up so that her delicate blue-veined little hand would dangle from her wrist like the head of a broken lily. The company always laughed.

The sun, moving over the black and white grazing cows, was just a little brighter than the rest of the sky. Looking down, she saw a darker shape that might have been its shadow cast at an angle, moving among them. She uttered a sharp cry and turned and marched out of the house.

Mr. Greenleaf was in the trench silo, filling a wheelbarrow. She stood on the edge and looked down at him. "I told you to get up that bull. Now he's in with the milk herd."

"You can't do two thangs at oncet," Mr. Greenleaf remarked.

"I told you to do that first."

He wheeled the barrow out of the open end of the trench toward the barn and she followed close behind him. "And you needn't think, Mr. Greenleaf," she said, "that I don't know exactly whose bull that is or why you haven't been in any hurry to notify me he was here. I might as well feed O.T. and E.T.'s bull as long as I'm going to have him here ruining my herd."

Mr. Greenleaf paused with the wheelbarrow and looked behind him. "Is that them boys' bull?" he asked in an incredulous tone.

She did not say a word. She merely looked away with her mouth taut.

"They told me their bull was out but I never known that was him," he said.

"I want that bull put up now," she said, "and I'm going to drive over to O.T. and E.T.'s and tell them they'll have to come get him today. I ought to charge for the time he's been here—then it wouldn't happen again."

"They didn't pay but seventy-five dollars for him," Mr. Greenleaf offered.

"I wouldn't have had him as a gift," she said.

"They was just going to beef him," Mr. Greenleaf went on, "but he got loose and run his head into their pickup truck. He don't like cars and trucks. They had a time getting his horn out the fender and when they finally got him loose, he took off and they was too tired to run after him—but I never known that was him there."

"It wouldn't have paid you to know, Mr. Greenleaf," she said. "But you know now. Get a horse and get him."

In a half hour, from her front window she saw the bull, squirrel-colored, with jutting hips and long light horns, ambling down the dirt road that ran in front of the house. Mr. Greenleaf was behind him on the horse. "That's a Greenleaf bull if I ever saw one," she muttered. She went out on the porch and called, "Put him where he can't get out."

"He likes to bust loose," Mr. Greenleaf said, looking with approval at the bull's rump. "This gentleman is a sport."

"If those boys don't come for him, he's going to be a dead sport," she said. "I'm just warning you."

He heard her but he didn't answer.

"That's the awfullest looking bull I ever saw," she called but he was too far down the road to hear.

It was mid-morning when she turned into O.T. and E.T.'s driveway. The house, a new red-brick, low-to-the-ground building that looked like a warehouse with windows, was on top of a treeless hill. The sun was beating down directly on the white roof of it. It was the kind of house that everybody built now and nothing marked it as belonging to Greenleafs except three dogs, part hound and part spitz, that rushed out from behind it as soon as she stopped her car. She reminded herself that you could always tell the class of people by the class of dog, and honked her horn. While she sat waiting for someone to come, she continued to study the house. All the windows were down and she wondered if the government could have air-conditioned the thing. No one came and she honked again. Presently a door opened and several children appeared in it and stood looking at her, making no move to come forward. She recognized this as a true Greenleaf trait—they could hang in a door looking at you for hours.

"Can't one of you children come here?" she called.

After a minute they all began to move forward, slowly. They had on overalls and were barefooted but they were not as dirty as she might have expected. There were two or three that looked distinctly like Greenleafs; the others not so much so. The smallest child was a girl with untidy black hair. They stopped about six feet from the automobile and stood looking at her.

"You're mighty pretty," Mrs. May said, addressing herself to the smallest girl.

There was no answer. They appeared to share one dispassionate expression between them.

"Where's your Mamma?" she asked.

There was no answer to this for some time. Then one of them said something in French. Mrs. May did not speak French.

"Where's your daddy?" she asked.

After a while, one of the boys said, "He ain't hyar neither."

"Ahhhh," Mrs. May said as if something had been proven. "Where's the colored man?"

She waited and decided no one was going to answer. "The cat has six little tongues," she said. "How would you like to come home with me and let me teach you how to talk?" She laughed and her laugh died on the silent air. She felt as if she were on trial for her life, facing a jury of Greenleafs. "I'll go down and see if I can find the colored man," she said.

"You can go if you want to," one of the boys said.

"Well, thank you," she murmured and drove off.

The barn was down the lane from the house. She had not seen it before but Mr. Greenleaf had described it in detail for it had been built according to the latest specifications. It was a milking parlor arrangement where the cows are milked from below. The milk ran in pipes from the machines to the milk house and was never carried in no bucket, Mr. Greenleaf said, by no human hand. "When you gonter get you one?" he had asked.

"Mr. Greenleaf," she had said, "I have to do for myself. I am not assisted hand and foot by the government. It would cost me $20,000 to install a milking parlor. I barely make ends meet as it is."

"My boys done it," Mr. Greenleaf had murmured, and then—"but all boys ain't alike."

"No indeed!" she had said. "I thank God for that!"

"I thank Gawd for ever-thang," Mr. Greenleaf had drawled.

You might as well, she had thought in the fierce silence that followed; you've never done anything for yourself.

She stopped by the side of the barn and honked but no one appeared. For several minutes she sat in the car, observing the various machines parked around, wondering how many of them were paid for. They had a forage harvester and a rotary hay baler. She had those too. She decided that since no one was here, she would get out and have a look at the milking parlor and see if they kept it clean.

She opened the milking room door and stuck her head in and for the first second she felt as if she were going to lose her breath. The spotless white concrete room was filled with sunlight that came from a row of windows head-high along both walls. The metal stanchions gleamed ferociously and she had to squint to be able to look at all. She drew her head out the room quickly and closed the door and leaned against it, frowning. The light outside was not so bright but she was conscious that the sun was directly on top of her head, like a silver bullet ready to drop into her brain.

A negro carrying a yellow calf-feed bucket appeared from around the corner of the machine shed and came toward her. He was a light yellow boy dressed in the cast-off army clothes of the Greenleaf twins. He stopped at a respectable distance and set the bucket on the ground.

"Where's Mr. O. T. and Mr. E. T.?" she asked.

"Mist O. T. he in town, Mist E. T. he off yonder in the field," the negro said, pointing first to the left and then to the right as if he were naming the position of two planets.

"Can you remember a message?" she asked, looking as if she thought this doubtful.

"I'll remember it if I don't forget it," he said with a touch of sullenness.

"Well, I'll write it down then," she said. She got in her car and took a stub of pencil from her pocket book and began to write on the back of an empty envelope. The negro came and stood at the window. "I'm Mrs. May," she said as she wrote. "Their bull is on my place and I want him off *today*. You can tell them I'm furious about it."

"That bull lef here Sareday," the negro said, "and none of us ain't seen him since. We ain't knowed where he was."

"Well, you know now," she said, "and you can tell Mr. O. T. and Mr. E. T. that if they don't come get him today, I'm going to have their daddy shoot him the first thing in the morning. I can't have that bull ruining my herd." She handed him the note.

"If I knows Mist O. T. and Mist E. T.," he said, taking it, "they goin to say you go ahead on and shoot him. He done busted up one of our trucks already and we be glad to see the last of him."

She pulled her head back and gave him a look from slightly blared eyes. "Do they expect me to take my time and my worker to shoot their bull?" she asked. "They don't want him so they just let him loose and expect somebody else to kill him? He's eating my oats and ruining my herd and I'm expected to shoot him too?"

"I speck you is," he said softly. "He done busted up. . . ."

She gave him a very sharp look and said, "Well, I'm not surprised. That's just the way some people are," and after a second she asked, "Which is boss, Mr. O. T. or Mr. E. T.?" She had always suspected that they fought between themselves secretly.

"They never quarls," the boy said. "They like one man in two skins."

"Hmp. I expect you just never heard them quarrel."

"Nor nobody else heard them neither," he said, looking away as if this insolence were addressed to some one else.

"Well," she said, "I haven't put up with their father for fifteen years not to know a few things about Greenleafs."

The negro looked at her suddenly with a gleam of recognition. "Is you my policy man's mother?" he asked.

"I don't know who your policy man is," she said sharply. "You give them that note and tell them if they don't come for that bull today, they'll be making their father shoot it tomorrow," and she drove off.

She stayed at home all afternoon waiting for the Greenleaf twins to come for the bull. They did not come. I might as well be working for them, she thought furiously. They are simply going to use me to the limit. At the supper table, she went over it again for the boys' benefit because she wanted them to see exactly what O.T. and E.T. would do. "They don't want that bull," she said, "—pass the butter —so they simply turn him loose and let somebody else worry about getting rid of him for them. How do you like that? I'm the victim. I've always been the victim."

"Pass the butter to the victim," Wesley said. He was in a worse humor than usual because he had had a flat tire on the way home from the university.

Scofield handed her the butter and said, "Why Mamma, ain't you ashamed to shoot an old bull that ain't done nothing but give you a little scrub strain in your herd? I declare," he said, "with the Mamma I got it's a wonder I turned out to be such a nice boy!"

"You ain't her boy, Son," Wesley said.

She eased back in her chair, her fingertips on the edge of the table.

"All I know is," Scofield said, "I done mighty well to be as nice as I am seeing what I come from."

When they teased her they spoke Greenleaf English but Wesley made his own particular tone come through it like a knife edge. "Well lemme tell you one thang, Brother," he said, leaning over the table, "that if you had half a mind you would already know."

"What's that, Brother?" Scofield asked, his broad face grinning into the thin constricted one across from him.

"That is," Wesley said, "that neither you nor me is her boy . . . ," but he stopped abruptly as she gave a kind of hoarse wheeze like an old horse lashed unexpectedly. She reared up and ran from the room.

"Oh, for God's sake," Wesley growled, "what did you start her off for?"

"I never started her off," Scofield said. "You started her off."

"Hah."

"She's not as young as she used to be and she can't take it."

"She can only give it out," Wesley said. "I'm the one that takes it."

His brother's pleasant face had changed so that an ugly family resemblance showed between them. "Nobody feels sorry for a lousy bastard like you," he said and grabbed across the table for the other's shirtfront.

From her room she heard a crash of dishes and she rushed back through the kitchen into the dining room. The hall door was open and Scofield was going out of it. Wesley was lying like a large bug on his back with the edge of the over-turned table cutting him across the middle and broken dishes scattered on top of him. She pulled the table off him and caught his arm to help him rise but he scrambled up and pushed her off with a furious charge of energy and flung himself out the door after his brother.

She would have collapsed but a knock on the back door stiffened her and she swung around. Across the kitchen and back porch, she could see Mr. Greenleaf peering eagerly through the screenwire. All her resources returned in full strength as if she had only needed to be challenged by the devil himself to regain them. "I heard a thump," he called, "and I thought the plastering might have fell on you."

If he had been wanted someone would have had to go on a horse to find him. She crossed the kitchen and the porch and stood inside the screen and said, "No, nothing happened but the table turned over. One of the legs was weak," and without pausing, "the boys didn't come for the bull so tomorrow you'll have to shoot him."

The sky was crossed with thin red and purple bars and behind them the sun was moving down slowly as if it were descending a ladder. Mr. Greenleaf squatted down on the step, his back to her, the top of his hat on a level with her feet. "Tomorrow I'll drive him home for you," he said.

"Oh no, Mr. Greenleaf," she said in a mocking voice, "you drive him home tomorrow and next week he'll be back here. I know better than that." Then in a mournful tone, she said, "I'm surprised at O.T. and E.T. to treat me this way. I thought they'd have more gratitude. Those boys spent some mighty happy days on this place, didn't they, Mr. Greenleaf?"

Mr. Greenleaf didn't say anything.

"I think they did," she said. "I think they did. But they've forgotten all the nice little things I did for them now. If I recall, they wore my boys' old clothes and played with my boys' old toys and hunted with my boys' old guns. They swam in my pond and shot my birds and fished in my stream and I never forgot their birthday and Christmas seemed to roll around very often if I remember it right. And do they think of any of those things now?" she asked. "NOOOOO," she said.

For a few seconds, she looked at the disappearing sun and Mr. Greenleaf examined the palms of his hands. Presently as if it had just occurred to her, she asked, "Do you know the real reason they didn't come for that bull?"

"Naw I don't," Mr. Greenleaf said in a surly voice.

"They didn't come because I'm a woman," she said. "You can get away with anything when you're dealing with a woman. If there were a man running this place. . . ."

Quick as a snake striking Mr. Greenleaf said, "You got two boys. They know you got two men on the place."

The sun had disappeared behind the tree line. She looked down at the dark crafty face, upturned now, and at the wary eyes, bright under the shadow of the hatbrim. She waited long enough for him to see that she was hurt and then she said, "Some people learn gratitude too late, Mr. Greenleaf, and some never learn it at all," and she turned and left him sitting on the steps.

Half the night in her sleep she heard a sound as if some large stone were grinding a hole on the outside wall of her brain. She was walking on the inside, over a succession of beautiful rolling hills, planting her stick in front of each step. She became aware after a time that the noise was the sun trying to burn through the tree line and she stopped to watch, safe in the knowledge that it couldn't, that it had to sink the way it always did outside of her property. When she first stopped it was a swollen red ball, but as she stood watching it began to narrow and pale until it looked like a bullet. Then suddenly it burst through the tree line and raced down the hill toward her. She woke up with her hand over her mouth and the same noise, diminished but distinct, in her ear. It was the bull munching under her window. Mr. Greenleaf had let him out.

She got up and made her way to the window in the dark and

looked out through the slit blind, but the bull had moved away from the hedge and at first she didn't see him. Then she saw a heavy form some distance away, paused as if observing her. This is the last night I am going to put up with this, she said, and watched until the iron shadow moved away in the darkness.

The next morning she waited until exactly eleven o'clock. Then she got in her car and drove to the barn. Mr. Greenleaf was cleaning milk cans. He had seven of them standing up outside the milk room to get the sun. She had been telling him to do this for two weeks. "All right, Mr. Greenleaf," she said, "go get your gun. We're going to shoot that bull."

"I thought you wanted theseyer cans. . . ."

"Go get your gun, Mr. Greenleaf," she said. Her voice and face were expressionless.

"That gentleman torn out of there last night," he murmured in a tone of regret and bent again to the can he had his arm in.

"Go get your gun, Mr. Greenleaf," she said in the same triumphant toneless voice. "The bull is in the pasture with the dry cows. I saw him from my upstairs window. I'm going to drive you up to the field and you can run him into the empty pasture and shoot him there."

He detached himself from the can slowly. "Ain't nobody ever ast me to shoot my boys' own bull!" he said in a high rasping voice. He removed a rag from his back pocket and began to wipe his hands violently, then his nose.

She turned as if she had not heard this and said, "I'll wait for you in the car. Go get your gun."

She sat in the car and watched him stalk off toward the harness room where he kept a gun. After he had entered the room, there was a crash as if he had kicked something out of his way. Presently he emerged again with the gun, circled behind the car, opened the door violently and threw himself onto the seat beside her. He held the gun between his knees and looked straight ahead. He'd like to shoot me instead of the bull, she thought, and turned her face away so that he could not see her smile.

The morning was dry and clear. She drove through the woods

for a quarter of a mile and then out into the open where there were fields on either side of the narrow road. The exhilaration of carrying her point had sharpened her senses. Birds were screaming everywhere, the grass was almost too bright to look at, the sky was an even piercing blue. "Spring is here!" she said gaily. Mr. Greenleaf lifted one muscle somewhere near his mouth as if he found this the most asinine remark ever made. When she stopped at the second pasture gate, he flung himself out of the car door and slammed it behind him. Then he opened the gate and she drove through. He closed it and flung himself back in, silently, and she drove around the rim of the pasture until she spotted the bull, almost in the center of it, grazing peacefully among the cows.

"The gentleman is waiting on you," she said and gave Mr. Greenleaf's furious profile a sly look. "Run him into that next pasture and when you get him in, I'll drive in behind you and shut the gate myself."

He flung himself out again, this time deliberately leaving the car door open so that she had to lean across the seat and close it. She sat smiling as she watched him make his way across the pasture toward the opposite gate. He seemed to throw himself forward at each step and then pull back as if he were calling on some power to witness that he was being forced. "Well," she said aloud as if he were still in the car, "it's your own boys who are making you do this, Mr. Greenleaf." O.T. and E.T. were probably splitting their sides laughing at him now. She could hear their identical nasal voices saying, "Made Daddy shoot our bull for us. Daddy don't know no better than to think that's a fine bull he's shooting. Gonna kill Daddy to shoot that bull!"

"If those boys cared a thing about you, Mr. Greenleaf," she said, "they would have come for that bull. I'm surprised at them."

He was circling around to open the gate first. The bull, dark among the spotted cows, had not moved. He kept his head down, eating constantly. Mr. Greenleaf opened the gate and then began circling back to approach him from the rear. When he was about ten feet behind him, he flapped his arms at his sides. The bull lifted his head indolently and then lowered it again and continued to eat. Mr. Greenleaf stooped again and picked up something and threw it at him with a vicious swing. She decided it was a sharp rock for the bull leapt and then began to gallop until he disappeared over the rim of the hill. Mr. Greenleaf followed at his leisure.

"You needn't think you're going to lose him!" she cried and started the car straight across the pasture. She had to drive slowly over the terraces and when she reached the gate, Mr. Greenleaf and the bull were nowhere in sight. This pasture was smaller than the last, a green arena, encircled almost entirely by woods. She got out and closed the gate and stood looking for some sign of Mr. Greenleaf but he had disappeared completely. She knew at once that his plan was to lose the bull in the woods. Eventually, she would see him emerge somewhere from the circle of trees and come limping toward her and when he finally reached her, he would say, "If you can find that gentleman in them woods, you're better than me."

She was going to say, "Mr. Greenleaf, if I have to walk into those woods with you and stay all afternoon, we are going to find that bull and shoot him. You are going to shoot him if I have to pull the trigger for you." When he saw she meant business, he would return and shoot the bull quickly himself.

She got back into the car and drove to the center of the pasture where he would not have so far to walk to reach her when he came out of the woods. At this moment she could picture him sitting on a stump, marking lines in the ground with a stick. She decided she would wait exactly ten minutes by her watch. Then she would begin to honk. She got out of the car and walked around a little and then sat down on the front bumper to wait and rest. She was very tired and she lay her head back against the hood and closed her eyes. She did not understand why she should be so tired when it was only mid-morning. Through her closed eyes, she could feel the sun, red-hot overhead. She opened her eyes slightly but the white light forced her to close them again.

For some time she lay back against the hood, wondering drowsily why she was so tired. With her eyes closed, she didn't think of time as divided into days and nights but into past and future. She decided she was tired because she had been working continuously for fifteen years. She decided she had every right to be tired, and to rest for a few minutes before she began working again. Before any kind of judgment seat, she would be able to say: I've worked, I have not wallowed. At this very instant while she was recalling a life time of work, Mr. Greenleaf was loitering in the woods and Mrs. Greenleaf was probably flat on the ground, asleep over her holeful of clippings. The woman had got worse over the years and Mrs. May believed that now she was actually demented. "I'm afraid your wife has let religion warp her," she said once tactfully to Mr. Greenleaf. "Everything in moderation, you know."

"She cured a man oncet that half his gut was eat out with worms," Mr. Greenleaf said, and she had turned away, half-sickened. Poor souls, she thought now, so simple. For a few seconds she dozed.

When she sat up and looked at her watch, more than ten minutes had passed. She had not heard any shot. A new thought occurred to her: suppose Mr. Greenleaf had aroused the bull chunking stones at him and the animal had turned on him and run him up against a tree and gored him? The irony of it deepened: O.T. and E.T. would then get a shyster lawyer and sue her. It would be the fitting end to her fifteen years with the Greenleafs. She thought of it almost with pleasure as if she had hit on the perfect ending for a story she was telling her friends. Then she dropped it, for Mr. Greenleaf had a gun with him and she had insurance.

She decided to honk. She got up and reached inside the car window and gave three sustained honks and two or three shorter ones to let him know she was getting impatient. Then she went back and sat down on the bumper again.

In a few minutes something emerged from the tree line, a black heavy shadow that tossed its head several times and then bounded forward. After a second she saw it was the bull. He was crossing the pasture toward her at a slow gallop, a gay almost rocking gait as if he were overjoyed to find her again. She looked beyond him to see if Mr. Greenleaf was coming out of the woods too but he was not. "Here he is, Mr. Greenleaf!" she called and looked on the other side of the pasture to see if he could be coming out there but he was not in sight. She looked back and saw that the bull, his head lowered, was racing toward her. She remained perfectly still, not in fright, but in a freezing unbelief. She stared at the violent black streak bounding toward her as if she had no sense of distance, as if she could not decide at once what his intention was, and the bull had buried his head in her lap, like a wild tormented lover, before her expression changed. One of his horns sank until it pierced her heart and the other curved around her side and held her in an unbreakable grip. She continued to stare straight ahead but the entire scene in front of her had changed—the tree line was a dark wound in a world that was nothing but sky—and she had the look of a person whose sight has been suddenly restored but who finds the light unbearable.

Mr. Greenleaf was running toward her from the side with his gun raised and she saw him coming though she was not looking in his direction. She saw him approaching on the outside of some invisible circle, the tree line gaping behind him and nothing under his feet. He shot the bull four times through the eye. She did not hear the shots but she felt the quake in the huge body as it sank, pulling her forward on its head, so that she seemed, when Mr. Greenleaf reached her, to be bent over whispering some last discovery into the animal's ear.

Rinehart Editions